KU-752-622

A SISTER'S TEARS

by

Meg Hutchinson

Magna Large Print Books
Long Preston, North Yorkshire,
BD23 4ND, England.

British Library Cataloguing in Publication Data.

Hutchinson, Meg
    A sister's tears.

    A catalogue record of this book is
    available from the British Library

    ISBN   978-0-7505-3307-2

First published in Great Britain in 2009 by Hodder & Stoughton
An Hachette Livre UK company

Copyright © Meg Hutchinson 2009

Cover illustration © Larry Rostant

The right of Meg Hutchinson to be identified as the author of this
work has been asserted by her in accordance with the Copyright,
Designs and Patents Act, 1988

Published in Large Print 2010 by arrangement with
Hodder & Stoughton Ltd.

All Rights reserved. No part of this publication may be reproduced,
stored in a retrieval system, or transmitted in any form or by any
means, electronic, mechanical, photocopying, recording or otherwise
without the prior permission of the Copyright owner.

Magna Large Print is an imprint of Library Magna Books Ltd.

Printed and bound in Great Britain by
T.J. (International) Ltd., Cornwall, PL28 8RW

0465876

All characters in this publication are fictitious and any resemblance to real persons, living or dead is purely coincidental.

FOREWORD

The workhouse of the town has very bad water in the well and they are obliged to fetch it for washing and drinking several times a day...

Findings of a government commission investigating conditions of Wednesbury town in 1845

...the good folk of Wednesbury go on their sooty way happy in the knowledge that nothing more dreadful than life in their own town is likely to occur...

Daily Mail, 1898

1

'It is little enough to give in return for all I have done for you ... do not forget the choice is yours, but it is a choice whose refusal you will be given cause to regret, and believe me, my dear, you will regret deeply...'

Oblivious of the rain driving against the black tulle covering her face, deaf to all save the words hammering in her brain, Emma Lawrence watched the coffin lower slowly into the earth.

It had been a week since the funeral, a week since cold wet earth had closed away the coffin holding her beloved sister.

'If, as you have requested, you wish a token of your sister you had better take it now for I intend the room be cleared.'

So impersonal it might have been spoken by a total stranger, the ultimatum fell flatly.

There had been no tears. Emma turned to face the figure standing with hands crossed over a tightly corseted stomach. Henrietta Gilmore had shed no tears over her dead niece, nor had she offered comfort to the sister whose world had so suddenly broken apart; there had been no sympathy in those cold grey eyes, no compassion had softened features which when the body had been carried into the house seemed to narrow even more. Lips which were always tight and censor-

11

ious when speaking to her nieces had thinned into nonexistence as she ordered no one was to enter the bedroom, that she herself would attend to the laying out.

'Well Emma, the choice is yours, which is it to be?'

'*...the choice is yours...*'

Like a blow to the head memory snatched at Emma's breath. *He* had said the very same words, Fenton Gilmore had used that same phrase – then followed it with a threat!

As dread, cold and cloying, kept the breath from her lungs she stared at her aunt then with a gasp almost ran from the room.

It *had* been a threat. Heart thumping from fear of what had slid like a serpent into her mind, Emma stood with her back pressed against the door of her sister's bedroom.

'*...you will be given cause to regret...*'

How could it have been otherwise?

'*...you will regret deeply...*'

How could it *not* have been a threat?

Denial she wanted to believe in suffocated beneath the almost audible memory of her uncle's voice.

'*Don't forget my dear...*'

He had come closer, the smile touching his mouth carnal and vindictive.

'*...where you have refused there is another; one who will not be given that choice.*'

Had he meant Rachel? Were those last words, flung like the hiss of a cobra, meant to imply he would force himself upon her sister?

'*...newspaper reckons death be due to stranglin'...*'

12

Whispers she had overhead, gossip in the kitchen hastily ended whenever she came near, sounded now in Emma's brain.

'Ar, that were what finished the poor little mite, but it weren't all as was done to 'er...'

'Not all! What do you mean, Mrs Coley?'

'I means...'

The reply had tailed away and for several seconds it seemed to Emma she would hear no more but just as she had made to enter the kitchen the murmurs had begun afresh.

'I means that wench were put through a lot more afore them 'ands choked the life outta 'er; why d'you think the mistress would 'ave none but 'erself see to the layin' out?'

'I thought meself as how that were strange but then I supposed it were grief, mistress were so overcome her couldn't bear the thought of less lovin' hands touchin' Miss Rachel.'

Poppy the housemaid's musing reply had met with a snort.

'Lovin' hands!'

A thump like that of a ladle being brought down hard on the table had followed the cook's exclamation.

'Lovin' hands y'says! Then y'best tell me when it were y'seen the mistress touch a lovin' hand to either that wench or 'er sister. I were in this house the day them Gilmores walked into it and I ain't never once seen no sign o' love on the part of 'Enrietta Gilmore, no nor that husband of hers neither.'

'Well if it be like you says, and come to think on it I agrees about mistress, why then would her let nobody but herself prepare Miss Rachel for her buryin'?'

13

'Why! I'll tell you why!'

There had been so much anger in the voice, so much disgust it had seemed to claw Emma into itself, holding her so she had to listen.

'Cos her upstairs d'ain't want nobody becomin' privy to what that husband of her'n be up to! Her don't be stoopid, her knowed the ways of Fenton Gilmore ... may the Devil tek him! Her knows his temper, felt his fist on her many a time when things ain't gone as he would 'ave 'em.'

Unconscious of the action Emma raised a hand to her face, to the spot which had borne the mark of the savage swipe of her uncle's hand when she had threatened to call out, to awaken the household to the fact he was in her bedroom.

'An' there be others as knows...'

Bella Coley's vilification had hardened.

'...women he's paid to keep silent about the blows they've suffered, for it teks more'n a roll in bed to satisfy Fenton Gilmore...'

'Eeeh!'

Polly's exclamation had sounded clearly beyond the partly open kitchen door.

'D'you reckon that be the reason of Sally's leavin'? Her were covered in bruises, I seen 'em clear when her were dressin' ... you think it could have been the master's doin'?'

'I think it best you keep out of his way and y'keep the door of your room locked at night!'

Had that been an indirect affirmative?

Questions of her own vied with the dialogue running rampant in Emma's mind. Sally James had been parlourmaid at Beechcroft a little over a year when she had been summarily dismissed.

Why had her aunt ended the girl's employment – and so suddenly?

'*Laundrywoman says as how Sally had gone and got herself pregnant...*'

Conversation which had held Emma captive on that day held her fast again. Spine pressed hard against the door she recalled Polly's voice.

'*...said her'd got herself a parcel of bruises to go along with it; an' them got not a mile from this wash house!*'

Bruises! Pregnancy! Could what Polly had heard in the wash house be the real cause of Sally James' rapid dismissal?

'*...an' them got not a mile from this wash house!*'

Emma's brain whirled.

The laundrywoman's hint, the veiled accusation, could there be truth behind it? That truth being Fenton Gilmore had coerced Sally James into becoming his mistress, that he had succeeded in that vileness he had attempted with herself?

'*Gossip and truth don't always be strangers...*'

Bella's answer revolved in the maelstrom of Emma's thoughts.

'*...and scandal be like tar, it don't easy wash away. 'Enrietta Gilmore be more'n aware of that, one whiff reachin' the ears of her fancy friends and you wouldn't see their arses for dust, so Sally were seen off.*'

'*I can understand that.*'

The pause in Polly's answer had been reflective. '*But ... but there couldn't be anythin' of that sort with Miss Rachel, surely Gilmore wouldn't ... not his own niece!*'

Bella's reply had resounded with scorn. '*The likes o' Gilmore preys on them as needs 'old their*

15

tongue if they wants to hold to their livin'! He teks the like o' Sally James, God help the poor wench!'

'Exactly!' Polly answered decisively. 'So it be less than likely he would set his sights on Rachel! 'Sides, as you says, he likes to treat women to more than what be between his legs but he don't go around a'stranglin' of 'em. It has to be what the police reckoned, her were come upon by somebody up to no good. He were afraid of her reporting him to the authorities so he killed her. That much were written in the newspaper for everybody to read so I don't see as there was anythin' mistress gained by refusin' to allow you or me to be with her in that bedroom.'

'That be cos you d'ain't see what Bella Coley seen. The 'igh and mighty 'Enrietta thought her had checked well enough, and so her had; I've known this house for well on thirty year an' I knows when a room has bin gone through with a fine-tooth comb, an' that be what her ladyship had done, her'd searched Miss Rachel's room top to bottom.'

'Searched for what?'

It had not been only Polly's query, Emma's brain also had asked the question ... a question to which she wished she had never heard the reply. But she had, she had heard it spoken in that hushed tone, as she heard it again now.

'That I don't know, but this I does. That little wench were raped, raped afore her were strangled.'

Raped! Legs trembling, refusing to support her, Emma sank to the floor covering her ears with her hands. But the words refused to be blocked out.

'...don't be easy strippin' clothes from a body who be dead, 'specially when there be none save y'self a'doin' of it. 'Enrietta Gilmore must have found it particular'

16

difficult an' in the struggle the garments dropped to the floor got shuffled 'neath the bed. That were where I found 'em. Gone to Webb's the undertaker had 'Enrietta for to choose a casket and took Miss Emma along to the town to buy mourning clothes. That were my opportunity. I had vowed that somehow I would kiss that child one last time... I thank the Lord He med that possible. I went up to the bedroom; folks says a body always looks peaceful in death but that face still wore a look I would swear were fear; an' though it was probably the gleam of the lamp left beside the bed it seemed the glint of tears lay on them eyelashes; I did as the Lord had granted, kissed that cold little face, then as I knelt to pray I felt somethin' touch against my skirts. It were on pickin' that bundle up I knowed what Miss Rachel had bin put through for the dress were torn, every button on the bodice snatched away, an' the cotton bloomers, they was ripped near in two. I couldn't believe what my brain were tellin' me, it were an evil thought and I didn't want to believe, to see, yet I felt if I didn't I was somehow lettin' that child down. So I drew back the covers, lifted the nightgown and saw what 'Enrietta Gilmore thought nobody to see, black and purple bruises, marks of violence all over that body, the marks of rape! I learned what that sweet face were tryin' to tell me, I learned, but I knows I'll never be able to prove that terrible deed nor point to the beast who committed it!'

Bruises! Rape!

'...you will be given cause to regret...'

'...where you have refused there is another...'

'... will not be given that choice.'

The words of Fenton Gilmore rang as silent screams in Emma's brain but all were overridden

17

by words louder still, words crying like night-driven banshees, each a shrieking demon rising as if from the very bowels of hell twisting, turning, spiralling into a vortex, a whirlpool of horror sucking Emma into its own black heart.

'Sorry to intrude, miss, but mistress says to clear out things no longer needed.'

When had she risen from the floor? When had she come to sit beside the bed?

Still deep in the torment of her thoughts Emma looked blankly at the young woman she was unaware had entered the room.

'Mistress were adamant, wouldn't have me wait no longer, said it were to be done now ... eeh Miss Emma, I be real sorry,' Polly apologised again, 'I'd leave you for as long as you wants but ... well, you knows the mistress.'

'It's all right, Polly.' Emma struggled to throw off the shadows darkening her mind. 'I have finished.'

'Miss Emma!'

Polly glanced at the open door of the bedroom and when she spoke again it was in barely a whisper.

'The mistress... Mrs Coley believes her had already gone over every nook and cranny of this room so her knows all that be in it, but that don't go to say her won't claim somethin' be missin' after I be done sortin' Miss Rachel's belongin's, so...' She paused, the look she gave Emma remorseful as her spoken apology had been. 'Well, I realises how painful all of this be for you but ... but if you could bring y'self to stay along of the room 'til I be finished then mistress couldn't hardly say I'd stolen anythin'.'

I can't! I can't! Oh God, I can't watch every trace of Rachel being removed, please Polly, please don't ask me to do that! It was a cry in Emma's soul but one which, as she looked at the girl so obviously afraid of being accused of theft, remained there in silence.

'...I knows when a room has bin gone through with a fine-tooth comb...'

Perhaps thinking conversation to be preferable to silence Polly had chattered as she worked.

'...them be Mrs Coley's words, said that be what her ladyship, beggin' y'pardon, miss, but that do be what Mrs Coley said ... her ladyship searched Miss Rachel's room top to bottom.'

Her aunt had searched Rachel's bedroom! Returned to her own room Emma stood at the window, the drapes of which had been opened a few inches each day of the week following the funeral until now they stood wide.

What had her aunt been looking for? Had she expected to find something hidden there? But what would Rachel have to hide?

'...there is another...'

The words hissed at her and the shadowed darkness closed a clammy hand about Emma's throat.

'...her upstairs d'ain't want nobody becomin' privy to what that husband of her'n be up to...'

'...a parcel of bruises ... got not a mile from this wash house...'

'...'Enrietta Gilmore be more'n aware...'

Hot as a recurring fever, in wave upon wave the

19

remembered words burned their brand.

'*...I learned what that sweet face were tryin' to tell...*'

That last thought resounded in her brain as Emma gasped.

Was it possible her aunt had seen that same look? Had she thought, as had Mrs Coley, it was a look which said 'rape'?

'*...her knowed the ways of Fenton Gilmore...*'

So did she! A trembling breath ran the length of her as Emma turned from the window. She knew him for a would-be rapist, she had felt the sting of his blows. Had her aunt known of his visits to her bedroom? Was she fearful that he was possibly gratifying his carnal desires with a younger niece? Had that been the reason for her search, to find any evidence Rachel might have left?

One hand clamped to her mouth to hold back the sickness threatening to erupt, Emma stared at the bed.

Bruises! Attempted rape! Fenton Gilmore had proved himself capable of both; was he also capable of murder?

2

'I know you would like these.'

Emma looked down at the simple bunch of wild flowers she had placed on her sister's grave, a haze of tears spilling colour one into another; stately golden rod, rich purple meadow rue and

20

the gentle white of gypsophila merging into a brilliant kaleidoscope.

'I picked them in our favourite place,' she whispered, 'along by the canal. We both knew we ought not to go there, that Aunt Henrietta would be very angry if she knew. Remember how cross she was the Sunday you tore your dress; I warned you against rolling in the grass, I told you your dress would get stained and likely torn but you wouldn't listen. It seemed my ears rang for days afterward with Aunt's screeching. But it was worth any admonishment seeing you run free, hearing you laugh, the two of us escaping if only for an hour from...'

The whisper dying on her lips Emma blinked the moisture from her eyes. She really should not think that, should not let it enter her head! But how could she blot out the truth? How could she deny the misery she and Rachel had felt growing up in that house, the joyless atmosphere, the constant displeasure of an aunt they instinctively knew did not love or want them?

So many times they would plot how they would leave, the two of them happy together.

'You talked of running away to live with the gypsies,' Emma murmured through a fresh mist of tears, 'we would live in a caravan you said, you would beg a carrot or an apple from villages we passed through and feed it to the horse; or if the gypsies would not have us then we would stow away on one of the narrowboats we sometimes waved to as they passed along the canal. But they were pipe dreams, Rachel, like the dreams we shared before sleeping; tales of how one day we

21

would be free of Beechcroft and the unhappiness it holds, of how when you were of an age we would leave that house together. But you did not grow up. Oh Rachel!'

So much grief rose inside, filling her whole being as if it were an empty vessel, that Emma cried her agony, the pain cutting deep in her heart. 'Why, why did it happen, who could have been so evil?'

Carried on a soft breeze across the silent cemetery the words vanished leaving no solace, no alleviation of Emma's torment, no answer to the anguish tearing her apart; like the sister she had loved they were gone, leaving only an emptiness life would never fill.

'Where have you been?'

Henrietta Gilmore's demand cut across the sitting room meeting the young woman as she entered.

'Well?' The harsh voice trilled again. 'I asked you a question, Emma, you will please to give me an answer.'

Pleased to give an answer! Emma glanced at the tightly drawn features, the rigid hold of the body announcing her aunt's displeasure. Give the answer she longed to give? Tell this woman she was no longer a child, that she would not submit to constant interrogation? She forced down a desire she knew could only result in further misery and instead answered quietly. 'I have been to the cemetery.'

Quiet as the first snarl of a dog defending a bone, Henrietta's 'For what reason?' held the portent of yet another emotional storm.

Perplexed at being asked such a question whose answer was so self-evident Emma hesitated, then as the question was repeated answered, 'I took flowers for Rachel.'

'Flowers!' The word cracked irritably from between thin lips. 'You took flowers! And what do you suppose is the good of that! The dead have no need of empty gestures; laying flowers on a grave is no more than a waste of money, money you, Emma, do not have to earn.'

Anger the strength of which she had never known before suddenly convulsed in Emma. Hard and cold it drove up from the very deepest part of her being, rising like an iceberg until its huge surfacing wave rolled over her, swamping control until she could only stare at the woman for whom she had never felt love, who in that very instant she came to hate.

'Empty gestures,' she said frozenly. 'Who better than you, Aunt, would know about empty gestures? They are all you have ever shown Rachel or myself, you have never wasted a moment in affection for either of us; but then neither have I wasted money I do not earn, nor was it money earned by your husband that bought Rachel the flowers I took for her. They were picked from the ground bordering the canal.'

'The canal!' Henrietta Gilmore's eyes flashed cold fire. 'Have you no more sense, no more thought than to wander off alone after what has happened, have you no consideration for the suffering it would cause your uncle and myself should you meet with...'

'No more, Aunt!' Emma met fire with a douche of ice. 'Don't add empty words to empty gestures. We both know were I to meet with the same fate as has my sister, it would bring no sorrow to you, rather it would remove the affliction imposed upon you with the requirement of...' She paused, a shake of the head adding definition. 'No, I cannot say of caring, for you never cared for Rachel or for me, so let us say it would relieve you of the burden, the ordeal of pretence you have been forced to present to the outside world.'

'You will hold your tongue while you are in my house!'

'Yes Aunt.' Emma's reply was cold. 'Hold my tongue as I have always held it; but I will not be in your house for much longer; what I thought to be seven years of living in the misery of this house, of waiting until Rachel became old enough to leave with me, ended with her death.'

'You are not yet twenty-one, you are not of an age to say whether or not you remain beneath this roof, until you are–'

'Until I am,' Emma cut across the savage reprisal, 'yes, Aunt, I will abide by your wishes, but even you cannot halt time; within a few days I will no longer be a ward, Fenton Gilmore will no longer be my guardian and you will lose the spite I could never understand yet have always known you felt for the children of your sister.' As she turned to leave Emma halted at the door. 'I will leave no love behind,' she said quietly, 'but I will leave pity, pity for you, Aunt, for the woman cold and empty as the grave she will one day occupy.'

I will not apologise, I will not! Anger still cold

inside her, Emma fought away the feeling of guilt. Let her aunt take whatever steps she would; Rachel was beyond the reach of spite, beyond reach of punishments and so very soon would she herself be. But perhaps she need not remain here for those days. Like a whisper in her mind the notion began to grow. It had been made so patently clear, so very obvious she and Rachel had not been wanted, that they had been given a home on sufferance only due to Henrietta being sister to their mother.

It had happened so quickly: one day they had been a happy family yet the next that happiness had been snatched away. Though fifteen years old she had not really understood her parents leaving their daughters at home. If mother and father were going on holiday why could they not take herself and Rachel with them? But it had not been a holiday which had taken her parents away.

'Stop weeping, child! There is nothing to be gained by tears!'

Henrietta had snapped at a tearful Rachel before casting a passionless look at Emma who instinctively had placed a protective arm around the distraught girl.

'There will be no more behaviour of this sort, understand me, Emma, I will have no tantrums from either of you. Such displays are evidence only of selfishness. From now on you will both remember the presence in the home of others suffering the loss of loved ones; I forbid you add to that grief with what can only be described as insensitive exhibitionism.'

Memory flooding on memory Emma let herself be carried on the tide.

'*You have to be brave,*' she had told a heartbroken Rachel in her arms, '*you have to be brave for us both, Mummy and Daddy would have wanted that.*'

'*But I'm not brave,*' Rachel had sobbed. '*I am afraid, Emma, I am afraid of Aunt Henrietta, afraid of Uncle Fenton. I don't like them Emma, I don't want to live with them.*'

That was a sentiment they had shared. But for herself there had been another, a hazy impression, a feeling which at that time she had not understood, an apprehension which very soon had hardened into definite fear; fear of Fenton Gilmore.

At first she had told herself she was imagining things, that the expression which sometimes crossed his face when he looked at her was no more than 'parental' interest, yet even then something deep inside warned that Fenton Gilmore's interest was other than paternal. And so it had proved.

Revulsion which had become an almost constant companion spread its shadow over Emma.

Why had her aunt not seen his conduct for what it was? Why had she not objected when he came to the bedrooms of each niece, which he did without her company? Did she believe her husband the loving uncle he pretended to be, that the purpose of his visit was no more than to say a fond goodnight? Or could the darker truth be she was aware of his motives?

'*... her knowed the ways of Fenton Gilmore ... felt his fist on her many a time when things ain't gone as he would 'ave 'em...*'

Words heard outside the kitchen rang afresh in

26

Emma's mind.

Did that explain why Henrietta turned a blind eye to her husband's nocturnal wanderings, why she ignored his visits to the room of Sally James? Was she so afraid of him she would ignore his infidelity?

But it was more than infidelity when he came to act out his loathsome desires on his own niece, it was tantamount to incest, a base depravity nothing could excuse. No one in this house would prevent it happening again.

Again! Abhorrence enshrouded Emma in its dark folds, which parted to show brief displays, images which made the breath clog in her throat, images it snatched back into darkness only to replace with even more repulsive scenes, which despite tight-shut eyes brought the same cold fear that for so long had haunted her nights.

Had it begun in all innocence? Fairness must allow the possibility.

Emma opened her eyes and stared into the stillness of the sun-kissed garden, a garden painted silver on that night.

As if they were a stage performance she watched the pictures in her mind, pictures she did not want to see yet was unable to banish.

Dressed in a plain cotton nightgown with which Henrietta had so soon replaced Emma's softer lace-trimmed lawn one, claiming such were a waste of money when cotton served equally well, she had been standing at the window, her mind lost among the happy calls of two small girls running to throw their arms about a man coming to meet them, his own arms spread wide, his smile

27

travelling to the woman who sat on an intricately wrought garden seat, her cream organdie dress setting off to perfection deep auburn hair and soft hazel eyes. She had watched the woman rise, heard the voice reply to her greeting: but it had not been the voice of her father.

'I simply wish to say goodnight, my dear.'

Daydream shattered she had turned to see Fenton Gilmore, his pallid eyes gleaming ghostlike in the moonlit shadow.

'Your aunt is a little tired, she asks I come in her stead.'

He had smiled as the lie tripped so glibly from his tongue, an untruth they were both aware of, for given knowledge of his wife's attitude toward her sister's children, her only too obvious antipathy, he could not but have known what it was, and never in the years of them living at Beechcroft had it been Henrietta's practice to come to the bedrooms of her nieces to wish them goodnight.

'So my dear...'

He had stepped nearer, his already hushed tone dropping to a whisper.

'...We will say goodnight, may your dreams be pleasurable as I know my own will be.'

Emma shuddered. He had stood close and though he did not touch her the look in those pale colourless eyes had seemed to pass beyond the barriers of cloth, to stroke every part of her body.

'...may your dreams be pleasurable as I know my own will be.'

The insinuation, the look which had followed

28

had said clearly what that pleasure would be for him, while for her it brought trepidation, fear of his coming again to her room.

Innocent! Turning from the window Emma almost cried aloud. If an innocent practice why had it not ceased when she asked! But he had merely smiled at that, a sly vulpine smile finding no reflection in cold eyes as he had refused.

Nor had Henrietta reacted differently.

'Your uncle will not hear of locks being placed on the doors of family bedrooms, he feels that in the event of any emergency locked doors would prove an added danger.'

She had not even asked the reason! Anger laced the thought. Her reply had come so quickly it might almost have been prepared in readiness!

So the visits had continued. Irregularly, sometimes a couple of weeks between, but always they had come and always the smile, the look that seemed to touch.

Afraid to sleep, afraid to enter the oblivion she longed for, she had taken to sitting long into the night, fully clothed, listening for that dreaded step, for the opening of her bedroom door; watching the lamplight flicker on the small elegant French clock above the fireplace, its slender pointers marking seconds each of which had seemed an eternity, hoping, praying he would never come. But her prayers had not been answered.

Revulsion clamping her lips Emma tried to fight off memories, to banish the scenes still showing so vividly in her mind, to push away the horrors, yet still they remained.

She had been to say goodnight to Rachel but

caught as she was in her own fears she had failed to notice how quiet, how withdrawn and unresponsive her sister had been.

Why? It rose like a sob in Emma's throat. How could she not have seen! But she had not and now she never could, she could not ask if Rachel was suffering the same as herself.

She had returned to her own room to sit staring at the door. Perhaps it had been the warmth of the summer night, the airless silence wrapping the house, but the somnolent lull of the ticking clock made her doze, drifting in that half world between sleep and waking, floating gently where the borders of reality merged with unreality, happy in the dream of her mother's arms holding her, of her mother's kiss; but her mother's arms were gentle! Her kiss the tender essence of love!

Half in the grip of sleep, bemused by a sweetness which was somehow sour, she must have moaned for the kiss which had been a brush against her mouth had hardened, the oppressive demand of it cutting off her cry as it snatched her back to consciousness.

Fenton Gilmore was holding her, his mouth pressing down on hers. Memory flushed ice through Emma's every vein.

'Had you thought I would not come?'

Thick, turgid, the words murmured in her brain.

'But then you should have known I would.'

Loathing and dread shot her fully awake and she had tried to twist away, but the arms holding her had been too strong.

'How could I not come when there is so much pleasure waiting here in this room, pleasure I cannot

deny you, my dear.'

Swift as a striking snake one hand had fastened over her mouth, stifling the cry. His head had lifted then and in the brilliance of moonlight bathing the room those pale, opalescent eyes had glittered, the stare they held betraying an obscenity, a bestial gleam devoid of all but lust.

'Ahhh...'

He had laughed softly, a brutal sordid sound catching in his throat.

'But then I had forgotten, you do not share in that sensation; that is unfortunate ... but only for you my dear; as for myself it is regrettable, but then a man cannot have all he might wish for and neither can a woman, so you, Emma, must simply enjoy your displeasure.'

'No!'

Muffled by the hand covering her mouth, the plea had made no impression on the silence.

'Shh!'

The sound had been soft, a mere breath on the stillness, but the flash of those moon-painted eyes had carried a warning, a noiseless threat booming loud as thunder in her frightened mind.

'It would be senseless to cry out, senseless and useless my dear.'

He had brought his face close to hers and though his hand was still on her mouth the fumes of brandy on his breath filled her nostrils.

'You see...'

It had come on a laugh of pure lechery, a putrescence of sound which as it echoed again in the deep reaches of Emma's brain had her limbs tremble.

31

'I have thought of everything. You cry out and I say I came in place of your aunt whom you have worn out with your endless cries in the night, cries claiming a man is in your room when of course no one is ever there; I can have you proclaimed mentally disturbed and placed in an asylum: oh yes all of that is within my jurisdiction as of course is your sister.'

Rachel! He had the same rule over Rachel as he had over her!

She had tried to twist away but the gleam in those animal eyes showed such struggles only served to excite him.

'You are telling yourself I would not impose a lifelong sentence on one so young, so innocent, but believe it Emma I would and I will supposing you do not co-operate. After all, my dear, that you pleasure me is little enough to give in return for what I have done for you.'

In the soft glow of moonlight, he had seen her recognise the truth of this, that unless she did all he asked then Rachel would be shut away for the rest of her life. She had so desperately wanted to twist from his grasp but as his hand had released her mouth, had with deliberate tormenting slowness released the buttons of her gown and chemise then fastened over her breast, she had felt the mantrap of lust close about her.

It had lasted no more than minutes, minutes in which her soul had screamed, and then abruptly he had stepped away.

'We will not taste all of the sweetness tonight...'

At the door he had looked back and there had been evil in the voice coming quietly to her.

'We have so many nights before us, nights filled with pleasure for myself and in time for you also Emma, *however do not forget, the choice is yours but it is a choice whose refusal you will be given cause to regret … and believe me my dear you will regret deeply, for where you have refused there is another, one even younger, one who will not be given that choice.'*

'No! Not again, please God not again!'

Locked in her own private nightmare Emma's cry rang in the hushed room as a hand touched her shoulder.

3

'No! No more! Never again, you will never do that again!'

'Eh miss, I apologises; I wouldn't 'ave touched you 'cept you didn't seem to hear when I spoke to you, eh Miss Emma I be real sorry…'

'Don't lie, you've lied enough already!' Emma's retort was half cried, half screamed.

'Lied!' Pained feelings echoed in Polly Lacy's voice, 'I ain't never lied to you Miss Emma.'

Where were the bruising fingers, the snarl as she was pulled to her feet, the thick victorious laugh as the hand closed over her breast?

'I wouldn't never do that Miss Emma, you should know I wouldn't.'

Miss! He was calling her miss! But why, for what reason? Fenton Gilmore never addressed her as miss!

'I apologises again…'

Neither did he ever apologise!

33

Pushing slowly through the trauma of revulsion Emma struggled to separate reality from nightmare, giving a gasp of relief as she surfaced from the dark realms of loathing and disgust.

'Polly!' She frowned, not yet completely free of the horror which had gripped her senses.

'I said as I be sorry, miss, please don't say anythin' to Mrs Coley, her be cross with me enough already and if you tells her you be cross with me an' all...'

'Cross!' Emma's frown deepened. 'Polly, why on earth would I be cross with you?'

Nonplussed, her own brow creasing, the maid regarded Emma with puzzled eyes. 'You were cross on account of me touchin' you, I ... I wouldn't 'ave done so 'cept you seemed not to hear when I spoke; but I d'ain't lie to you Miss Emma, honest I d'ain't.'

What had she said? Had she spoken a name? Had she disclosed the abomination which took place in this room? Doubt a turmoil threatening once more to suck her into that dark pit of odium and despair, Emma caught at the lifeline of tears she saw glint in the other girl's eyes.

Rising quickly to her feet she caught the maid's hand. 'Polly I'm sorry to have hurt you, I ... I was half asleep, forgive me please.'

'It's all right, Miss Emma.' Polly smiled through the hazel gleam. 'I guess you must 'ave been daydreamin' and my touchin' you on the shoulder scared you; I should 'ave had more sense.'

'No Polly, I should have had more sense.'

'Ain't none of us has a lot of sense when we be dreamin'.'

'Even so.' Emma shook her head. 'I ought not to have reacted in such a way ... and as for accusing you of lying, Polly, that is unforgivable.'

Blinking remnants of moisture from her lashes, her smile becoming an impish grin, Polly replied. 'Only if half a lie be unforgivable; you see Miss Emma, it were only part truth when I said I wouldn't never lie, one half be I wouldn't lie to you but the other half is there be some folk I wouldn't be so particular about.'

A sound from the landing caught her ear; Polly glanced at the door standing ajar then, her eyes returning swiftly to Emma, their look requesting understanding, she said, 'I'll bring you up a nice cup of tea Miss Emma, and I'll ask Mrs Coley for one of her powders. They always works wonders.'

'Powders! For what, Emma?'

Henrietta's demand seemed to penetrate every corner of the room.

'Miss Emma is...'

Henrietta's look of iced slate swivelled. 'I did not address you girl, until I do you will remain silent! Now Emma, *you* may answer.'

There was more than coldness in those eyes, more than enquiry. For a moment Emma was uncertain what she saw, what lay behind the look now directed at herself, then in a flash blinding in its clarity she knew; it was apprehension. Her aunt was concerned, but that concern was not for her niece. The realisation lent her confidence and she met the stare intended to dig its way into her mind. 'I have asked Polly would she please bring a cup of tea to my room; do you have an objection to that, Aunt?'

35

Recognising the challenge Henrietta ignored the question, her own a fresh barrage of ice. 'And the powder? What would that be, and why do you require it?'

Holding the glacial stare with one equally unrelenting Emma answered. 'Mrs Coley is kind enough to give me one of her powders when my monthly pain is strong.'

'You!' Henrietta glared at her maid. 'Tell me, what exactly is it Mrs Coley so kindly supplies?'

'That be Beecham's Powders, ma'am.' With relief that the strategy of the glance directed earlier to Emma had succeeded Polly went on. 'They be very good for 'eadache and for that pain Miss Emma be sufferin', a Beecham's Powder will see it gone in no time; will I go fetch it for her, ma' am?'

A nod granting permission, Henrietta waited until the door closed behind the departing maid, then in a tone matching the frost in her eyes said. 'I have cautioned you on previous occasions against gossiping with the staff yet you continue to disregard my instructions.'

'Gossip, Aunt!' Emma met the reprimand with open derision. 'I would hardly call asking a drink be brought to my room gossip.'

'And that is all you spoke of?'

There it was again! The concern she had seen in those eyes was now clear in the demand hurled at her. Fear of what? Emma sat down on the bed. Was her aunt worried the staff knew of her husband's predilection for night wanderings? That they might inadvertently let drop that information in her niece's hearing? Or ... Emma's heart thumped ... was her anxiety that of a woman with a yet more dreadful secret to hide than that of a seduced housemaid? Emma forced herself to speak calmly.

'What else would I speak of, Aunt?'

It was not so much question as confrontation! Henrietta's mien tightened like a screw. In the weeks following her sister's death the girl's attitude had become one of defiance, of provocation, a fast developing problem which must be stamped out. Nostrils flared with suppressed anger her voice stiff beneath the effort of control, she directed a glance of hostility at Emma.

'Your manners are to be regretted, Emma. Perhaps you would benefit from a period of confinement.'

'*...I can have you proclaimed mentally disturbed and placed in an asylum...*'

Almost the same words, the very threat Fenton Gilmore had used against her. Coincidence or complicity? Emma's veins throbbed with the sudden surge of blood. Had her aunt and uncle discussed the subject, had they talked together of how they might have her removed from Beechcroft without apparent blame to themselves?

'*You are telling yourself I would not impose a lifelong sentence believe it, Emma, I would...*'

They both would! Facing the truth contained in that caustic stare Emma felt the cold fingers of fear close about her heart.

'I couldn't think of anythin' else to say, I hope I don't 'ave caused you trouble with her lady – the mistress.'

'No trouble, Polly,' Emma assured the girl as Henrietta swept from the bedroom. 'You said exactly the right thing, my aunt knows the pain both Rachel and myself...'

As though only now did the full impact of the loss of her sister strike home, Emma's whole body trembled. Forgetting the different status of maid and daughter of the house, Polly placed the tray she held on to the bedside table then sat beside Emma and took her in her arms.

'I know what you be feelin',' she murmured, 'I know the pain of losin' them you love most, it be a pain so strong you think nothin' will ever cure it an' truth to tell nothin' does, not complete. Time...' Polly paused, her voice quivering as she went on. 'My mother used to say time was the Lord's poultice, it sometimes be slow drawing poison from a wounded heart but the healing be sure. That is what you must cling to, that and the knowin' Miss Rachel wouldn't want you to grieve for her; and as for that other one,' Polly's voice hardened, 'you 'ave no need of bein' worried, that cow of an aunt won't never find out nothin' from me nor from Mrs Coley; and any road up, her don't be one for pokin' among the laundry so her don't be like to see it ain't your time of the month.'

If it were that: simple, if the worry were only about Polly's well-meant white lie!

Swallowing hard on the tears Polly's compassion had resulted in Emma drew free of the girl's arms. 'Thank you, Polly.' She forced a smile but it did not hide the tremor in her words, the fear of her aunt's threat.

Polly rose and moved to the door, waiting several

seconds before opening it and glancing along the corridor to the landing. Satisfied her mistress had returned downstairs she closed the door quietly. 'Miss Emma.' She turned toward the figure still sitting on the bed. 'Please don't ask no questions there don't be time for the answerin', your aunt be already suspicious of we talkin' together.'

'Polly...'

'No, miss.' Polly shook her head. 'Not here, not now, please just listen. After Miss Rachel were brought home, afore anybody were allowed into her room ... well, Mrs Coley were certain the place had been gone over thorough like and that by your aunt. We don't know what her might 'ave been lookin' for or whether her found it but one thing her d'ain't find.'

'...*the garments dropped to the floor, got shuffled 'neath the bed...*'

Words the cook had uttered with such contempt echoed in Emma's mind. That was what her aunt had not removed, the clothes Rachel had been wearing, the clothing showing the evidence of her abuse.

'*Her never found it cos I did.*'

As memories invaded her head Emma was only half aware of Polly's continuing.

'It were among Miss Rachel's underwear, folded in a pair of bloomers so it weren't seen by just flickin' through the drawer. It dropped from the pocket when I shook out them bloomers – you remember your aunt said not to put any patched clothes among the things to be sold but put them aside to be sent to the pawn shop – that were the reason of my checkin' everythin' so

39

careful, the mistress don't take kind to her word bein' ignored.'

'...*if you wish a token...*'

It had held no sympathy, conveyed no tenderness of feeling, a face rigid in its apathy emphasising a callous lack of interest. Henrietta Gilmore had issued the favour with the sensitivity of a judge sentencing a felon. Drawn ever deeper into the past Emma heard only the cold accusation.

'Nothing, you have taken nothing? It is inconceivable you would want no token. I warn you, Emma, I do not care to be deceived. There is no necessity for you to hide the fact of your keeping a memento from your sister's belongings; I demand you tell me what it is!'

'I never meant to keep it, Miss Emma, and that be the gospel truth but when I heard the mistress's step on the landing I ... well I thought should her see me with it in my hand her might go sayin' as I was stealin', that were when I slipped it 'neath my skirt. I know I shouldn't 'ave but somethin' seemed to tell me not to let the mistress 'ave it and though you was there along with me I couldn't 'ave explained my feelin', not afore your aunt reached the room. It were wrong of me I knows that but I ain't no thief, Miss Emma, I d'ain't never intend the keepin' of it.'

'...*the fact of your keeping...*'

Unaware the words pounding in her brain had slipped from her tongue Emma was startled by hands grasping suddenly at her own.

'Oh please, Miss Emma ... truly I never meant to keep it.'

Almost in tears Polly shook the hands she held, the movement bringing Emma to the moment.

Emma looked up with consternation at the maid, seeing distress where usually a smile would have been, noticing that tears were threatening to spill. 'Polly.' She stood quickly, all her attention now on the girl. 'Polly, what is wrong ... what is it?'

Polly glanced toward the door, to check that it was still firmly closed. Reassured, she slipped a small cloth-wrapped parcel from the pocket of her skirt. 'It be this. I took it from Miss Rachel's room but I wasn't thinkin' to steal, cross me heart and hope to die.'

The heartache so obvious in the oath, in the quick touch of fingers signing brow and chest, stopped Emma's quick smile. Whatever it was Polly had or had not done was clearly the cause of some anxiety. 'Polly,' she said as she dropped the object unthinkingly on to the bed then reached for the other girl's hands, 'Polly, of course I believe you would not steal.'

'The mistress wouldn't, her would be only too quick to condemn, that be why I thought at first to throw it away, get rid of it in the rubbish heap. That way nobody would never know of it but ... well, that would 'ave been stealin' just the same, so I asked Mrs Coley what were best to do, I showed her what it was and explained how come I didn't give it to the mistress, I thought Mrs Coley would chide me for that but her never. Her looked at what I'd handed her then said it had to be given back but not to the mistress, that seein' as it had belonged to Miss Rachel then I should give it to you, that—'

Halted abruptly, Polly swung round at a sound beyond the door. Soft, muffled, it had not caught

Emma's attention but to the girl, her acuity of hearing heightened by nervous tension, it cracked like a pistol shot.

'Hide it, miss.' Swift as were the whispered words her hands were quicker as she caught up the package and thrust it at Emma. 'Please,' she whispered agitatedly, 'don't tell the mistress I–'

Once more she broke off in mid-sentence. Taking up the neatly wrapped powder, handing it and the teacup to Emma, the request repeated clear in her eyes as Henrietta returned to the room Polly said, 'You take that, miss, you'll feel better in an hour or so.'

'I see no cure for pain in idle chatter!' Henrietta stared sourly at Emma, then to Polly snapped, 'Return to your duties!'

Would the woman have seen, would she demand to see what it was Emma had instinctively dropped behind her back, to be given the package now being sat on? Without question that would lead to a charge of attempted theft. With only a glance as a way to transfer these thoughts to Emma, to silently plead her cause, Polly bobbed a curtsy then took the tray and left the room.

'That girl finds far too many excuses to leave her work, I am thinking to give her notice.'

'Polly is very conscientious in her duties. You may have difficulty in finding someone as willing and helpful as she.'

'Pah!' Henrietta spat away the defence. 'Willingness to stand gossiping is that girl's only quality and it is one fast transferring itself to you, but I tell you a last time, that will stop or I will be forced to take action.'

Superficial calmness concealing the flurry Polly's anxious words had produced in her mind, Emma met the innate threat with a cool derision. 'Action?' She paused as if engaged in some mental search, then with one eyebrow raised in recognition went on. 'Ah yes! The confinement to an institution. Thank you, Aunt, your concern for my welfare is so very heart-warming ... just as it always was for Rachel.'

The last, a barb tipped with acid, found its mark. With a sharp snatch of breath, her hands held across a corseted stomach clenching together, Henrietta's thin lips tightened to vanishing point but the eyes glaring at Emma spewed fire. For several moments that fire burned against the ice of Emma's stare then with a snapped, 'You will regret your insolence!' she swept from the room.

'...*you will regret deeply...*'

Heavy with lust, reptilian in their horror, the words slid uncontrollably into Emma's mind, words Fenton Gilmore had used to subdue her to his will.

4

'You knew, didn't you? You knew and yet you did nothing, you knew and you let him do it!'

Emotions which had torn like a rip tide, emotions she had fought so hard to restrain in the hours since Polly Lacy had left her with that small package, trembled afresh in Emma.

Across the immaculately neat sitting room Henrietta Gilmore also trembled though her tightly held body showed none of the perturbation inside her. Servants' ears were forever open. Though thin lips barely moved nothing of the viciousness was lost in the quiet hiss.

'Control yourself, Emma!'

'Control!' Emma's gasp was one of disbelief. 'How?' she demanded, 'tell me, Aunt, how do I do that, is it by shutting myself in my room, sitting there telling myself it is all in my imagination? Do I lie to myself as you did on all those nights your husband spent in your housemaid's bed?'

Henrietta's glance flicked nervously toward the closed door then returned to Emma filled with iced venom.

'How dare you!'

'How dare I what, Aunt? Speak the truth? It is the truth, is it not?'

How could she have learned of that incident? That trollop of a housemaid had been paid to keep silent. There was only one answer: the girl had reneged on her agreement, disclosed all to those below stairs and they in turn had told it to Emma; but to whom else might it have been told? Who outside of this house was privy to that scandal?

Juggling with thoughts that had her nerves scream, Henrietta forced a frigid calm as she said:

'What you have said, Emma, is beyond forgiveness. I shall speak with your uncle on his return. He will judge what is to be done with you.'

Again the thinly veiled threat, but this time Emma was not to be cowed. Head up, eyes bright with anger, she retorted sharply, 'We will both

44

speak with him, we will both ask if what I have said is the truth or a lie.'

'It *is* a lie!' Henrietta's snarl rasped across the room.

'In that case he should be given the opportunity to deny it for himself.'

What had come over the girl? Henrietta felt a nervous twitch pull at her stomach. She had always been easily quelled, quickly put down in any controversy, but today ... today she showed little of that former self. The death of her sister would in some respects account for a temporary change of attitude but not for open defiance, and that was what was displaying itself now.

'Why?' Henrietta snapped over the tumult of thoughts. 'Why would I believe so outrageous an accusation, why would my husband want a housemaid when he has me?'

Facing the woman with whom she had lived for so long Emma saw the answer in the cold hard eyes. Fenton Gilmore never preferred his wife.

A twinge of pity at that silent admission stirred in Emma; that was a terrible knowledge for any woman to hold.

'I see you realise your mistake!' Henrietta continued bitingly. 'You comprehend that whoever furnished you with that information has sadly misled you; I warned you so many times about listening to gossip. See now where ignoring my instructions has led you; it is the act of a wicked, spiteful girl who would accuse her own uncle of committing so dreadful a crime when all he has ever done is care for her; but then you were ever ungrateful, you and that sulky, petulant ill natured brat of a sister. I advised you were both placed in an institution, one where you would reap the benefit of lying, but your uncle was too soft-hearted. But now ... now when he hears of this latest transgression he will not be so lenient!'

Sulky, petulant, ill-natured. She could say that of a child who had never once answered back, never disobeyed, a child who had only ever wanted love. Whatever had stirred in Emma, whether pity or simply regard for a woman stoically defending a husband she knew to be unfaithful, died instantly. All of the despondency, the heartache and wretchedness with which this woman had helped make the life of Rachel so full of misery rushed together in Emma, consolidating into animosity so strong it took a moment for her to speak, but when she did it was with a bitterness so profound the words cracked like ice.

'The mistake is not mine but then you know that. You advised an institution for Rachel and myself; the sadness is your advice was not acted upon. Had it been then my sister and I would likely have been happier than living in what you made a prison of distress. Also I would not have been, as you put it, "furnished with gossip".' Pausing fractionally, her eyes surveying that taut unrelenting face, Emma felt animosity turn to loathing. This woman had virtually destroyed the childhood of her own kin, given Rachel a lifetime of unhappiness, a life which had ended in that same misery! Biting back tears crowding on that thought she went on:

'This, Aunt, is not gossip. It is incontrovertible truth and once more I say you knew and yet took

46

no action to prevent your husband molesting the children of your sister, that you stood by while Fenton Gilmore abused both Rachel and myself.'

Henrietta's eyes expressed a sudden sharp fear, but again her reply was steady. 'Abused!' she grated. 'Since when was caring for children termed abuse!'

Anger Emma had managed to curb, though it burned like a fire in her chest, suddenly flashed with mercurial swiftness along every nerve as her reply blazed across the room:

'And since when was rape termed care!'

Breath drawn through tightly held lips Henrietta glanced again at the door before her own words burned the air.

'That is a vile and loathsome accusation and it is one you will be given cause to regret!'

'Given cause to regret,' Emma repeated. 'The very words spoken to me when I tried to fight Fenton Gilmore, to twist from his hands, hands which pawed my body while he threatened my refusal to pleasure him would result in his taking advantage of Rachel, his actual words being, *"Where you have refused there is another, one even younger, one who will not be given that choice."*

'That is a foul lie!'

'It is no lie.' Emma answered fire with ice.

'You have no proof.'

'Of his abusing me? Maybe not, but of his rape of my sister there is proof.'

It was like a bomb had exploded in the room, an explosion followed by thick, intense silence.

'Proof?' Henrietta gagged on the word.

'Yes.' Emma nodded. 'Proof even you will be

unable to contest. Not satisfied with defiling one niece your husband abused then raped a younger one; he raped a thirteen-year-old child.'

Alarm flashing across eyes hard as lead, the closing of tight features, nervous fingers twisting together like a lapful of serpents evidencing the turmoil in her brain, Henrietta's reply was nevertheless sibilant, hushed yet redolent with threat.

'Rape!' she snarled. 'No man can be accused of rape when he is taking what was freely offered; yes *freely* offered. If he raped your sister then she asked for it, both of you did, smiling and flaunting yourselves whenever you were in his company. If he came to your rooms, did what you profess then it was because you both invited him there. That little slut of a sister and you yourself are the same as your mother. She was a whore, she would open her legs for any man; my husband should be praised, not vilified, he should be praised for finding a home for the offspring of a whore, taking you in when nobody else would. He saved you from the workhouse and this is the reward he gets!'

'No!' Emma cut across the tirade. 'No, his reward was not given, it was taken, taken when he forced a child to play his evil games.'

'Forced!' The half laugh curdled on Henrietta's lips. 'Forced! When it was she went to him, enticed him with soft arms twined about his neck, with kisses not to the cheek but pressed on to the mouth, a tongue caressing his, seducing him to the wickedness inside her; that will be my answer should you speak any of this beyond this room. I will vow she came to him, that I saw her enter his bedroom, that it was I followed her there, I

48

returned her to her own room thus saving my husband from her wickedness, from an inherited evil, an evil that filled her and fills you yet; you will be seen as spawn of the devil, like mother like daughter, all three whores.'

Holding firm to those cold eyes Emma answered calmly. 'Then you will have convicted him out of your own mouth, you will have reinforced evidence written in Rachel's own hand, written evidence of his raping her.'

Henrietta's half laugh sounded again. 'Evidence!' she said snidely. 'What evidence?'

Should she reveal what she had been given? For the briefest moment Emma hesitated then said, 'Rachel's diary, Aunt, I have Rachel's diary.'

As from a slap to the face the older woman's head jerked on her neck, breath seeming trapped in her throat while trepidation drew furrows of anxiety across her brow.

As she watched the sudden transformation, the certainty that what that package had revealed had been no fiction, no product of Rachel's imagination, quickened in Emma.

'It was that you searched her room hoping to find it, wasn't it?' she went on, needing to know if what was in her own mind was more than suspicion. 'You looked for anything Rachel might have written, but that was not the sole reason for banning anyone from entering her room. You were afraid of something else, something you feared might link her death to this house, to your husband. You know his sadism, the pleasure he gets from inflicting physical injury on those he violates sexually, and what you know so do others.

Should they tell of those proclivities, should that be coupled with what is written in Rachel's diary and the marks on her body...'

'There were no marks on her body!' Henrietta threw the words as though flinging daggers. 'The only mark of violence was that on her throat, those left by strangulation!'

'No.' Emma shook her head. 'That was the only mark visible when Rachel was carried into the house, but you feared there might be more, and when you prepared her for burial you saw what you feared, the bruises to her stomach and inner thighs, dark blood-filled contusions on her lower parts, all of them marks of lust-driven violence. Was it concern for social standing made you try to keep that secret? Were you afraid reaction to such a scandal would be less than friendly or is the truth of the matter you knew what your husband had done to Rachel on previous occasions, that he had forced himself on her? Were you anxious that he was the one had come upon her in that barn? That it was he had raped her and in that frenzy had strangled her!'

'Enough!' Henrietta was on her feet, her eyes blazing fury behind whose flames burned the colder gleam of dread. 'I put up with the foolish behaviour of you and your sister, endured your disobedience for the sake of family, but no more. When your uncle returns he will hear the atrocious slur you have cast on his name, the foul accusations you have made. He, like myself, will realise that such maligning of his character cannot be allowed to go on, that you must be placed where no one will pay any attention to your ravings; in a word, Emma, an asylum!'

'In a word, Emma, an asylum.'
The words rasping in her head Emma stared at the door her aunt had slammed behind her. Was that an empty threat, one made to frighten her? No! Emma's heart jumped at the answer which came to mind. It was real, real as the fear she had seen flood across those hard, cold eyes when hearing of her husband's assault upon a child and of his attempt to do the same with her sister, fear real enough to have Henrietta Gilmore do anything to avoid her associates learning of it. The name Gilmore was respected in Wednesbury, it carried regard and a certain esteem, it afforded that much-valued social standing which in her aunt's eyes was paramount, something that nothing and no one must be allowed to taint; and that look, that swift flash of fear, had evidenced the same much more clearly than any spoken word. Henrietta Gilmore would not hesitate to sacrifice anything on the altar of pride, and certainly not a niece she had no love for. And what of Fenton Gilmore! Emma felt the trap tighten about her. He as much as his wife needed to safeguard his reputation; like her, he would not relish social disgrace, and if to avoid it meant incarcerating the girl he had abused then that was what he would do. And she would have no voice! Flutters of panic flicking across her chest, Emma moved restlessly about the room. Fenton Gilmore was her guardian; the law gave him total control, placed her completely within his power to do with as he saw fit. It gave him the authority of a

parent, a parent whose love was not for the child but solely for the nauseating pleasure of possessing the body of that child. Sickened at the thought Emma tried unsuccessfully to stem the next. Having her closeted behind locked doors for the rest of her days, shut away in life as Rachel was in death, would give rise to no regret on the part of Fenton Gilmore; it would simply prove a very satisfactory solution to a problem.

If only her parents had not taken that decision to go away on holiday leaving their daughters behind. The cry of that thought so loud in her mind brought Emma to a standstill. Why? This question had often tormented her in the years of her growing, one which had been especially potent those nights Fenton Gilmore had come to this room, a question which had become a silent scream as he had pawed and kneaded her breasts, had forced her to lie naked on the bed while he had stripped away his own clothes. Then each time before lowering himself beside her had come that quiet throaty laugh, that obscene depraved sound which seemed even in his victory to challenge, to dare her to cry out. That was the vileness of the man. Emma lifted her hands to her mouth to press back the moan already risen in her throat. He had known she would not cry out, that she would suffer any depravity to save her sister. Yet it had not saved Rachel. She too had been subjected to Fenton Gilmore's lascivious demands, to that evil debauched desire which had led him to rape a defenceless young girl.

Why had he not taken that step with herself?

Why had he not raped her?

Fingers still firm against her lips Emma stared at the bed, its covers drawn neatly up to crisp white pillows, a bed which had witnessed her misery.

Following that first time, the time of his making that threat against Rachel, his visits to this room had followed a kind of pattern.

Remembering, Emma watched the invisible scenes in her mind.

Silent as a prowling cat Fenton Gilmore entered the bedroom, his shadow cast by the glow of the one oil lamp a black menace on the shadowed wall.

'My dear...'

He smiled as he spoke, a sly atavistic smile barbarous as the ruthless intent behind his coming.

'I trust I have not kept you too long in the waiting...'

The smile never reached his eyes. He crossed to where she sat and the mere memory of the touch of his hand drawing her from the chair made Emma shudder.

'...but I promise, my dear, the wait will prove worthwhile.'

Low, intense with the promise of what was to come, his voice had throbbed on the silence, yet to Emma, standing immobile as a statue, it carried no sound above the tumult of loathing crashing inside her head.

'Come, my dear, let us make up for lost time.'

From the soundless stage of memory Fenton Gilmore reached for the buttons of her dress, unfastening each one with deliberate slowness, the anaemic yellow glow of the lamp playing on those pale colourless eyes revealing only too clearly how he savoured the trembling Emma could not prevent.

Watching as if from outside herself yet feeling every nuance of horror, as first her dress then chemise and petticoats fell to the floor, Emma's nerves jolted at the thick rasp of breath which followed the removal of her drawers.

How long had he stood, just his eyes moving as they stroked her nakedness? Probably no more than moments yet each had seemed a thousand times that of eternity, an endless time in which the evil inside him grew.

Unconscious of her step backwards Emma withdrew from the hands reaching to her breasts, her teeth clamping hard on the cry of revulsion as long fingers clasped the soft mounds, squeezing hard until the nipples rose like ripe cherries. With a guttural half laugh he took first one then the other into his mouth, his tongue licking greedily, sucking them deep inside as a child sucks on its mother. Then, her breast still in his mouth, he had forced her to backtrack, releasing her only when the press of the bed against her legs threatened to topple her.

'So delightful, I regret having to let go...'

The smile he had given on lifting his head had been an obscenity, a gross lewdness not lessening as he went on. *'...but then Emma, I have only moments to wait before engaging once more in that most agreeable entertainment.'*

Agreeable entertainment was what he had called the defiling of a girl he knew had no defence against the corruption burning inside him; a girl who must suffer his debauchery if she were to save her sister.

Watching as she might actors in a play Emma saw within the night shadow of her room the man she loathed press her down on to the bed then angle the lamp so it shed a pale gold radiance over her naked form.

'*Beautiful.*'

It seemed to rasp again.

'*...even more appealing than...*'

As someone on the verge of making a mistake he halted, a quick frown of self-reproach creasing his brow. Then it vanished leaving a nefarious smile to accompany the stripping away of his own clothing.

Emma saw her own eyes close, her own head turn away from the figure beside the bed, a figure naked as her own, one clothed only in the gleam of lamplight; but though none of this was physical reality the acid of nausea stung in her throat, a sickness threatening to erupt as memory returned to her the lowering of that figure to the bed, the pressure of flesh hard against her thigh, the abhorrence increasing at the phantom touch of his hands on her breasts, the trail of fingers over her stomach, the encroachment into that soft vee at its base, and all the while that coarse snatch of breath testified to the emotions driving him.

But though his hands had invaded, though he had forced her legs apart, had lain atop her, he had not raped her.

'*Not yet...*' he had said thickly, '*soon, my dear, but not yet.*'

'*Soon, my dear, but not yet.*'

55

As the pictures faded from her mind words remained to clang like bells. Fenton Gilmore intended to rape her yet had quite intentionally turned from committing the final act.

Why? Once again the question forced itself to the surface only for Emma's breath to catch in her throat as a fresh thought struck her.

Rachel! Emma reeled at the enormity of what screamed in her brain. Was the evil of Fenton Gilmore so entrenched he would work up a passion by pawing one sister then with premeditated intent go and fulfil the craving it induced by raping another?

'Soon my dear, but not yet.'

It seemed to smile at her, smile with the same sly atavistic gleam of those many nights.

A sound from outside of the house caught her ear. Emma glanced from the window, her nerves twanging as she saw her uncle descend from his carriage.

Fenton Gilmore, hearing his wife's account of what had passed between herself and their niece, would without doubt consign that niece to an institution for the deranged; but Fenton Gilmore was, as he often stressed, a man of his word.

'...*soon*...' It whispered again to Emma.

Rape! That ultimate violation would take place before she was locked away.

5

He had not meant for things to go so far.

In a first-class compartment of a train carrying him from Birmingham Fenton Gilmore stared through the window but the scene he looked at was not that of trees and fields. Instead he saw the shadowed darkness of a barn.

He'd intended only to lie with her, to satisfy the urge which had risen as he had watched the slight figure walking across the meadow below Beech-croft House. He'd known who it was he watched, had recognised the long auburn hair freed of its ribbons float like strands of dark silk in the breeze, a breeze pressing a flimsy skirt against colt-like legs, and he'd smiled in the recognition and again in the knowledge he would meet no resistance.

With the thought he set spur to the horse, the animal's cry at the sharp jab causing the figure to turn. For several moments it had remained still, its shape outlined against the sunlit sky, then as he galloped forward it had started to run.

That had been a bonus!

Positioning his top hat high on his knees he covered the erection memory ordered to rise.

Seeing the figure run had aroused more than the spirit of the chase, it had thickened the desire beginning to burn along his veins. It had been a hopeless chase, the girl could not possibly outrun a horse, but to add thrill to it he had reined the animal to a trot; a fruit gathered and tasted was fine fare, but one lingered over, the flesh of it admired, caressed with fondness which became fervour; that became a feast.

And he had feasted.

Beneath the cover of his hat thickening flesh jerked, adding a further flush to the heat beginning to sting his veins.

She had looked back twice, a small frightened face with breeze-whipped strands of auburn hair lying across its clear creamy skin like dark wounds, and though across the distance separating the hunter from the hunted he could not truly see the fear in those wide eyes, he sensed the pleading they must hold that he turn away. He had known that fear was there, known the familiar silent cry so many times before and as at each of those times a tide of triumph surged in his blood.

The figure had darted toward a barn and he had laughed. The moth had danced to his flame; now its wings would be scorched.

He had not hurried his satisfaction.

He had used the horse as a shepherd would a sheepdog to herd animals in the direction it was wished they go, only he had shepherded a young girl, turned her in the way he wanted her to run.

And run she had.

Staring solidly at the window Fenton almost gasped at the remembered thrill.

She had described a zigzag pattern, a course taking her ever nearer a large barn, a barn he knew was used only to house winter feed for cattle. No one would be in there, no one to witness his activities.

He had reined the horse to a halt, prolonging the moment, smiling at the figure darting away in the hope of escape.

He had watched the figure hasten into the barn then setting his mount once more to a trot he had ridden up to the door.

Again he had not hurried. He had taken his leisure in dismounting, strolling almost lazily into the barn, his mind already feeding on the pleasure yet to come.

He could almost see it now, the gloomy shadowed interior slashed with narrow beams of golden sunlight filtering through rotting timbers, could almost smell again the heady sensuous scent of fresh cut hay; but it had not been the aroma which sent his pulses leaping but the promise of what that hay was hiding.

He had found her soon enough.

Beneath the rhythm of train wheels crossing the points Fenton seemed to hear half-swallowed sobs, sobs which could not be held back and which had led him surely as any intended call.

She had cried aloud as he had kicked away the hay she had dragged across her body, tried to scramble away but one snatch had pulled her back, his legs astride the thin form preventing further attempts at escape. Still she had begged to be released. But as with that scramble her entreaties had fallen on deaf ears.

Beyond the window of the compartment fields and hedgerows went unseen, only the pictures in Fenton's mind alive to him.

He had stared down at her, stared into tear-filled eyes, but they had made no impression other than to fuel even further the fires in his blood.

He had removed his clothing slowly, savouring not so much the shedding of each garment but the sob of terror it produced. Then had come the last article. He had let the under-breeches slide slowly from his waist down over the bulge of hard pulsing flesh, a laugh drowning the girl's cry.

She had tried yet again to scramble from him. That he had not expected; she had cried times before but never struggled, never attempted to fight him off as she had fought that afternoon flailing out with both hands, her fingernails tearing along his cheek and neck.

It had to have been the scuffle had caused events to develop as they had.

Her struggles had quickened the swirl of blood along his veins, intensified the intoxicating rush that came with the feeling of mastery, of domination; it had all combined together, erotic sensuality adding itself to heightened physical desire until he was no longer aware of anything other than hair red-gold in the splashes of sunlight, of brown eyes glistening molten bronze beneath a sheen of tears, eyes which radiated fear: he had been alive to nothing but the need to satisfy the carnal demands of his own body.

She had twisted like a live eel.

She had very nearly escaped.

Pictures flashing one on the other Fenton watched the scene unfolding in his mind, his breath catching at the scene.

The terror-stricken face, the childlike body beneath him, the cries as he snatched at her dress, as he tore away her bloomers, cries becoming screams as he forced those thin colt-like legs apart.

Then the screams had stopped.

Everything had been so still, so silent.

Fenton's eyes closed at the memory but eyelids could not shut out that mental picture.

Ripples of sunbeams were gliding across piles of hay, glistening fingers of light caressing a throat held in his clenched grip, a kiss of yellow gold touching a face whose wide eyes were held in the stare of death.

Shaken by the vivid intensity Fenton shuffled in his seat. It didn't do to linger in the past, he must rid himself of such memories.

'Wednesbury ... Wednesbury in two minutes.'

The call of the conductor announcing the train's approach to Wednesbury station had the only other passenger in the compartment juggle frenziedly with newspaper, Gladstone bag, cane and silk top hat, the latter falling several times to the floor before the flustered owner thought to set it on his head, but even then the palaver with bag, cane and newspaper continued until with the jolt of the halting engine the man pitched forward, his ample frame coming to rest half across the opposite seat, his shoulder bumping against Fenton's arm.

'I apologise ... I'm so sorry ... clumsy of me, I do apologise...'

Red-faced, perspiring with the effort of manipulating his several belongings, the stout little man struggled to regain his footing repeating several more apologies as he scooped his renegade possessions hurriedly into his arms.

Rising from his seat Fenton opened the car-

61

riage door. Standing aside allowing his flustered co-traveller to alight he drew a long tension-clearing breath.

One man's problem had proved another man's relief. Taking his own bag he stepped out on to the platform.

That fellow's contortions with bag, cane and hat had provided time enough for Fenton Gilmore's particular dilemma to resolve itself. Smiling at the thought he placed his own hat on his head.

Fashionable enough for Wednesbury!

Fenton's inner smile became one of derision as he glanced after the rotund figure walking toward the exit. The attire of tan-coloured jacket reaching two-thirds of the way past the thigh, double breasted to fasten high on the chest, narrow collar and entirely without cuffs either high or low buttoned, screamed the style of thirty years ago.

Yes, fashionable enough. The smirk deepened. Adequate for mine owners and the industrialists of this smoke-plagued, dirt-encrusted town but not stylish enough for Fenton Gilmore. Then again, neither was Wednesbury.

Setting down leather Gladstone he fastened the buttons of his smartly tailored dark grey morning jacket. He had chosen the tailor carefully, insisting the man follow explicitly his instructions as to short reveres and high button cuffs which were the latest statement in fashion and suiting elegantly the lighter grey creaseless pinstriped trousers cut to come well down on mirror-shined shoes, a silk top hat finishing off the ensemble.

Taking up the bag he followed in the wake of

that one other passenger. Like this town he was drab and uninteresting but then, much like Henrietta, Wednesbury had served its purpose. Now that purpose was nearing its end; Fenton Gilmore had a new venture, one which meant money and the freedom to spend it as a refined and cultured gentleman ... a recently bereaved gentleman!

And Henrietta's niece, what of Emma?

Taking train ticket from a pocket of his stylish coat Fenton's snide smile deepened. He would be taking no excess baggage with him into his new life. That which was discarded could like last season's clothing be replaced with newer, more titillating commodities. But for the present the delicious Emma would suffice.

'Evenin' Mr Gilmore, sir, there be a 'ansom just along of the street. Will you 'ave me call it for you?'

Handing his ticket to the smiling stationmaster Fenton shook his head, replying that he would first take a cup of coffee in the nearby Great Western Hotel.

'Evenin' sir, would you p'raps be wantin' of some company, some entertainment? Wouldn't cost y' no more than 'alf a sovereign.'

Company! Fenton glanced at the woman who had barely given him time to step clear of the station before approaching. A prostitute. He glanced at her again. But one who as yet still had a presentable face.

Entertainment! Flesh which so recently had responded to efforts to quieten it flicked again.

Half a sovereign? That would pay for a room and

a meal in the hotel. And the woman? He nodded at the dark-haired figure, a cheap blue frock all but revealing the nipples of a pair of ample breasts as she thrust back the shawl set about her shoulders. She would provide the solution to the demand rising ever stronger at the base of his stomach. A temporary solution admittedly, also one which would earn no more than a florin.

Sufficient for the purpose. Ignoring the woman following at his heels Fenton smiled at the quotation learned as a boy.

'Sufficient unto the day is the evil thereof.'

Sweeping up a key passed across the wide-topped reception desk, issuing instructions regarding a meal and a bottle of wine, Fenton turned toward the impressive curved staircase. The woman would prove that for one evening her brand of 'evil' could match his own.

And in the evenings yet to come?

The door of the rented room closed and Fenton watched his lady of the night slowly unfasten the buttons of the cheap cotton frock.

For evenings yet to come there would be Emma.

When the blue dress dropped to the floor he ran a discerning glance over the woman, the smile she thought to be enticing having less effect than the bulge of breasts.

The breasts he had uncovered in that barn had been small, little more than buds, the nipples almost too small to take into his mouth; but not those of Emma. Not copious like those he looked at now, Emma Lawrence's breasts were just as he preferred, soft yet firm, mounds which fitted into the hands, pretty breasts topped with cherry nipples, breasts which wrenched at a man's loins.

'I see you be ready to play.'

The woman laughed, bringing her body to press against the pulse of flesh straining to be loosed.

Play! Fenton grasped the chemise, pulling it away from the overfull breasts. That was what he had done with Emma Lawrence. He had tormented her with the threat of rape while never taking that step. But the time for games was over; when he next visited Emma Lawrence it would not be merely to fondle those delicious breasts, to stroke that slender naked body; on his next visit he would take her virginity.

He would not find her sitting in her chair. This time he would not find her too afraid to resist.

Stiff from the fear and tension which had gripped since witnessing Fenton Gilmore's return to the house the previous evening, Emma grasped a heavy brass-based oil lamp which she raised high above her head as the handle of her bedroom door began to turn.

He would not suspect; after all she had proved docile enough the nights he came to this room, the nights he used her to fuel his filthy intentions. But he knew that docility had been a way of protecting Rachel! Emma's sudden thought had her grip the lamp more tightly. Rachel no longer needed her protection. Fenton Gilmore would have realised the difference this would make, he must know the girl he had so long abused would no longer be the passive victim. That would make him wary in his approach.

Every sense alert, Emma had listened to the soft tread along the landing. That was how he always came, carefully, trying to mask each footfall yet each time her jangling nerves had detected that soft muffled sound just as it had now. She watched the doorknob turn but watching it she seemed to be far distant, with a detached feeling that she was there but played no part, almost as though caught in some nightmare. But a corner of her mind told her the nightmare was real enough, that in the next seconds the real horror of it would become manifest: Fenton Gilmore would enter her bedroom.

She must act quickly, to hesitate would allow time enough for him to avoid the blow.

The blow! Emma's stretched nerves twanged like plucked fiddle strings. Brought down across the head it would render him unconscious. But if it killed him! Out of the darkness of fear the voice of reason spoke and for a moment Emma's determination wavered. She did not want any person's death on her hands, not even a swine such as Gilmore, but she would not let him degrade her again and this was her only chance to prevent that happening.

What of the consequences? Soft as before, reason posed its question.

Prison! Emma's brain answered. Her justification for striking would be seen as a lie, Henrietta would back any claim to her husband's innocence and as a consequence a term of imprisonment would be given. But whether locked in one of her Majesty's gaols or in a mental institution, Emma knew her fate was sealed.

The doorknob had turned full circle. Watching the door begin to open Emma's breath caught in her chest. Above her head the heavy oil lamp began to descend.

Fate had decreed her future, but that future would not be sullied by Fenton Gilmore.

6

The handle had turned full circle.

Spine pressed hard to the wall, the heavy lamp poised above her head, Emma held her breath.

Somewhere almost beyond the brink of sanity the voice of caution whispered.

Wait! Fingers tightened ever more painfully about the lamp. Wait until he was fully inside the room. Strike too soon and he would fall in the corridor, in view of his wife should she be watching.

He would not suspect, he would not think to meet resistance. Breath screaming to be released, exhausted from being too afraid to sleep Emma felt her head spin, then as it seemed she must fall the almost soundless click of the doorknob flicked like electricity along her nerves, jarring her back to wakefulness.

'Emma.'

Like a thunderclap in her ears the whisper drove all sense of caution from her mind. Let them send her to the gallows. Her life was a small price to pay in exchange for that of Fenton Gilmore!

With one short gasp Emma brought down the

lamp with all of her force, her spinning brain registering a figure stumbling forward before blackness folded her in deep shrouds.

'...Emma, Emma...'

Deep in the comfortable darkness which held Emma a voice spoke softly, a voice saying a name she did not know. Weariness pressed like a weight on every limb and Emma tried to shut away sound, yet the voice probed its way to her ears.

'Emma...'

Urgent in its softness, it beat against the consciousness she tried to close against it.

'Emma, please...'

Emma? Who was Emma? Why did she not answer? A pang of irritation stirred in Emma as the comfortable quietness was again disturbed.

'Emma ... please wake up.'

Emerging out of the mists enveloping her, pushing hard against mental resistance, the words admitted the first light of recognition into Emma's brain.

Rachel! The voice calling was Rachel! And she ... *she* was Emma!

Struggling to shake off the strands of fatigue still intent on holding her Emma called to her sister. 'I'm coming, Rachel, I'm coming.'

'Oh Miss Emma, thank God you be woke up!'

'Rachel.' Emma blinked to clear her vision, then saw the figure helping her to her feet.

'Ain't Miss Rachel, it be me, miss.'

'No.' Emma shook her head. 'It was Rachel, I heard her call, I have to go...'

Lowering the suddenly silent figure to the bed

68

Polly Lacey's head shook with sympathy at the memories she knew were flooding over Emma.

'Sit you still a minute,' she murmured, 'Give y'self a minute and things'll fall into place.'

Things would fall into place.

Her memory was fully recovered now. Emma stared across the room at the lamp lying broken on the floor, the stain of paraffin spreading into the carpet. But where was the man she had struck down, where was the body of Fenton Gilmore?

'I hit him?' She frowned confusedly. 'I struck him with the lamp ... I saw him fall.'

The maid answered, a faint smile touching her mouth. 'No miss, you hit me with the lamp, that is you almost hit me. It be fortunate light from the landing cast the wall of this room with shadow of an arm and a hand holding of that lamp, give me warning enough to duck beyond the full force of the blow or I'd have been a goner for sure.'

'But I saw him, I saw...'

'No.' A brief shake of the head added emphasis to Polly's denial. 'It were me you seen, I stumbled when I dodged away from the blow, nearly measured me length on the floor.'

'You.' Still slightly dazed Emma frowned the protest. 'But it had to be him, it is always he comes.'

'You means the master!' Polly's plain features registered contempt. 'Yes miss, we downstairs knows of his coming to you and to Miss Rachel, God rest her soul, that be why Mrs Coley sent me to ask would you come down to the kitchen. There be something her be wanting to speak of

69

and there be less likelihood of being overheard than here in your room.'

'But my aunt...'

'Be sleeping, miss, her and the master had words or so it seems for her took herself a drop of poppy juice to settle her nerves, that and a drop more Mrs Coley slipped into the cup of tea her called for will see her sleep like a babe for several hours.'

'My uncle...'

'Left some half-hour since, said he'd be late back but there be no certainty of that so please, miss, won't you come talk with Mrs Coley while there be chance.'

'I apologises for takin' the liberty of askin' you to come to the kitchen, I knows it don't be my place to go doin' of such.'

Emma smiled at the plump cook housekeeper. 'Please don't apologise, Mrs Coley, visiting the kitchen has always been a pleasure for me and Rach–' A choked sob filling her throat, Emma broke off.

'You was always welcome.' Bella Coley lifted the corner of a spotless white apron to her eyes. 'You an' that little 'un, Heaven rest 'er, it were ever a pleasure to me havin' you both sit at that table with a cake or a scone that one upstairs knowed nowt of...' She sniffed, dabbing her eyes a second time, then with a decisive stroke she smoothed the lowered apron and glanced at Polly before continuing. 'Me an' Polly, we wanted you come downstairs cos that way there be less chance of 'Enrietta interferin' afore I says what I

70

'ave to say, the kitchen bein' too menial a place for 'er ladyship. It were seeing of that book, reading what your sister wrote in her diary, the facts about that filthy lecher Gilmore, had meself an' Polly determine to up stakes and walk out of this 'ouse for good.'

'Leave!' Emma was astounded.

Glancing again at Polly bending to reach into a cupboard set alongside the large well polished black iron cooking range Bella Coley nodded. 'Ar miss, an' that today. An' if you'll be advised by me then you'll be doing of the same. That man won't leave off what he enjoys, he'll continue in his evil; the only way for you is to go, me an' Polly both believes that.'

'Mrs Coley is right, Miss Emma, you have to leave lessen you ends up the same way Sally James did.'

'Fenton Gilmore won't let no such happen again,' Bella put in dourly. 'Bitten once be enough for him, the next wench he gets pregnant'll be put away an' whether that be in some House of Correction, a lunatic asylum or a grave won't make no odds to Gilmore, an' that wife of his would back him up; that be why I says to you leave now, afore you have more to grieve along of grievin' for your sister.'

'...*you are not yet twenty-one, you are not of an age to say whether or not you remain beneath this roof, until you are...*'

She wanted only to turn her back on Beechcroft, to leave behind the many unhappy memories; but as her aunt's words resonated in her mind Emma said quietly:

71

'I cannot, not until I have attained my majority. Until that time I remain a ward of my aunt and uncle and as such must abide by their ruling. I have to stay here in this house whether I wish it or not.'

'Hmmph!' Bella Coley folded her hands over her ample stomach with a pronounced snort. 'And you thinks that be your salvation do you! You thinks once you reaches that comin' of age you'll be your own mistress, that Fenton Gilmore'll no more pester you, there'll be no more of his night-time visitin' of your room. Forgive me in the sayin' of this next bit, Miss Emma, but it be my belief you thinks that with Miss Rachel gone, Gilmore can have no more hold over you. Well, I says you be wrong in that, he be too fond of his nasty pleasures to give them up, leastways 'til he be ready to do so, nor as I told Polly will he follow the same road as was teken with Sally James; Fenton Gilmore nor the woman he married will not risk anything being said of his doings in this house.'

Coming to stand beside the table dominating the centre of the kitchen Polly dropped a cloth-wrapped bundle on to the chenille-covered surface saying as she did so, 'You should listen to Mrs Coley. I know you haven't seen much of life closeted so close in this house but you have to realise the lengths the Gilmores will go to in order to protect themselves. They won't never let you rule your own life, Miss Emma, they won't never let you free.'

'...I can have you proclaimed mentally disturbed and placed in an asylum ... that is within my juris-diction...'

72

To Emma, the words of her aunt still echoing in her head, the threat Fenton Gilmore had uttered had the blood curdle in her veins. What Polly said was true: Gilmore would see her locked away sooner than run any risk to his reputation. Mrs Coley and Polly had advised she leave – but to go where?

'Miss Rachel be gone... the Lord in His mercy tek 'er to Him.' Bella crossed herself piously, adding with a tearful sniff, 'And the Lord's justice catch up with the one who killed 'er. As for you, Miss Emma, y' must look to yourself, go from here while you still be able.'

'There is nothing I want more,' Emma answered the woman who for so long had been her friend. 'But they would only bring me back and by law I have no stand against them, they would be within their rights.'

For a long moment it seemed cook and maid agreed the hopelessness of what they had urged. In the silence broken only by the deep-throated tick of the large kitchen clock they glanced at one another. Then, the cap covering her grey hair flopping like some enormous snowflake, Bella Coley snapped derisively:

'The law! And what law be Fenton Gilmore abidin' by – that which he made for hisself. I reckoned on never saying this, I told meself it were none of my business, that Gilmore would tell it all once you was of age. Now I realises that wouldn't never 'appen and with readin' of your sister's words I've come to think as it do be my business.'

Drawing out a chair, motioning for Emma to

do the same, Bella sat heavily with her hands clasped together on the table.

'Miss Emma.' She paused, then with a short determined breath went on, 'Miss Emma you 'ave always believed your mother and father left you and Rachel behind while they themselves went holidayin', but that don't be true. Your mother had a growth in her stomach, it were your father told me the advice the doctor had given, it were of a surgeon in London who might be able to remove the tumour; but the man were leaving for the Continent before the end of the week so if your parents wished to consult him they must needs leave the next day. They would be gone for just a few days but even so your mother was loath to leave you and your sister behind; that were when the Gilmores come on to the scene. They were asked would they come stay at Beechcroft for the time your parents were away, your mother think-ing them comin' here would be less stressful for 'er children than 'aving them go stay in a strange 'ouse along of folk they'd only met once or twice, but...' She paused again, reaching for the corner of her apron and dabbing at moist eyes. 'But the Lord in His wisdom decreed otherwise, though it be a wisdom Bella Coley won't never understand.' Several swings of her head set the frilled edges of her white cap bouncing as she looked across the table to Emma. 'We was taught never to question the Lord or His works,' she sniffed loudly, 'an' that I abides by but there be summat I'll no longer keep from you. Your mother... rest 'er soul, thought 'Enrietta Gilmore be the best one to 'ave care of yourself and Miss Rachel.'

'Surely Mother was right.'

Apron flung back over her knees, white cap seeming to dance with a life of its own, Bella Coley's retort came sharply. 'Ar, and so 'er might 'ave been 'ceptin' 'Enrietta Gilmore don't be sister to your mother!'

A frown conveying her confusion, Emma could only stare.

'You be right to be flummoxed,' Bella said, interpreting the look, 'you've never been given cause to question and though I sees there be question now in your mind let me say lyin' never buttered no parsnips. Sooner or later them as indulges in it gets found out.'

'But...' Emma's short exhalation of breath had the words stumble out, 'but why would they not have told me? If Henrietta is not my aunt why has she not said so?'

'Ain't no "if" about it. I knowed that one from way back. Her were the oldest of seven, lived a few yards from my grandmother along of Drew's Court. Her mother died of consumption, the father followin' soon after. Never 'ad a decent pair of bloomers to 'er name, did Nellie Platt, but 'er weren't goin' to let that stand in 'er way, like 'er weren't havin' them brothers an' sisters stand in 'er way, they was all bundled off to be cared for by the parish. Nellie was deemed old enough at fourteen to look to carin' for 'erself. Seems your mother met her at the Methodist Chapel, Nellie pretendin' to religion none of 'er family ever practised, no doubt seein' the chapel-goin' as a way of meetin' a higher class of folk. It were but a few months later after my own grandmother passed away I were put to work as scullery maid in Oaks-well House. I worked my way up to be undercook then hearin' of the position of cook becomin' empty here at Beechcroft I applied an' was given the post. Imagine the surprise I got when 'Enrietta turns up to dinner, her then bein' Mrs 'Enrietta Gilmore no less. Well like I says I thought it no business of mine who your mother be friends with, an' if it pleased 'er to call 'Enrietta sister then that again weren't nowt of my business. As I've told you we thought it to be no more than a week afore your parents would be back to Beechcroft but then come news of an accident.'

In an instant Bella Coley's voice became that of Sally James calling across the garden.

Henrietta had sent the maid to bring both children to the sitting room. It seemed to Emma she felt again the cling of her sister's hand, heard her whisper as they followed to the room.

'...*we have done something wrong, is ... is she cross with us, Emma?*'

Emma's heart twisted at the memory. Rachel had ever been afraid of Henrietta.

They had stood, two frightened youngsters in a room where two days before their mother had held them in her arms, her gentle voice filled with love, telling them she and their father would be back home within the week; that Aunt Henrietta and Uncle Fenton had consented to stay at Beechcroft to be with them. '*You will have so much fun...*' The last echoing like a taunt, Emma almost cried aloud.

Fun had left Beechcroft with her parents.

'*Your parents will not be returning...*'

Cold, dispassionate, the words had greeted herself and Rachel.

'...*there has been an accident, they were both killed.*'

Where was the comfort, the assurance they were loved, they would be cherished and cared for? Was that not the natural reaction of an aunt who supposedly loved their mother?

'*Emma...*'

Rachel's tremulous voice reached again into Emma's mind.

'*Emma, I want mummy ... tell her I want my mummy.*'

'*Don't be so stupid, child!*'

It had been the snap of a vice.

'*...I have just told you, your mother and father are both dead. You are old enough to understand that, you are also old enough to understand that crying will not bring them back so you will stop it at once. From now on you will be the responsibility of Mr Gilmore and myself.*'

A responsibility! Young though she had been Emma had realised at that moment that was all Rachel and herself were to these people, a liability.

'It were the sound of a train...'

As if from afar the cook's words floated into Emma's brain banishing the ghosts of a sobbing young girl holding fast to an older sister who herself choked on tears.

'...they be monstrous things, shouldn't never be allowed!' Bella Coley shook her head in condemnation, her white cap adding a nodded vehemence.

'All that noise an' smoke be enough to stop a body's heart. It were the roar of that thing, the clanging of its iron wheels and then that scream

77

of its steam whistle had the horse bolt, tipping the carriage with your parents in it; instant it was.' Bella sniffed again. 'The Lord in His mercy let them feel no pain.'

7

'The Lord in His mercy let them feel no pain.'

The resentment of a child suddenly deprived of all it loved and cherished flared in Emma, freeing thoughts she had blocked for so long, potent anguished reflection which fought with beliefs passed to her by her parents; these now conflicted bitterly with the comfort Bella Coley had thought to give by saying it was not given to folk to question the ways of the Almighty, when asked by two heart-broken little girls, why if God loved them had He taken away their mother and their father?

But how could she not question!

'Mrs Coley and myself knows it's been hard for you.'

Though speaking quietly Polly's voice had challenged the emotion threatening to engulf Emma, breaking the coils of anger already wrapped round her, having them fall away so Polly's words and not her own thoughts sounded in her ears.

'We know it's been more so since Miss Rachel...'

The quiet voice had stilled but then at a nod from the cook had gone on, '...but we be convinced it will get harder yet, and if you be honest with *yourself then you'll admit there is nothing here for you but more misery. Life in this house won't go getting any more pleasant though I venture to say it will get a sight more the opposite.'*

'More the opposite.'

Emma's brain replayed Polly's warning while asking, was that possible? Could life at Beechcroft become more offensive? As quickly, the answer had come: yes, life for her would become ever more repulsive.

As she knelt beside a grave still so new it bore no sign of the gentle cover of grass, Emma touched the letters carved into stone.

Sacred to the memory of Rachel Lawrence
1880–1895.

'Rachel.' The half-sob made no impression on a silence so deeply potent yet so soft, holding in peace the loved ones entrusted to its care.

'Rachel, I know what he did to you, that he raped you, that you kept silent in order to protect me.'

Words she had read from the diary lanced like knives as Emma stared at the soft black earth.

'That was a trick,' she whispered again, 'the same one he used on me. I endured his abuse thinking that way to keep you from that very torment, yet all the time he... Oh Rachel... I was so blind! Why didn't I see, why didn't I see!'

'You leave her be!'

Deep in misery Emma was unaware of the shout sending several crows squawking indignantly from trees interspersed among the graves, their drooping branches brushing tenderly against headstones grey with age.

'You ain't tekin' her.'

A second determined shout coming on the heels of the first increased the noisy agitation of the birds. It penetrated Emma's conscious hearing.

'I don't want to ... don't let him make me, I don't want to.'

'...*Don't let him make me...*'

The cry stabbed at Emma, echoing in her mind. Rachel! It was Rachel crying out, Rachel being threatened.

'I'm here...'

Enmeshed yet in the shadows of the past Emma called to her sister.

'I'm coming Rachel, I'm coming.'

'*Don't let him take me, I don't want to go to that place.*'

The barn! Fenton Gilmore was taking Rachel to the barn!

Pitiful in its distress the sobbed cry had Emma mindful of nothing except the need to save her sister. She ran blindly in the direction of a voice which set her veins tingling.

'*You're coming with me, girl; and as for you, one word, just one word, and you'll be found with the life choked out of you.*'

'*No, please...I'll go with you, just don't hurt...*'

'*Don't hurt Emma.*'

Memory supplied words from the diary; Emma's cry, almost lost among the screeching of disturbed crows, answered the phantom in her mind.

'I'm here, Rachel, you don't have to go, he

won't make you do that ever again!'

Halted by a small figure hurling itself at her, her own arms closing protectively around it, Emma touched the head burying itself in her skirts. The hair! Bemused, she frowned. What had happened to Rachel's hair? It was no longer rich auburn but a brown so light as to be almost fair; and the clothes ... the dress was ragged and far from clean.

'You... I don't know who you be but like I told the boy, you'd best get lost unless you wish to wind up dead.'

The snarled words brought Emma's head up sharply. Fenton Gilmore! Confusion which until that moment had misted her brain cleared as though touched by sunlight. The man glaring at her was not Fenton Gilmore, and the girl. ... she glanced down at the fair head ... she was not Rachel!

The girl was not Rachel. But the fear was the same, the trembling of the thin figure attested to that, and the cause of her fear... could that also be the same as Rachel's had been?

'Don't let him tek her, don't let...'

'I don't warn twice!' threatened the man. The boy who had come to stand beside Emma held a stout branch gripped between both hands.

Her whole body taut as a wire, rendering movement stiff and jerky, Emma thrust a detaining hand in front of the boy, stepping defiantly forward to meet the threat.

The man did not look like Fenton Gilmore, but other aspects were chillingly similar. Cold unfeeling eyes, the air of dominant arrogance, no account taken of the fright of a young girl or the

81

boy trying to protect her. This man gave mind only to what *he* wanted. It was all too familiar.

'That goes for you as well.'

The cold stare had switched to Emma.

'I won't be tellin' you again neither, hand over the girl and get y' self gone afore you be given cause to regret.'

He was thickset, strong; if he should attack, strike out at them, they would have little chance against him. Emma trembled but even as he reached to pull the child from her she stepped back, evading the hand.

The man's eyes narrowed, his breath came hissing between yellowing teeth. His hand remained on a level with his waist, then its fingers closed into a fist and it began to rise.

Caught as if in some awful dream, transfixed as a rabbit held by the merciless gleam of a snake's eyes, Emma watched the arm lift; for an endless age it descended, slowly, slowly, it brought its promise nearer, then as it drew almost level with her face it dropped away, a shout of pain screaming over the quiet grounds sending a flurry of furious crows flapping toward the sky.

'You ain't hittin' nobody, mister, an' neither be you tekin' my sister.' The branch which had landed hard on the raised arm was brandished again. 'Now I advises you follow after that you give to us and get y' self gone afore you gets summat you'll really regret.'

With his lips curled into a snarl, a menacing half-laugh snatched back into his throat, the man stared at the branch then lifted a hate-filled stare to the young face.

'You dares to threaten me!' The words grated between teeth bared like fangs. 'You snipe-nosed little scum, I'll rip your bloody gizzard out!'

'Not with two broken arms you won't.' Quick as the retort the boy skipped aside, the make-do club cracking down hard on an arm nursing the one injured moments before.

It seemed sheer pain and fury would hurl the man at the figure blatantly defying him.

'*...I want mummy, tell her I want my mummy!*'

In Emma's mind the girl's cry became that of Rachel, but instead of drawing her deeper into a miasma threatening again to cloud her reason it seemed to clear her mind further.

She had not been able to help her sister but she must help the child clinging to her skirts, the boy adamantly protecting her. Twisting the girl about, thrusting her behind her skirts, Emma stepped forward to place her own body as a barrier between the man and the boy anger said he was prepared to kill.

'Get out of m way!' It was an animalistic growl his face twisting, yet as rage overrode pain he made to sweep Emma aside. Swift as mercury the boy darted round her, the branch thudding into his palm.

'You don't learn, d'you, mister?' The branch thumped again. 'But I be patient, I don't mind givin' the teachin' over again.'

As though wiped away with a cloth rage disappeared from the jowled face leaving it wreathed with supercilious scorn.

'I'm gonna tek that stick and beat your bloody head in,' he laughed, 'and then do the same to her as thinks to save you ... then I'll tek the little 'un.'

Nudging his body against Emma, his glance never leaving the face of the man bent on taking his sister, the boy urged. 'Run, Lily! Run, and you, miss, both of you run, I won't let this swine follow.'

Mustering every atom of courage Emma grabbed the improvised weapon, surprise releasing it from the boy's hands. She held her gaze steady to their opponent's face, a determined ring to her voice masking the fact that beneath the cover of her skirts her legs trembled as she said firmly, 'No! You go, go now, take Rachel and run!'

'Rachel?'

The boy's voice sounded puzzled but to Emma, quivering with nerves, it made no impression; she repeated the instruction that he should run.

'Quite the brave one, ain't we?' A snide grin underlay grunted words. 'Big sister stays to face the music while the little 'uns meks a run for it, but I don't know how you expects that twig to do anythin', it won't fight off what be in store for you!'

'P' raps it won't, but I'd lay odds some of that lot would, and enjoy the doin' of it.'

Following the boy's glance to where a cart bearing a plain coffin rumbled through the tall wrought-iron cemetery gates, the man saw a group of mourners following it, among them several men no doubt grudgingly permitted an hour's freedom from their employment to see a loved one to a last rest. They were still dressed in spark-pitted moleskin trousers identifying then as iron foundry workers, a rough jacket and muffler covering the special addition of a shirt donned in honour of the occasion. Emma's would-be attacker assessed his situation. He needed to take the younger girl; things would not go well for him turning up empty-handed, but it could prove even less to his benefit to risk a run-in with that lot.

Yards away stood the black-robed priest, white-lace-edged cassock bravely catching the last remnants of the setting sun. The mourners walked sombrely between rows of tombstones, some tall and imposingly topped with carved statuary while others, broken with age, stabbed upward from ivy-covered ground like jagged teeth.

'...I am the Resurrection and the Life...'

He recited from memory rather than the open book carried unconsulted in his hands, the intonation drifting on a silence now returned with crows once more settled in the trees. The priest turned on to a side path leading the pitiful cortège directly toward where Emma stood, the branch resolutely in hand.

His glance remained on the small procession as the man continued his mental computation. A move unexpected by the others, a quick grab for the girl, it could work but then a cry for help would not be ignored and those iron workers ... he looked quickly at each of the male attendants, their faces streaked with sweat-grimed dust wiped with a cloth, time not allowing a proper wash. These men would certainly answer a woman's cry as they would that of the girl, and even more certainly would leave a child snatcher with more broken bones than any doctor could put together again.

His venom-filled look flashed again to Emma;

words spitting against clenched teeth he ground out, 'This don't be the last of our meetin', mark that well ... it don't be the last!'

Bella Coley glanced at the line of small brass bells mounted on a board fixed to one wall of the kitchen of Beechcroft House, one of them ringing imperiously.

'That'll be 'er ladyship wantin' of a cup of tea.'

'Will I add a spoonful of the mixture?'

'No need.' Bella eased her ample frame in the chair set beside an empty table. 'The wench is gone so don't matter none 'er upstairs bein' in 'er full senses.'

'What will I say if her asks after Miss Emma?'

'You tells the truth, that you seen 'er walkin' in the garden, that you ain't seen 'er since.'

'Supposin'...'

'Supposin' you goes answerin' of that bell afore it drops off the wall!'

'But we had decided...'

'Decidin's can be broke!'

The emphatic retort signalled all argument was at an end; Polly reluctantly left the kitchen. Pausing at the closed door of Emma's bedroom she pondered a moment. Should she enter, make sure all was as it should be? But then the notes of yet another jangle of the bell reached faintly up through the silence of the still house. She tapped at a door a little way along the corridor and entered Henrietta's room. Heavy velvet drawn across the windows held the room in near-darkness, the heat of the fire Henrietta demanded even in the height of summer lending a dry airless feel.

'You rang, mum.' Polly dipped a diminutive curtsy.

'Several times!' Henrietta snorted, aggrieved at being kept waiting, then snapped irritably, 'Don't just stand there, open the curtains, then you can bring me tea.'

Yes mum, no mum, three bags full mum! Exercising sarcasm only in her mind Polly parted the drapes, comforting herself with the delightful prospect that today would see the end of Polly Lacey's having to be at this woman's beck and call.

'No.' Henrietta rose from her satin-covered bed. 'You may serve tea in the drawing room; ask the master to join me there.'

A gratifying smile lay hidden as Polly turned from the window. 'Master isn't home, mum.'

Halfway to a well-appointed dressing table Henrietta turned abruptly. 'Not home?'

'No mum.' Polly forced the smile to remain concealed. This bit she was going to enjoy. 'Left no more than an hour from his arriving.'

'Did he say what it was had him leaving so soon?'

Watch the mouth, the eyes, the whole expression! Polly savoured the promise of the next few moments, of the result her next words would bring, but it must appear she had no desire to utter them.

'Never said nothing of that, said only...'

Her glance dropped to the expensive Turkish carpet, its rich blue matching the exact colour of the drapes; Polly hesitated.

'Said?' Henrietta snapped. 'Said what, girl?'

'I ... I don't feel I should say, mum.'

Irritation developed rapidly into suspicion while Henrietta's lips tightened over teeth tight as a closed trap. What was it the girl did not want to say? What had she heard? Or was it something she had seen?

Emma! It flashed like ice yet its coldness lacked the effect of cooling the flames of jealousy and mistrust suddenly flaring along Henrietta's every vein. Fenton had left without coming to this room, without speaking to her, but had he visited Emma's room? Had he given way to the temptation she saw driving him harder each night, had he at last availed himself, given way to a craving she, his wife, knew he harboured? One which had many times resulted in violence, Fenton striking her whenever she had dared intimate the impracticality of his visiting the bedrooms of both Rachel and Emma, because of the suspicion this might arouse among the servants. But Fenton paid no regard to the possible gossip of servants; money would always silence a wagging tongue. Would it be called upon to buy that service again? Caught in the heat of passion Fenton would have paid no heed to anything other than his own desires, given no thought to being observed; and was that what the girl standing before her now had witnessed, a half-open door revealing Fenton lying with Emma?

Lying with Emma!

Almost choking at what she was envisaging, Henrietta forced words past clenched teeth.

'Did ... did the master speak with Miss Emma?'

'Went to Miss Emma's room.' Polly did not

need to raise her glance, her mistress's sharp intake of breath clearly expressing seething emotions.

She would not ask more, she would not demean herself to a mere servant! Emma then? No, it would be even more humiliating to enquire of her, to ask what had transpired between her and Fenton; it would also be hazardous, for should the girl speak of such a conversation to Fenton his rage would know no bounds and his wife would feel the brunt of it. Yet how else was she to find out?

Henrietta hesitated, thought clashing with thought, but jealousy, the driving need to know, prevailed:

'Did the master remain long with Miss Emma?'

Should she prolong the agony, make this woman pay if only a trifle for the hurt she had so often caused Emma and her sister? Should she lie, tell 'her ladyship' that due to duties in the drawing room she could not say how long her husband had spent upstairs? Revenge was a sweet dish but to swallow it whole was to shorten the pleasure of its eating. Pushing guilt aside Polly met the next thought with determination. She would take hers one bite at a time.

'Don't exactly know how long, mum, but...'

'But?'

The ice was cracking. Polly almost felt the impact of suspicion. One more bite and it would split apart.

'He...' She paused again, allowing the moment to ferment the poison in the other woman's mind. 'The master, I come out from cleaning the drawing room as he come down the stairs and well, mum, he looked right pleased with himself.'

Henrietta's silence was screaming louder than any words. Polly hugged satisfaction to herself; none of this could rebound on Emma, she was gone from this house, finished with the Gilmores for good.

Pleased with himself! Bitterness sliced like a knife through Henrietta. Fenton Gilmore was pleased with himself and devil take the rest. The devil had come so near to doing precisely that: the business of molesting children left in his care, the beating of a wife who tried to prevent it would not have shone a favourable light on him; even if unproven it would have been enough to bring about his downfall, yet she had held her silence, she had protected him and this ... this was her reward!

Her breath short and hard, her spine stiff and straight, Henrietta forced out a question to which she was reluctant to hear the answer.

'Did the master enquire after me?'

This would be the sweetest bite of all. Maintaining the entirely false pretence of unwillingness, her glance remaining lowered, Polly sniffed, implying that to answer was painful.

'He...' She sniffed again. 'He asked were you in the drawing room, when I said you was upstairs resting and should I ask you to come down he said...'

'What, what did he say?' The incisive demand slashed at Polly's hesitation.

'He... Oh mum, I don't want to repeat...'

Henrietta breathed a longer, harder breath.

'What?' she demanded again. 'Tell me, girl, what is it you do not want to repeat?' Then feeling this might not bring an answer added, 'Refusal will result in your instant dismissal.'

If only she knew the uselessness of that threat! Her inner laugh exuberant, Polly's tone nevertheless became suitably tinged with apprehension. 'The master...' She swallowed on a lump only pretended in her throat. 'He ... he laughed and said why would he wish to speak with a dried-up prune of a woman.'

8

'I thanks you for helpin' my sister, miss, but I could've seen him off.' Brown eyes glinting, the tow-haired lad glared after the figure making toward the entrance to the cemetery.

'Yes miss, you have my thanks along of Timmy's.'

'You shouldn't have come 'ere in the first place!' Still gleaming anger the chestnut glance switched to the girl, her hand as yet holding Emma's skirts. 'I've told you 'til I be sick of tellin', it don't do for you to come wanderin' to this place on your own.'

'I wanted to talk to mum, I wanted to be with my mum.'

The gleam of anger replaced by a gentler look, the boy drew his sister protectively into his arms, his words murmuring softly above the head pressing against his shoulder. 'I knows you misses,

Mother, we both does, but comin' to sit along of her grave don't do no good Lily, you have to learn, ain't nothin' can bring her back.'

'But I can talk to her, Mum hears me, I know her does.'

Over the sobbed reply, fighting tears filming his own eyes, the boy looked at Emma saying quietly. 'Been this way for weeks, ever since Mother died, I can't get her to see it be useless to come here; the dead can't listen nor can they answer, that be right don't it, miss?'

Heartbreaking in its appeal the girl's look lifted to Emma. 'My mum does hear, don't her, miss?'

Instantly the pages of memory flicked open showing Emma two girls, the younger one turning an innocent gaze to the other while asking, *'Mummy does hear, doesn't she, Emma?'*

A different graveside, different children; but the same grief, the same need for understanding. Emma's heart went out to the girl whose toffee-brown eyes filled with the same plea as had been Rachel's. But did she have the right to answer as she had then, offer someone completely unknown to her the same comfort she had given a sister? And the boy, would he understand or would he view anything she said as interference? Caught in the cleft stick of indecision Emma was silent.

'See Lily, I told you it be daft, talkin' at a grave don't do no good, this woman agrees on that.'

'No, no I do not agree, not in the way you think.' She had not intended to speak but catching the unhappiness on the girl's face as her brother turned her to leave, Emma's words had slipped out.

'Ain't no other way!' The defiant denial found emphasis in the glance flashed at Emma.

'Maybe there is.' Emma let it hang in the air.

'What way be that then?'

It had taken several moments, time in which he had stared at her, pondering whether to take up the inherent challenge or walk away.

Trying to hide the tremor left by the picture memory had shown Emma said quietly, 'I knew a girl, who like Lily would sit beside the grave of her mother, she also would talk.'

'Surely you don't believe–'

'What *I* believed was not important.' Emma cut gently across swift cynicism. 'What was important was understanding of how someone other than myself deals with a sorrow so strong it seems it could never heal. Lily needs your understanding as Rach ... as that other girl ... needed mine. Talking to her mother is Lily's way of dealing with her heartbreak, of easing the pain. The need will not be with her forever, it will pass, but in the meantime you must be patient.'

Passing beyond the gates they had reached while talking, the boy shook his head. 'Be all right to speak of patience miss, but how do I work wonderin' where my sister be, of not knowin' is her biding by what I've said or run down to Wood Green Cemetery, and even worse has her been teken off like almost happened today.'

Taken off! It rang in Emma's mind. The diary had said Rachel was going away; had she come here to the cemetery, had she come to stand beside their parents' grave, to 'talk' with them as she had so often done when she and Rachel had come here together, had she been 'taken off' as this girl almost had? Taken to be raped then murdered.

The thought a sickness in her mind she looked at the pair, the boy protectively holding his sister's hand. If only Rachel had confided in her, she could have protected her.

'We thanks you again, miss, it were good of you to 'elp.'

'Wait ... please.' Emma reached involuntarily to the boy beginning to move away her hand dropping quickly when he turned to look at her. 'The man, do you know who he is, his name, where he lives?'

'Don't know none of that miss, but I, knows what he ain't.' The boy's mouth twisted disgust. 'He ain't no whipper-in, he don't be after takin' back kids who be runnin' from the workhouse, but even if he was he wouldn't be takin' Lily. My sister ain't never goin' into that place not so long as I be breathin'; that there...' he nodded his head toward the cemetery, 'be preferable; that workhouse be a place where the livin' would be better off dead, and houses many who wishes they was.'

Following the flick of the tousled head Emma stared across the now-deserted burial ground. Memorial stones reached upward drawing down the gathering evening, draping grey about grey, merging colour with colour, hiding away their sorrows within it. But how did one hide the sorrows of the heart?

'Emma, look Emma, see what I have made!'

It seemed to come out of the shrouded mists settling over pitted headstones, words followed by the light laugh of a delighted child seeming to echo between frowning tombs. Rachel! Emma's heart called to the illusion her mind showed, to two smiling girls both enveloped in aprons reaching to their feet, their faces smudged with flour, their aunt's absence affording moments of happiness.

'Rachel!' The whispers died on her lips, the hand she had reached toward the girl present only in her mind dropped again to her side. Emma's throat trembled on a sob. Those had been the happy times and few though they were they left a warmth in her soul, memories she would hold there forever.

'The girl, miss, the one you says would sit along of her mother's grave, would talk with her believin' what her said bein' heard, was her kin to you?'

A tug at her skirt banished recollection, exiling the smiling children once more into the past. Emma looked at the thin face turned innocently toward her.

'Lily!' A sharp snatch pulled the girl away. 'Ain't I said it be wrong to go askin' questions what 'ave nothin' to do with you! Ain't I told you it be rude!' Then with a swift glance at Emma he added, 'I 'pologises on account of my sister, miss.'

She had heard the girl's inherent sympathy, felt the bond built of mutual heartbreak and wanted to answer, to tell her of Rachel. But even as Emma prepared to speak the boy took to his heels, pulling his sister along with him.

'...*Refusal will result in your instant dismissal.*'
'Her said that?' Bella Coley watched the younger

woman's face crease in a mischievous smile.

'...*instant* dismissal!' Polly Lacey imitated the haughty expression of her mistress.

'I bet that had you worried.' Bella smiled.

Polly struck a dramatic pose, her eyes twinkling. Hands clasped, lips trembling, she said brokenly, 'Oh mum, please ... I ain't being disrespectful, it ... it's just ... well I wouldn't want to cause you no hurt.' Then the twinkle gave way to the hardness of contempt as she added, 'Like hell I wouldn't!'

'Language, Polly Lacey! I'll 'ave none of that!' Bella admonished but could not entirely hide her amusement. 'Now tell me in good Christian language just what you did say to 'Enrietta.'

Polly chuckled softly. 'I told her ladyship naught but the truth.'

'An' that were?'

'Exactly what Gilmore said, and I agrees with him.'

'What you agrees or don't agree with don't be what I asked!' Bella retorted. 'Now you give me a straight answer my girl lessen you wants to feel a ladle about your shoulders!'

That wouldn't happen. Bella Coley had often threatened but she was too soft-hearted to put threat into action – or at least she had been up until now. Deeming it expedient not to tempt providence Polly resisted the urge to continue with her teasing saying in a level controlled voice, 'I'd already told he'd asked was her in the drawing room and I'd said no, the mistress were in her room resting; then when I asked did he wish me to bid her come downstairs he'd laughed and said why would he wish to speak with a dried-up prune of a woman.'

'You told 'Enrietta that!' Bella's voice echoed surprise.

Polly's answer was defiantly sharp. 'Why not, it were the truth her asked for so the truth her got, and the look on her face at the hearing of it were worth a year's pay.'

'*A dried-up prune!*' Bella could not help but savour Polly's reply. Having that said by a domestic servant, knowing that servant could, and very well might, repeat it to others in the town, repetition likely to reach the ears of employers, the very social circle with which the Gilmores associated, would have galled the hoity-toity Henrietta. An embarrassment ... but little justice for what that pair had put Emma and her sister through.

'Emma,' Bella said as a thought registered. 'Did 'er upstairs ask of Emma?'

Freed from her frilled lace cap Polly's curls gleamed, a shake of her head catching waxen yellow reflections from the kitchen's gas lamps, spreading richer amber glints among soft hazel. 'I thought when going to answer that bell it would be Miss Emma I would be told to fetch; I admit I was at a loss as to what I would answer when it were discovered Miss Emma weren't in the house nor were her in the garden, but luckily none of that were called for.'

'No.' It was the turn of the older woman's hair to catch the gaslight as she glanced at the small brass bell jingling in its place on the wall. 'That call were not asking Miss Emma be fetched, but this one most likely is.'

'I don't have to answer.' Polly's lower lip jutted.

Rising from her chair Bella Coley glanced at the dresser, where a neatly folded white apron together with a frilled cap lay on its polished surface. 'No,' she said quietly, 'you don't, but for meself I wouldn't forego seein' the expression on 'Enrietta's face when 'er learns there be no longer any staff to this 'ouse. I only wishes I could tell 'er Emma be gone as well; I wouldn't miss the seein' of the look that would bring, not supposin' the cost were twice a year's wage.'

And again that ain't likely to happen! Smiling at the thought, comforted by touching a pocket holding the year's salary paid to her no more than two days since, Polly followed the ample figure leading the way to the drawing room.

'Why are you not in uniform?' Henrietta's demand met the woman entering the tastefully furnished room.

''Cos I don't 'ave a mind for wearin' of it.' Bella's reply, bland in the extreme, fuelled an already well-built fire of irritation.

'You don't have a mind!' Henrietta snapped. 'Well maybe you have a mind for dismissal!'

'That I 'ave mind for!' Bella nodded. 'But the dismissin' be of my doin' an' not of yourn.'

'What do you mean?'

Complacent as before Bella smiled as she answered. 'I means *I* be dismissin' *you*.'

'Don't be ridiculous! Whoever heard of a menial dismissing her mistress.'

Carpet bag over one arm, the hat she had placed

on top of piled-up grey hair bobbing with a splendid array of feathers, Bella's smile remained.

'Ridiculous is it,' she said, 'an' how ridiculous will it seem when folk finds you got nobody to cook or clean, what'll you say when you be asked why? And afore you answers let me tell you it won't be easy findin' a body to take my place, an' for certain it won't be a body *I* gets to talk to.'

'That goes for me an' all.' Polly stepped to Bella's side. 'You want a maid to fetch and carry then you be having to look elsewhere for I'm leaving along of Mrs Coley.'

Like grey ice Henrietta's glare moved from one face to the other but when she spoke her voice held a veiled warmth of triumph. 'Very well, leave, but you will both do so without remuneration.'

'Huh!' Bella's scornful toss of the head had feathers dance again. 'Menial and remuneration! Them be big words; don't be many along of Drew's Court 'ave the understandin' of them.'

Sitting stiff and straight in her chair, only the sharp twist of fingers betraying her sudden apprehension, Henrietta's breath caught in tight lungs as Bella continued scathingly.

'But then Nellie Platt were quick to learn anythin' that would be to her benefit, such as leavin' her brothers and sisters to the workhouse rather than herself workin' to keep 'em ... like pretendin' to be sister to Mary Lawrence, the true mistress of Beechcroft. But you don't be the only one to 'ave learned,' Bella's head shook again, 'Bella Coley's also done a bit of that and now her be goin' to add some to your own; such as the things a so-called "guardian" gets up to in this 'ouse. Yes Nellie!' Bella paused at the other woman's swift intake of breath. 'I sees you knows I be on about that the changin' of a given name, but let me share summat else with you. I seen the marks on the body of the child that were carried into this 'ouse, a child you thought kept hidden; but Bella Coley saw, her saw the bruises on them poor legs, the purpling on that tender stomach: they was the marks of rape, bruises the same as the ones were left on the legs and stomach of Sally James after your husband took his pleasure ... a pleasure you fears he took with a fourteen-year-old girl. Weren't nothing said to the police cos of havin' no proof but remember, Nellie, the Lord might take His time a-metin' out His justice but He never fails in the doin' of it.'

Following after Polly as she walked to the door Bella hesitated, looking back to Henrietta who sat like stone. 'Oh,' she said, hitching the carpet bag higher on her arm, 'there be one more thing ... re-muneration, the fancy word you used, it alludes to wages Polly an' me be entitled to for the year...' She paused, allowing the words to penetrate before adding, 'You don't need to piddle your drawers a worryin' over that, Gilmore paid the both of we afore he left.'

Had Fenton been informed of their intention to end their employment in this house? Henrietta stared at the closed door, her thin lips clenched with bitterness almost to invisibility. Was that one more thing he had not wished to discuss with his wife? His 'dried-up prune' of a wife!

9

She had not meant to stay so long. Standing alone beside the tall ornamental iron gates of the cemetery Emma glanced back toward where her family lay, their graves becoming lost amid the rapidly falling evening. She had thought to spend no more than a few moments beside that patch of black earth, its only relief a small knot of faded wild flowers, a few minutes which might somehow ease the burden lying heavy on her heart, a weight of guilt that she had not protected Rachel as she ought.

'I didn't know, Rachel! I didn't know!'

Caught as though by unseen hands the cry drifted away to be lost among rustling leaves of trees whose branches seemed to reach for the shadows drawing the darkness in and around themselves, longing to become one with the night, yearning to forget the sorrows of the day.

Forget!

Soft as breath the song of leaves brushed against her mind.

A sigh in the velvety dusk, gentle, lulling, the trees sang their counsel.

Forget!

For a moment it reached into Emma's very soul, its promise of peace, of blessed forgetfulness drugging her senses, numbing them to all but that tranquil murmur; but with the call of a

101

roosting bird the trance fell away.

Forget! Tears choked her throat at the thought. She would never forget... nor would she ever forgive.

'*All Fenton Gilmore 'as, all him an' 'Enrietta lives on belonged to your father...*'

Words spoken while Polly had opened the bundle she had placed on the large kitchen table replaced the whisper of trees.

'*...they've lived like gentry while keepin' you an' your sister – God rest her soul – in little more'n poverty, begrudgin' the very clothes you wore even though they be the cheapest 'er dared buy.*'

'*These don't be of the best neither but you be welcome supposing you'll take 'em... Mrs Coley and me thinks you'll be less noticed if you wears these rather than coat and bonnet. Anybody searchin' of you won't go looking for a woman dressed in skirts and shawl.*'

Polly had taken several articles of clothing from the bundle and with Mrs Coley's urging had helped Emma remove her dress then replace it with white cotton blouse and dark heavy cotton skirt, patches of wear attesting to both age and usage.

'*It ain't what you should 'ave to wear, Miss Emma,*' Polly had lamented as she fastened small cloth-covered buttons to secure the sleeves of the blouse about each wrist.

'*You shouldn't 'ave to be got up like this, it ain't right, it ain't right at all.*'

'*Ain't right but needful all the same.*'

Bella Coley's reply sounded again in Emma's mind.

'Er upstairs'll set folk to searchin' for a wench in a blue coat with bonnet to match, her'll think, Miss Emma, you left wearin' your Sunday go to church outfit.'

'But when she sees them in my room?'

'Her won't!' Bella's curt reply had cut short the question. 'Her won't find no sign of 'em 'cos the minute you leaves this 'ouse that hat an' coat be goin' into the fire and may Heaven's justice have the Gilmores go into a much hotter fire, her for the lyin' an' cheating that's robbed you of what be rightfully yourn, and him, Fenton Gilmore, for...'

For the rape and murder of your sister.

Emma's mind said the words Bella had not. Beneath the brown chequered shawl Polly had draped about her shoulders Emma touched the diary that lay in a pocket of the rough twill skirt.

'... all Fenton Gilmore 'as ... belonged to your father.'

In the silence of her heart Emma answered. Beechcroft and all that goes with it Fenton Gilmore could keep; the abusing of a helpless young girl, the evil he forced upon Rachel, for that he would pay.

Lifting the shawl over her head, holding a corner of it to hide the trembling of her mouth, the thought became a whisper on her lips. 'I swear to you Rachel,' fervent and soft it spilled into the listening shadows, 'I swear Fenton Gilmore will pay!'

She was alone.

From the shadowed doorway of the Golden Cross public house a figure watched the solitary woman with a shawl drawn over her head.

Not old. Narrowed eyes challenged the deepening gloom. The movements, the walk, it was not that of an old woman. Yet she was no babe.

No child.

Eyes alert, gaze following the draped figure, possibilities brought a smile to a face half hidden by the turned-up collar of a rough jacket. Not to move yet! caution advised. Could be her was with one of the stallholders, yet if so why not stand alongside, why flit from one to another? Being friendly, taking time to exchange a word or two with each? That had to be considered.

Shoved impatiently by a customer wanting access to the pub the shrouded figure reacted swiftly, drawing an empty box from the jacket and shaking it then slurring, 'Bloody box be empty, how do a bloke light a pipe wi'out a bloody match!'

The ruse had worked before and it had worked again. The sly smile returned beneath the raised collar. That customer to the Golden Cross would remember – if he ever bothered to think – only that a man already three sheets in the wind had wanted a match to light his pipe. But he wasn't drunk. The smile spread. And it wasn't the smoking of a pipe he was after.

That one weren't after buying. Watching intently, the man's gaze followed the movement from stall to stall, registering the fact the figure carried no basket nor did it reach out to examine any article; he had observed too many women going about their shopping in Wednesbury market place, seen the way they inspected every last item, heard them haggle down to the last farthing to be fooled by this one.

So what was her about? He returned pipe and box to their respective pockets; a stumbling gait was propelling him from the doorway when, followed by a cloud of tobacco smoke, two men strode from the tavern. Though keeping to the pretence of taking too much drink his eyes scanned the buildings surrounding the market square. There were too many folk around as yet to risk making his move, he must bide his time; but where best to bide it? Lose sight of the woman and he mebbe wouldn't find her again for with shawls drawn against the night women in the market all looked the same. But underneath them shawls they wasn't. P'raps this one was plying her trade among the stallholders, a trade more often practised in the vicinity of the railway station or the town's more stylish hotels. If the one he watched was indeed a prostitute then he was wasting his time, that soul wasn't on his shopping list. But trade had not been of the best for a week or more so mebbe he should see what was on offer.

But approach the wrong one! Caution again stepped in. Do that and all hell could break loose. Though circumspect in their shopping the women of this town were less so when something annoyed them; their shouts could alert half the nation.

Crossing the gradually emptying marketplace, sidling into the equally shadowed doorway of Benjamin Wright's watchmaker's and jeweller's shop, closed and shuttered some half-hour since, he again decided upon caution. With his hands pushed deep into pockets ready to pull the matchbox trick should the need arise, he leaned deeper into the cover of the doorway. He would wait a while, be more sure of his quarry, not just because of the penalty the law imposed on those engaged in his line of business; no, not so much the magistrates, there was another, one who would impose his own sentence and that wouldn't be to the benefit or the advantage of Jud Perry.

Customers began to emerge in twos and threes from the several public houses bordering the market place, men dressed in moleskin trousers teamed with flat cap, jacket and neckerchief, workers from the coalmines and iron foundries making their way home after taking a nightly glass or two. Would the woman he watched belong with one of them, a father, a brother, a husband?

'Bugger it!' Seeing a man detach himself from a laughing trio and walk across to the woman Jud Perry swore softly into the collar half covering his mouth. He'd stood about for nothing! That one might have been suitable, certainly none that frequented the taverns or flaunted their dubious invitation outside the Green Dragon or even the more salubrious Talbot Hotel would be acceptable. His glance flicking across to the further corner of the market square he surveyed the latter. Might it be worthwhile? But even as he gauged the luck of finding a new and as yet inexperienced 'lady of the night' a shout of laughter recalled his attention. The man had rejoined his companions leaving the woman shrinking back against the wall of a darkened shop. Luck! The smile revived. That lady had not deserted Jud Perry.

A few more minutes! Most of the candlelit jars shedding meagre light on the stalls were already extinguished, the traders having packed their wares and left for the night; only a greengrocer remained and he was lifting empty boxes on to a handcart. A few more minutes! Removing his hands from his pockets, turning down the collar of his jacket as the final candle was blown out, Jud Perry watched the cart being wheeled away, then stepped out from the doorway.

Why had the maid not hurried to take his coat? Fenton Gilmore stood in the hallway of Beech-croft House. Why were the gasoliers unlit? A frown creasing his brow, he listened to the silence. There was nothing unusual in that, the house was always quiet, yet – the frown deepened – it was more than the silence, the whole aura was ominous ... almost as though some threat waited to pounce.

That was absurd! Impatient as much with him-self as with the maid who would receive her dis-missal forthwith he threw coat and cane to the floor.

'They ... they gave no reason.' Henrietta's glance fell before the stare of the man who had stridden into the sitting room. Fenton was already angry; how to answer without making him more so?

'They gave no reason.'

The mimicked reply sending warnings along her spine, Henrietta felt more than saw him angrily snatch a taper to light in the embers of the fire, then with it touch the gasoliers set one each side of the ornamental fireplace.

Mimicry was replaced by scorn, that same

107

emotion seeing the taper hurled into the dying fire. Fenton turned slowly.

'They gave no reason.'

Protracted, unhurried, each word lingered in the space between man and woman. But Henrietta knew from times past the quietness of their delivery was no guarantee of receding anger. Fingers twisting nervously, she kept her gaze lowered.

Waiting for the reply which did not come Fenton felt again the foreboding that he had encountered in the hall and underlying it the certainty his wife was not telling the all of their servants' peremptory exit from the house. Unease adding an extra cutting edge to his voice he gritted:

'Are you saying they left these premises without a word? If so then perhaps you will also inform me as to how you came to be in receipt of that information?'

Not to answer would be to inflame the ire already so evident, would be to invite the blows her husband was ever fond of treating her to.

'I,' Henrietta swallowed against the constriction fear placed in her throat, 'I ... I...'

'No lies, Henrietta!' It lashed the room, snapping like a whip.

Lies! Henrietta's silent laugh was disparaging. Wasn't their whole life a lie, a fabrication which had begun with their coming here to Beechcroft? But then lies on her part had begun long before that; they had started back in Drew's Court, stories told by a girl determined to leave the life of poverty behind; and Fenton Gilmore, what lay hidden in those years before she had met him?

Adopting a nonchalant pose, one highly polished boot resting on the edge of the hearth, an elbow on the mantelshelf, Fenton tapped his fingers rhythmically against the smooth marble, but it was the caustic bite of his tone that broke Henrietta's thoughts.

'The last time we were together you, my dear, were not deaf.' Spread fingers drummed a slow emphatic beat. 'Stupid yes, but not deaf. Perhaps I should have you examined by a doctor after all!'

Stupid! Henrietta stung beneath the slur but mention of medical attention, with its underlying threat, clamped hard in her stomach. He used that weapon against her more and more often.

Glancing furtively at the figure half turned away from her Henrietta was not duped by the stance. Fenton was never casual.

'I ... I apologise,' she said quickly, the stilling of his fingers adding to the warning tripping along her spine. 'I meant they gave no explanation as to their decision to leave.'

Across from her a long irritated breath marred the pause.

Henrietta knew she must expound further but to repeat all that was said would serve only to turn annoyance seething behind that seemingly unconcerned manner to rage.

'I rang for afternoon tea, I expected Lacey to answer as was her duty but when she eventually came to this room she was accompanied by Coley and both were attired in outdoor clothes. I asked the meaning of that seeing neither of them was due a free afternoon, then when they replied they were leaving I told them they would forfeit any wage due them.'

Leave it there! Henrietta's sixth sense whispered judiciously. Don't let him learn he had been forestalled, that cook and parlourmaid had been wise enough to wait until after they had been paid before taking the course they had.

The resulting silence could mean her explanation had been sufficient, that he would ask nothing more, but Henrietta's hope was smashed as he said quietly, 'Emma, you have not mentioned Emma. She was in this room with you, I trust.'

Emma! Senses flaring wildly Henrietta had to clamp her jaws to prevent the exclamation escaping. She had not thought of the girl, not thought to check she was in her room, but then where else would she be? Pushing aside thought and question, the momentary delay they caused in her reply being enough to alert him to that omission, she said quickly, 'Emma had been a long time in the garden, when she came indoors I advised she go upstairs to her room, to rest until dinner.'

Despite her stress the lie lay easily as to the truth of that statement.

'You of course accompanied her, saw to it she was comfortable before retiring to your own room, a practice I know you observe each afternoon.'

It had taken time in coming, the reply which was in itself an accusation. Henrietta's nerves jarred again. 'She ... she was quite comfortable.'

'I am pleased at your thoughtfulness, my dear.' He turned then, an almost feline smile touching his mouth. 'Now perhaps you would bring her here; maybe she will be able to throw a little light on the problem of why the staff have left.'

10

'Emma, Emma wake up!!'

In the doorway of the unlit bedroom Henrietta frowned impatiently. Fenton's mood would not be improved by being kept waiting.

'Emma,' she called more sharply. 'Not to answer is childish behaviour that will avail you nothing, so you will accompany me to the sitting room ... unless of course you wish your uncle to come for you himself'

Fenton would not be averse to that; rather, he would relish it. No household staff to witness his visit, a wife for whose feelings or concerns he didn't care tuppence, yes, Fenton would welcome the opportunity to come to this room; but he would not get it! Jealousy curdling her blood, Henrietta stormed into the bedroom.

There were matches with the lamp on the bedside table, obviously the stupid girl had overlooked that. In the dim moonlight filtering through the window she made her way across the room and lit the oil lamp.

'Now!' Turning to look down upon the bed the words she had been about to utter trailed into nothingness. The girl was not lying there! Grabbing the lamp, holding it high, she stared at the shadows drawing back before its glow. The room was empty! She was not here! She was not downstairs! Did that mean...! Had she left along with Bella Coley? Henrietta's nerves flared, her hand trembled, causing the lamp to cast long flickering shapes across the walls, shadows to dance on moonlit windowpanes.

Window! Henrietta's mind stumbled to reach forgotten words, then as memory obliged she breathed relief. Lacey had said Emma was walking in the garden. That must be where she was now. At the window, the lamp held close to the panes, she peered into the gloom below but within seconds that swift flash of relief ebbed away. Emma was headstrong but she was not foolish enough to sit in the garden alone and at night.

That encounter this afternoon! That angry exchange!

'...*it is incontrovertible truth*...'

It seemed the words rose from the night-cloaked garden.

'...*you knew and yet took no action ... you stood by while Fenton Gilmore abused both Rachel and myself ... I have Rachel's diary.*'

Incontrovertible truth!

Blood pounded in Henrietta's veins.

Rachel's diary!

It had been said with utter conviction, the emotion driving words of ice-cold anger; anger strong enough to make Emma hand that diary over to the police?

A sound from the stairs reached beyond the flurry of thought. Fenton! It could only be him. With a supreme effort Henrietta brought the trembling of her hand under control as she faced the open doorway.

'*She is in the house, she has to be, she would not go anywhere without my permission.*'

'*And that you did not give!*'

Fenton's supercilious answer had chilled every fibre.

They had returned to the sitting room. Sitting there once more alone Henrietta hugged both hands to the handkerchief held to her face.

'*You did not give your permission and of course she would not leave the house without it!*'

Seeing for himself Emma was not present he had stood in the doorway, his whole body emanating threat, then, every word the snap of splintering ice, had said:

'*So of course her outdoor clothes are still in the cupboard!*'

She had not thought to check. He had given her no time to reply but had snatched the lamp, going with it downstairs to the large cupboard inside the hall. Holding its light to the door he threw it wide.

Emma's coat and bonnet were missing.

In the lightning seconds following the discovery she had tried to speak but her faltering words had proved their own confession. The girl had left the house and she, Henrietta, had not prevented it.

His eyes reflected the light of the lamp, glittering like the tips of daggers. He had shoved her roughly aside, to stride into the sitting room.

'*You stupid fool!*' he had screeched at her following after him. '*You stupid fool!*'

Hurled into the fireplace the lamp had smashed, paraffin spreading a sheet of flame across the hearth, but Fenton had ignored the danger. Rage

113

burning every bit as hot inside him he had launched himself at her, grabbing her by the shoulders, shaking her so hard her head had bobbed on her neck.

'Do you realise what this means ... do you?'

He had released her but only to drive a closed fist to the side of her head, a blow which had her senses reel, yet still his voice had thundered as though rising from a well of deep water.

'Unlike you that girl is no fool, she may well talk to folk who knew her parents. She could ask questions, such as who was her father's solicitor; even you must know the outcome of that! We would lose everything!'

She had stared at the figure which came to stand over her, a tall shape swaying back and forth. But Fenton had not swayed, she had realised later, her lurching senses had made it seem that way.

'In your case that would not matter...'

The bitter laugh rang again in Henrietta's mind.

'...you can slip back into the slum of Drew's Court, you would fit well seeing you are as dried and sour as the drudges who live there.'

'Fenton please ... I'm sorry...'

Handkerchief pressed to her face, Henrietta shuddered with the memory of being snatched to her feet, another stinging slap biting against her mouth.

'You are sorry!'

He had grasped her face to force her to look into his, into rage-blackened eyes narrowed to slits, the hiss of pure venom filling every word.

'You do not yet realise the true meaning of "sorry", but should I not find that girl then, my dear, you will experience that emotion in its fullest depths! So you *had better pray, pray very hard I do not return alone.'*

He had flung her aside as a child might throw down a worn-out rag doll then had stormed out of the house.

Wincing from the sharp sting as she removed the handkerchief from her cut lips Henrietta lowered her hands to her lap.

'Do you realise what this means?'

Like spilled acid it burned in her brain.

Staring into the flame-blackened hearth she smiled against the pain throbbing in her head.

'Yes,' she whispered, fingers twisting the blood-stained handkerchief. 'Yes Fenton, I realise what it means just as I realise the root of your anger is fear, fear not solely of losing house and business, of never having been appointed guardian of the children of Austin and Mary Lawrence, but of the world coming to see you as you are, the abuser of those children, a cruel, violent rapist.'

Fingers suddenly still, she let her glance rove over the splinters of broken glass, the brass base of the shattered lamp gleaming in the pallid light of the gasoliers, then back to the hearth.

'Search for her, Fenton.'

She lifted one hand to touch her broken mouth.

'Search thoroughly for Emma Lawrence while I do as you ordered and pray; I will pray fervently you fail in that venture but,' she smiled again, 'I will pray God, I will pray very hard the fears I know you hold in your heart will one day be realised.'

She had not expected it to be like this; but then

had she thought carefully she would have known it could not possibly be the same.

The last candle extinguished, the last stall-holder having cleared his pitch and vacated the market, Emma stood alone and bewildered in the near total darkness.

She had visited the town before of course, but only ever in the daytime and that in the company of her aunt. Her aunt! A picture of the hard unsmiling face rose spectre-like in her mind; she drew the shawl closer as if to ward off the image. She need never address that woman as 'aunt' again, need never meet her or Fenton Gilmore.

But your promise. It seemed the words whispered from surrounding shadows. Your promise to see him pay for what he has done.

A promise made in the grip of misery and guilt; one more time she had not considered the implications. She had murmured to Rachel, given her word; but how to carry it out! She had paid that problem little attention just as she had the question of where she would go on leaving Beechcroft.

'You don't know what you be lettin' y'self in for, ain't like you've ever 'ad to fend for y'self, I tells you it be best you come wi' meself and Polly.'

Why had she refused Mrs Coley's offer?

The Golden Cross spewed a noisy group of men into the street. Emma shrank back against the wall, afraid the very sound of her breathing would draw their attention.

The shawl covering the tremble of her lips, set teeth holding back the sob of fear, she watched the figures melt away in the darkness. But the sounds emanating from the public house said those men would not be the last, there would be others, others who possibly spotting her would think as that man had only minutes ago, that being alone she must be a woman of easy virtue. Oh Lord, why had she not listened to Mrs Coley, why had she not at least asked that woman where a suitable lodging might be found?

Lodging! For a moment Emma felt stunned; then her returning senses brought with them a further alarm. A room in a hotel would cost money and that also she had refused to accept from Mrs Coley. But she could not stay on the street all night. Beechcroft! Perhaps Polly and Mrs Coley had not yet left the house; she could go to the kitchen door, they would hide her there and tomorrow she could make some plan for her life.

But even the kitchen was not safe from Fenton Gilmore!

Like a trap the thought sprang. Discovering she was not in her room he would search the entire house, question and requestion both his wife and his servants ... but Mrs Coley and Polly would not tell him where she had gone. For a comforting moment Emma basked in the warmth of the thought, then gasped as the cold flood of reality washed over her. Fenton Gilmore was as shrewd as he was evil. It would be the work of a moment for him to deduce that no matter where she thought eventually to go she would not do so without first visiting the cemetery, that same insight telling him also the love she had for Rachel would have her linger at that grave, that in all probability she had not left herself time enough to get clear of Wednesbury.

He would know! Fear turned to ice clamping tight on every nerve. He would know and he would come, he would search every street until he found her.

'You can't stand here all night.'

A hand firmly gripping her elbow shattered the last of her hold on her senses. Emma felt the world circle around her.

'You can't remain 'ere, I'll take you 'ome.'

Half immersed in the mist shrouding her brain Emma smiled at Mrs Coley.

'It'll be coming on to rain afore much longer, we should go now.'

Mrs Coley! Emma smiled again. She would take her home.

'I said we go now, so move!'

The grip on her arm was painful; why had Mrs Coley snatched at her?

'Move!'

The grated command and accompanying jerk turned Emma's smile into a frown. Mrs Coley was angry, but at what? What was it had so annoyed her? Half formed, the question struggled to surface from beneath the shrouds cloaking Emma's reason and with it came realisation. It was not Mrs Coley speaking, it was not that woman's hand holding fast to her!

Fenton Gilmore! Not quite free of clogging mist, her brain reeling afresh, Emma stared at a tall figure, a figure whose grip on her tightened, a figure beginning to drag her away.

118

'Whatever you thinks to be about you'd best be forgettin' of it.'

Emerging from deep shadows another figure came to stand at Emma's side.

'It be nearin' time for Father to be comin' home and I wouldn't give a wooden robin for your chances be it he finds no hot meal a waitin' when he gets there.'

'You'll need more than a robin if you try interferin' with me; doctors require more than a farthing for the treatin' of broken bones and undertakers ask even more for the buryin' of 'em so I advises you leave while you still 'ave legs to carry you!'

She had heard that voice before. Emma frowned. That same harsh greeting, the threatening mocking tone. Fenton Gilmore! Fear chasing the last wisps of fog from her brain she tried to snatch herself free but the hold on her closed, the viciousness of it a warning she remain silent.

'You've med one mistake, now go before you mek another.'

The acerbic voice sent a shiver along Emma's spine though it seemed to have no effect upon the figure standing to her other side, a figure which answered breezily, 'The mistake be your'n, mister, if you thinks to make away with my sister!'

The boy, the boy from the cemetery! Recognition had Emma glance quickly at the owner of the voice. But why would he claim she was his sister?

'I've advised you, don't interfere...'

Fenton's voice rasped, cleaving the question.

'...now I be warnin' you, afore that advice be given in stronger language.'

The boy had obviously taken her for someone else, but Fenton Gilmore would make no allowance for that; he enjoyed hurting people, that 'stronger language' would be real physical pain. She could not let that happen. Trying to insert conviction into words she felt must sound tremulous she said:

'I'm sorry, you really have made a mistake in thinking me to be your sister, it can happen easily in darkness.'

'There, you've 'eard for yourself her don't be your sister.'

It was exultant, gloating, a note of victory she had heard so many times before, a nuance of tone Fenton Gilmore could not keep from his voice each time he forced his loathsome attentions upon her.

Switching her glance to him now, to the face the capricious dance of moon and cloud first highlighted then obscured Emma felt breath catch in her throat.

'Oh I 'eard it all right.' Breezy as before, the reply laughed from the shadows. 'Same as I'll hear her cry out when Father lathers her arse for talkin' with a strange man, then gives her a further taste of the belt for the sayin' of her be no sister to me ... that meanin' her don't be no daughter of his; won't take kind to that, won't Father.'

The hand still clasping her own tightened, the raising of the other above his head declared a positive intention to strike. Emma thrust herself forward but was immediately snatched back with a hissing snarl.

'Then p'raps your father'll tek kindly to my teaching his son it don't do to interfere with things no concern of 'im!'

'Father always 'ppreciates teachin'.' The boy skipped aside, dodging the blow aimed at his head. 'P'raps you'll kindly do the same for him, this be him now comin' from the Cross.'

Beside Emma the tall figure turned its head in the direction of a well-built man, a rough jacket hanging loose over a muffler tied about the neck offering no disguise to the muscular frame illuminated beneath the lantern above the entrance to the public house.

The boy spoke again. 'The Golden Cross be a favourite place for foundry men. They also be 'ppreciative of teachin' though they prefers the givin' of it rather than the takin'. So now I be givin' you advice, mister, take your dirty paws off my sister afore I gets them to do it for you!'

11

He would have known it was a lie. He would not have let her go.

Half pulled off her feet by the boy dragging her along behind him Emma tried to reason out the past few minutes.

He had appeared from nowhere, or so it had seemed in the gloom of the empty market place. Authoritative, commanding and demanding,

121

every aspect that of the man who for so many years had blighted her life. But the man who had caught at her, who had attempted to take her away with him, had not been Fenton Gilmore. The man who had claimed to be her uncle would have known she was not the boy's sister; he would not have stood bandying words but more likely would have struck the boy down.

But if not Fenton Gilmore then who? Why would a perfect stranger – and seeing it was not Gilmore then he was a perfect stranger – wish her to go with him? Emma's mind stumbled over questions rising one over another. And the boy? The boy now pulling her with him, why would he claim she was his sister? Why? Why go so far as to threaten to call those workmen to help him fight off the man?

'You shouldn't go standin' about like that!' The boy stopped so abruptly Emma almost fell against him. Releasing her hand with a sharp throw, reprimand was strong in his voice as he went on, 'It were a crackbrained thing to do, you made easy pickin's for Perry, same as you was easy pickin's on your own along of that cemetery, the scum would've had you away hadn't it been for me.'

'Away! I, I'm sorry...'

'Sorry!' It snapped out from the gloom. 'You would've been if Jud Perry had his way. Lord, where was your mother when you was growin' up!'

Her confusion was dashed away by the asperity of the words flung at her and Emma answered in the same way. 'My mother, since you are kind enough to ask, was in her grave during my childhood.'

'That were you, weren't it? It were you in the graveyard, you helped Lily. I couldn't be sure of it in the dark but when I 'eard you speak then I knowed.'

Was it apology she heard in his tone? Was he regretting the rudeness of his words? Emma drew the shawl which had flapped loose during their flight more securely about her shoulders. No matter whether it was or not, she would thank him then leave.

'An' go where?'

Part challenge, part genuine enquiry, the boy's reply to her polite thanks for his assistance robbed Emma of an answer.

'Where be it you be goin'?'

Darkness added potency to the demand, a demand she herself had requested an answer to; one which Emma could not supply.

Waiting for her reply, the boy's thoughts ran in his brain. Perry had watched her from his shelter in that doorway. Watched her move from stall to stall, seen her hesitate then go to stand close against the wall, and guessed that the girl in the shawl was not going *to* but was rather running *from*, running from somewhere ... or was it someone? Emma's silence provided her agreement with the thought so he went on but this time more gently.

'I don't be wishin' no offence miss but, but would the truth be you ain't got...' he hesitated, a quick cough covering the slip, '...you ain't decided where it be you'll spend the night, I means which 'otel you be choosin'?'

Embarrassment made Emma falter. 'I ... I am

not familiar with the town's hotels.'

The way she spoke, it were the way he'd heard the women who rode in carriages speak, women whose husbands' wealth dripped from fingers and throat in sparkling stones and golden chains; but this one wore no fine clothes nor jewellery costing more than a foundry man could earn in a lifetime. In the darkness the boy frowned. He would bet a robin, no he would bet all of the six pennies he had earned that day, this woman did not have a single farthing, yet there was a pride about her, a pride he felt would not allow the truth, nor could be demean it. This last was uppermost in mind when he spoke as though perusing each in turn.

'There be the George, though that be costly. Then there be the Talbot, it be a fine place but likely no lighter on the pocket; now the Turk's Head...'

She could not let this go on, she could not have the boy stand in the cold while all the time believing the lie that she wished to find a hotel, nor should she herself let him continue in the belief.

'Thank you, I...'

'But the "Turk" be bound to be full as most like will be the George and the Talbot,' the boy's chatter flowed over Emma's attempted dismissal, 'this time of year sees a lot o' trade comin' into Wednesbury an' the folk bringin' it needs places to stay.' He laughed lightly. 'So like the Lord's holy mother it be like you'll find no room at the inn.'

No room! Emma swallowed hard on the bitterness of that. She had been so definite in not accepting the money offered by Mrs Coley, money which would have provided a roof over her head.

''Course,' the boy's laugh sounded again, 'if like Her you don't be above the offer of somewhere not so desirable as a 'otel then you be more'n welcome to spend the night along of Lily an' me.'

Fighting tears of relief Emma could only nod.

Huddled in the shawl, damp and chilled from the night air, the drum of rain beating relentlessly against the roof, Emma shivered. The boy and his sister lived here! She glanced about a room lit by a single candle, a fire so small it was unworthy of the description doing next to nothing to fight off the cold. Her aunt would have called it a hovel. Her aunt! Emma stared into the red embers. Life had never been pleasant under that woman, there had been so much ill nature, her constant un-remitting reproach of two young children a bitterness which had many times reduced Rachel to tears. But all the bitterness of Henrietta Gilmore, the rancorous spite she had visited on them, was nothing compared to the lie she had allowed them to live with.

'It was not true, Rachel, none of it was true.'

'Who be Rachel?'

A twitch to her skirt went unnoticed; Emma remained in the past.

'It was a lie.' Scarcely a breath the words whispered past lips stiff with cold. 'It was all lies. Oh Rachel if only I could have told you...'

The child Lily looked up from where she sat at Emma's feet. 'Rachel were the name you spoke when you said for Timmy an' me to run from the cemetery. Was it her you was there to visit with, did you want to talk to her same as I was talkin'

125

with my mum?'

'Lily!' Sharp with rebuke the voice rang in the dimly lit room but in the next breath softened. 'Lily, how many times do I needs tell you, it don't be polite to go askin' folk of things which be no concern to you; it don't be good manners; what would Mother have said?'

The gentle reprimand made the young head droop, the girl answering quietly, 'Her would 'ave said to say sorry.'

'So?' Tender yet firm the boy's urging had the desired effect, bringing his sister to whisper:

'I be sorry. I asked what I shouldn't, I were meanin' no rudeness.' Then as if in explanation she rushed on, 'I could hear her were hurtin', I heard it, Timmy, her were cryin' inside an' ... an' I thought...'

The rest was lost against his shoulder as the boy darted from the gloom-filled corner of the room to catch his sister swiftly in his arms, his look and words defensive as he faced Emma.

'Lily ain't had much learnin' of the ways of the world miss, her don't always think to what her says but her asks your pardon an' I puts my own askin' along of it an' begs you accepts.'

Pregnant with tears, Emma's answer was soft. 'Lily was being kind and that can never be thought rude. As for apology that must be mine. I am the one lacking in manners, for I have not yet thanked you both for your hospitality in bringing me to your home, but I do so now with much gratitude.'

He had turned his head, obscuring his face from the faint light of the fire, not wishing to betray the dejection visible in his young features, but to Emma it carried clear as a beacon in the gruff reply. 'It don't be much to offer, I only wishes it were more.'

Seated in the one chair to grace the almost empty room, a chair given to her to rest in, Emma searched for a way in which to express the emotions churning inside her, a way to say what was in her heart. The boy had nothing yet beneath his poverty lay a graciousness that went beyond wealth, a compassion unknown at Beechcroft after her parents' leaving.

A stifled sob caught in Emma's throat as the memory of her parents rose vividly in her mind. It was caught by the girl, who whimpered, 'I didn't mean to make her more unhappy, honest I didn't, ask her to know that Timmy, ask her to know that!'

The distressed cry returned Emma's thoughts to the present, to the girl sobbing in her brother's arms. The boy had risked a possible beating from that man in the cemetery and again when facing up to another in the market square; he had placed himself in danger to safeguard her, a woman he did not know, someone he had never met before; but more than that. Listening to his whispered comfort Emma's pulse jolted: he had chanced the wellbeing of his sister! It had not been a random act, something done on the spur of the moment! Even before the notion was fully formed Emma had dismissed it. The boy cared deeply for his sister's welfare yet still he had chanced that in order to protect a stranger from a hazard she herself had not recognised, for had he been injured then that child also would have been taken, and from the explanation given while walking home neither Lily nor herself would have seen the inside of any workhouse. It had been an act not only of bravery but of unlimited kindness, a charity of the soul which she was repaying with thoughtlessness. Reproach adding to the flush of shame sweeping hotly through every vein she said, 'I know you did not mean to make me unhappy...'

'But I did!' The girl answered quickly but remained in the protecting arms of her brother. 'It were me made you cry when I asked was it Rachel you was wantin' to talk with along of the cemetery, I shouldn't ought to have done that, like Timmy says, it were rude.'

Soft as the meagre light of the candle Emma's reply brushed the moment's stillness. 'No Lily, it was nothing you said...'

Freeing herself from the boy's hold the thin figure turned to Emma, the childlike voice shrill with new concern. 'Then ... then if it were Timmy he be sorry, he–'

'No.' Emma's quick reply cut off the unwarranted apology. 'Neither of you have done or said anything to cause distress.'

'But you was cryin' ... I heard you!'

'Yes.' No more than a tremble on Emma's lips, the admission was gathered up by shadows coiling it away into themselves.

Her anxiety seemed to melt away into those self-same shadows. Lily came to stand beside the crude wooden chair saying quietly, 'I knows what hurtin' be like, it be a pain no medicine nor no words have the curin' of and though the speakin' brings no comfort still I be sorry for the 'eartache you be sufferin', and if the Rachel you spoke of be the one lyin' along of the cemetery then I asks God be lovin' to her same as I asks He be lovin' to my mum.'

Too strong to be held any longer Emma's tears coursed between fingers lifted to her face.

'Now see what you've done!' Embarrassed at what he saw as yet another of his sister's blunders the boy caught her arm. 'Best get y'self away to bed afore you puts your other foot in it.'

In reply the girl uttered a soft half cry. Emma heard through her own heartache that of a frightened child.

'Don't be cross with me, Timmy.' It was an entirely different emotion, the girl's voice raw with an underlying fear. 'I be feared when you gets cross, feared you'll leave me like Mother...'

Smothered into his chest the words were lost beneath the anguish of his own. Silent tears threading each one he said softly, 'Mother didn't leave cos her wanted to, her tried hard to stay along of us, but God seen as her were sufferin' bad and that were why He sent His angels to fetch her up into heaven, so her could be made well again.'

'But God be all powerful, least that be what was said at Sunday school. If that were true then He could have made Mother well without takin' her into heaven!'

'There were another thing said along of Sunday school, God acts for the good of us all, you have to remember that, Lily.'

'But what if God takes it into His head to send His angels to fetch you? I be feared of that

129

Timmy, I be feared of bein' left on my own.'

Thick with emotion he could not swallow the boy's answer, murmured against the head pressed to his chest, came quietly to Emma.

'I won't never leave you, Lily, nothin' won't make me do that, not so long as you be needin' of me, that I promises ... now,' he sniffed, 'it be time you was sleepin' so say your goodnights.'

'...*God acts for the good of us all...*'

Listening to the breathing of the boy asleep in a corner of the room Emma's heart challenged what he had said. Had it been for the good of her sister and herself their parents had been killed in an accident? Was it for Rachel's good she had been raped and murdered? And for whose benefit was it that evil men such as Fenton Gilmore were allowed to exist? And these two children, how could having to live like this be said to be beneficial?

'Like Timmy said we don't have much, but you be welcome to take my bed, I can sleep here alongside of the grate.'

The girl had smiled as she made the offer. Her stare fixed on the long-dead fire, Emma listened to another voice, a voice murmuring in her heart.

'These two have come to you in friendship, they offer you their all. Do not reject that, accept what is given, take them into your heart, Emma, care for them as you would for me.'

Sleep resting heavy on her eyes Emma's heart whispered its reply. 'They are there already, Rachel, they are there already.'

12

He had not found her! Fenton Gilmore stood in the high-windowed room, barely registering the company of the man watching from the further side of a wide desk. He had gone first to the cemetery but not finding her beside that grave had gone into the church. He had stood there, flickering candle-thrown shadows sidling in and out of darkened alcoves, silent watching forms stealing along ancient stone walls; grey ghosts observing him while his eyes had searched every pew. But Emma Lawrence had not been in any one of them. So where had she run to? She had no kin, no relative to whom she could go for shelter. Friends then? But he and Henrietta had kept both girls close; a few minutes of conversation after Sunday morning church attendance was all they had allowed with anyone and any invitation to visit had been politely refused until eventually they had ceased to be made. Without friends she would have no refuge! He had smiled at the thought, waving away the black-gowned priest quietly enquiring if he could be of assistance, jubilation turning the smile into a laugh as he returned to his carriage. Cold, wet and miserable as a stray dog she would be walking the streets, only now realising where her actions had brought her, only now understanding the plight of being homeless. Alone, and if fortune favoured

Fenton Gilmore, already terrified by the attentions of some drunken lout, Emma Lawrence would be only too happy to be taken back to Beechcroft, to the comforting arms of her 'uncle'.

Comfort! The laugh had thickened in his throat as he had set the carriage toward the town. He would demand a special kind of comfort, demand and be given it time and again. There would be revulsion on her part! The laugh had returned, soft and elated. Shudders of abhorrence would ripple beneath his touch, quivers of loathing at the offence of his mouth; but all of that would serve only to increase his own pleasure, his amusement in knowing the cries she would be unable to subdue would not be those of rapture. No, those emotions would be his, his the gratification of having her subject to his every demand, his every *diverse* and *totally* fulfilling demand.

'These are the very finest.'

Fenton frowned deeply as he glanced in the direction of the interruption to his thoughts. The finest? What was the man talking about?

'Came from the Chandler plantation.' As if the question had been spoken the other man supplied the answer. 'That is the finest in all of South America, brought in by the *Sea Witch* just two days ago.'

Two days ago! Fenton's mind cleared instantly. With a nod he acknowledged the words. 'Chandler's, you say!'

Slight frame twitching like some nervous bird, his beak-like nose sniffing several times, the other man touched a wooden box placed on the desk. 'As you can see.' A long finger traced dark lettering printed elegantly on the smooth lid. 'Not only do these originate from that plantation, they are of the finest matured leaf, each one rolled and packed under the most vigilant supervision; I think you will find them most satisfactory.'

He lifted the lid of the box and Fenton inhaled the rich aromatic scent of Cedrela Odorata, the tropical American timber used only in the making of the finest of cigar boxes. It was definitely not for the market he supplied, for those .... miners, foundry workers and labourers ... the cheapest of anything would be good enough, and most certainly that was so with tobacco! He kept the snide thought to himself as he accepted a cigar from the proffered box, rolling the slim form between his fingers, then lifting it beneath his nostrils to sniff appreciatively the aroma of the tobacco. These were not for men who toiled at hewing a living from beneath the earth or for those tied to factories; these were for gentlemen of worth, for his other, more special customers. Replacing the cigar in the box he smiled inwardly. A fine quality corona provided an excellent finishing touch to an evening's entertainment, the enjoyment of which helped soften the expense!

He signalled approval, as much for his thoughts as for the tobacco, with a nod. 'I'll take a dozen boxes along with my usual order; you have that, I trust.'

'That' meant the poorest quality leaf roughly crushed and mixed with a generous helping of corn maize but sold by Fenton under the trade name of Exemplary Cigarettes, as misleading as was his Old Roly Superb, a pipe tobacco as inferior as the other. His disapproval subjugated by that same desire for profit, Noah Wilkins closed the lid of the cigar box before consulting a large black bound ledger lying beside it on the desk.

He ran a finger down the page, stopping at an entry in elegant copperplate, the handwriting flowing gracefully across the page, then nodded. 'Yes.' He tapped the column. 'One cask of cigarette tobacco and one of slab-cut pipe tobacco.'

'When will delivery be made?'

Gilmore well knew the day his order was to be delivered. Whatever the reason for this visit an enquiry as to that date was not it! Allowing none of his musing to show Wilkins switched his glance to a brass calendar stand. Flicking several pages he said, 'That will be on the twelfth.'

Eight more days! It was too long! Fenton's teeth bit down on the bark rising to his tongue; he waited several moments to allow an enforced calmness into his voice before remarking casually. 'The clipper arriving two days since, does it leave again soon?'

Was this the reason for Gilmore's unexpected arrival in this office? Once more Noah Wilkins kept his curiosity veiled, answering in the same bland manner.

'She leaves two days from tomorrow.'

'As soon as that.' His cursory tone was meant to appear casual rather than indicate any real interest; Fenton turned to glance from the window down on to a yard busy with men heaving crates of every size on to several wagons each harnessed to heavy dray horses. 'I would have thought after a sea voyage men would have wished to remain longer on shore, to spend time with their families.'

'A berthed ship makes no profit.' The reply came immediately. 'And that is not acceptable to Samuel Holt. He prides himself on having cargo unloaded, a new one taken aboard and his boat made ready for sea in record time.'

'What cargo would that be?'

'Captain Samuel Holt don't hold no preference.' Moving to stand beside Fenton the other man looked down on the scene below. 'Sometimes it be a shipment of tea for delivery to Cuba, while the crates you see being taken out now, they hold tools and machinery for use in the sugar industry. They will be on the night train and in Liverpool by first light tomorrow. It be in that town the *Sea Witch* will take on food and water for a crew must needs be fed and it is still several weeks' voyage to the South Americas even for a clipper as fast as she is, and there is no place to take on provisions once you leave Ireland behind. The Atlantic...' He shook his head. 'It is a wide ocean, a very wide ocean!'

Wide indeed! Fenton acquiesced silently. Wide enough to lose things in! Turning from the window, all interest in the activity taking place below seemingly entirely dissipated, he said brusquely, 'I have received a request, a customer it would be imprudent to refuse if business is to remain on an equally profitable basis. Therefore I trust you will understand my request for a cask of Superior Royale to be delivered to my premises no later than this evening.'

Watching the other man return to stand at his

desk, long-fingered hand cradling the gold hunter pocket watch removed from a dark waistcoat, the beak nose virtually twitching as the small bird-bright eyes surveyed the dial, Fenton felt distaste touch his palate. Noah Wilkins was a man he had no liking for, a man he would prefer not to do business with, but needs must when the devil called and Fenton Gilmore's devil had certainly called last night.

'This evening.' Noah Wilkins returned the watch to its pocket. 'I fear that is not possible, Mr Fenton, I have no deliveries scheduled for Wednesbury before...' Once again he consulted the ledger. 'Yes, it is as I thought, the soonest date is the same as that on which your own consignment is to be despatched, that is the twelfth.'

The twelfth! Fenton's hands tightened viciously about the rim of his top hat, his reply the crack of a whip. 'That is as may be but I must have the Superior this evening!'

Bent over the ledger, grey thinning hair lying like a layer of dust barely covering a pink scalp, Noah Wilkins smiled to himself. The request Fenton Gilmore had specified would not entail a great expense but the service ... that would add a great deal to the cost.

'I understand your anxiety to please a client but as you saw for yourself all of the wagons are in use. Of course,' he lifted his glance, 'it may be possible to procure a conveyance, though that would add considerably to the overall expenditure.'

Of course a conveyance could be procured! Fenton's mouth tightened, a white line of anger edging lips thinned almost to invisibility. Noah

Wilkins would procure the moon supposing the profit margin were wide enough. How he would like to take that scrawny neck and squeeze 'til the little eyes popped; but that urge could not be gratified, not that was unless some other proprietor of the import and export business was found to deal in that Superior brand. Suppressing the desire he snapped coldly, 'See to it!'

The door banging shut behind his departing customer Noah Wilkins smiled as he closed the ledger. There would be no record of this particular order, no entry registering the request for or delivery of a cask of Superior Royale tobacco.

The woman was not of the type she would have preferred to engage. Henrietta looked with apprehension at the sallow complexion, the greying hair scraped back and caught under a black bonnet. Thirty years old! She had caught back a sniff of disbelief on being given that information. Had the woman owned to being fifty it would have been almost as unbelievable, seeing the number of lines marking a face narrow and pinched as an undernourished mouse. And she came with no references; that alone regardless of the worn-out look of her should have seen her from the door but there had been no other applicant for the post of cook-housekeeper.

'...let me tell you it won't be easy findin' a body to take my place, an' for certain it won't be a body I gets to talk to.'

Bella Coley's words rang in Henrietta's mind. Was that the reason there had been no other women seeking employment at Beechcroft, had

137

Bella Coley been true to the threats she had made? But threatening to advise others against working in this house had not been that woman's only ominous remark! As she sat poker-straight, hands locked together, Henrietta felt a cold trace of worry accompany the words rushing into her head.

'*...I seen the marks on the body of the girl that were carried into this 'ouse... saw the bruises on them poor legs, the purpling on that little stomach, they was the marks of rape ... a pleasure you fears he took with a fourteen-year-old child...*'

Had Coley or the girl Lacey talked of that? Was it already being spread abroad in the town? If so, how long would it be before Fenton learned of it? Worry which had been a cold trickle locked an ice barrier around Henrietta, paralysing her thought processes.

'I don't 'ave worked in no 'ouse ma'am, that be the reason of me 'aving no paper, no what you called reference, but I can cook an' I can clean along with the best of 'em.'

Standing opposite Henrietta, the woman waited for a reply then when none came added quickly, 'Bert were put out of his job when the gaffer – the ... owner of the factory...' the woman amended her explanation, 'well, when Josiah Perks died the son d'aint want no part of the lock makin' so he up an' sold takin' hiss elf off to live abroad. There were no other ready to take men on so it were a case of move to some place other than Willenhall or starve, that caused Bert and me to come 'ere to Wednesbury. You can follow up my words, ma'am, you'll find the truth of 'em same as when

138

I says Bert and me we ain't neither of we had no trouble with the law, we ain't never had no dealin's with the police.'

The last remark broke through the ice and Henrietta's nerves twanged. Police! The woman had talked of the police! But what had she said?

Catching the swift glance of cold grey eyes, interpreting the look as one of suspicion, the woman tried again, saying quietly, 'I realises the fact of my 'aving no word to tell of my capabilities as to cookin' and housekeepin' be against my bein' given employment, and there ain't nothing I can do as to that but as for the other, I be willin' to go with you to the station along of Holyhead Road, or if that don't suit then I be willin' to call back in a few days, that'll afford you time to enquire of a magistrate as to the truth of what I claims.'

Her mention of the police, it had been nothing to do with Fenton! Holding back the breath of relief threatening to issue from her lungs Henrietta gave a brief shake of her head. She wanted no truck with the law in any shape or form. Now her brief alarm was stifled she spoke sharply:

'That will not be necessary, though I warn you, should you be given a post here then misconduct of any sort while in my employ will be dealt with severely!'

'As it should be, ma' am.'

Beneath the black bonnet unwavering eyes had Henrietta almost flinch. Had there been a note of contempt in that reply? The woman might be seeking employment but she was not begging. Disconcerted by the steady stare Henrietta fished a handkerchief from the pocket of her pearl-grey gown, dabbing the flimsy lace edged square to her nose several times before saying imperiously, 'Your husband, no doubt he also will be seeking employment with this house.'

'I don't 'ave no husband, ma' am.'

'That is not what you said a moment ago!' Henrietta's accusing glare fixed on the woman. 'You said you and your husband came to Wednesbury looking for work after he was sacked.'

'No.' The woman shook her head. 'What I said were Bert and meself come to Wednesbury.'

'Exactly!' Henrietta snapped. 'That is what I said. Do you take me for a fool!'

Sharp and bitter, the reprimand was flung at the woman but she answered levelly:

'What you said, it weren't right. Bert don't be my husband, Bert be my brother.'

This was not at all what she had expected. Henrietta snatched the handkerchief back and forth between her fingers. The woman showed no deference, no anxiety to please a prospective employer and of even more concern was the lack of respect she observed for a woman so very much better than herself! Dismissal already on her tongue Henrietta hesitated. No other woman had enquired as to service in this house; the maid who had shown this one into the sitting room was a girl taken from the workhouse. Humiliation which had swept hot in her veins on going to that place tingled again. She had made it seem taking a girl from there was no more than an act of charity but though the superintendent had remarked on the graciousness of that act yet she had suspected the woman had known the true cause. She could not

140

apply there for a cook! Desperation flicked at Henrietta's senses. Beechcroft without staff was already resulting in raised eyebrows; to be much longer without domestics would be to invite question and questions of any sort appertaining to the business of this house were to be avoided. Better then to take this woman than risk being without staff any longer; after all it was as easy to dismiss as it was to appoint and when a more suitable candidate presented herself then this one would be shown the door that same day.

Consoled by the thought yet not wanting to appear over eager Henrietta allowed several more seconds of silence before saying, 'The brother you speak of, he will of course need to be interviewed by Mr Gilmore regarding a position. Should my husband approve of him and appoint him to the staff he will take his meals in the kitchen but will not be provided with a room in the main house. His sleeping quarters will be above the carriage house.'

A twitch of the mouth, a slight gleam in the eyes, a quick suck of breath, all signs of thankfulness, obviously the brother needed work as much as did the sister. Henrietta smiled to herself, mentally reducing the salary Fenton had formerly paid their domestic servants; this was one time he would follow her advice.

'I be sure were Bert 'ere he would thank you for himself, but the fact be he don't 'ave need of no offer, he already found a job along of the town and as to a room he's already teken one along of a house there.'

The twitch of the lips, the gleam of the eyes, the

breath… Relief? Or amusement! Again caught off balance by what now could be deemed an almost impudent reply Henrietta's own inner smile drowned in a rush of acid. The pleasure of dismissing Bella Coley had been denied but that loss would be more than amply recompensed when time came to dismiss this woman! Henrietta drew a long breath to imply a review of the conversation and returned the handkerchief to her pocket. Then, lips repressively tight, she rose from her chair to tug viciously at a brocaded cord hanging beside the fireplace.

'Very well.' Hands folded across her stomach she looked at the woman she had deliberately kept standing. 'I will give you a two-week trial period. If at the end of that time you have shown yourself favourable then we will discuss a more permanent arrangement.'

Permanent arrangement being your instant dismissal.

Somewhat mollified by the thought Henrietta glanced at the girl who had come to answer the summons of the bell cord.

A disparaging frown settled on her brow as she repressed a sniff at the bob of a curtsy. A housemaid! The girl was far from that but thanks to the training given at the workhouse she was docile and biddable. But the main point in her favour was the scar marking her cheek; combined with her innate drabness and the fact she would be sharing a bedroom with a cook-housekeeper drab and unattractive as herself would deter any nighttime visit Fenton might otherwise have thought to indulge.

A scarred face! Watching the door close behind woman and girl Henrietta's frown gave way to a thin smile. Even Fenton Gilmore would turn away from that.

13

'...*I am so afraid. I pray every night he will not come again, why are my prayers not answered?*'

'*I cannot ask Aunt Henrietta to speak with him, Uncle Fenton says I must not tell anyone of his coming to my room, that it is our secret and if I break it he will send Emma away to some place where people will do those same horrible things to her, that men will pinch her breasts and make her cry as Uncle Fenton pinches mine, that they will hold a hand over her mouth while they force their body into hers as Uncle Fenton does. I don't want that to happen to Emma, for people to hurt and frighten her...*'

'To hurt and frighten her.'

Tears blurred the words running one into another yet they stood clear in Emma's brain. For all the horrors visited upon her by Fenton Gilmore, Rachel's wish had been to protect her sister, to keep her from the hands of a vile lecher who called himself their guardian.

Guardian! Anger hot and blinding as the tears flooded swiftly through Emma. The only thing Fenton Gilmore had guarded was his own evil.

'*I must not tell anyone ... he will send Emma away...*'

Those were the words of a man not wanting to protect a child but to protect himself, to keep the world from knowing Fenton Gilmore for what he truly was, a cruel sadistic man who to satisfy his perverted lust had subjected a young girl to mental as well as physical abuse; and all the time using those same threats, that emotional blackmail, to enable his abuse of her sister.

'Why do you read that book when it always 'aves you cry?'

Unaware of the child watching her from the bed Emma closed the diary with a startled snap.

'You does,' Lily said again, 'you cries whenever you reads of that book, I knows 'cos I've seen you; why does you keep it when it makes you sad?'

Glancing at the slim volume, moisture in her eyes making it appear to swim in her hands, Emma answered softly:

'I keep it because it would make me more sad to part with it.'

'Why?'

Her glance still on the book, Emma searched for an answer. How could she explain? How did you tell a child this book was a last link with Rachel?

'It be special, don't it?'

It held such quiet conviction, a perception that was sympathetic but at the same time matter of fact, a maturity of understanding unexpected in someone so young.

'That be Rachel's book; the sister you told me and Timmy of, it be hers an' that be the reason you treasures it.'

Surprised once more by the apparent insight, Emma could only nod.

'I have a treasure.' She fumbled beneath the pillow, drawing from under it a scrap of faded blue cloth. Holding it to her breast, eyes glittering with tears valiantly held back, she went on. 'This belonged of Mother. It were the only pretty thing her ever owned. Time was often her intended to pawn it but then her knowed inside her wouldn't never have money enough to redeem it. It were with her when...' The voice broke on tears refusing to beheld, '...when her died; next door who come to wash her for buryin' said for me to have it.'

Glancing at the tiny bundle held out to her Emma felt her heart twist. This child and her brother had been turned from the home their mother had worked herself to death to keep for them.

'It were sickness of the lungs.' Lily had as usual been held protectively in his arms while Timothy's explanation had been given through gritted teeth. *'Were brought on 'cos of breathin' steam from washin' in the brewhouse, of havin' wet sheets draped across the livin' room when weather were too wet to have them on a line in the yard; that an' the ironin' her stayed up most of the nights to get finished then trudgin' through all weathers tekin' stuff back to them houses. Parish doctor said were naught could be done 'cept to tek her into the poorhouse and Lily along of her, but Mother wouldn't have none of it, her said only the Lord would separate her from her children ... and in the end He did.'*

She had asked why, seeing he was capable of earning a living, had they not remained in the house, when surely their neighbours would have helped.

'*They had no more'n we.*' The boy's reply had been laconic. '*They each put a penny towards the cost of a funeral but even so it were nowheres near enough. The parish would have seen to it but I couldn't stomach a pauper's buryin'...*'

He had paused, obviously struggling with emotions, but then had gone on:

'*I told Lily the meanin' of how paupers were put into ground furthest away from the church like they was some criminal an' like meself her d'ain't want that, her thought – we both thought – Mother deserved a proper restin' place so we sold every stick, everythin' which would bring a farthin' and with it we give Mother a proper grave though its marker be no more'n a cross I made meself from two pieces of wood! It were no longer than a day from the funeral we was turned into the street. The house belonged of the colliery, they had let Mother rent it seein' how Father had been killed by a fallin' coal seam but said Lily an' me couldn't look to ourselves, we would be best teken into the workhouse ... a new family moved into the house that same mornin'.*'

So who did they rent this house from? Her question had been answered grimly.

'*We don't pay nobody no rent along of nobody knowin' we be here. We keep it that way by Lily leavin' with me soon after first light an' not comin' back 'til it be dark. The market women looks out for her an' I manages to bring her a drink and a bite at dinnertime.*'

That had accounted for so meagre a fire, for smoke rising from the chimney would alert any passer-by to the fact that the property was occupied. Timothy could not take that chance ... but what of Lily? How long before she succumbed to

146

the harshness of such an existence? How long before pneumonia claimed her life as it had her mother's?

'You can look at it, I don't mind.'

Immersed in thought, Emma frowned.

'My treasure!' Lily said again. 'I don't go showing it to anybody, but you be different, you knows what treasure means.'

Yes. Emma smiled at the watching child. She knew that no matter what lay hidden in that scrap of cloth it meant the world to Lily. Slipping the diary back into her pocket she took the offering, carefully peeling back the layer of wrapping.

'...*the only pretty thing her ever owned ... wouldn't never have money enough to redeem it...*'

Had that been the real reason the woman had not pawned this 'treasure' or was the truth of it she had guessed no pawnbroker would loan a penny against a piece of cheap glass?

'It is very beautiful.' She smiled at the face wreathed in pleasure at the words. 'Your mother must have loved it very much.'

'Her did.' Lily nodded. 'Her said it were a present from Father along of her saying her would marry him.'

An engagement gift! Emma touched the brooch. A cameo of green glass, probably purchased from a pedlar during the May Fayre, but loved and valued more than gold by the girl it had been presented to.

'Your father chose well, it is a very pretty brooch.'

'It be a cameo.' With pride shining in her eyes the child shared her knowledge. 'It be called such on account of havin' a woman's face on it so Mother told me. I think Father reckoned it were beautiful as Mother's face and that be the reason he chose it.'

'That would be my thinking also, Lily. Thank you for showing it to me.' Folding the brooch back into the cloth Emma returned it, noting the reverent way the girl took it, how she brought it to her mouth to kiss before slipping it into its hiding place.

'Emma.' A whisper in the shrouded gloom of candlelight, it had Emma return to the child she had tucked beneath the covers. 'Emma.' Eyes which had lost the gleam of pride stared up from the pillow. 'What Timmy says about ... about when somebody be dead they can't speak back to we...'

The child was hurting as much as she was, the grief and pain of losing her mother was raw. Lowering to sit beside the figure so thin and small it hardly showed beneath the blanket, Emma stroked a wisp of hair from the pale forehead.

'...He says it be naught but imaginin'...'

'Shhh!' Emma soothed but the whisper went on.

'...that I only tells meself Mother answers when I talks to her, that it don't be real, that I be tellin' meself lies; but it don't be no lie, I hears her Emma, I hears in my heart.'

I hear in my heart. Emma swallowed as a lump rose in her throat. It was a description the wisest of sages could not have bettered.

She smiled at the upturned face. 'No, Lily. It is not a lie, or if it is then it is one I also tell myself.'

'You means Rachel, you hears her inside just

148

like I hears my mum?'

'Yes, in my heart, just like you.'

Lily's eyelids were closing and it seemed sleep had claimed its victory but as Emma made to move the whisper came again.

'But the other thing Timmy says about nothin' can't bring them back, that be right, Emma, your Rachel can't be with you no more...' The eyelids lifted and in the pale ambience of the candle Emma saw shadows of uncertainty flick in golden-brown depths while the hushed voice lowered further by a sudden shyness murmured, 'But I could be a sister if you wants me to.'

Stunned by the surge of strong emotion that robbed her of speech Emma sat motionless.

'I understands.' Lily sniffed silent tears. 'Rachel wouldn't be happy for me to be sister to you.'

The girl's stifled sob released her senses and Emma caught the small figure in her arms. 'No Lily,' she said softly, 'Rachel would not be un-happy, she would be as delighted as I am to have a new sister.'

From a narrow iron-framed bed set opposite that in which Lily lay asleep Emma stared into the darkness. These children had shared everything they had with her. Unlike Fenton and Henrietta Gilmore who had lied and stolen, who between them had destroyed one young life and tried hard to do the same to another, Timothy and Lily Elsmore had been kindness itself. They had brought her to this house, provided food and shelter, brushing aside her protests of having nothing with which to repay them. Timothy that first evening had brought back bedcovers bought from a pawn-shop insisting on making up a bed for her in his sister's room, a bed he could easily have put into the living room for his own use.

A roof over her head, a bed to sleep in, food shared freely.

Listening to Lily's quiet breathing Emma's heart swelled with gratitude.

Each of those were a generosity, a charity borne of the heart, but greater still was that gift made moments ago, that charity of the soul, the whisper which had said, 'I could be a sister.'

The delivery had been made as he was confident it would be. Standing in the locked storeroom attached to Lawrence Fine Tobacco, Fenton listened to the footsteps of the carter die away. The man would spend the next couple of hours in some bar drinking down the half-sovereign he had been paid.

The money would be deducted from the reckoning submitted by Noah Wilkins; that man profited well from this particular service, well enough to pay for the inconvenience of a night-time delivery as well as to ensure the carter did not refuse an even later delivery back to Wilkins' yard.

Assured the carter was gone Fenton listened for a moment to the medley of sounds coming from the Street: calls of men leaving the Golden Cross public house, the quicker tap of a woman's feet; a woman who had bargained a last-minute deal at a market stall or one set on a bargain of a different kind? That which would ease some man's devil.

But that particular devil was not so easily satisfied. It returned again and again.

As his own devil did. Staring through the darkened window at the street beyond Fenton felt the conviction of that truth jerk at the base of his stomach, a flicker that spoke of desire. But his demon was not always appeased by the services of a prostitute.

Shifting his glance from the window he let it ride into the depth of shadow enveloping the storeroom.

The fiend which lived in him mocked willpower, its inexorable demand breached all effort at denial; but then he offered it none, he took pleasure from its risings, delighted in its hedonistic sensual grip, abandoning himself to the ecstasy of the moment.

As he had done in that barn; as he had again the evening he had searched for the runaway Emma.

She had been coming from a doorway.

Conjured from shadow a young girl, shawl draped around a large jug held in the crook of her arm, stood a moment beneath a lantern fixed above a door, its yellow light temporarily bronzing her mouse-brown hair. Then with a wriggle of the shoulders attesting to the coldness of the night air she had turned in the direction of Upper Russell Street. She could have been returning to any one of the close-packed back-to-back houses lining both sides of the narrow road, the only light escaping from those which sported any at all being the flickering dance of flames from a fireplace. She had walked quickly, her sure step in the darkness attesting to the fact she knew the area well. Would he have time enough? Would another person enter the street before he caught up to her? Questions had tapped a matching rhythm to that of the girl's feet and for a moment he had harboured the notion of turning the carriage in a different direction, but that moment had died a swift death, submerged in the hot rip tide surging through him.

The devil had awakened.

Fenton's fingers tensed as they had when giving a flick to the rein setting the carriage in motion; then he watched in his mind as once he drew almost level with the girl he snatched viciously again on the straps, the pain of the bit cutting into the animal's mouth making it rear in protest, causing the carriage to swerve dangerously. Startled, the girl had jumped back, the jug falling from her arms to crash on the ground.

He had leaped from the vehicle, apologising profusely, asking was she injured? After she assured him she was not he had said of course he must pay for the broken jug and also its spilled contents.

There was a saying, 'the devil looks after his own.' In the deeply shadowed storeroom Fenton smiled. He had certainly looked after his own on that occasion.

'Mother'll think that be all right,' the girl had answered his offer of remuneration, 'but Father won't tek kind to 'avin' no beer with his supper. Like as not I'll feel the strap about me backside.'

Not a belt! Fenton's senses had jolted. That little backside would not feel a belt ... until it had felt something else! His answer had been swift.

'That must not happen. I will speak with your parent, explain it is all my fault.'

It had sounded full of concern for the girl but the only concern had been for himself, that his intent would be forestalled by someone coming from the houses.

But it seemed the devil had been once more prepared.

'No sir!' The girl had answered, drawing the shawl closer about her shoulders as if already feeling the bite of her father's belt. *'I thanks you but that would mek things worse, Father would swear I'd been up to no good an' I'd still get a beltin'.'*

The pretence of reflection had been masterful as was the reply it produced.

'Look.' Another moment's hesitation had added credence to his apparent indecision as to the propriety of such a proposal but then he had gone on. *'My shop is not far from here, it carries a variety of jugs one of which I am certain would suit the immediate need. If you wish to come choose one I could have you returned to the hotel in just a few minutes.'*

'Aint no 'otel!' The girl had scoffed. *'Father don't pay the fancy prices they asks for drink, he gets his from Joby Newton's beerhouse, that be just along the street aways.'*

Was she about to refuse? Aware of the prospect he had played his next card quickly.

'That is all to the good.' He had smiled, opening the carriage door. *'It means we can collect the jug and the beer and have you back home soon enough for your father to have no concern.'*

A replacement jug, a fresh quart of ale, half a crown in payment for the inconvenience and a ride in a carriage. The girl's long-drawn-out 'Oooh' had relayed all of those thoughts.

He had driven to the rear of Lawrence Fine Tobacco's premises drawing the carriage well into the yard, closing the tall gates against any prying eyes. Then, quickly releasing the locks on the door of the storeroom, he had ushered the girl inside and on up the narrow back stairs, saying the better quality jugs were kept not in front of the shop but in a room above.

He had lit only one lamp, and the thick curtain drawn across the window ensured even this pallid light did not spill beyond it. The High Street with its market place on which the shop faced was rarely empty, especially so at this time of night, hence the precaution of entering the premises in the fashion he had.

'Where be these jugs then?'

The girl's query had followed a wide-eyed stare around the comfortably appointed room, at its deep armchairs and wide – very wide – day bed.

'First things first my dear.'

Memory showed him the fear leap to that young face. Fenton warmed to the thrill it had given him, a thrill heightened by the cry that had followed his reaching for her, a cry that became a scream as the shawl and dress were snatched away.

It had been so easy, duping her into accompanying him. He had laughed at that, lust keeping the sound low in his throat as he gazed at the slight figure thrown naked on to the day bed. A pity he was forced to gag and bind her, he would

154

have enjoyed the cries of fear, of pain; but then he could not allow the screaming to continue, could not risk attention being drawn to premises which to all intent and purposes were closed for the night. Justifying the blow which had knocked the girl unconscious, a smile of satisfaction curving his mouth, he had removed his own clothing.

Staring through the curtain of memory he watched the eyes open, saw stark terror darken them from blue to black as the girl's senses returned, heard the stifled gurgle in her throat when realisation dawned, the muffled gasp as he straddled her which became one of pain as he pinched and squeezed the small breasts, the tears swim along her cheeks as he drove deep into her.

Perhaps the binding of her wrists to prevent any attempt at fighting him off had lessened the enjoyment, precluded the pleasure of domination. Precluded but not entirely banished!

'*...like as not I'll feel the strap across me backside.*'

The words echoed in his mind as appetite had reared again.

Risen from the bed he had bent over the weeping girl intending to flip her over on to her stomach but another thought entered his mind. He had straightened. Why deny himself the extra amusement of seeing her reaction to that next delight?

Crossing to a cupboard unobtrusively set into a recess he had lingered over the contents, fingering first one and then another of several closely twisted cords. Eventually he chose one augmented with an ivory-handled whip, slim intricately plaited leather braids shining gently in the glow of lamplight as he held it to the girl's face.

155

In her terror she had kicked out at him. That had been exhilarating, it had given him a taste of the desire rape of her had not fully sated.

In the quiet dimness of the storeroom Fenton's loins twitched, aroused by the scene continuing to play in his mind's eye.

She had struggled to prevent him from tying the cord about her ankles, her eyes pleading through the sheen of tears; all of which had served to enhance the fervour coursing through his every vein.

'Now my dear.' Standing over her he had smiled at features contorted with fear. *'Let us proceed with our little pastime.'*

He had turned her.

A harder flick at the base of his stomach had Fenton catch a quick breath as it seemed he saw again that small pink bottom, watched himself trail the leather braids back and forth across nerve-quickening flesh, the submission to desire which raised the whip bringing it stinging across the girl's backside. Time and again it rose and fell, the slap of leather against flesh an aria in his ears, a soaring anthem of passion rising, rising, filling his being, burning it with an intensity he could no longer resist, a frenzy which saw him throw aside the whip then mount the girl, thrusting himself into that blood-whealed backside.

The girl was alive! In the calm of the aftermath reason had returned. She had seen his face, could recognise him, lead others to this place; others meaning the police. But that of course could not be allowed to happen!

Cold as moments before he had burned he had

156

removed the cord fastening her ankles, then passing it around her throat had twisted it tight. Only then had he washed the stains of blood from his own body.

She had been no burden to carry.

Fully in the here and now Fenton glanced at the small figure he had brought from that upstairs room. Twice locked as were the doors of the storeroom it had been safe to leave the body until it could be dealt with, the only keys to both never leaving his possession.

Now it could be removed. Smiling to himself Fenton picked up the cold inert figure.

14

She could not go on living here, she could not continue to daily take from these children while giving nothing back.

As she looked around the room she had cleaned as much as was possible, at the folded blanket which served as a bed for Timothy, set beside the cold empty fireplace, Emma's guilt which had weighed heavily since coming here pressed heavier still.

Timothy was still a child though he would not suffer being told so. He had taken on the role of a man, but at fifteen he should not have to carry the burden not only of providing for a younger sister but also for someone in no way related to them.

'...*I could be a sister...*'

Remembering Lily's whispered words Emma felt the same rush of emotion as when the child had spoken them. Timothy and Lily had taken her into their hearts, to them she was part of the family. But families should take care of each other; how could she take care of these two when she could not even take care of Rachel!

She had not known then, had not known the burden Rachel carried for her sake, the dreadful things she had suffered just so her sister would not be made to suffer the same.

'I did not know, Rachel.'

The words a tremble in her throat Emma pressed a hand to the diary in the pocket of her skirt.

'I did not know the affliction I placed on you, Rachel, the torment you endured in order to keep me free of Fenton Gilmore. But I am not so blind now, and though the horror which existed at Beechcroft does not exist here yet I know the encumbrance my presence causes; that is why, love Lily and Timothy as I do, I must leave them.'

'What be you doin' here?'

The harsh authoritative demand had Emma turn quickly, her hand automatically dropping away from her pocket.

'I asked what be you doin' here?'

The tone, the same unquestionable ring of authority! Her heart pounding, Emma stared at the figure stood in the doorway. Fenton Gilmore ... he had tracked her down.

'It be a simple enough question, and one you best be answerin' of.'

The mode of speech! Fenton Gilmore never spoke the way she was hearing now. But the man was full of tricks and this could be another one. She stared at the figure silhouetted by the bright daylight.

'Well if you don't be goin' to answer then I'll tell you. This be private property and no gypsies be tolerated, so you'll be leavin' right now.'

It was not him, it was not Fenton Gilmore! With relief Emma sucked air deep into her lungs and though her limbs still trembled from shock she looked steadily at the man staring back at her.

'I am not a gypsy, sir...'

'Huh!' It cut sarcastically across Emma's reply. 'You say you be no gypsy yet you parks yourself anywhere, on this property with no regard as to who it belongs to; but that don't be goin' to 'appen, not here, you and your brood will move on afore I brings men to see to it you do.'

Your brood! He meant Lily and Timothy, but this house was the only place they had found. Concern lent Emma courage. She said firmly, 'As I have told you, I ... we are not gypsies. We came here thinking the house abandoned, no longer wanted by anyone.'

'Did you now!' Again the reply was heavy with sarcasm. 'Or was it you thought to live free, to pay nothing for the use?'

'We don't pay nobody no rent along of nobody knowin' we be here...'

Timothy's words sounded in Emma's mind. But he had not thought to act unfairly, the house had been vacant, unoccupied, its derelict condition

159

strongly suggesting it had been that way a long time; yet neglect did not mean it had no owner.

Thought emphasising the rightness of the argument Emma's reply was quietly apologetic.

'We ought of course to have enquired as to ownership; you have my regrets.'

'Regret be one thing,' he snapped, 'rent be another and that be called for.'

Rent! Emma's pulse skipped. How much would he ask? Whatever the amount how would she pay? She hadn't a penny and even if Timothy had money he would not have left it in the house.

Anxiety laying a fresh trail along her nerves Emma tried to sound calm.

'Of course.' She nodded. 'If you would tell me the amount to be paid.'

Was his silence a mark of surprise, did he think that gypsy or not she had the means with which to pay? Watching the fleeting pull of heavy brows Emma waited with bated breath.

'That don't be left to me,' he answered at last. 'That decision be up to Mr Halstead, him bein' the owner of this property and all else hereabout.'

If this man could not answer as to the amount of rent to be paid then maybe he could not order them from the house! Maybe that decision also must be made by Mr Halstead.

Only half aware of the notion suddenly entering her head Emma gave it rein saying smoothly, 'In that case I shall speak with him; will you kindly inform me as to where I might find him.'

'Won't do no good.' The man's head swung dismissively. 'He's too busy to give time to the like–'

'To the like of gypsies!' It was Emma's turn to

160

snap. 'He leaves that to you does he? Well sir, either you tell me where is the place I may speak with the man or you may tell him should he want his rent then he must come collect it for himself.'

Let him accept the reply she had given, let him leave now, give her ultimatum to whoever he must.

Trying desperately to keep anxiety from showing in fingers already trembling Emma forced herself to stare calmly at the face whose features did not entirely conceal a flicker of admiration.

Please! she prayed inwardly. Please, if he leaves I can go to the town, warn Timothy not to return to this house.

'Right, you win.'

The nod, the half smile of agreement: it could only mean he was leaving. Silently thanking the Fate which had come to her assistance Emma moved to close the door behind the man.

'I'll speak with Mr Halstead...'

He smiled, one hand preventing the door from shutting.

'...and you be coming with me!'

'Why bring it to me?'

Emma glanced toward the room from which a slightly irritated voice emanated.

She had not known where the man she had been made to follow was bringing her, no idea of what she might expect, but it had certainly not been this.

And what exactly was this? In the minutes since she had passed through a wide entrance and crossed a large cobbled yard she had asked herself the same question as a series of shouts and clangs ringing out from a long low brick building set her already tense nerves jangling.

'Did she indeed!'

Had irritation 'been diluted by amusement or was the seemingly altered tone coming now from that room simply a product of her own imagination, a little wishful thinking?

'Well, let us hear how your gypsy woman answers to a charge of trespass.'

Definitely wishful thinking! Emma breathed deeply. Whatever happened she must protect Lily and Timothy.

'I am informed you are living in a house belonging to me.'

He had given her no 'good day', offered her no seat and there was no trace of humour in those clear eyes, no token of leniency in the crisp voice.

'Might I ask when and by whom you were given such permission?'

The sharp question carried a breath of warning. Should she reply truthfully then Timothy would find himself answering to this man; but to lie...! Caught between the two, Emma hesitated.

'Gypsies don't ask nobody permission Mr Halstead, they just let up wherever fancy teks 'em.'

Again he had called her gypsy. Emma turned to the man who had accompanied her to what must be the office of some factory. Giving a slight nod of acknowledgement she said, 'Thank you for helping with that explanation.'

'Yes, thank you Adams, but it is obvious your "gypsy woman" has a tongue, therefore we should let her answer for herself; so I ask again, when and by whom were you given permission to use that house?'

He had the right to ask, but no right to ask acrimoniously! Senses which moments before had tripped with apprehension suddenly tingling with annoyance, Emma swung her look to the figure seated at the desk.

'Sir,' she answered coldly, 'I may not address you otherwise, not having been accorded the courtesy of an introduction, neither do I feel it the act of a gentleman to couch a question in so sardonic a tone even though that question be put to a gypsy woman. But good manners not being the sole province of a man of property I will answer. I had permission of no one to stay in that house.'

Quite a reprimand, a sound slap to the wrist! The strident blare of a hooter made immediate answer impossible; Mark Halstead surveyed the slight figure whose reply had been more than a little reproving. Adams had reported her as a gypsy, a woman giving little consequence to what or what was not hers, and the clothing – his glance took in the dark skirt, the brown chequered shawl held tight about the shoulders – it was much the type he had seen gypsy women wear at the spring and autumn fairs; yet something did not quite fit the image in his mind. Those women at the fair had olive complexions but hers was light, untouched by wind and weather, and her hair was red-gold, not the black of the Romany. But more than either of those things it was this woman's way of speaking which set her apart.

163

'That be the afternoon smelt, the crucible be ready for tipping. Will I see to it, sir?'

Mark Halstead nodded in answer to Adams' enquiry and waited for the door to close behind his works' overseer. Then, rising to his feet, he said, 'Forgive my unfortunate lack of manners but seeing there is no other person present to do the honour of introducing me may I do so myself. My name is Mark Halstead.'

It had been said with no evidence of a smile, but then it had held no derision. Emma watched the slight bow of the dark head as she declined the offer of a chair. She had no desire to lengthen the proceedings; she wanted only to reach the town, to warn Timothy against returning to that house. But having alluded to his manners Emma had no recourse but to answer with her name.

He had already been remiss in the practice of manners. Smiling wryly to himself Mark Halstead remained standing.

'Well Miss Lawrence,' he said as Emma again fell silent, 'as you have admitted you were given no permission to enter that house you must also admit you acted illegally.'

Emma nodded. 'Yes.'

'Are you also aware trespass is an unlawful invasion of property?'

Emma nodded again. 'Yes.'

She was by no means stupid, her previous replies had demonstrated that fact, so were these monosyllabic answers some devious ploy, a method of getting him to dismiss the whole affair? If that were so then John Adams' 'gypsy woman' was mistaken. Turning to glance through the win-

164

dow Mark Halstead took a moment with the thought before saying, 'Then I am quite justified in sending for a constable and having you arrested. What have you to say to that, Miss Lawrence?'

What could she say? She could not deny her crime.

Emma stood in silence but beneath the façade of calm her whole body tensed with anxiety. Prison! She had brought the threat of that upon Timothy; children of his age were given terms of imprisonment, and Lily – her heart missing a beat she almost gasped – could Lily also be imprisoned?

'...*my sister ain't never goin' into that place so long as I be breathin'* ... *workhouse be a place where the livin' would be better off dead...*'

Adamant, fiercely protective, Timothy's vow to keep Lily from the workhouse rang in Emma's mind bringing with it a hardening of her own resolution: Mark Halstead must not learn of those children ever having occupied that house. Her arrest would achieve that; with her removal from his property he would have no call to go there and when she failed to return Timothy would have sense enough to move on. About to answer the man once again facing her, Emma's breath caught on yet another thought. Newspapers! Report of arrests were published in newspapers! Some of these were taken at Beechcroft; Fenton Gilmore would see her name, he would certainly intervene, pay this man the sum required and she ... she would be forced to return to Beechcroft, be subjected again to the horrors of the past.

Since his question met with silence Mark

Halstead had been about to pose another but seeing the look of revulsion on Emma's face, the words stilled on his tongue. His mention of sending for a constable had drained the colour from her, and her hands ... his glanced flicked to Emma's fingers clutching at her skirt. It seemed they were unable to stop trembling; could the reason be this woman was already involved with the law? That trespass was not her only transgression? Then why did he not call for Adams, tell him to send a boy to bring a constable? Why? He looked again at the stricken face, at the hands twisting the cloth of the cheap black skirt, and felt as he had a moment before, that concept and conviction were not one, notion and belief were not completely hand in hand in his mind and that being so he would take the matter no further.

'Miss Lawrence...' he began but was halted by Emma's shake of the head,

Prison or Fenton Gilmore it did not matter: either was preferable to having Timothy and Lily separated, to bringing them even more hardship and unhappiness.

'Mr Halstead.' Emma looked directly at the man responsible for her decision. 'I have not denied my unlawful habitation of your property nor will I; it was a breach of the law and I must take the consequences. To that end I propose you have Mr Adams send for a constable.'

Again that way of speaking! It denied the roughness of her clothes, it did not match the local dialect nor did he suppose it that of an itinerant. So just who was this woman and why was she living in a derelict house, and why so determined upon being arrested?

Intrigued, wanting answers but not in the way she proposed, he said, 'That is one way of settling this business but would it not be more sensible for you to pay what is owed now rather than suffer the indignity of a magistrate's court, the ordeal of a prison sentence which would part you from your family? You did I believe give Adams to understand you had the means by which to do this.' Had that been a lie? Mark Halstead watched the flash of colour rise swiftly to pale cheeks then felt a touch of admiration at the quiet response.

'I did imply as much, but that I confess was untrue. I do not have the money to pay; as for being parted from family my parents are both dead and so is my sister. There is no one else: you need not fear any other person will suffer on my account, Mr Halstead, so please send for the constable.'

She was asking to be arrested! Watching Emma, seeing the resolution with which her soft lips had compressed to a white line, Mark Halstead's curiosity deepened. No woman in her right mind would act this way, but as he had concluded already Emma Lawrence was not stupid. The only answer had to be she was protecting someone, yet the shimmer of tears filming her eyes as she had spoken of her family had confirmed what she said about them. Their being dead was no lie; so what, if not family, would have her opt for incarceration?

He masked his growing interest with a show of supposed contemplation, taking several moments before voicing the idea that had taken less than one to form in his mind.

'Miss Lawrence.' He paused, a wry lip adding to the illusion of consideration. 'Miss Lawrence, a magistrate will need to know of any damage caused to my property in order to fairly assess his ruling. You will agree I could not supply that information without first carrying out a full inspection, and to ensure you the same fairness I insist you return to that house with me.'

15

'I saw no sign of her, no one I spoke to had any knowledge of her, she must have left Wednesbury altogether.'

'Rubbish!' Fenton Gilmore spat angrily. 'You know as well as I do she would not leave this town, she would see that as turning her back on her sister.'

'But Rachel is dead.'

Flinging his brandy glass against the fireplace he whirled on the woman watching him, her spine stiff with fear.

'How very observant of you, Henrietta, had you been as attentive on your visit to the town you would have seen the people you spoke to were lying, that some of them had to have seen the girl.'

'Fenton, I had to be careful who I spoke to, I had to be discreet, it wouldn't do for people to know ... to find out Emma had left without your permission.'

'And what if they should learn the reason? What if she decides discretion is not to her advantage?'

'She would not speak to anyone of...'

'Of?'

Venomous as his glare the word snarled at Henrietta. Not to answer would be to add to his ill humour, yet to finish the sentence would make his bad temper turn to rage.

Lips so tight they barely permitted words to pass yet knowing she must reply she said, 'What I meant was Emma has always been a very private person. Even as a young girl she kept very much to herself; I cannot recall her once having shared a confidence with me and I doubt she would do so with anyone else.'

She had never shared a confidence! Going to the sideboard Fenton poured a liberal measure of brandy into a finely cut crystal goblet. Taking it across to stand before the fireplace he stared at the glowing coals. Emma Lawrence had shared no confidence ... but did that apply only to her relations with Henrietta?

'Emma has always been a very private person...'

He tossed brandy into his mouth, the bite of it stinging his throat as the words circled his brain. That might very well be so between her and the woman sitting in this room; Henrietta was not the most inspiring of women, it was not surprising the girl had shared no intimacy with her. But would it have been that way between sisters or would one have shared confidences with the other, might the younger one have divulged a certain secret? He drank again, alcohol steadying the sudden flurry of nerves. Rachel had been terrified of him, terrified not only of his using her body but of his abusing it, the pain of his twisting and pinching her breasts. Fear and pain. He smiled into the crimson bed of the fire. They had proved a distinct asset in loosening the tongue but for all his questioning as to her conversations with her sister, despite the breath-stopping pain accompanying those little tête-á-têtes, there had been not the slightest intimation of the happenings in either bedroom ever being spoken of. And Emma herself? Smiling again he drained the glass. She had been too considerate of a younger sister, of the threat against her, the threat she knew very well he would fulfil; no, Emma Lawrence would not have spoken to anyone while her sister lived. The question now was, could he be as certain she would keep silent now that sister was dead?

Staring at the goblet in his hand he heard the answer in his mind. He could never be certain, he could never be certain until Emma Lawrence was as dead as her sister!

Turning slowly he cast a glance over Henrietta, distaste adding to the acid of his temper.

'You searched for her!'

It slithered across to Henrietta, the poison of its inherent warning making her blood turn cold.

'You asked had she been seen, did anyone know of where you might meet with her.'

'Fenton, I told you–'

'Yes, you told me!' The malicious snap cut Henrietta's reply. 'Now I am telling *you*. I want Emma Lawrence back in this house, I want her where she can be of no threat, so you my dear had best look for her again.'

'Fenton please...'

'Find her!' The glass went crashing with its twin, the shout bounced against the walls. 'Find her if you want to go on living in this house, if you want to go on enjoying what you stole from her.'

'I was not alone in that, you too have stolen.'

'Me.' Cold, serpent-like, Fenton smiled. 'What have I stolen? I have simply cared for the children of my wife's sister.'

'The business, the house.'

'The business,' he smiled again, 'what of it? I have administered it but it remains in the name of Lawrence. There can be no charge of stealing as a result of that. As for this house I agreed to abide by your and your sister's request her children be cared for in their own home; how can that be described as theft? No Henrietta, yours is the blame. It was you claimed kinship with Mary Lawrence, yours will be the penalty should that ever be brought before a court. Think of it, my dear, a prison cell with rats for company, and that so I am led to believe, is not the only vermin living within those walls.'

With a laugh in his throat he crossed the room. Turning to look at her, the door open beneath his hand, the laugh echoed sarcastically.

'There is one way you can be saved such un-pleasantness.' He paused, sending a long glance over the room. 'Though for myself I find that solution rather less agreeable; having you in jail would relieve me of the bother of having you placed in some other institution. So if you wish to avoid either prospect then I advise you find Emma Lawrence, find her so she can be put alongside her sister.'

Slamming the door shut Fenton did not hear the soft footfall of steps along the corridor, the quiet click of another door leading to the kitchen.

This was the very last thing she wanted, the decision she had prayed he would not make. Seated in the horse-drawn trap Mark Halstead was driving, Emma hugged the thought in her mind. She had wished him to send for a constable, hoped he would have her taken from that office and so put an end to it; but that had not happened. Instead he had elected to visit the house, insisted she be with him when he did. Why? Why would he bother to do that?

She had seen her own query reflect in John Adams' eyes when his employer had called for the trap to be brought to the yard, watched the perplexed frown pass fleetingly across the man's broad forehead, as she had been ushered into the vehicle. The frown had returned when he learned it was not the police station his master was driving to but the house at Lea Brook.

'There'll be others along of that place sir, a gypsy won't be on her own. There'll be men somewhere around and they can be a nasty bunch; I thinks it best meself and a couple of the hands goes along with you.'

The protest had given her fresh hope of a change of mind, so that Mark Halstead would abandon this intention in favour of that threatened earlier and have his overseer call for a constable. But again hope had crashed around her. Emma drew the shawl close as though somehow the action would shut out the words from her mind but inexorably they continued.

'*Thanks, but I want you here when those moulds are broken. That job has to be perfect, we can't chance it being flawed either in the casting or chipped with a hammer while being freed of the moulds. A lot of people ride in trains, every wheel must be flawless.*'

A lot of people ride in trains ... and some are killed because of them! With the thought came a sudden mental picture, a vivid scene of a toppled carriage, her parents lying crushed beneath it, a great iron monster screeching as it thundered past. Echoes of the shock of Henrietta's disclosure rippling through her Emma shuddered, a cry escaping her throat.

'There is a rug beside you, use it.'

'Thank you but I am not cold.'

'Then why did you shiver? And there is no need to cry out, Miss Lawrence, I am not about to harm you.'

Had she shivered? Had she cried out? Holding herself tense Emma denied the tremor beginning to assert itself.

'You need have no fears in that direction,' he said over her silence, 'my only interest is in that property, in finding the extent of any damage done to it.'

But was it? Was inspecting a property he had known to be derelict his only reason for doing as he was? Guiding the horse to the left, directing it from Potters Lane into Great Western Street, Mark Halstead refused the answer his brain was attempting to give. He had no interest in the woman beside him! No interest at all apart from wondering why she so obviously wanted him to hand her over to the police, why she was so keen to prevent his visiting that house.

What was she hiding? He had mulled over that question driving the rest of the journey past the railway station and on along the busy Lea Brook Road and now as he pulled into the yard of the tumbled building of an old malthouse and its cottage he asked it again. There had to be more than she had confessed in his office alongside the iron foundry. Catching sight of the tightly compressed lips of the woman he handed from the trap Mark Halstead knew whatever that 'more' might be he would have to find it for himself.

She might never find Emma! Fenton Gilmore flicked a short-handled whip above the flank of the chestnut stallion. Henrietta was a disappointment, no ... he flicked again, the crack of it bringing the animal's ears upright. Henrietta was more than a mere disenchantment – not that she had ever been in any way gratifying – she was a disadvantage, an impediment to the life he would very soon be leading. But then drawbacks could be remedied. Find Emma or not, it would be of no advantage to Henrietta. The carriage drew level with Wood Green cemetery; he glanced across the field of headstones, of huge draped urns, of figures of angels, stone wings spread, arms reaching out, beatific smiles on carved faces. His own smile a reflection of the corruption of his thoughts. Henrietta and Emma, 'aunt' and 'niece'. Both would soon be lying there.

Perhaps he might mark his wife's resting place with the effigy of an angel? The cemetery fell

174

away behind him as he laughed with quiet contempt. Now why would he waste money on a woman he wished only to forget.

His amusement at the notion still lingered when he handed carriage and horse to the ostler of the George Hotel and strode into its plush interior. Dinner here with a few glasses to embellish it made for a pleasant evening, and another hour or so spent with a lady of the night would make it that much more enjoyable; but it must be an hour without the added company of his particular devil, the demon that drove desire to passion, appetite to lust; a craving on which those struggles and silent screams, that fear in the eyes of a partner bound and gagged, fed and fed until nothing but physical violence satisfied it.

'Gilmore, I was hoping to see you here.'

Drawn from the fantasy of pleasures yet to come, Fenton's hands pressed down on the newspaper he had lowered across his stomach in order to cover signs of stirring emotions, his eyes flicking open.

'Sorry old man, didn't realise you were asleep.'

He wasn't, the pictures in his mind forbade sleep, yet Fenton let the illusion live a little longer. Blinking a few times, groaning quietly in his throat to give himself time for the pull of his flesh to subside, he sniffed himself 'awake'.

'Too good a dinner.' He removed the newspaper, laying it aside.

'Not to mention the brandy eh!'

'That also.'

'Then what say we enjoy another?'

He wasn't wanting company, at least not of this

kind. Concealing chagrin with a nod of acceptance Fenton looked at the slightly rotund figure
waving a hand toward a black-suited waiter. With
his bald egg-shaped head and trousers stretched
tight over a too ample stomach the man re-
sembled nothing less than the Humpty Dumpty
of the children's book he had once glimpsed in
Rachel's room.

Rachel! Fenton felt the familiar twitch. He'd
had so many good times... but not here, not now!
He pushed the memory away.

'So.' Lowering himself heavily into an armchair
facing Fenton the plump man smiled. 'Business
good, is it?'

Taking a glass from the tray the waiter offered,
holding it in an attitude of salute toward his un-
wanted companion, Fenton replied, 'Flourishing
... and yours?'

'Never better, never better, which is why meeting you here tonight is so fortunate. It'd been my
intention to come see you at your place but we
can do business just as well here.'

This did not take first place in his choice of
diversions but business was business. Fenton
sipped from his glass, and, given the kind of
money this man paid, then for the moment
business was top of the agenda.

'That last batch was most acceptable; a bloody
good brand of cigar, bloody good!'

And the business you have in mind now, will
that require the same standard of quality? Fenton
watched the heavy jowls bob as alcohol was
tipped and swallowed.

'I'm glad you approve.'

'Approve, yes I do.' The glass he had emptied with one swallow was put aside. The corpulent figure leaned forward, his voice lowered several degrees. 'So do the customers I passed that consignment on to, they approved highly, so high they've placed a repeat order.'

Fenton's mouth pursed, he frowned; the attitude of uncertainty made the other man inch forward in his chair.

'There be no problem with that, does there, Gilmore? I wouldn't want to lose good custom and I reckon you don't either.'

'Of course not,' Fenton answered. 'I just don't have the amount you ask for in my storeroom.'

'But you can get it?'

Lips twisting wryly, head swinging slowly back and forth, Fenton nourished the apprehension he saw flick across the fleshy face. Difficulty attached to the process of providing what was wanted would, as Noah Wilkins regularly quoted, 'add significantly to the purchase price', and making profit – excess profit – was almost as exhilarating as that other indulgence.

'Well!' The demand coming louder than was meant the man made a show of coughing into his handkerchief as several heads turned in his direction. Then as glances switched away he went on quietly. 'I told my customers there would be no problem of supply.'

'Perhaps you should have enquired as to supply before taking requests.' Fenton studied the brandy in his half-full glass.

'There are other suppliers! You don't be the only one dealing in tobacco!'

It had been said with all the vehemence of a threat. Fenton smiled to himself. Now to see the biter bit. Rolling a sip of brandy around his tongue he savoured the other man's unease. This was an entertainment worth the temporary postponement of the delight which would round off his evening.

'As you say,' he nodded, 'there are other suppliers, perhaps one of them can find what you want.'

The other man's eyes half closed beneath heavy overhanging lids, as his reply cracked from tightened lips.

'Dammit Fenton, you know it be best not to spread business among too many, that way profit gets thinned!'

But it was not going to be thinned for Fenton Gilmore. He waved away the offer of another drink. Deals such as this needed a clear head.

'My own principles entirely,' he agreed as he watched the other man tip brandy into his throat, 'but one has to take business where it can be completed.'

'Then you can't find what's needed?'

'I believe what I said was I did not have the amount of tobacco you require in my storeroom.'

'Yes, yes.' Fat fingers waved impatiently. 'What I wants to hear now is be it possible to get more?'

'Hmm.' Fenton leaned back in his chair, allowing silence to do the rest.

One minute ... two. Opposite Fenton the portly figure moved restlessly. Another minute. Fenton let the tension build, then hid a smile of satisfaction as the man bobbed to his feet like a cork from a bottle. Hands fastening on the lapels he eased the coat too closely, wrapping his ample frame, saying as he did so, 'A hundred, there'll be a hundred more on the price supposing you deliver what be asked.'

A hundred. Alone with his brandy Fenton smiled into his glass. Delivery would be made.

16

He could not possibly hold her to account for the state of this property, he could not seriously judge her responsible for walls partly demolished, for doors ripped from their hinges, yet the look Mark Halstead had shot at her as he had walked around the several badly damaged outbuildings had clearly conveyed the fact he was very seriously thinking just that. But she had confessed to having no means by which to pay rent much less whatever the law might see fit to impose as a fine.

Nerves becoming ever more taut, Emma watched the man who had returned with her.

Was he getting some sort of satisfaction from all of this? He knew her anxiety, he had seen it when questioning her in that room at the iron foundry. Did prolonging it this way afford him a type of retribution, a substitute for the money she could not pay?

In the tiny living room of the ramshackle house Emma's tight nerves threatened to snap as the glance he was casting around caught the folded blanket placed neatly on the pillow in the alcove beside the fireplace.

'Did you say you lived here alone?'

She could not look away, could not lower her glance before the one seeming to cut into her; that would be to invite suspicion.

'I may have misheard when we spoke in my office; if I am wrong then forgive me, it is just I believed you to have said you were alone here.'

The look in those clear eyes was steady, demanding an answer. She did not want to lie yet how else to protect Timothy and Lily?

Emma felt the bloom of colour rise to her cheeks. Drawing a quick short breath she said, 'You did not mishear, Mr Halstead.'

Was the pull of the mouth a sign of his disbelief, a conviction intensified by the glance he cast again over Timothy's place of sleeping? Offering no more than that brief reply, only nodding when he said he would take a look upstairs, Emma waited to hear the tread of footsteps on the bare boards of the bedroom then quietly opened the door, scanning the way Timothy and his sister must come. If she could see them, warn them to turn back, not to come any nearer the house!

'Are you expecting someone, Miss Lawrence?'

Intent on looking for the youngsters Emma had not detected the step on the stairs. Hastily she pushed the door closed, managing only a shake of the head in answer to the markedly derisive question.

'A breath of fresh air then? That at least is believable, however what I cannot understand so well is why a woman living alone needs two beds to sleep in; and it is quite obvious that both are in use otherwise why have them made up with pillow and bed linen? Perhaps, Miss Lawrence, you can throw light on the problem?'

There had been no way to prevent his going up to that room, and having done so there was no way of denying the evidence of two beds, yet she had to try.

'I ... they...' Emma stumbled over an explanation she could not make without revealing the truth.

Censure clear in the snapped word as in the look directed straight at Emma, Mark Halstead's controlled irritation rang back from the damp brick walls. 'They! Are you, by use of that definition, alluding to those beds or was it a slip of the tongue, a slip which would betray the fact you are lying when you say you are the sole occupant of this house, that you are here quite alone?'

He would bring a prosecution against her, he would have her imprisoned and that was his right and as such she would accept it. Now she must accept his calling her a liar. Resentment flooded every pore, washing away the anxiety which until now had held her nerves rigid, and Emma's reply came hot and swift.

'Mr Halstead.' Head held high, eyes bright with controlled asperity, she returned the stare directed at her. 'You will believe whatever you wish to believe; I neither have nor wish to have any effect upon that so at risk of curtailing the evidently clear amusement you are deriving from bringing me here, may I ask we do what you intend and go now to the police station.'

181

Why so anxious to be gone from here, so anxious she would prefer a prison cell? Watching the head held high, the steady stare fixed on his own, Mark Halstead felt a warmth of admiration. Whoever this woman was, and for certain he felt she was not what John Adams had termed a 'gypsy woman', she was shielding someone, someone she would venture prison in order to protect. But who could be so important to a woman she would run so dreadful a risk?

He felt unprepared for the sharp stab to his senses that came with the answer slipping into his mind. He opened the door, but as he walked from the house Mark Halstead's brain repeated its reply.

A husband! Emma Lawrence was protecting her husband!

'But why would he walk off, why not give you over to the police like he threatened?'

'I don't know.' Emma answered the question her tale of first John Adams and, then of returning here to the house with Mark Halstead had provoked.

'He said you'd be out of here come mornin' yet nothin' of havin' the constable fetch you!' Timothy frowned. 'And why leave things 'til mornin'? By that time you could be miles away.'

Was that why Mark Halstead had stridden from the house, a terse 'You will be out of this house come morning' his only words as he had climbed into the carriage and driven away? Was he thinking she would disappear therefore avoiding any consequence of using his property, behaving, as might be expected of a gypsy woman?

'I don't know his reason, I only thank heaven for it,' Emma answered truthfully. 'It gives you time to collect your things and leave.'

'Leave!' Frown deepening, Timothy shook his head. 'I don't be goin' nowhere.'

'But you must, if you are found to have been living here then you as well as I will be taken before the magistrate.'

'He already knows there were somebody here along of you.'

'But he does not know who, and he won't if you are sensible and go while there is still a chance.'

Timothy shook his head, his tow-coloured hair catching the gleam of the single candle on the narrow shelf above the fireplace, his squarish chin lifting in defiance that the glint of brown eyes emphasised.

'An' leave you to dance to the fiddler's tune! A right fossack that would 'ave me.'

Huddled close to the fire Timothy had insisted on building Lily broke the silence she had observed since being told of Mark Halstead's ultimatum. Looking at Emma she said quietly, 'It means one who be no good.'

'And that's just what I'd be if I turned me back, if I left Emma to pay for what were my doin'. No, Emma!' Timothy shook his head, seeing her about to reply. 'I ain't goin' to do no moonlight flit. I'm goin' to see Halstead, tell him straight it be me took over his property and it'll be me will pay the penalty.'

'...it'll be me will pay the penalty.'

183

Morning light was lifting the room from shadow as Emma glanced at the girl lying asleep in the opposite bed. They had sat, the three of them, long into the night, she trying to get Timothy to see his adamance would serve no purpose, that to a man as determined to get justice as was Mark Halstead then having two people jailed would afford more satisfaction.

But not only two people would pay. There was Lily; maybe hers would be the hardest sentence of all. The girl had not wept, she had not begged her brother to think again, but the sobs muffled by the bedcover pulled over her head when cold had driven them to their beds spoke of the fear inside her, fear not only of being separated from her brother but of being placed in the workhouse.

She could not do that to her, she could not have Lily threatened in any way, and she would not let Timothy pay that price either. The intention born during the few remaining hours of darkness hardened into resolution and Emma slipped from her own bed. She would be gone before they woke.

Pulling on the dark skirt, her hand touching the book tucked into its pocket, Emma's whisper barely touched her lips.

'I am doing the right thing, aren't I, Rachel? I can't see any other way; I can only pray Timothy will understand, that he will forgive me.'

Looking once more at the sleeping figure curled into itself Emma felt her heart twist. Rachel had slept that same way. How often had she seen her curled into a ball almost hidden by bedclothes, and how often had she smiled, thinking Rachel lay that way naturally. But that had been one more misapprehension. There had been nothing natural about Rachel's tightly drawn-up knees, the head pulled deep on to her chest: that had been her way of shutting out the horror that had been Fenton Gilmore, her attempt to hide from fear, to close away the pain and terror of rape. Now Lily too was hiding a fear, a fear of losing her brother.

Wanting to kiss the fair head, wanting to whisper of a love that had grown so quickly Emma took a half step then paused. It would be so much harder to do what she determined if Lily were awake. Suppressing the emotion welling into her throat, tiptoeing carefully down the staircase, Emma glanced toward the alcove where Timothy lay then quietly lifted the latch and slipped away.

'I thought you'd be tryin' that.'

A half scream rose in her throat as Emma stared at the figure which had stepped on to the track in front of her.

'I guessed you'd leave as soon as could be, well them sly gypsy ways don't work with me, I be up to your tricks and many more you might never think to; you be goin' to pay your dues ... one way or another.'

'I ... I intend to do that, I am going to the police station to tell—'

'Just you yourself be goin' to the station, so what about the other one livin' in that house, why is he lettin' you take all the stick? Gypsy or not he don't be much of a husband to slip off while a woman goes to jail.'

He had said she would be gone from the premises come morning but somehow she had not felt Mark Halstead to be a man would set another to keep watch on her movements, to think her so dishonest she would leave before he returned. Obviously she was wrong. Chin lifting over the tingle of disappointment flicking inside, Emma answered firmly.

'There is no one, I have no husband.'

'Done a moonlight has he, went on his way while you was sleepin'? Be a proper gypsy what does that, take what you wants and leave somebody else to do the payin' for it.'

It would be useless to argue, useless as it had been yesterday. This man was convinced she was a liar, convinced as Mark Halstead was. So let them believe as they would, let them hold to their convictions. None of that mattered against Timothy's not being prosecuted.

'Mr Adams.' Head still held high, Emma looked directly into eyes watching her shrewdly. 'Gypsies have their ways as does your employer, both seem to prefer to have others do what they themselves find distasteful. But in this instance Mr Halstead was mistaken. He need not have had you stand watch; if it is of any consolation you have my sympathies for a wasted and most uncomfortable duty. Now if you will please accompany me … just to satisfy yourself this gypsy will not "do a moonlight", then may we proceed to the police station.'

Whoever or whatever, gypsy or not, this woman had fortitude and you had to give her full marks for that. John Adams felt again the quick wave of

186

respect he had experienced when speaking with her that first time. Of course she was shielding someone, but a man prepared to let her take the consequence of law was not worth the shielding. He glanced over her shoulder to the way she had come, in hope of seeing a figure going in the opposite direction, a man he could bring to book, who if he would not take full responsibility for trespass then at least to make him stand beside a woman prepared to do so.

Was he thinking to go to the house, to see for himself if it was empty as she claimed? Catching the glance going beyond her Emma's nerves quickened. If Timothy was not yet wakened ... but even if he were then had Lily been given time to dress? Were they gone or were they still in the house? Questions raced in her mind so that Emma almost cried her desperation; but to give this man the slightest inkling of her fears would have him do just that. Calling on every reserve of willpower, forcing herself not to turn and look in that same direction, she drew the shawl firmly about her shoulders saying, 'Mr Adams, I see no sense in standing in the cold so with or without you I am going to the police station.'

John Adams met the gaze of the woman regarding him with clear determination and again respect surged in him, but regard for Mark Halstead beat the stronger; he would not have that man fooled. Ignoring the fact he also felt the nip of cold he said, 'Now that might not be the best thing to do, I mean a young woman, 'specially one pretty as you, wouldn't be liking the sort of life the justice would be deliverin' you up to, locked away with all sorts of riff-raff; as for meself I wouldn't feel right knowing I'd let you do what that man of yours hadn't guts for so I be goin' to turn a blind eye, you can go on your way, go wherever you please.'

'And have your employer believe you failed to apprehend me? No, Mr Adams, you see I would not feel right in allowing you to lie on my behalf.'

He had given her the opportunity to get away yet she had refused; that was the way of no gypsy he had ever had dealings with. In the face of her set-lipped resolution John Adams' own sense of justice pricked sharply. He wanted only to protect the man who provided him with a living, a man who was friend as well as employer.

'I would not feel right in allowing you to lie on my behalf...'

Words spoken seconds before met with a voice speaking in his mind, one which said though he himself were prepared to lie if it meant the best for Mark Halstead, that man would not welcome it. He would not hide behind any misrepresentation.

'Miss Lawrence...' He paused. This was more difficult than dealing with men, men who would think not twice but half a dozen times before talking back to him as she had, 'Miss Lawrence, I ... the fact is, Mr Halstead did not set me to keep watch on that house nor on yourself. Were it not that I'd wanted to second check some special mouldings afore the molten iron be poured into 'em then I'd not have been comin' by at this hour.'

'...that job has to be perfect ... every wheel must be flawless.'

Mark. Halstead's remarks returning to her mind Emma asked, 'Those special mouldings, would they be for railway trains?'

Adams nodded. 'Yes. Don't do to tek chances with a job like that, too many lives depends on them trains.'

And some are taken by them! Holding her breath to quell the stab of pain the thought aroused, Emma lifted the shawl over her head as if in response to the cold then with a trace of a smile said, 'Then I suggest I come with you, that I wait at the foundry until you are satisfied all is as it should be and then you can escort me to the police station.'

17

'You'd best wait in the office.'

Having entered the wide yard fronting the iron foundry John Adams pointed to a building set apart from the larger low-slung one from which even at so early an hour sounds like the pounding of demons emanated.

Emma glanced to where he pointed. Though the outside of that smaller edifice was as dust-covered as its larger counterpart the inside had proved remarkably clean. Was that the reason for his suggestion she wait there or was it another ruse? Another chance for her to run away?

'Mr Adams,' she said as he began to lead the way further across the yard, 'thank you but I will remain with you.'

'I be going into the foundry, miss.'

'Yes, so I understand, I will go in with you.'

Adams shook his head.

'That can't be allowed, foundry be no place for women.'

'I see.' Emma smiled. 'Then, Mr Adams, you will have to wait with me here or, as you suggested, in the office.'

'Crucible be ready, Mr Adams.'

Glancing at the workman who had come from the main building Adams hesitated. He needed to oversee the whole process before allowing molten metal to be poured.

Throwing a curious glance toward Emma the workman slipped a blackened neckerchief from about his throat, wiping it over his sweat-stained face. Then glancing back to Adams he said, 'Rommin' be finished 'alf-hour since but we couldn't lift the patterns 'til the work 'ad been seen by y'self.'

He had given that order himself. It would not be disobeyed, yet every minute the job was kept waiting resulted in delay to the start of the next one and as Halstead had told him, the transport job had a definite deadline. Go beyond that and the order would be written off.

'Will I 'ave the next load o' pig brought in, Mr Adams?'

'Yes ... no! Just ... just tell the men to be ready to tip.'

'They be that already, 'ave been for some time since.' Retying the cloth about his neck the workman glanced again at Emma before turning back into the dark building.

'Miss Lawrence.' Adams had watched the man walk away, heavy metal-studded clogs ringing on the uneven cobbles of the yard. 'Miss, I have to make sure everything has been done the way it should be, the men ... they can't carry on 'til I've given the OK.'

'You have to make sure everything that has to do with you has been done to your satisfaction,' Emma smiled coldly, 'therefore you will understand when I demand no less for myself; even a "gypsy woman", Mr Adams, has that right. I have broken the law in occupying property belonging to your employer, that I have owned to and intend to do again before a magistrate. I have been called a liar, accused of being a thief by using what was not mine then attempting to leave without making payment. Both of those accusations I have no argument with, but Mr Adams, you will not add "shirker" to the list of wrongdoings you have no doubt compiled in your mind, you will not brand me with the name of one who runs from responsibility. I intend to go to the constable and you, I intend, shall go with me.'

'Miss Lawrence–'

'Mr Adams.' Drawing her shawl in a tight determined gesture Emma interrupted sharply. 'I could not help but hear the workmen have already waited some half-hour or so and you yourself have said they can proceed no further until your inspection of their labours has been carried out so unless you wish to delay those men further would it not be sensible to proceed with that inspection?'

'Then you will wait in Mr Halstead's office.'

As quick and sharp as before, Emma's reply rang out in the early-morning air. 'No, Mr Adams, I will not!'

He had thought the woman to be seeing sense, to be recognising the fact she would be more comfortable in the other building, but seeing the set of that mouth, the firm no-nonsense tilt of the head, John Adams felt reassurance drain away.

'Miss Lawrence please, I can't let ... I mean the foundry ... it don't be the place...' he floundered, then explanation giving way to exasperation went on thunderingly, 'You seen for yourself the holes in that man's shirt, they weren't left by snowflakes, you seen the spots and blisters on his arms, they don't be caused from strolling too long in the hot sun, and them breeches ... they don't be no fine cloth nor no gabardine, they be made from moleskin, a real tough leather, yet they was riddled with holes burned clear through 'em so how do you think them skirts o' yourn would fare once inside of there!'

He could have any one of the workmen man-handle her into that smaller building, have him keep her there until that so important inspection was finished and the annoyance in his voice, accentuated by the stab of the finger pointed toward that dark, almost forbidding entrance through which a fresh cacophony of shouts erupted, said he was ready to do exactly that. But despite what her ears told her Emma refused to be cowed. Then her glance caught yet another figure emerge from that black mouth. Allowing her eyes to follow a lad, Emma's conviction hardened. His torn jacket barely covered the thin chest, its sleeves hanging loose and ragged below the elbow; numerous small holes were visible in trousers so worn patches of flesh showed through and the expanse of leg left unprotected between the calf and metalled clogs was pin-pricked with tiny scars where showers of sparks had burned. Keeping her voice steady though her heart ached in sympathy for a lad who might not be even as old as Timothy she answered calmly.

'The clothes of a gypsy woman need be no concern of yours Mr Adams, and as for the foundry, if it is a place safe enough for a lad as young as the one I see now then it is safe enough for me.'

Following the direction of her glance John Adams' mouth became set. 'That don't be what it appears,' he said, watching the lad scoop sand into a bucket. 'Mr Halstead don't have lads young as that one go anywhere near the furnace nor will he have them inside the foundry while metal be poured into moulds; but lads 'ave to work if they and their families are to be fed so here they be given work carryin' sand to the moulders.'

'But his clothes, the burn holes ... his legs!'

'None of that were got at Halstead's.' John Adams watched the lad carry sand into the building. 'That lad came askin' for work a week or so back, seems he worked alongside his father in an iron works along of Bilston.' He paused, his head shaking before adding, 'Not all ironmakers operates the policy we 'ave here, some don't care how young a lad be supposin' he can load pig or help carry a crucible; that lad seen his father burned to death when a container of molten iron tipped down on him when he tripped while carryin' it. House and job being one then both were lost with the man's death... that's how the lad and his mother come to be in this town.'

'I ... I'm sorry.' Emma's quiet apology brought Adams' glance back to her and as she met his eyes she felt suddenly shamefaced at her behaviour. By steadfastly refusing to wait in another building, by adamantly demanding to go along with him into that foundry she was adding to a burden of responsibility which must already weigh heavily upon his shoulders. About to tell him she would remain where she was until he was able to return Emma jumped at the sound of a voice at her back.

She was not sparing herself. Listening in silence to Emma's explanation of how she came to be at the iron foundry Mark Halstead watched the play of morning light flash auburn darts with each movement of her head, the sparkle of gold-flecked green eyes that stayed unremittingly on his own, the hands held tight together in her lap. He had heard the story of her setting up home in that half-demolished place but of the reason she came to be there nothing had been revealed. So what was the truth of the matter, just what had brought a well-spoken, obviously educated woman to such circumstances? She had been making her way to the town, to report her unlawful activity to the constable, so she had told Adams. Looking at Emma now he believed it.

'Perhaps, Mr Halstead, you would set one of your workmen to walk me to the police station,

194

that way you can be–' A series of shouts from the yard had Emma break off, her glance following the tall supple figure rising to cross to the window overlooking the cobbled yard.

'Get along now, I told you he won't see nobody 'til the tippin' be over; you come back in an hour or two.'

A voice deep and gravelly could just be heard above the noise emanating from the foundry.

'I don't care whether tippin' be done or not, I come to speak with the gaffer an' I don't leave until I do.'

'I told you...'

Vibrant with defiance, cutting across the deeper voice a lighter one rang its reply. 'An' I be tellin' you, I ain't leavin' 'til I've done what I come to do!'

'Then we'll just 'ave to let my clog do the persuadin'.'

'Good God!' Part amazement, part admiration, Mark Halstead's exclamation had Emma rise to her feet but a quick movement of his head had her remain still.

'Y' should 'ave thought twice afore lifting your clog mister, I don't be no wench y'can frighten.'

'He didn't see that one coming.' Mark Halstead shook his head, then as yet another figure joined the mêlée leaned a little closer to the dusty glass.

'What be goin' on here?' Demanding, authoritative, a voice Emma recognised as that of John Adams seemed to hit against the windowpane, then from what seemed tight clenched teeth, halting every few seconds as if faced by a barrier of pain, she heard the reply.

195

'This one... he come bustin' through the gate sayin' ... sayin' he wanted to talk ...

'To talk with the gaffer, that be what I intends, mister, so lessen you wants to feel my boot where he felt it you'll get outta my way!'

'The next boot will be mine!' John Adams' irate answer rang clear. 'I be the gaffer here and it be me tellin' you to get y'self out ... or maybe I should give myself the pleasure of draggin' you from this yard.'

'You be the gaffer!' The response throbbed with contempt. 'Then you be the brave soul who faced a young woman all by 'imself! You be the man with courage enough to confront a woman! Bold enough to threaten her with jail before givin' y'self the pleasure of draggin' her along of here yesterday, well let me tell you, mister gaffer of a bloody iron foundry, you ain't talkin' with no wench this time, your bully boy ways might frighten a woman as it seems they do for the men I sees here, but you don't frighten me.'

'Obviously not.' Unaware he had uttered the words aloud Mark Halstead smiled then turning to look at Emma said dismissively, 'A skirmish in the yard, Adams will take care of it.'

'I warned you, mister...' Followed by a shout of pain the next words became muffled as if the speaker were engaged in a tussle but then, 'You tell me, mister, tell me what you've done with Emma!'

'Timothy!' For a moment Emma stood rock still, the blood draining from her face. Then as Mark Halstead made to reach for her she was gone, racing back downstairs toward the yard.

Mark Halstead's frown denoted none of the admiration felt inside of him as he looked at the lad standing now in his office, one hand protectively clutching that of Emma. Ragged yes; his glance slid over the worn jacket and threadbare trousers; young, hmm, yes! He looked at the defiant face, the tilt of the head, the direct meeting with his own eyes. What this lad had said to John Adams about holding no fear of him was clearly apparent in that steady stare, a stare which repeated, 'You don't frighten me.'

'You have caused quite a commotion...' He paused, interrupted by the quick light patter of feet running along the corridor from the stairs then as the door was flung open added, '...and it appears not to be finished yet.'

'Lily.' Before Emma could taken in what was happening Timothy was already holding a weeping Lily in his arms, his countenance threatening all manner of harm to the man who had followed to stand in the doorway.

'I couldn't 'old 'er, Mr Adams.' Flat cap twisted in dust-stained hands the man mumbled his explanation. 'The wench be quick as a flea, another second or two would 'ave seen 'er runnin' through the foundry an' we couldn't tek no risk of that so I thought it best to bring 'er along to the office seein' as 'ow you be 'ere.'

'You did the right thing, thank you.' He had spoken to the workman but Mark Halstead's attention was with the three grouped together, his frown deepening as he saw Emma's arms now about both boy and the girl he held so protectively. She had lied after all, here was the family she had denied existed; now where the husband?

A coldness rising inside he nodded assent to his overseer's query should he return with the other man to the workplace.

'Please sit down, Miss Lawrence,' he said as the door closed, 'I am sure you can lie as eminently well sitting as you do when standing.'

'Lie!' Emma looked at the man sitting calmly at his desk. 'I have told you no lie, Mr Halstead.'

His glance travelled tellingly over Timothy and Lily, then Mark Halstead looked again at Emma. 'You told me no lie?' He smiled contemptuously. 'You told me you had no family, that your parents and sister were dead, that there was no one else yet here you are with two people who clearly are not strangers to you, how do you explain that?'

'Don't be none of your business!' Timothy had thrust himself in front of Emma though the hand stretched behind him held on comfortingly to the still trembling Lily. 'That man Adams were mistaken in supposin' it were Emma took over your property, that were my doin'.'

'But Miss Lawrence was found there, she has not denied she was living there.'

'At my invitin'!' Timothy blurted. 'Her come only 'cos Lily and me asked her to.'

'I can understand how easy it must have been to accept the invitation of one as pretty as Miss Lily.' Mark Halstead's smile met the eyes peeping from behind Timothy's back, then his glance hardened as it met Emma and he added, 'As it must have been to impose herself on my property.'

'Mr Halstead.' Emma stepped forward. 'I have already said to yourself and to Mr Adams that I accept what you say and am fully prepared to face the outcome. Now please may we go to the police station.'

'You don't be goin' to no police station, the doin' were mine, Emma, an' it'll be me answers to it.'

'Not family!' Mark Halstead's glance moved from one to the other. 'You still did not explain, Miss Lawrence, and though I am somewhat markedly informed it is not my business perhaps you, if not your champion, might be inclined to humour me as to the relationship.'

'I be Tim ... Timothy Elsmore and this,' Timothy pulled the resisting Lily forward, 'this be Lily, my sister.'

Mark Halstead smiled again, this time rising to his feet as he said, 'How do you do, Lily, my name is Mark Halstead.'

'And you be the one wantin' of his pound of flesh.' Timothy snatched Lily's hand from the one extended to her across the desk. 'So, mister, let's you and me go see to the cuttin' of it.'

'And your sister,' Mark's stare swivelled to Timothy, 'what is to happen to her while you and Miss Lawrence are serving a spell in prison? You see, Miss Lawrence being as much culprit as you she will also be required to answer to the law.'

'Timmy and Emma don't need worry for me, I ... I shall go to the workhouse 'til Timmy can come for me.'

Had they discussed separation before coming here? Could these two young people possibly

199

know what life in a workhouse was like? Looking at the young face staring at him with such innocent eyes Mark Halstead felt confused. They had owned there was no family tie, no filial relationship, and yet each was willing to risk much for the other, even to walking willingly into the workhouse!

'I think we can discount that, Lily.' He took a slim blue-bound ledger from a drawer of the desk and looked soberly at Timothy asking, 'Exactly how long have you been at that house?'

Brow creasing with thought Timothy took a moment to answer then said, 'It were the day of Mother's funeral, I heard folk sayin' that bein' orphans then it would be the duty of the parish to look to Lily, I knowed that meant puttin' her into the workhouse and I couldn't let that happen so ... well we run off, that were...' He paused again, assessing, the length of time then, 'I can't tell how long ago that be since I don't know the date of today so my answer can't be held accurate. If you thinks that be a way of shortenin' any account of the magistrate then you can put your own reckonin' to him, but near as I can fathom I thinks Lily and me 'ave been livin' at Lea Brook some six, p'raps seven weeks.'

They had lived in a vermin-infested, derelict house for some seven weeks, they had eaten and slept in squalor in order to prevent the girl being taken into the care of the parish ... and he had asked himself could these two children possibly know what life inside of a workhouse was like! With something akin to self-disparagement Mark Halstead stared at the unopened book. He was

200

thirty years old yet it would seem a boy half his age already knew more of life than he did.

Opening the book he stared a moment longer at the unblemished page then reached for a pen, the seconds affording him time to come to terms with the emotion risen so suddenly.

'I said I 'ave no knowin' of the date but Mother ... Mother were taken a week on from her birthday and that be January tenth, her were laid in the churchyard four days followin' so I reckons you can count the days from then.'

'I see.' Mark Halstead glanced at the face regarding him with a defiant honesty, then using the barrel of the pen, twisting a brass-bound calendar so Timothy could see it said, 'Today is the sixth of March, if my calculation is correct then you have had the use of my property for...' He hesitated, running over the figures again in his mind before continuing. 'Seven weeks and two days. Do you have any query with that reckoning?' Then at Timothy's shake of the head asked, 'You, Miss Lawrence, would you have any disagreement regarding my reckoning... Miss Lawrence?'

'What ... I beg your pardon,' Emma drew her glance from the calendar. 'No, no I have no dispute.'

She had been caught off guard, her answer had been clear proof her mind was elsewhere ... with the husband? Dipping the pen into a crystal inkwell Mark Halstead found himself wondering just where had the mind of Miss Emma Lawrence been, what thoughts had brought a tinge of colour to that pale face.

Writing the date in clear bold print he looked again at Timothy, saying politely, 'You will forgive my asking but do you read? I ask only in the event you might wish someone to oversee what I write in this book, I would want no air of deception between us.'

'That be civil of you, Mr Halstead.' Timothy's expression of defiance softened. 'But yes I does read and so does Lily, Mother seen to that and to our both bein' able to write, though I confess that don't stretch to no lawyer words.'

'Then we shall avoid lawyer words.' Hiding the smile the boy's reply brought to his lips he wrote a while longer then, handing the book to Timothy, waited while he and Lily read the plainly scripted words.

Taking the book back, waiting for the blare of the foundry hooter to recede, Mark nodded at the boy's acceptance of what had been shown.

He glanced again at the neatly written page then back to Timothy saying quietly, 'I pay my watchman here at the foundry one shilling and sixpence per night which amounts to ten shillings and sixpence a week–'

'Mr Halstead,' Timothy interrupted quickly, 'I don't 'ave whatever that might amount to, there be no way I can pay anywhere near so why draw this out?' A red flush stained his cheek; he hesitated then with head held high, eyes firmly on those of the man who raised his own head, he went on. 'I 'adn't took you to be one who likes to stab afore cuttin' of his pound of flesh!'

'Please, Timothy did not mean...'

'There is no need to explain what was meant.'

Mark shook his head at Emma's intervention. 'I fear I have given the wrong impression; if I might continue.'

Compliance, but no compromise! Mark Halstead caught the flash of challenge dart from angry brown eyes, the determined set of the square jaw. Timothy Elsmore owned nothing in the world and owed nothing to it; he was a lad living a man's life, a youngster caring for a younger sister, a lad fighting to hold together the last that life had given him. A lad? Mark Halstead answered the question. No. The boy he looked at was every inch a man, and that a man of consequence.

Glancing again at the book he continued. 'Ten shillings and sixpence for seven weeks amounts to three pounds thirteen shillings and sixpence, plus two nights more at one and sixpence brings a total of three pounds sixteen shillings and sixpence. That,' he looked up at Timothy, 'is the sum I owe to you since you have acted as night watchman to that property at Lea Brook.' Ignoring the boy's exclamation he proceeded. 'Miss Lily also must be reimbursed. She has carried out the duties of housemaid and scullery maid which combined I feel must carry a wage equal to that of night watchman. So if you are both in agreement my cashier will furnish you with both amounts.'

'That be all very well, and don't be thinkin' as me and Lily don't be grateful.' Timothy straightened from listening to his sister whisper in his ear. 'But from what we sees of all this is Emma bein' left to face the law on her own. That don't do for Lily and me, we thanks you again but we won't 'ave Emma pay while we goes scot free.'

Had he expected more? Continuing to write a note of payment Mark Halstead knew he had not. But a germ of perversity made him continue, 'Miss Lawrence, so each of you have informed me, is not family, in which case I fail to see why you should feel any allegiance toward her.'

Glancing at Emma, taking her hand in one of his own while grasping Lily's with the other, Timothy replied quietly. 'You be right, Mr Halstead, Lily and me don't be family to Emma, not in the sense you means family, we don't be children of the same blood but we be somethin' as strong, we be children of the heart. Where Emma goes Lily and me goes, even though that be prison and the workhouse!'

It had been said with such softness, such a wealth of feeling, that it could only be called love. As he bent his head once more to the book Mark Halstead felt suddenly humble.

18

'*Where Emma goes Lily an' me goes.*'

Her heart had surged at the words yet for all they meant to her she had known she could not let Timothy go through with his decision. It had been filled with affection but it was too rash, he must not deprive himself and especially not Lily of a home where they would be warm and dry, a home not riddled with damp and vermin. But despite her pleading, her reasoning, he had stood firm. There had been only one way she could see to rectify the situation, to make Timothy think again; she had to tell him she was moving on, that she was leaving Wednesbury and – this would be the hardest of all – she must tell him she did not want himself and Lily to accompany her, she wanted their friendship at an end.

Watching the cart which had been loaded with the paltry few possessions the Elsmore children owned driving away, Emma felt her throat constrict with pent-up emotion.

Lily had cried out at the announcement, her small face twisted with disappointment, tears brimming in wide disbelieving eyes while Timothy stared, his mouth held in a taut line. She had wanted to hold the both of them, to confess her statement a lie, to tell them she was thinking only of them, of their well-being, but with fingers clasped bitingly into her palms she had resisted the call of her heart. Glancing to the man seated at his desk she had thanked him once more then, knowing to speak to Timothy and Lily would breach the dam holding back her tears, had turned to leave.

'Miss Lawrence...'

The voice in her mind sounding so clear Emma started slightly, a tinge of pink creeping to her cheeks as she remembered the look Mark Halstead had bestowed on her, a look which had said she lied; but had he thought the lie lay in what she said about not wanting the Elsmores, or in her earlier claim of having no other companion?

He had not said and she could not ask. Emma watched the cart lumber on to Lea Brook Road, turning to go in the direction of Wednesbury.

She had been already at the door when he had spoken.

She had not welcomed the delay, every moment of hearing Lily's stifled weeping cutting like a knife but good manners dictated she must hear what Mark Halstead had to say, so she had halted and he had gone on.

'I fear I have left my proposition too late, I had not expected you to be moving on.'

'Proposition?'

He had nodded at that. *'I had meant to ask would you consider putting my father's papers in some semblance of order.'*

'Mr Halstead,' she had replied quickly, *'I have no knowledge of the iron-making industry, no familiarity with terms such as I heard used to Mr Adams.'*

'You mean "romming".'

'That and a "load of pig". I would never associate the need for pigs with producing metal.'

He had laughed, his eyes echoing amusement.

'Nor would I expect you to have,' he said. *'"Romming" is the mens' word for the hard packing of sand firming the patterns prior to filling them with molten iron; as for "pig" that refers to pig iron, a rock-bearing iron mineral, this is extracted when the stone is crushed and burned off in the furnace, but that is not what I had thought to discuss with you.'*

She had made no answer, not wanting to prolong the pain of parting from two young people who she knew she had become fond of but until that moment had not fully recognised the depth of that feeling, an emotion that had leaving them pull her apart.

He had paused but when she made no response had continued.

'My father travelled widely during his lifetime, he was passionately interested in architecture and culture of foreign lands but that passion did not spread to the filing of information gathered along the way. It is his written notes together with his watercolour paintings I wished to be properly recorded and catalogued so ultimately they could be bound in book form. It had been my idea you could carry out the work in the house I offered to...' he had glanced at Timothy, *'to Mr Elsmore, but seeing he has refused that offer and you yourself are moving on then I must suffer the disappointment of my intention.'*

He had thrown her a lifeline, but it was one she could not grasp.

'I thank you for your confidence in thinking me capable of ordering your father's work,' she had answered, forcing herself not to react to Lily's cry she accept, *'but you have overlooked the matter of rent. What I could not pay before I cannot pay now.'*

'I sometimes prove to be more my father's son than I think I am.' Mark Halstead had shaken his head. *'I am as inattentive in this as he was in ordering his writings; I should have informed you the employment I ask you undertake carries with it a salary.'*

'What be salary?' Lily's voice had piped across the small room only to be immediately answered by Timothy's exasperated. *'Lily! Ain't I said you be never to ask questions where you don't be concerned, now come on, we be finished here.'*

'Please,' Mark Halstead had said quickly. *'Don't leave until you allow me the pleasure of answering Lily's question.'* He had smiled at the child, a smile

which seemed to light his face. Remembering the catch it had brought to her throat, the colour already staining Emma's cheeks deepened.

'Salary,' he had said, '*is payment for work being done.*'

Resisting her brother's urging they should leave, Lily had stepped closer to the desk. '*You mean wages?*' she had asked innocently, '*be salary a posh way of saying wages?*'

'*Yes.*' Mark Halstead had chuckled softly. '*It is what your brother would call lawyer's words.*'

'*So if you paid Emma wages then her could pay rent for the house you talked of and ... and her wouldn't have to leave Wednesbury.*'

'*As you say.*' He had lifted his glance from Lily holding it steadily fastened on herself. '*She would not have to leave Wednesbury.*'

It had been more than a lifeline for her. Emma watched the cart pull out of sight. It had been a way of keeping Lily, Timothy and herself together, a way of holding a roof over their heads. But again she had not reckoned on Timothy's pride.

'*I knows why you said it.*' He had later answered her heartfelt explanation behind the reason she wanted to sever their friendship. '*I seen your mouth tremble and knowed you was lying but like I tells Lily, a person's business be their own and shouldn't 'ave the interfering of others.*' His head had lifted in that proud self-sufficient way she had come to know so well and though his next words had been said quietly there had been strength in his voice. '*You and Mr Halstead 'ave reached a business together, Lily and me be pleased at that.*'

With that he had taken Lily's hand, instructing

her to say goodbye, then both had walked away.

Was it her? Henrietta watched a slight figure crossing the busy junction of Upper and Lower High Street, noting the dark rough cloth of that skirt, the brown chequered shawl all so typical of mineworkers' and nail makers' wives. Henrietta's nose wrinkled in distaste. They were not the garments she had thought to see Emma Lawrence wearing, she – if the figure she watched was that girl – should be dressed in a blue coat and bonnet; they were the outdoor clothes missing from her closet; but then the sly ways of Bella Coley and Polly Lacey would likely have taken care of that. It wasn't above either of them to have furnished Emma with second-hand garments while taking hers and selling them to some pawn shop. But then she could be mistaken, in thinking the figure was Emma. Henrietta's steps slowed. After all she had scoured the town several times without once glimpsing the girl, yet this time ... tutting loudly at a woman blocking her view of the rapidly disappearing young woman Henrietta circled around her. This time there was the hair, that rich auburn hair ... this time it had to be Emma Lawrence.

This was the chance she had hoped for but not the place. Ignoring the woman answering her tut of irritation with equal annoyance Henrietta wrestled with the problem of whether or not she should follow. A crowded market place was hardly the choicest ground on which to confront a girl who'd run away from home: there were too many eyes, too many ears, any of which might well put two and two together and if there were a scene help Emma get away again, probably to disappear even more effectively. But not to take this opportunity, to let it slip through her fingers, would mean living with the fear the girl would at some time realise what it was she had lost, what was still being kept from her, and with that realisation the Gilmores' days at Beechcroft would come to an end.

Emma Lawrence claiming her rightful inheritance might not be all Fenton and herself need fear; there was the problem of Rachel. The child's death could not be linked to Fenton but once suspicion had pointed its finger ... and the diary, should that prove real, should what was claimed prove actually to be written in it then socially it would bear a sentence as condemnatory as any passed by a magistrate. They would be disregarded by anyone of note, unaccepted even by the few who did proffer the odd invitation. Watching the bright head disappear into a shop Henrietta weighed the for and against of the situation then, turning a haughty stare on the driver of a cart shouting for her to move out of the way, crossed deliberately in front of the vehicle to walk quickly in the direction taken by that dark-skirted figure.

'Emma, Emma my dear, I am so very glad to see you. Oh my dear, your uncle and I have missed you dreadfully.'

'Aunt!' Surprise made Emma gasp.

'How lovely to meet you,' Henrietta gushed on, 'Your uncle will be delighted to have you home with us.'

'I have no intention of returning, I won't ever...'

A hand flashing to Emma's arm Henrietta

hissed quietly. 'Do not make a scene, we do not want the whole town knowing our business.'

'I am sure you do not.' Emma shook the hand away.

The girl was going to be awkward. Henrietta's mouth tightened, her cold grey eyes flashing a warning though her voice kept a lighter note.

'Emma,' she forced a smile, 'Your uncle and I–'

Disdain thickening her throat Emma's interruption rasped out. 'Uncle,' she shook her head, 'you dare call him that, a man who–'

'Emma!' Henrietta's own intervention snapped like a dried twig. 'Control yourself!'

'Control myself!' Emma's reply echoed disgust. 'As your husband controlled himself!'

'Be silent!' It had snapped out too sharply. Alarmed by the very slip she hoped to avoid Henrietta glanced to each side, relief sweeping her when it appeared her reprimand had been that of a mistress to a servant thus drawing no attention. 'Emma,' she began again, careful to keep her voice low, 'what happened at Beechcroft, it was unfortunate.'

'Unfortunate!' Emma stared disbelievingly at the woman in front of her. 'You call the rape of a fifteen-year-old girl unfortunate. What kind of hypocrisy is that!'

Eyes like chips of grey ice regarded Emma while the snide reply slithered from smilingly scornful lips. 'You have no evidence.'

'Oh but I have.' Emma met the sneer calmly. 'But perhaps you forget I have Rachel's diary.'

She had not forgotten. Henrietta squirmed under what must for a moment be reckoned a

211

threat. Were that looming solely over Fenton then it would cause her no heartache but its reflection would cast its shadow; though not directly accused of compliance in his wrongdoing there would be an inevitable suspicion, the sins of the husband would in some form be visited upon the wife. It was a possibility she could not risk, one which must be destroyed quickly and thoroughly.

Acid biting inside at the knowledge she must placate a girl she had dominated for years she said soothingly, 'Emma, my dear, you must know Rachel's death was not at the hands of her uncle, you know deep within yourself your uncle would never harm either of you.'

Anger which had lain at the pit of Emma's stomach writhed, coiling upward, its tentacles gripping with a force that suppressed the air in her lungs, holding it there until it seemed her very heart must burst.

'Uncle!' It broke from her at last, pulsing with every last ounce of abhorrence the years had built in her. 'Never,' she cried, 'never refer to that man as Rachel's uncle; he was her tormenter, her abuser, a vile loathsome wretch who raped her not once but many times yet even that was not enough for Fenton Gilmore, he had to abuse her sister also.'

This was not going as she wanted. The anger Henrietta had restrained washed like a tidal wave through her veins. Accusing Fenton, voicing her denunciation of him here in the street, it was bound to be overheard.

Mastering an almost overriding desire to slap away the indictment blazing in the eyes staring back at her, to slap away contention as she had so many times previously, Henrietta was forced to swallow repeatedly before she could infuse a superficial calmness into her tone.

'Emma my dear,' it was so nearly a purr, 'of course losing Rachel has hurt you deeply, the loss of one you love, is so very painful, and when that person is your sister...' She broke off, allowing a sigh to escape. 'I too have lost both brothers and sisters so I understand the hurt. The feeling of sorrow, the pain of knowing you will never see them again is almost too much to bear but making such wild allegations can only result in more unhappiness, it can only cause you more hurt in the future, once you come to recognise how wrong your aspersions were. Now my dear, let us say no more. Come home to Beechcroft, you will feel much better once you are there.'

Go back to that house, deliver herself into the hands of the man she detested. Her stomach retching at the prospect Emma turned on her heel.

'Emma.' Henrietta had caught again at her arm. 'Please, remember your parents, they would want you in your own home, want you to be with people they trusted.'

Turning slowly, her eyes tracing the hard features of the woman who had never once treated her with compassion, Emma snatched free her arm. 'My parents,' she said scathingly, 'my father, the man you and your husband have consistently robbed, my mother, the woman you claimed to be your sister, one you called a whore, they trusted you, but I never will.'

Henrietta raised her hand to strike but pulled it

quickly down as she glanced again at people passing around them. Someone was bound to recognise her sooner or later. Drawing a tight breath she hissed, 'Hold your tongue, there are people who will hear!'

Hold her tongue ... wasn't that what Rachel had done, held her tongue for fear Fenton Gilmore would send her sister away? But now that fear no longer held sway and neither did this woman.

Emma had not missed Henrietta's quick covert glance. 'That is your worry, isn't it? That people will come to hear of the true Fenton Gilmore. Well, you must live with that as I must live with the knowledge of what he did to two young girls he had pledged to care for.'

Henrietta's eyes narrowed. 'You think Fenton will allow you to threaten him. No, Emma, by this evening he will have brought his ward back to Beechcroft and you may be certain you will not leave its walls again.'

'Ward!' Emma shook her head. 'Rachel and I were never legally that, but even had your husband obtained any legal right of guardianship, it is now at an end; you see, Mrs Gilmore,' she almost spat the title, 'I obtained my majority a week ago; I am now at an age to answer for myself.'

He had refused the money. Mark Halstead stared at the entry he had written in the slim blue-bound ledger, an entry now marred by a heavy black line going straight across it. That young scamp had flatly refused to accept the payment he and his sister had been offered, an amount he had probably never seen in his whole life and certainly an amount he could not hope to earn in months; tatting about in the market, running errands, helping load and unload carters' wagons, a way of life which paid tuppence here, sixpence there, a way barely affording those two a living; yet the lad had rejected the money. But that was not all he had said no to.

Thinking the matter of illegal possession settled with the Elsmores he had supplemented it with the offer of a house which he'd said could be theirs supposing the lad made an evening check on the building to be erected on the site once the remains of the malthouse and adjoining buildings were demolished. Only then had he turned his attention to the young woman who stubbornly had chosen to stand throughout the whole proceedings.

'*As for Miss Lawrence...*' His own words running through his head, Mark Halstead gazed at the spot where Emma had stood, memory filling the empty space with a slender figure dressed in rough black skirts, a shawl hanging loose from her shoulders, a figure whose delicate features were a contrast to the rough clothing, the creamy porcelain skin accented by the gleam of rich auburn hair, the wide green-gold eyes it had taken several repetitions of her name to draw away from the calendar her stare had returned to, a figure which had so nearly prevented further words. Not fully assessing the sudden swirl to his veins he had made an issue of replacing the pen on its stand before beginning again.

'*Miss Lawrence, seeing you were a guest in that house I do not propose to take the matter further. You can return to wherever it was and whoever you were with before you came to be in that house with the full assurance this matter is at an end.'*

'No, Mr Halstead, it ain't...'

Timothy Elsmore had not bent to his sister nor had he so much as glanced at the young woman whose hand he clutched but chin lifting, eyes firm and steady, he had gone on unhesitatingly, *'It ain't finished. I thanks you for this.'*

He had released Emma's hand and taking up the payment slip placed it squarely on the closed ledger.

'I also thanks you for the offer of a house but Lily an' me won't 'ave the takin' of it. You see, Mr Halstead, like I told you some minutes gone, Emma be family to Lily an' me, we be sisters an' brother to one another as much as had we been born of the same father an' mother, an' that bein' the way it is then where Emma goes Lily an' me goes.'

Slipping the ledger into a drawer of the desk Mark smiled. As he had once told himself young Timothy Elsmore was already a man of consequence.

19

It was too soon, it would be too much of a risk!

Fenton Gilmore stared from his study window out across the expanse of garden stretching away from Beechcroft. Those buyers had made a reorder as though the goods requested were no more than sacks of potatoes. Potatoes did not fetch the kind of money they were prepared to pay and neither did tobacco, but then he wasn't dealing with either.

Money! His fingers curled as though already clutching banknotes. That was what it took to live in the style he wanted, the style he intended to have; money and plenty of it was the only way of fulfilling that desire.

He could not turn that business away, could not refuse to accept that order. To do so would be to lose those customers for good; they would turn to someone else to acquire what they wanted and Fenton Gilmore would be left with nothing but an almost failed tobacconist's business.

The shop in Wednesbury market place. His fingers tightened further, a spasmodic jerk of reaction to the thought springing to his mind. If that too had to be sold then...

As if caught by steel clamps the thought skidded to a halt in his brain. There was one way to make certain Lawrence Fine Tobacco remained viable: find Emma Lawrence, bring her back to this house, have her sign everything over to him.

Barking a reply to a tap at the door Fenton made no effort to conceal aversion as the young maid entered. What the hell had Henrietta been thinking, taking on a scarface? But then his wife had never displayed taste, in anything, she totally lacked refinement in appearance and judgement ... the education gained in Drew's Court! Contempt marking his face he ran a glance over the girl dropping a light curtsy. Where would she find herself once dismissed from this house?

With Henrietta in that slum of a place, find

herself a husband there? Fenton's laugh rumbled in his throat. Even the lowest of Drew's Court wouldn't take a scarface for a wife.

'Mr Perry to see you, sir.'

'I told you never to come here!' Once the door had closed behind the girl Fenton rounded as the man strolled into the room. 'Not only do you disregard that, you also gave your own name!'

'So who should I say be callin', don't hardly be the time for Father Christmas.'

The man thought himself so sharp! Fenton frowned, the gall of anger replacing contempt. But like Henrietta he also lacked judgement, a shortcoming which one day could culminate in a positively lethal accident; but for a while longer the distasteful had to be tolerated.

Concealing the nature of his thought in his tone Fenton crossed to stand at the stone fireplace, taking a moment before asking, 'Have you told anyone of your coming here?'

'Now that I were careful of, I ain't the fool you seems to think I be.'

Let us hope not for both our sakes! retorted Fenton silently, glancing across the room. That girl could be at the other side of that door, she could be listening. Interpreting the look Jud Perry snatched open the door. Closing it again after a swift check of the hall he smirked. 'Nervous be we, Gilmore?'

'This is no parlour game, Perry, you would do well to remember the undertaking we engage in has, if caught, only one conclusion: the gallows!'

'Not for Jud Perry.' The other man laughed. 'He don't be the one a sellin' of young wenches.'

218

Again the man had made a misjudgement. Not only was he a fool, he was a complete fool! Unleashed fury, cold and dangerous, writhed and coiled inside Fenton, its venom etching the hiss of words spat at his visitor.

'You don't be one selling young women! Then just what is it Jud Perry sees himself as doing? What is it he takes money for?'

'For findin' wenches employment,' Perry answered blithely. 'Ain't no wrong in that. I done only what were asked by yourself, to find suitable girls to work in your cigarette factory; Judge won't condemn me for that, won't be Jud Perry will dance at the end o' the rope.'

Maybe not the gallows, maybe not by sentence of the court but soon and by whatever mode of despatch Jud Perry would be hurled through the doors of hell. Contrary to his own belief Perry was not indispensable, kill one snake and you need only kick over a stone to find another! Consolation a balm to the anger seething a moment before, Fenton answered calmly.

'No one will dance at the end of the rope provided we take precautions, one of which is not to be seen together in the town. The fewer people seeing us together, possibly hearing any discussion between us, can only be for the better...' He paused, a frown marking the fleet arrival of doubt. 'The lad, the one I sent to say I wished to see you, where did he find you?'

Feeling in the pocket of his worn jacket Perry withdrew a smoke-darkened clay pipe, answering as he packed the bowl with shavings of black tobacco.

'Found me in the Turk's Head and afore you jigs like a biddy with a flea in her bloomers let me tell you the lad give me the wink to go outside, we talked in the yard, weren't nobody else there.'

A scowled 'not here' informing the other man the pipe was not to be allowed Fenton went on sharply. 'What message did he give?'

Denied the pleasure of smoking Jud Perry tapped the slivers of tobacco back into a stained pouch. Offence at the perceived affront evident on every feature he returned pouch and pipe to his pocket, patting it several times before saying acidly, 'He were to tell me Mr Smith would like to speak with me.'

'That was all?'

'If there were more then you ain't been given all of your money's worth! You should 'ave written a note if you wanted to be certain what you asked were what I learned.'

Committing any of his dealings to paper was a practice he had no intention of following. There must be nothing, however vague, to link him with the trade in young girls. There had been a hue and cry over the one gone missing from Russell Street. The broken jug had been found where it had fallen, men from the surrounding streets had banded together searching the outlying heath but found no sign of the girl. Nor would they. Fenton congratulated himself. It was a perfect way of getting rid of a dead body. The return of empty tobacco tuns to the plantations was an everyday occurrence at the Liverpool docks, one which gave rise to no speculation, and if one were lost at sea it was unfortunate but of no great significance and the fact of it carrying the body of a girl with it to the bottom of the Atlantic Ocean would never come to light.

'So what be it you wants, "Mr Smith"?'

Perry's question cut across his thoughts; Fenton looked at the face wreathed in sarcasm. Smith was an innocuous name, a suitable choice for a pseudonym, so many people bearing it made distinguishing one from another a complicated task, but Perry...! Had taking him as a partner in the business of procuring been the wisest of decisions? The man liked his drink, the money he was paid went on beer and women, and who could say when one or the other might loosen his tongue? And what had possessed him to come to this house instead of their usual meeting place, the railway goods station at Lea Brook? There they could talk without drawing attention; he was merely a gentleman enquiring after a consignment of goods. The workers employed in carting materials into sheds having no official uniform meant Perry in his rough clothing blended in well, no one sparing him a second glance.

Annoyed at this departure from the norm Fenton snapped, 'Why did you come here and not the goods station?'

'Why d' ain't you say if you wanted a meetin' there!'

Coming to this house, disregard for the usual meeting place, questioning the method of request for that meeting, announcing his real name to the maid instead of the alias: all were in blatant contravention to previous agreement. The man was becoming a liability and that was not good for any business. But liability must be weighed against immediate need. Fenton suppressed the anger gathering in a cold pool inside. Within days need would have been met, that order dispensed, and along with it the liability; Perry could be got rid of. It would mean finding a replacement to carry out the business of finding suitable goods, however – Fenton smiled to himself – money, the right amount of money, would solve that problem. Satisfaction coming with the thought he chose to disregard Perry's retort to the question about the meeting place, saying instead, 'I have been approached with a request for further supply, the same quality as previously of course.'

'Oh of course!'

Had there been an undertone of insolence in that reply, a jeer? Apprehension flicking his senses Fenton shot a quick glance at the man whose attitude since coming into this room had been one of offensiveness. The man would be paid for that, well paid, but not in coin! Holding the thought as a shield against a fresh arousal of ire, a forced congeniality disguising what lurked inside, he said, 'Requesting goods of the same quality is an assurance, a customer's way of denoting confidence in your choice of material.'

'Ain't had no complaints up to yet.'

'Nor will we have, I'm sure. You have the knack of selecting exactly what is required.'

'So what be required?'

Again that air of condescension, of almost blatant mockery. Holding on to his patience was becoming ever more difficult. Fenton took a gold hunter pocket watch from his waistcoat, checking it against the time displayed on the carriage clock on the mantelpiece above the fireplace.

'Four.' He slipped the watch back into his pocket, only then looking at Perry. 'Four,' he reiterated, 'but there is a stipulation.'

Normally unappealing features rendered the more so by heavy brows lowering over eyes agleam with distrust Perry growled, 'A stip ... you what? What the hell be that to mean?'

Revelling in a moment of gratification at the other man's lack of understanding Fenton allowed nothing of that pleasure to sound in his reply.

'Nothing to worry about, it simply means the client has imposed a condition.'

'A condition.' Perry's look was sour, 'An' what condition might that be?'

'It is merely a limit of time.' Fenton shrugged. 'The goods are to be with them two days from now.'

'Two days.' Perry nodded. 'Then I hopes you can come up with them goods.'

'What do you mean?' Apprehension flicked again in Fenton.

Removing pipe and pouch once more from the pocket of his shabby jacket, refilling the bowl with the shavings of tobacco, Jud Perry struck a match. Holding the flame to the bowl, looking across it to Fenton, he smiled.

'I means I don't be goin' to be findin' no more wenches for that "cigarette factory"'. He drew on the pipe, exhaling a cloud of unappetising smoke. 'It means you be 'aving to do your own dirty work.'

'You can't...'

'Can't I?' Perry laughed, blowing out the match then flicking it to where Fenton stood at the fireplace. 'I believe I already 'ave, taken my cards so to speak; I don't work for you no more.'

'But why? if it is a case of money we can come to fresh terms, say ten pounds a head.'

'I've already agreed fresh terms.'

'With whom?' Consternation rushed Fenton's question across the room.

Perry drew again on the pipe, a fresh stream of smoke emanating from pursed lips before answering.

'D'ain't give no name, done somethin' better; he come with money ready in his hand, more'n you've ever come up with or ever be liable to: weren't no waitin' of payment as be the case with you, I were given cash in hand and that before producin' the goods. That beats what I had with you so Gilmore, you an' me be finished.'

Nerves fluttering like moths in her stomach, Emma moved restlessly about the living room she had tidied and retidied for the fourth time. Meeting Henrietta in the town had unnerved her, their conversation circling over and over again in her mind.

How could she have had the temerity to ask her to return to Beechcroft, to say knowing what she did that Fenton Gilmore would never harm either Rachel or herself? But Henrietta Gilmore had inadvertently spoken one truth during that confrontation.

'...*you may be certain you will not leave its walls again.*'

224

Hearing it again as clearly as if spoken aloud Emma's whole body trembled. Should he find her, force her back to that house then she would be no better than a prisoner, a prisoner kept for the amusement of her jailer.

But he could not force her, she was of age, he could no longer exercise jurisdiction over her. But a man as evil as Fenton Gilmore, a man whose wickedness had ruined Rachel's young life, had contributed towards her death even if he had not actually ended her life himself, would not contemplate jeopardising all he had gained by allowing Emma to remain free.

A sound at the door made her nerves scream; Emma reached instinctively for the poker from the fire irons beside the hearth. Gilmore! She stared to where the living room door gave directly on to the street, Henrietta must have told him of their meeting, now he was here. Blood racing at a second knock she clutched the poker. He would not find it easy taking her back.

He would not knock ... he would not knock; slowly, as if wading through mud, words struggled to reach Emma's conscious mind, finally breaking through as the knock was repeated.

Gilmore ... he would not knock ... he would not wait out there ... he would walk straight in.

Logical thoughts like this followed rapidly one after another, their effect helping to calm the storm shaking her senses, yet still Emma held on to the poker while opening the door.

'I apologise for disturbing you at your work.' Mark Halstead glanced at the poker.

'No you didn't ... you haven't...' Emma

blushed, pushing the poker behind her.

'I had arranged to meet with the builders on the site of the old malthouse which meant my passing this way so I took the opportunity of bringing you another batch of my father's papers. I hope I have not inconvenienced you too greatly.'

Striving against a fresh onslaught to her senses Emma took refuge in a brief shake of her head. 'No,' she managed a smile, 'you have not inconvenienced me.' Then opening the door wider she added, 'Those you had delivered last week are finished, so if you would step inside I will get them for you.'

She had added a woman's touch to the room. Left alone while Emma went to collect the work from what he knew was a small front parlour Mark Halstead glanced approvingly at pretty chintz-covered cushions and curtains then to the cast-iron grate, its black surfaces polished to silver. Even the brass fire irons gleamed. He smiled to himself. Opening the door she had looked ready to use that poker on someone's head – thank heaven she had not brought it down on his.

'I hope what I have done will prove satis-factory.' Emma reentered the room. 'Some of the notes were a little difficult to decipher.'

'My father's handwriting.' He laughed. 'As with his record keeping, not of the neatest.'

'I can forgive him that seeing his beautiful watercolours, they are fascinating. Your father is to be congratulated on giving time to writing at all. I could not have torn myself away from those places long enough to sleep.'

'They do look rather magnificent, little wonder

he preferred travel to running an iron foundry.'

'Did you not wish to go with your parents?'

'My wishes could not be considered, my education was not to be interrupted. I reckoned that a pretty rough deal at the time, I remember it had me feeling rather abandoned; shame on me but I confess I might have shed a tear or two.'

'It is painful when parents ... Rachel and I–'

'Rachel?' He voiced the enquiry.

'Please inspect the work thoroughly, Mr Halstead. If it is not to your liking then I will do it over again.'

She had brushed aside the query. Mark Halstead looked at Emma whose glance dropped to the box she held out to him. But she had not been so adept in controlling her voice; that had trembled, her mouth quivering, and he had caught the sheen of tears filming her eyes as she looked away. Was Rachel the sister she had said was dead? Had they, as himself, been left behind as children?

Letting questions lie he took the box, allowing his glance to rove over the crude wooden settle, a chintz-covered seat its only saving grace. His glance moved, taking in plain chairs drawn to a table on which had been placed a brown earthenware jug filled with wild flowers, the dresser with an assortment of crockery; this was not as he would have wanted.

'This house,' he said, unaware the displeasure rustling in his voice, 'it was meant for one of my foundrymen.'

'Of course,' Emma answered tightly. 'I will leave tomorrow.'

He frowned. 'I was not implying you were to vacate this house but that I will arrange for the furniture to be replaced with something more comfortable.'

'Please do not trouble on my account,' Emma replied quickly. 'What is here is perfectly adequate; thank you, but I have inconvenienced you enough.'

Adequate! Discontent already plaguing Mark Halstead's veins flared with fresh life. It might be adequate for a foundry manager but it was not good enough for this woman; he ought never to have offered this place.

Proposing to explain he was halted by Emma's own quick words.

'Mr Halstead.' Her head lifted, she looked directly at him. 'We both know your providing me with employment and with a place to live is no more than a kindness on your part and truly I appreciate it but I must face one fact, that fact being that sooner or later I must find another home and means by which to support myself I think it best I do so as soon as possible.'

Why did he suddenly feel at a loss? The woman was nothing to him, why should he care how soon she left his life? But he did care. Mark Halstead felt his nerves tauten at the realisation. He had cared from the moment John Adams brought her to his office. Taking a moment to bring emotion under control he said, 'Do I take it you no longer wish to continue with my father's work, that you find it perhaps too arduous?'

'It is neither of those. I simply feel that perhaps it better you find someone permanently resident in the town, someone who can devote the time and patience the work deserves.'

'More simply said than done.' He forced a smile. 'Wednesbury is a town of mines and factories, the majority of its population working in one or the other, their employers seeking to expand their business in order to maintain their workers in employment. So you see, Miss Lawrence, it is not a town rich in persons with time, ability and inclination to take on a project such as I asked of you. Therefore I ask again, will you not stay until the work is completed.'

'But this house,' Emma protested, 'it is needed for one of your workmen.'

'That will not be until the iron works to be erected across the way is finished.' He glanced through the window to where the malthouse lay in a heap of bricks. His smile returned as he looked back to Emma. 'And iron works, as Rome, are not built in a day, which renders your protest irrelevant, do you not agree?'

She had enjoyed reading his father's papers, unravelling handwriting which at times became no more than a scrawl, of resolving a complicated method of shorthand, matching it to a particular watercolour as one might fit the pieces of a jigsaw puzzle ... but was that the only reason she wanted to say yes she would stay on here, stay for however long he asked? The last bringing a tinge of colour to her face Emma replied, 'Nor are they as beautiful, judging by your father's depiction of that city.'

'Indeed.' He glanced at the box in his hands. 'Rome is beautiful but it is not alone. There are many other pictures just as impressive among my father's portfolio, it will be a great disappointment to me should they be left to lie in a cupboard, which they will, for I could not rest easy sending them away to be indexed. To me they are more than a series of notes and paintings, I see them as a man's legacy not merely to his son but to history, a way of preserving what sometimes sadly is not seen to be of value or else must be demolished to make way for the needs of the present.'

This was more than an acknowledgement of art, more than a tribute to his father she saw deep in those eyes, it was Mark Halstead's way of holding to a love he had been denied. Compassion a lump in her throat Emma said quietly, 'It would be a privilege to see those other paintings; perhaps the construction of your iron foundry might take time enough.'

'Thank you.' Mark Halstead's smile deepened. 'Now to my other reason for stopping by: I would like a word with the Elsmore lad.'

Emma's own smile faded. 'I'm sorry, Mr Halstead. Timothy is not here, neither is Lily.'

20

Allowing the book she had been trying to read to rest in her lap Henrietta gave in to the intrusion of thought.

It had been a risk, an expensive gamble, but one she had to take. The man had taken one look at the money partly concealed in her hand and agreed instantly to her proposal. Fifty pounds! She stared blindly at the book. She had thought long and hard about spending so much of the money she had hidden away, money Fenton knew nothing of. Nor must he ever know – to even suspect she had money would be to have him beat her until she gave it to him. But she had been careful and Fenton had not missed the articles she had sold over the years. She had never taken more than one piece at any time, selected solely from rooms Fenton rarely entered; but then since the Lawrence girls were no longer in the house his time saw him mainly in the study or in his own bedroom; the latter certainly not every night.

But that had suited her very well. Her husband made no pretence of his preference for other women's beds and that, together with his absence from the house most of the day, allowed her freedom to conduct her own affairs. As she had conducted them two days ago.

The idea had developed in her mind for some time. She had gone over it day after day, refining it, arguing the possibility of success ... and the outcome of failure. But then the evening before last had come her decision. Fenton had asked again what she was doing about finding Emma Lawrence. It had been on the tip of her tongue to tell him of seeing the girl, talking with her in the town, asking her to return to Beechcroft but before any of that could be said he had flared, accusing her of not searching at all. She had pointed out that would not have been in her interest or his but it was her additional remark that two people searching might bring a quicker result which had made him turn to stare directly at her.

'*Two people.*' His mouth had twisted, his eyes narrowed to glacial cracks. '*Two people.*' He had snarled, then a fist had lashed against her temple as he had grated, '*Fenton Gilmore don't keep a dog then bark himself!*'

A dog! Henrietta touched the purpling mark. That was all she was to Fenton Gilmore. In that moment the idea which had been for so long no more than that, which up to then had been just hypothesis, became resolution.

Next morning she had acted. Toward midday Fenton had replied he would not be home for dinner but would take a meal in Birmingham, then looking casually at the darkening flesh across her cheek and beneath her eye had sneered, '*I had thought nothing could ever be an asset to your looks, but that is an improvement.*'

There was something else suited her. Henrietta's fingers closed tightly about the book. Given past practice his visits to Birmingham had seen him return late in the night, so his absence in the city provided her with the perfect opportunity.

With his leaving she had informed the maid both she and the cook might take the rest of the day off and need not return before supper. The cook, Henrietta's mind lingered, the woman she had hired to replace Bella Coley. They had scarcely spoken, the young scar faced girl carrying messages between them. Nothing so very odd, Bella Coley and herself had scarcely found it necessary to meet but when need dictated they must she had not sensed the strange feeling of unease this

232

woman aroused in her; but servants could be replaced. Henrietta's mind moved on. She had waited, seen cook and maid leave the house then had taken the money from its hiding place.

Fifty pounds. She had laid the large white banknotes side by side on the bed, a pale splash against the deep blue of the bedcover. She had stared at the money. It was such a large amount to risk, there was no guarantee it would buy her what she wanted, yet what would she do if not take that risk? She had stood there in her room mentally debating the dilemma, then had scooped the notes together.

She had taken the tram into Wednesbury, alighting at the High Bullen and walking along Upper High Street to the market place, her eyes alert for one figure. She had seen them on several occasions, Fenton and the man she sought, talking together outside the shop Lawrence Fine Tobacco and had guessed it was not merely the time of day they discussed.

He had not been there. Several men had gone into that shop but none had been the one she hoped to see.

The market had been busy with women hurrying from stall to stall so to remain in one spot any length of time would have been to invite attention, yet pretending to shop she still felt conspicuous. She had been an hour dawdling between the butchers' stalls trading in the Shambles and the assortment of general dealers, their stalls filling the market square and had resigned herself to returning to Beechcroft when she had seen him. He had paused to stand before the tobacconist's shop and her pulse had quickened. Had he come to meet Fenton?

She had waited several minutes, observing him as he took a pipe and tobacco from his pocket, taking his time in filling and lighting it. She had to be sure; one man in flat cap and rough jacket looked very like the next.

But she had come this far, too far to turn away without ever trying. She had begun to cross the square when he had turned away. Quickening her step she had followed but before she caught up with him he had entered the Turk's Head hotel. Though that establishment was several cuts above the beer houses in and around Drew's Court still she was loath to go inside. Would he stay for one drink? She had laughed at herself for thinking so. Most likely he would be there for several. That could take the remainder of the afternoon, maybe on into the evening; to stand about so long was to invite suspicion.

Unconscious of the long breath she drew Henrietta watched memory flash its next picture. She had stared at the somewhat impressive façade, with its painted effigy of a man, a colourful turban wound about the head, the face walnut brown, the dark eyes seeming to watch her; then pulling the hat she wore lower over her brow, drawing the collar of her coat higher about her neck while lowering her chin deeper into the scarf tied about her throat, she had walked into the bar room. It had been acrid with the smell of pipe and cigarettes, a thick bloom of smoke lying grey and heavy over the small round tables each encircled by men seated on stools, tankards at hand. For a moment she had been back at Drew's Court, had smelled that same pungent odour of smoke and beer and for a moment had been ready to turn and run. Then she recalled where she was and why. When she realised that her presence had drawn no attention she had glanced around the room. He had been sitting alone in an alcove beside an ornate fireplace, raising no glance as she took the one vacant seat.

Dialect she had employed until her relationship with Mary Lawrence returned easily to her tongue, and with the naturally low control to the timbre of her voice coarsened by the harshness she injected into it she had said quietly, *'I be told you does business wi' a bloke the name o' Gilmore, be that right or do it be nowt' but coddin'?'*

He had not lifted his glance nor had he affirmed whether what she claimed was truth or lie.

'Word be you does jobs forrim.'

She had seen the fingers tighten about the tankard but they had not lifted it.

'Be that fact or be it I be barkin' up the wrong tree?'

The same silence greeting this further enquiry seemed to say he would not answer. She had been about to leave when with tankard lifted to his lips he had said over its rim, *'What if it do or don't be no wrong tree, what be it to you?'*

Relief had poured air into her lungs. His question was as good as assent to his knowing Fenton. Letting it rest a second or two she had asked, *'Does Gilmore pay well?'*

He had drunk deeply, wiping his mouth on his sleeve, eyes narrowing, an undercurrent of

235

warning in the reply.

'I asks again ... what be it to you?'

She had reached into a pocket and as he watched had, with fingers deliberately darkened with soil, riffled the corners of the banknotes.

'This.' She had opened her hand, displaying a little more of the notes. His breath had caught sharply, his eyes transfixed on the money.

'There 'as to be–'

'Fifty.' She had cut short his guess, her hand closing away the money.

'Fifty!' He had swallowed hard then lifting his glance had croaked, *'What do a man 'ave to do to earn that? I reckons you be after summat or you wouldn't be flashin' of that kind o' money.'*

She had told him then, told him what she expected her money to buy, saying were the result to meet with her approval then there could be more where that came from but, she had allowed her palm to open revealing the folded notes, should loyalty to Fenton prove too strong, should he already be paid more than was offered here then he was to say so and all conversation would be forgotten.

'Loyalty be all well an' good.' His eyes had gone again to the money. *'Business be summat else again; as for money I'll tek yourn.'* He had grinned, smoke-yellowed teeth bared like an animal prepared to devour a meal, *'Better a whole loaf than a slice from one.'*

Bargain agreed upon, she had left him sitting there.

One man's faults could prove another man's

lesson. Had she been at fault trusting to the loyalty of the man she had done business with? With that money in his pocket would he honour their agreement or turn his back and smile on his good fortune? She could have no comeback if he did. Fifty pounds! It could prove a costly lesson. Perhaps. Uncertainty had hammered at her mind; recalling the happenings of those minutes spent in that smoke-filled bar room had caused her to pause halfway along Wood Green Road, then cross to stand at a tall wrought-iron gateway; perhaps the need to think, to clear her brain of the tumult raging in it had been the cause of her entering the cemetery. There had been no mourners present, no funeral taking place, no visitor she could see paying respects before a grave. The entire cemetery appeared empty, devoid of people, its wide expanse clothed in serene peaceful calm, a quiet gently sunlit haven.

She had not intended to go in yet somehow had found herself standing at the furthest side away from the church, staring at the bare ground reserved for pauper burials, the spot where her own parents had been unceremoniously put to rest. Being orphaned had caused her no heartache. Her thoughts had winged to the past, to the humiliation, the degradation that had been Drew's Court and the bevy of brothers and sisters she had been left with, a problem she had solved by passing the burden of it on to the parish.

'You won't find no markers there.'

The voice had piped back at her.

'That ground be kept for the burying of folk who don't have money for to pay for a proper funeral, they

237

have to be buried by the parish, they don't get given no stone with their name on it.'

She had turned to face the voice which asked a question innocently.

'Do you have somebody restin' along of there?'

She had felt her skin tingle, felt the breath catch in her chest, had wanted to release words of rebuke but had managed to hold irritation at bay. Cemeteries might be quiet but they were not isolated; there might be mourners following a coffin, visitors to a grave. People could appear at any time and angry words drew attention.

'My mum and dad be over there.'

The small figure had pointed.

'...and my sister be close against them.'

She hadn't wanted a discussion. Henrietta's fingers toyed with a page of the book. But her glance had automatically followed the direction of the pointed finger.

'I picked some daisies and honesty from the heath, my mum liked flowers, they looks real pretty though they be only white, would you like to see them?'

The child had made to take her hand but she had walked away without a word, keeping her glance from the area of the cemetery where Mary and Austin Lawrence were buried.

She had forgotten the incident, her mind reverting back to thoughts which had filled it before entering the cemetery, and had continued to preoccupy her as she had walked on toward Beechcroft. But as she had neared the house her brain had cleared. Her timing had been perfect as always. Henrietta nodded to herself. Dusk had lent shadows which wreathed the house. But she had not approached the building; instead she had circled round it to the rear. Even then she had exercised caution, waiting some moments, ensuring she was not observed before slipping through the low gate set into the wall protecting the rear of the property. No one had seen her come into the garden and no one had seen her slip into the long disused potting shed conveniently hidden on one side by the boundary wall and on the other by a tall yew hedge shielding it from sight of the house. It had been a good ruse telling the staff she was paying a call on her sister; they in turn would take advantage of their free time until the last moment. And Fenton? Fenton also would be taking maximum pleasure.

In the silence of the house Henrietta smiled to herself as mental pictures glided on.

Once in the potting shed she had removed the clothes donned to go into the town. Dressed once more in skirt and blouse left there she had carefully returned the rest to a hiding place behind shelves of pots then strolled leisurely up the pathway and into the house.

No one would assume she had been anywhere but there, and Fenton? She smiled again. He would never guess what his latest bout of temper had given rise to.

It had been yesterday Fenton had received a visitor. She had been in her room when she had heard the doorbell ring, the lighter voice of the maid being answered by the deeper, more gravelly one of a man. Feeling it preferable to remain where she was she had stayed until once more the sound of voices in the hall proclaimed the caller was taking his leave. Even then she had sat some time in her room thinking Fenton would be gone front the house, so relieving her of possibly having to speak with him.

But it had not transpired that way.

Henrietta's hands stilled, memory flipping the pages of time.

She had eventually gone downstairs, ringing for the maid to bring a tray of tea. It was then Fenton, his face dark with fury, had slammed into the room.

'*Bloody man!*' he had roared, heaving a kick at the chair she was sitting on. '*Don't work for you no more he says, been paid more by somebody else, cash in hand so it seems; but Perry won't get away with things so easy as he thinks, nobody double crosses Fenton Gilmore without paying dearly.*'

'*Is something amiss at the shop? Has the tobacco not been delivered?*'

Watching the pictures in her mind Henrietta saw her husband turn, the look in his eyes saying what was in his head, that she was a fool.

'*Tobacco!*' he had snarled. '*I'm not talking about no bloody tobacco nor no shop neither, I'm talking of Perry; he thinks I can't do without him but he is wrong...*'

He had gone to stand at the fireplace. Feet slightly apart in his usual arrogant stance he had glared black fury.

'*What Perry did can be done by another, his quitting won't affect my business.*'

'*If it is not the shop and not the delivery of tobacco then what is it this Mr Perry will not be allowed to affect? What other business do you have?*'

'The sale of—'

He had stopped short and though she had known the danger of probing she had frowned questioningly then asked, '*Sale? Sale of what, Fenton?*'

For a moment he had stared at her, his look changing from one of contempt to one of disgust.

'*You don't ask me no question,*' he had ground, '*you don't never ask no question.*'

'*Surely I have a right...*'

'*Right!*' He had laughed, a sneering grate of a sound. '*Since when did Drew's Court riff-raff have rights?*'

'*Since one of them helped you steal another man's home and business, since—*'

She had got no further, a stinging blow to the side of her head rocking her in the chair.

'*Watch your mouth, keep it closed lest I close it for good.*'

It had slithered across the room, twining itself about her spine like the cold coils of a snake, but for all its warning she had snapped.

'*Like I kept it closed while you abused Emma Lawrence, while you raped her sister ... did you close Rachel's mouth for good by strangling her in that barn!*'

There had been a tap to the door but in his anger Fenton had either not heard or had chosen to ignore it, screeching as the maid had entered with the tea tray, '*Yes, I closed Rachel Lawrence's mouth, same as I closed that of the one I took from Russell Street, same as I closed others and as I'll close yours.*'

He had broken off suddenly, aware of where

rage had led him yet even so it had not left him.

'Get out!' he had bellowed at the girl turned to stare at him. *'Get out, you ugly scarfaced bitch, get out before I put a scar on the other cheek!'*

The maid had darted from the room and minutes later Fenton had stormed from the house.

21

She had agreed to stay on until the work was finished. Mark Halstead looked at the papers he had taken from the box.

Emma Lawrence had done an excellent job. Each of the three paintings had been placed separately in protective tissue paper, the accompanying notes transcribed in a smooth flowing copperplate hand, his father's original scrawled writings set alongside.

He had said he would feel uneasy sending papers and pictures to some other town and so he would. He touched a finely scripted page. Be truthful with yourself, Mark, he thought with an inward smile. That was a lie and you know it, designed to play on Emma Lawrence's sympathy. You said it hoping to keep her here in Wednesbury.

Would she have recognised what he had said as not being perhaps entirely truthful? His glance moved to a delicate portrayal of the Nile River, its soft green waters embraced by gentle hills, their blush-pink profile kissed by the gold of a newly

242

rising sun. Yes. His mind once more forced him to accept reality. Whoever Emma Lawrence was, whatever had been her life before their meeting, it was evident she was educated. Chances were that though she might not have seen for herself the places she saw in these paintings she had been taught of them; it could also be counted probable that hearing what his father's work meant to, and represented for, his son, then he ought to have employed the skills of a qualified calligrapher.

Why had she not questioned his decision? Replacing papers and paintings in the box Mark's inner smile returned but now it was laconic. The answer was simple enough. Where he had offered employment in order to have Emma Lawrence remain in this town she had accepted it only as a means of providing herself with the wherewithal to leave it.

'...*we be family, where Emma goes Lily and me goes.*'

Those had been Timothy Elsmore's defiant words ... but the Elsmores had not been at that house when he had called. A man of consequence ... yes, he had thought that of Timothy Elsmore but was he also one of independence, so much so he had refused to take advantage of a home earned by the labours of a woman? That could be the only reason the lad and his sister were not at that house, they must after all have broken with Emma Lawrence and she, once her work on those papers was concluded, would have no other incentive to stay on; on her own admission her blood family were all deceased, the fact of her living in that derelict hovel pointed to the fact of her having no home ... but she had pride, a pride he felt certain would not allow her to accept any other commitments he might offer. That would be viewed as an act of charity and just as quickly refused.

Lips firming on the swift pang which followed on the thought, he crossed to a figured mahogany cabinet occupying a corner of the room. Pausing, he looked again at the box.

How long could he hope this work to take? How many days before the reason no longer existed?

Tell her. It whispered soft in his mind. Tell her what you already know, tell Emma Lawrence you love her.

Temptation was a fruit could often taste sour! Mark pushed it from his mind. Emma Lawrence was a young woman coming to terms with an occurrence in her life, a hurt that showed deep in her eyes, and though he desired nothing more than to reveal his feelings for her he would not add to the complexity of those emotions. Emma Lawrence needed time.

Opening the cabinet's elegant bow-fronted doors he placed the box carefully inside.

Should time prove Mark Halstead the loser? That would be his pain.

'...where Emma goes Lily and me goes...'

With a smile touching her mouth Emma added potatoes to the pot set above the fire.

She had reminded Timothy of those words when the three of them had left the iron foundry. He had held firm to Lily's hand, striding purposefully along Potters Lane and on into Great Western Street. He was not going to live in the place offered by Mark Halstead! He and Lily were not going to live in a house where the rent were earned solely by Emma! He had managed to find a roof for him and his sister and he would do it again!

Each of her reasonings had met with the same refusal.

'Timothy Elsmore takes nobody's charity.'

The cacophony of noise from the adjacent railway station, the shrieks of steam whistles, the rhythmic chuff-chuff of a departing train, the loud groan of iron wheels grinding on iron rails as yet another engine drew carriages alongside a platform; all this combined with the sounds of a street busy with carts and carriages had made conversation difficult.

She had caught at his arm, a woman asking was she in need of assistance while another, a laden basket on her arm, commented about the youngsters of today having no respect. But Timothy was not being disrespectful. His behaviour was that of consideration for her; maybe in his pride he would not own to such.

Adding salt to the pot Emma smiled again.

She had come to know Timothy Elsmore, she knew his talk of 'charity' was a way of covering embarrassment. He saw sharing a house without contributing toward its cost as taking advantage. But had she not done exactly that, had she not accepted his and Lily's charity, not only a roof but food as well?

The scream of a steam whistle accompanied by

a roaring belch of steam descending over the street like a thundercloud, its acrid soot-laden moisture souring the tongue and clogging the throat, made immediate answer impossible so she had waited before saying, *'I accepted when you offered to share your home.'*

He had shaken his head, his mouth set defiantly, toffee-brown eyes glinting resolutely.

'That were different,' he had retorted. *'You was a wench I could see hadn't never needed to find for herself you d'ain't have no idea of what to do nor where to take y'self me and Lily ... well we couldn't just leave you.'*

Taking a roasting pan from the side oven she basted three pork chops she had set to cook, spooning hot fat over the sliced parsnips placed around them.

'Wouldn't have been Christian...'

Lily's voice piped in Emma's mind.

'Mother always said it were a body's Christian duty to give help where it be needed; that were what Timmy were doin' when he brought you along of us.'

Christian duty! Emma felt the rise of emotion Lily's words had brought to her throat thicken there again.

If only Fenton and Henrietta Gilmore had been raised as these two young people then Rachel and herself would never have known so much unhappiness, they would not have been subjected to physical abuse, and Rachel... Emma swallowed on the pain of the thought ... Rachel would not have been driven to running away.

She had given no reply to Lily's explanation. Gathering utensils she had used in preparing the

246

meal Emma carried them into the small scullery, her mind revolving around that walk back to Lea Brook. It had continued in silence, she wondering how to convince Timothy his resolution was not the best policy. But how to do it without injuring that pride had posed a problem not easily resolved.

Filling an enamelled bowl with hot water from the kettle fetched into the scullery, Emma's thoughts continued as she washed then dried each cooking implement.

It had been when they had turned off the road and on to the open ground leading to the disused malthouse. As they passed that building, coming in sight of the tumbledown house, a horse-drawn cart standing in front of it, the idea had presented itself

She had caught the gasp of annoyance coming from Timothy at seeing the horse and cart and not wanting to add to that had almost rejected the notion which had sprung to her mind. But then it could not have made him any more determined to go his own way.

'Timothy.' She had spoken quietly. 'Did you not tell Mr Halstead that Lily, yourself and I are family? Did you not say, "Where Emma goes Lily and me goes"?'

'So what if I did!'

Glaring to where a roughly clothed man had come to stand beside the cart Timothy's reply had been truculent.

'Well,' she had persisted, 'it is my belief family should stay together so where you and Lily go I shall also go; if you cannot live in the house Mr Halstead *has offered then neither will I.'*

'*What Emma says be true,*' Lily had said again. '*You did tell Mr Halstead that, Timmy, you did say as we be family, it'd be tellin' of a lie to say as you never, and you shouldn't tell a lie Timmy, Mother said it be sinful to be speakin' a lie.*'

Hanging the tea towel on the drying rack set above the living room fireplace Emma smiled at the picture in her mind as Timothy turned, to his sister. The glint gone from his eye, his tone the infinitely gentle one reserved for her, he had asked: was staying with Emma what she wanted? Lily's answer too had been soft. Emma's heart caught at a word echoing from the past.

'*Emma be sister to we, Timmy.*'

It had conveyed more to Timothy than Emma herself could have hoped to do, carried more persuasion than all of her words. For a moment he had stood looking at the small face, wide brown-gold eyes regarding him with gentle censure, then had turned his glance back, meeting her own with that same level of determination they had held when talking with Mark Halstead.

'*You says family should stay together...*'

There had been no smile but no exasperation either, just a quiet air of ultimatum.

'*I says family should share. If Lily and me be to share a place you earns the rent for then it be for me to provide for the livin' in it.*'

Setting plates on the table she had covered with a plain white cloth Emma's inner smile deepened. He had saved face and Lily had saved a family.

'You deserves it Lily, you knows you do.'

Startled by the angry voice Emma looked up from the work which until that moment had engrossed her.

'I tells you and tells you yet still you does it.'

The sharp reprimand came through clearly to the front parlour. Emma put down the pen. What could have Timothy so vexed?

'Timmy, I d'ain't mean...'

'You always says that, you always says it Lily, says you don't never mean to do it but you goes and does it anyway.'

'Please, Timmy...'

'No Lily, there's been enough excuses, I ain't listening to no more; you 'ave to learn.'

The cry following had Emma move quickly to the living room to he almost bowled over by the weeping girl rushing to cling to her. Looking over the head buried in her skirts to where Timothy stood Emma felt words dry in her throat. The eyes that stared back at her gleamed not with anger but with fear. Her own pulse leaping, Emma led the weeping Lily to a chair drawn against the hearth then looked across at Timothy asking as steadily as her own fear would allow, 'What is wrong Timothy, what is it Lily has done has you so riled?'

'Done!' Throwing down the bag he carried Timothy snorted the reply. 'Been along to the cemetery be what her's done, been there on her own ... and after all the times I've told her not to.'

She could understand his anger though Lily might be too young to understand his fear. About to tell him so, Emma's explanation was blocked with Timothy resuming irately, 'I've tried givin' her reason for not going wanderin' off by herself, told her the wench gone missing from Russell Street ain't likely to 'ave disappeared of her own accord, that it be probable her were took off by some no-good, but Lily don't pay no mind, her don't never pay no mind.'

'Timmy I ... I be sorry, truly I does.'

'Sorry don't butter no parsnips!' Timothy's harsh retort had the tear-streaked face re-bury itself in Emma's skirts. 'From now on you stays behind. You listen to me this time, Lily, for I means what I says, you don't come with me into the town no more.'

Pressed against her knee Emma felt the tremor run though the sobbing girl. Timothy had every reason to be angry yet though she longed to mediate, to conciliate, Emma realised intervention at this stage was not the thing to do. Timothy had his sister's welfare at heart and in this matter he should not be gainsaid. It proved hard to hold to that decision and Emma looked again at Timothy, hoping to see a change to the angry look clouding his face, but even as she did he shook his head in denial.

'Emma...'

Lily's head lifted, her tear-filled eyes fastening imploringly on Emma's, her voice a broken whisper saying softly, 'I ... I d'ain't mean to anger Timmy, it fears me when he be angry, fears...' she choked, 'fears me he'll leave; tell him I be sorry, Emma, tell him I be sorry.'

Across from Emma the storm-darkened face cleared, the eyes, hard with resentment, softened, the tight set mouth parted on a swift indrawn breath. Then Timothy was across the room drawing the huddled Lily gently to her feet. Folding her to him, one hand holding the fair head pressed against his shoulder, a many attempt at suppression of tears Emma saw film his eyes not entirely eliminated from a voice trying vainly to retain some semblance of ill-humour, he said gruffly, 'That be summat else I be forever sayin'; I won't never leave you, Lily, not so long as you be needin' of me.' He paused, then lowered his head to kiss her hair, his murmur thick with emotion. 'Not so long as you be needin' of me.'

Contrition and forgiveness. It was best left at that. Rising from the chair Emma swung the trivet with its kettle over the fire. Lily was sorry for annoying her brother, but given Lily's nature it was a certainty contrition, like any avowal not to repeat her misdeed, would soon be forgotten.

22

He had lost that order, lost the money it would have brought. A wave of the hand displaying ill temper as much as the call for yet another glass of brandy, Fenton fumed inwardly. Damn Jud Perry and damn the one who had enticed him away. Who had that been? Perry had denied all knowledge ... but then money would have Perry deny his own mother. Snatching the brandy brought to him Fenton downed the drink in one swallow.

Cash in hand! He banged the empty glass hard down on the table. That was one thing Perry *had* said, he had been paid cash in hand! But payment could be made in other than cash. Rising unsteadily to his feet, ignoring the protests from tables he brushed against, he walked from the hotel.

Knocking away the hand offering to assist him into his carriage, Fenton grabbed at the whip. This would be the next payment given to Jud Perry. Oblivious to the danger of setting horse and carriage careering down a street already heavy with wheeled traffic as well as folk on foot he cracked the whip over the animal's head. Yes, Perry would have first a taste of the whip; then and only then would he receive payment in full.

How had it happened?

Fenton looked at the rug-covered heap.

He had taken several drinks in the George Hotel. That much he remembered clearly. 'Then he had taken his carriage and ... and what? That could be the only answer to how he had come to be there, but where was there?

Sounds of the street market drifted up to the private room above Lawrence Fine Tobacco but Fenton heard only the questions running through his brain. Eyes tight shut, he searched again in the fog. A shape ... squat and dark ... a finger pointing ... no, not a finger. He breathed deeply, holding the air a moment in his lungs before exhaling slowly and forcefully as if to blow away the miasma clouding his memory. Not a finger; he watched the emerging shape, the slow building of a spire, the spire of a church, a church set atop a hill.

St Bartholomew's Church! Clarity of mind rushing in, Fenton's eyes shot open. The undeveloped ground between Trouse Lane and Ethelfleda Terrace! Given its head the horse had wandered, finishing up grazing on that patch of heath.

Dusk had already begun to settle. Clear now, each detail sharp and vivid, Fenton watched the pictures form before his eyes. The girl had come from the direction of the church, a small figure bending now and then to take something from the ground. Flowers. He looked at the blossoms held in the small hands. She had been picking flowers. In his mind's eye Fenton saw himself climb from the carriage, saw the look of concern on the face turning to him, heard the quick, *'I ain't been stealin' from no grave, these be flowers from the 'eath, honest they be.'*

She had been afraid, afraid he might be clergy, or even worse a person from the law.

'I watched you pick them so of course I know they are not stolen.' He had smiled the answer, making no move away from the carriage.

Reassured, she had smiled back, saying, *'I picked them for my mum, it be her birthday today.'*

'I'm sure they will delight her, every lady deserves to be presented with a bouquet on her birthday and the one you have there is very pretty.'

'This,' the girl had lifted the flowers, their petals almost touching her chin, *'do this be a bow ... a boo ... a what you said?'*

'Indeed it is, and a lovely one. I am sure your mother will value it as highly as she will each of her

253

birthday presents.'

He had known the result of his words. Smiling to himself he saw again the crestfallen look wipe the pleasure from the girl's face, her quiet reply sounding in his mind.

'Her won't get no present, don't none o'we never get no present, mum says there don't be money enough to spare for that.'

Fenton glanced again at the bundle lying in a corner of the almost darkened room. A thin dress, its skirt adorned with a patch of a different colour, had hung from thin narrow shoulders, its hem reaching halfway between knee and ankle; a hand-me-down likely serving several girls before this one got it. Fenton recalled the sniff of revulsion he had managed in time to curtail. Poverty! It had shrieked its presence from head to worn-though shoes. There were more than enough of that ilk in Wednesbury; removing one could be doing some family a favour. Thought had been the spur, justification a warmth inside him, his smile a palpable benediction. Yet still he had guarded word and movement. Carefully, the smile still on his lips, he had withdrawn a coin from his pocket. Visible in his open palm, dying sunlight casting rose on silver, it had gleamed temptation.

'Take this.' He had proffered the half crown. *'Buy a present for your mother.'*

She had stood transfixed, her thin body almost a shadow merging with those beginning to gather round her. Like a silver orb, delectable and enchanting, a thing of magic, the coin called to her drawing her close, almost close enough to touch, yet though the familiar lurch at the base of his stomach had caught at his breath he had made no move other than to offer the coin. Be too hasty and she would be off like a startled colt. So he had stood in silence those long seconds she had gazed at the bright disc, swallowing the surge of anger when with a shake of the head she had said, *'Mother says not to take when it ain't been earned, though I thanks you for the kindness.'*

Kindness! That had played no part in the offer. Fenton withdrew his glance from the rug-enshrouded heap and at once mental images resumed their play.

An expression of regret colouring his voice he had said, *'Your mother is of course quite correct in her teaching, it was wrong of me to ask you to accept.'* He had smiled as he returned the coin to his pocket, adding, *'I hope my rudeness will not spoil your celebration and especially not your enjoyment of a delicious birthday cake.'*

Fenton watched his own image begin to turn from her, watched his hands reaching to pull himself back to the driving seat of the carriage, felt the smile which had touched his lips touch them again as the girl's soft reply echoed in his mind.

'Won't be no cake.'

'No cake!' He had managed a note of incredulity, a frown adding to it as he swung back to look at her. *'But everyone has a birthday cake.'*

The hands cupped about the posy had parted, dropping to her sides.

In the semi-blackness of that clandestine room Fenton's groin jerked as it had then.

A finger of breeze had traced the thin cloth of

255

the dress, laying it flat across the small breasts, etching it into the vee at the top of the legs.

The demon he could not deny had howled louder.

It had taken an almost supreme effort yet he had withheld the compulsion beginning to surge like a red-hot lava flow in his veins, the craving that was a thirst in his throat.

A shaft from the setting sun had brushed across brown hair, gilding it to ripe chestnut as the girl's head lowered.

'*Not everybody don't 'ave cake.*' It had been no more than a murmur though disappointment had sounded loud as a pealing bell. '*I ain't never tasted of cake.*'

The reply had been hell's gift to him, the boon of the devil, and he had received it gratefully.

'*Your mother, would she...*' He had hesitated, wanting what he said to sound more of an apology than a proposition. '*I mean, she is right in saying you should not take payment where it has not been earned but ... well, the fact is my wife packed a cake in my lunch hamper, a rather large chocolate cake,*' he had shaken his head, throwing in a smile for good measure, '*rather too much for me I'm afraid so ... well, would your mother object to your taking it home?*'

'*A cake! You be sayin' to give me a cake.*'

The head had lifted quickly, eyes wide with uncertainty.

'*Only if you are sure your mother would allow.*'

He had answered swiftly reading the refusal already beginning to replace indecision.

'*A cake!*'

She had breathed the words as though what he

256

offered were some divine gift.

'*A chocolate cake.*' He had flavoured an already delectable thought with a sugared sweetness, then had come the icing, the final layer of irresistible temptation. '*It will be thrown out with the kitchen scraps if I take it home.*'

'*Thrown out!*' she had stared disbelievingly. '*You means you throws food away?*'

'*My wife, she will have it thrown away ... a waste I know but she will insist on it.*'

'*Mum says wastin' o' bread be criminal; Lord knows what her'd say to the wastin' o' cake.*'

'*Then you will take it as a birthday cake?*'

The face had it up, the eyes dancing, acceptance a breath of pure happiness.

The contest was over.

He had smiled at the radiant face then turned, reaching into the carriage.

The reward was his, his and the fiend's driving inside him.

His hand fastening on the whip he had swung it about, bringing the heavy stock down on the small head.

There had been no sound, no cry.

Fenton stared into the mirror of memory.

He had brought the whip handle down, striking the head a second time, his free hand snatching the small figure and hurling it into the carriage. Then he had driven away, only a tiny heap of trodden wild flowers attesting to his ever having been on that patch of heath.

He had kept the horse to a steady walk choosing to return to the market place via Church

257

Street; anyone recognising him would think he had visited the Hawthorns, the large house kept by an acquaintance.

Lawrence Fine Tobacco was closed and shuttered as he knew it would be; even so he had taken the precaution of checking the rear of the premises before taking the carriage into the yard.

It had taken just a few minutes to complete the journey to the shop but each of those minutes had been fraught with worry the girl would wake, would scream. She had however remained unconscious as he carried her, wrapped in the travel rug, upstairs to this room. He had thrown her on to the daybed.

His glance sought the object, a shape black among black, shadow on shadow enveloping, hiding away. But the darkest of them could not hide the pictures from his mind.

How old could she have been? Mental vision wandered over the small body he had stripped, torn strips of dress binding wrists to ornate woodwork at the head of the couch, legs spread wide with the ankles secured at the couch's foot, a band of the material serving for a gag; but it was the eyes held him most, wide terrified eyes, their silent screams sending waves of lust tearing in his groin.

How old? It seemed he saw again the thin little body. Fourteen? It had not mattered; his satisfaction would be the same.

He had placed the candle near to the couch, where its light could show the slender rod he had fetched from the cupboard, and had revelled in the fear the slap of it against upholstery had added to that already blazing in those wide-open eyes. Fear and pain. He breathed a long slow breath. The instilling of both had ever been the vehicle in which the demon of desire drove through him and it had driven through him that night. He had slapped the rod again, laughing deep in his throat as the figure had twisted in its bonds. Then he had flicked at the young breasts, at the newly burgeoning nipples, his senses rocking with pure malignant pleasure as the slight body arched with pain. It was a pleasure he must repeat, must taste over and over again. And he had.

Standing in the increasing gloom, Fenton watched the scenes memory revealed.

The rod had risen and fallen, every stroke honey on the palate of lechery, every slap of cane against flesh adding savour to the heady wine of carnality, each gag-stifled cry stirring the dish of lust, mixing the whole into a feast of sensuality, a craving flooding the mind to wash away every thought, every feeling save the demand dragging in his stomach, the pulsing throb jolting the hardened column of manhood.

Desire had changed. He breathed again, a quick snatched breath of remembered lust. It had altered, mutated into need to inflict that different fear, that divergent yet equally amusing pain. He had thrown aside the cane, had stood a moment smiling down at those terrified eyes then bending low had traced the engorged head of his penis across the slight mounds of childhood breasts, had dipped it into the scarlet drips of blood oozing from her nipples then, that same laugh gurgling in his throat, had straddled the captive figure. Even then he had not taken that ultimate step. That potent force inside him had exacted yet one more tribute, one which he had indulged, the sheer gratification of the act augmenting the intoxicating, exhilarating rush in his veins.

Slowly, the smile still playing about his mouth, he had trailed the throbbing organ between her breasts, past her waist and on over the quivering stomach bringing it to the vee between those widely parted legs. Pausing, he had drunk in the plea of those terror-stricken eyes yet though his own gleamed denial he had listened to the whisper in his mind, a murmur saying to exercise compassion. He had understood and with that understanding had almost laughed aloud. The sacrifice he was about to offer to the fiend that was his master should be presented with a libation. With the thought he had rubbed one hand in the blood of those whiplash cuts, shaking droplets on to that enticing vee, then a carmine-stained finger had worked them inside that small tight cleft.

She had arched at the touch, tried to draw away, but the fetters of cloth had held, held while he thrust his swollen member deep into her.

Had it been that desperate twist of the body, the long drawn scream muffled almost to silence or the turning away of the head? In the aftermath of passion it had been difficult to ascertain. He remembered only grabbing the small head with both hands, forcing it about, pinning it so he could look at the terrified face, feed on the horror staring from tear drenched eyes; but in the craze of lust his hands had slid to the neck, blood-soaked fingers had tightened and in those final moments, that frenzy of passion as he had spent himself, both thumbs had pressed on the thin throat choking away all life.

Reawakened memory clasped Fenton's crotch with invisible fingers, flicking his senses, threatening to issue that same demand. But he must control it. In the greyness of weak moonlight he stared to where the body of the girl still lay. He could not afford to indulge in that pleasure ... not before this one was disposed of

23

The meal of leeks and bacon Mrs Coley had taught her how to cook during one of those stolen hours spent in the kitchen at Beechcroft had been well received by Timothy and Lily.

Readying herself for bed in a room so different both to the well-furnished one she had occupied at Beechcroft and that damp-ridden, musty-odoured one which had been part of the crumbling decrepit cottage Mark Halstead had caused to be demolished, Emma's thoughts harked back to the earlier evening.

She had smiled consent to Lily's request she be shown the correct spelling of a word.

'It be "treasure".' The girl had laughed happily. *'I be wanting to know how to write "treasure".'*

Already standing beside the table she had watched closely then slow and painstakingly had copied each letter as Emma wrote it.

'*There.*' She had turned to her brother, beaming as she waved the slip of paper like it was some hard-won trophy. '*Emma told me I could do it, her said big fancy words be no harder to write than little ones, her told me I could do it, that I could write that big word for oneself if I only tried, and I have ... look.*'

Drawing a comb through shoulder-length hair released from imprisoning braids Emma smiled at the picture formed in her mind.

Lily had pushed the paper so near her brother's face it had brushed the tip of his nose, while he laughed as he said, '*Hey up, I need to read it not eat it!*'

He had taken the paper, his eyes glinting a roguish message to Emma before returning to study the word written in unsteadily scripted letters. He perused the lettering again and gave Lily a hard look. Her gleam of triumph at the much anticipated approval was lost beneath one of trepidation.

'*What's this!*' Timothy's demand had been stern. '*You an' Emma be pullin' a fast one? You pair be tryin' to trick me, you thinks I be believin' this line to be wrote by you when it really be all of Emma's doin'!*'

Re-plaiting hair gleaming ruby darts in the soft candlelight, Emma's heart tripped as it had on seeing the crestfallen look which had greeted Timothy's taunt, the sheen of tears spilling beneath a fringe of lashes, of Lily's quiet sob, '*I did do it meself, I wouldn't say it were me if it weren't; Mother said not to tell lies, Timmy, an' I ain't.*'

'*Her also said you was a real clever wench, Lily*

Elsmore, an' this proves it.' Waving the paper, he had grabbed the tear-stricken Lily, laughing as he tumbled her to the hearth and rolled with her like a pair of playful puppies.

Lily's tears had vanished quickly as they came, her giggles mixing with the deeper laughter of the emerging man. They were so close. Emma looked again at the reflections in her mind. Brother and sister, the older one so mindful of the younger, Timothy's every action an unspoken assertion of his promise always to be there for his sister; of a love strong and steadfast.

As she should have been mindful of Rachel.

Emma's fingers stilled on the snippet of ribbon securing the thick plait of hair.

She should have understood that the sadness marking that face, the cloud which had come to rest ever more frequently over eyes which once sparkled with joy but had long become lost to laughter, was due to more than Henrietta Gilmore's heartless treatment.

She had seen but she had not asked a reason, not questioned the cause.

'Because I thought I knew, I did not query because I thought I knew!'

Only a whisper in the pastel glow yet the words were a scream of the soul, an echo of the grief Emma felt would never leave her.

'I thought the cause to be Henrietta, that her spite and cold-heartedness, her obvious aversion for both of us was the root of your despondency but it was not, it was not and I am to blame; I should have realised Fenton Gilmore would not be content with tormenting one sister, I should have realised and come to you with the question but I did not.'

Was that the real reason for Rachel leaving the house that day! Had Emma's failure to detect the full truth of her misery resulted in her death!

Emma caught her breath as she felt the sharp surge of guilt rise afresh, guilt which had racked her since she first read Rachel's diary, guilt which found no ease, no relief.

'...*so long as you be a' needin' of me...*'

Timothy's words rang adding to the anguish burning a brand in her heart. Rachel had needed her but she had failed in that support.

Trembling, gentle, it seemed a whisper came from the very centre of the pale yellow light shed by the candle.

No, it breathed. You did not fail me, you are not to blame ... accept that, Emma, accept and find rest.

It was Rachel's voice, it was her sister, it was Rachel speaking, she had only to reach out to take her in her arms...

Blind with tears Emma flung out her arms, her cry fracturing the silence when they closed on empty air.

'Rachel, Rachel come back ... please!'

All of the ache of longing, the pain of yearning had throbbed in the plea but there had been no answer in that void of silence, no reply from an emptiness life could never fill.

Find rest.

Like leaves in the breeze imagined words fluttered in Emma's mind only to be lost among the fragments of a breaking heart.

How could she find rest ... how could she ever find rest.

She had not heard the knock to her bedroom door, had not heard that other voice, only felt the clasp of arms about her shoulders.

'Rachel,' she had whispered again but it had been Lily had answered, Lily murmuring, Lily's sympathetic tears warm against her cheeks.

'I knows how you feels,' the child had whispered, 'I knows how it hurts deep inside, it be like a cut that gets no better, a wound you can't do nothin' for 'cept bandage it with tears; but love be a good ointment, love helps ease the sore nobody but you feels, and...' She had paused, a momentary shyness holding her tongue, then had gone on, 'Timmy an' me, we have plenty of that ointment; we can't bring you back your Rachel, we can only help with lovin' you and we does, Emma, we loves you very much.'

Wrapped in the shawl Polly Lacey had draped about her shoulders on leaving Beechcroft, Lily sat at her feet huddled in a blanket before a fire Timothy had coaxed back to life; Emma took the tea the lad handed to her. She had apologised for disturbing them, had said they should all go back to bed, but taking charge Timothy had insisted she come downstairs.

'*Tea be what be needed*,' he had said standing at the bedroom door Lily had left open when both she and Timothy had run to Emma's room on hearing her cry. '*A cup o' tea will help all o' we to sleep.*'

She had not argued with that logic but simply

followed brother and sister to the tiny living room. They had not broached the question of her tears, simply accepting the need to free a little of that same grief they also had experienced, the deep incising pain the loss of a loved one leaves behind.

'Emma.' Sitting cross-legged on the hearth Timothy nursed the thick pottery mug he had filled with tea but had not yet tasted. 'Emma,' he said again, his glanced fixed on the reawakened fire, 'what Lily said just now, about our lovin' you, that were no bunkum said to 'ave you feelin' better, Lily an' me we does care for you deeply but...'

But! Emma felt the sudden sharp stab of apprehension while against her knee the thin figure seemed to retreat deeper into the blanket.

'But...'

Timothy inhaled a long courage-seeking breath then rushed on. If what he had to say was not said now then it never would be.

'...the fact be, Emma, you be different to Lily an' me, you ... you ain't from no Foley's Yard nor the slums that be Dale Street nor them of Portway Road, the way you speaks be a provin' of that. We don't know of your background an' we ain't askin' of it but like I says we knows it don't be the like of ourn.' Slowly he twisted the mug, his glance going deep into it, then quietly said, 'Lily an' me, we've talked of the turn things'll have to take once the work you does for Mark Halstead be finished. This house will be teken back an' we will be out on the streets same as afore an' ... an' well, Lily an' me thinks you would do better for not havin' we tagged on to your skirts, that you stands a better chance of gaining work in one o' them posh houses if there be just you.'

In the warm silence dropped between them Emma watched the tow-coloured head lift, the shoulders in the rough worn jacket square as if faced by an enemy, caught the sound of a constricted swallow though no tea had been taken into the mouth, while the tension holding that figure taut and unmoving seemed to shout across the room.

'*...one o' them posh houses...*'

Suddenly Emma wanted to smile. She had known more affection in that tumbledown hovel, been shown more kindness by these two orphaned children than ever she and Rachel had received from Henrietta and Fenton Gilmore.

'Timothy.' She placed her cup aside. 'I lived in a house such as you describe.'

'Where?' Lily brought her face to look up at Emma. 'Where was the house? Were it really posh, did you–'

'Lily!' Timothy's sharp reprimand cut the stream of questions, then turning to look at Emma he said more quietly, 'Be no need o' sayin' more, don't be no business of ourn where it was you lived.'

Emma's reply was soft. 'But there is a need to say this. I have been happier living with you and Lily than ever I have been since my parents' death and I know my sister also would have felt that way. Rachel would gladly have exchanged Beechcroft for the chance of sharing a home with you.'

'Was you a servant there, did you scrub an'

clean, did they make you do everybody's washin' same as me mum, did–'

'Lily!' His voice heralded his mounting displeasure. Timothy was on his feet, his hand fastening on his sister's wrist. 'That be it! I don't be goin' to say no more, you ask Emma's pardon for puttin' your nose where it shouldn't be put then you get y'self off to bed.'

He felt a strong responsibility for his sister, a need to protect socially as well as physically, and though accepted as more than just a friend Emma felt she must not countermand Timothy who after all acted only to direct Lily's good manners. But she wanted to answer, the only question being how, without usurping Timothy? No time to plan a strategy, to think what words were best to express herself Emma plunged in as Lily, her face colouring from Timothy's disapproval, began the required apology.

'Please,' she glanced at the lad ready to squire his sister from the room, 'you said we were family.'

He nodded. 'I did. But that don't carry no right for the askin' o' questions.'

Emma smiled. 'I agree. But perhaps it might afford the chance for an explanation that is long enough overdue.'

A slight frown etching across his forehead Timothy's bemused 'explanation?' had Emma return.

'Of my leaving Beechcroft.'

'You don't 'ave to.'

'No I don't.' Emma smiled again. 'You and Lily have made it patently obvious you require nothing of me, no disclosure of where it was I came from, your acceptance had no other basis than friendship and it is in the name of that friendship, Timothy, I ask you permit me to answer Lily's questions.'

He had admonished Lily's lack of manners and so could not exhibit lack of his own by refusing Emma's request or that Lily might be allowed to stay and hear.

Stretched on his bed, arms folded behind his head, Timothy stared at moon-chased shadows.

He could not prevent that sudden spark of interest leaping to his eyes but as he had demanded of Lily he had allowed himself no question, simply releasing his sister to her position at Emma's feet then resettling himself by the hearth to listen in silence to the account of a life gone so swiftly from joy to misery. He had watched the nuances of emotion flit across her face, the shades of anguish darkening her eyes when speaking of the death of her sister, pain telling vividly that which Emma's tongue did not relate.

But what had caused that death? Emma had mentioned no sickness. Wrapped in the soft darkness of night Timothy saw again the distress of the woman he had grabbed from the clutches of Jud Perry. Had something of the sort happened to the girl called Rachel? Or worse, had she been attacked by some itinerant passing through the town? He had heard of young wenches going missing from home, even some being found dead, the crime blamed on a tinker or gypsy who was never found; but Emma had made no mention of such, she had said only that her sister had passed away.

269

But there was a darkness behind that meagre light. Timothy's eyes followed an intricate dance of moonlight across the walls of his room. Emma had said she wanted to share all with them but watching her he had felt something remained hidden, that some shadow followed on the heels of Emma Lawrence,

Shadow – or tangible reality?

'I don't want ... he can keep ... only my promise to Rachel...'

Memory replayed the scene Timothy had watched an hour before, returned the words to his mind. Emma's eyes had closed but the lowering of the eyelids had not shut off the hesitation, the broken half-finished sentences or the choking throat-filling sob that was hatred more than tears whenever she spoke of the man who had been guardian to herself and her dead sister.

Illusion? Timothy questioned the concept building in his mind. Was Emma's detestation of that man perhaps saying he was in some way responsible for her sister's death? Was he the shadow following still on her heels?

It had not been said yet it had been plain in her every word Emma Lawrence had endured a terrible despair, a wretched unhappiness in that house; but there had been more underlying those broken sentences, there had been a real positive fear.

Watching the flickering soundless dance, staring at shadow dark on moonlight Timothy acknowledged a deeper darkness settling over his mind, an unmoving cloud of suspicion.

A self appointed guardian, an 'uncle' who bore

no right to the title, a man who had assumed full authority over two young girls.

Behind his head Timothy's fingers clenched tight into his palms. Was he the shadow dogging Emma, was his the hand as yet reaching from that house called Beechcroft?

24

Damn Noah Wilkins, damn him to hell!

As he sat in the train carrying him to Wednesbury Fenton Gilmore's thoughts ran along a vicious path.

The bill would have been paid, hadn't he always settled his account in full?

'You does business your way, Noah Wilkins does business his way and that don't have no dealing with credit.'

Business! Bitter aloe, the word stung. Hadn't they done that together long enough for Wilkins to wait a few days for his money?

'Waiting sees a man grow older, it don't add to no bank balance,' Wilkins had answered the request for credit.

'A bank balance, helped nicely along by Fenton Gilmore.'

A hand resting on the ledger he had closed, Noah Wilkins had answered across the desk.

'Payment for service, Gilmore, payment for service.'

'Which can be got elsewhere.'

He had snapped the retort but the implied

threat had met with no more than a nod. Fenton stared through smoke-hazed windows seeing nothing but that poky office, the bird-like features of the man watching across a dust-topped desk the man who well knew service of the kind required was not found any place for the asking, knew had it been otherwise then his would not be the firm supplying it.

He had known and had played on the knowledge! Fenton's fingers gripped hard the rim of the silk top hat resting on his knee. Wilkins had bled money from him, had charged ten times the going rate for collecting empty tobacco casks; except not all of those collected from Lawrence Fine Tobacco were empty!

'It will be no more than a day or so, I am awaiting settlement for premises sold in Darlaston, it will all be finalised by the weekend and to show goodwill I will add five pounds to your bill.'

He had dangled the worm and the beak of a nose had twitched while above it blackcurrant eyes had gleamed. But the worm had not been snatched, the gleam of berry-bright eyes had not been that of avarice.

'That be gracious of you, and to show my own goodwill I will despatch that cask for the same hour payment for delivery ... and collection ... be on this desk.'

'And collection.' Anger bubbled in a fresh stream. Wilkins had emphasised the words, had quite deliberately underscored the fact that the amount asked covered more than simple collection of a tobacco cask. It paid for the keeping of a secret.

And how was this one to be kept?

Teeth clenched on the question Fenton had asked himself a score of times since leaving Wilkins' premises. How, without the convenience of a large cask, was he to remove the body of the girl lying dead in that room above the shop?

'Wednesbury next stop, sir.' Well-polished brass buttons shining bold against bottle-green uniform, the train's conductor smiled amiably from the doorway of the first-class compartment, a touch of fingers to his peaked cap accompanying the repeated 'Wednesbury next stop; two minutes, sir.'

How was it to be done? As he stood on the station platform with the hiss of steam from the train's engine, the grind of iron wheels obeying the signal for departure composing a medley of sound in his ears, Fenton heard only the question in his mind. How? Leaving the station, boarding a hackney to take him to Beechcroft, Fenton found no answer.

Had she acted too hastily? In the drawing room of Beechcroft House Henrietta mused over her meeting with a man she knew nothing of, a man whose dirt-ingrained fingers had closed greedily over that money.

Her only thought, her only reason for doing what she had done, had been that of revenge, to repay Fenton for his treatment of her, but had the step been taken unwisely?

The fellow had kept to the bargain struck in the Turk's Head Hotel. Henrietta's fingers tweaked the page of a book lying open in her lap. He had come to the house, the later raging of Fenton attesting to the cessation of any dealings the pair of them had together. But what had those dealings been? Could it be they were the only means of financial support left to Fenton ... and so to herself?

The full impact of what she had done grasped with cold fingers.

He had probably gone through the fortune rightly belonging to Emma Lawrence, had likely spent without thought of any but himself, of his own creature comforts, and undoubtedly without any for his wife.

It had been repayment of a kind. Henrietta's fingers worried again at the page. The only way she had of striking back, of returning the blows that had so often bruised her face and body, of easing the hurt of spite-filled words.

'Fenton Gilmore doesn't keep a dog then bark himself.'

Henrietta winced at the snarl echoing in her mind. That had proved the ultimate insult, that had hardened to stone a resolve which up to that point had been no more than a placebo, a thought soothing the pain of physical and mental abuse. And so she had gone into the town, sought out the man she had seen with Fenton then used her money to break off that relationship.

Revenge had tasted sweet but hindsight had that sweetness turn to acid in her mouth. The business Fenton was involved in, and the many sales of Lawrence Fine Tobacco shops clearly indicated it was not that commodity kept his pocket if not amply filled, then with at least money enough to indulge his appetite for prostitutes, to relieve him of taking to his bed 'a

274

dried-up prune of a woman'.

Revenge! She had eaten of that delicious dish and with Fenton's rage following Perry's call at his house had drunk deeply the heady wine of success, but – Henrietta's fingers tightened about the book – the glass had emptied, leaving the dregs of uncertainty. She had intended her action to merely discompose Fenton, to cause him a little of the mental perturbation he had so many times caused her to suffer; after all there were other men in Wednesbury, Fenton would have no difficulty recruiting a replacement for Perry. But the rage with which he had swept into the house an hour ago, the anger which had seen him throw the whole tea tray back at the frightened maid carrying it into the drawing room augured otherwise. And if the threads of Fenton's business could not be picked up...?

The slamming open of the door cutting off further thought Henrietta stiffened in her chair though every nerve tippled like waves on a wind-tossed lake. Wherever Fenton had spent the day it had not eased his temper.

'Bloody Wilkins...'

Judging no answer to be the best answer Henrietta rang the bell summoning the maid. Tea ... the pouring of it would give her something to do.

'...thinks he's the only one.'

Henrietta winced at the ferocity of a boot striking the fireplace.

'...wouldn't take a note, wouldn't give credit...'

Credit. Icy fingers which had grasped minutes before clutched again at Henrietta. Was Fenton already without funds?

275

'...said the job would be done only when money were placed on his desk, money...' he kicked again at the fireplace, 'I've poured enough of that into Noah Wilkins' pocket over the years, enough to have him allow a few days' credit, but oh no, he wanted payment there and then, he wanted cash before sending that cask to Wednesbury.'

'Noah Wilkins?' Too late to cover the slip of the tongue Henrietta's nerves trembled as Fenton turned, yet not to continue, to appear questioning, would only add to the anger already dark on his face. 'I thought you said the name was Perry.'

'Perry?'

It was barked more than asked. Making a play of placing the book on a small elegant table beside her chair Henrietta avoided having to meet a look she knew well, a look of cold fury which could so easily be vented upon her.

'Mmm,' she murmured noncommittally, 'the man who called to see you a while back, I thought you said his name was Perry, that he was the man you were speaking of.'

'Well you be wrong!' he snarled as the tea tray was carried in, 'wrong as both Jud Perry and Noah Wilkins be in thinking to put one over on Fenton Gilmore.'

'Where is Stokes?' Her question put to halt Fenton's unwise rush of words before a servant. Henrietta looked at the woman setting a laden tea tray by her chair. 'Why isn't she bringing tea?'

Her grey-streaked hair pulled severely from the forehead lent no softness to eyes deepening to a yet darker shade of grey. The cook-housekeeper met the enquiry with a blunt, 'Millie be away to her room.'

Henrietta's eyes recorded displeasure.

'Her room?' she demanded.

'That be what I said.'

A moment after the curt reply of her house-keeper Henrietta snapped, 'I gave no permission.'

A shake of the head allowing no movement of a fiercely starched cap the woman cast a deliberate glance over the face looking up at her before answering flatly, 'That be cos of my not askin' of it.'

'How dare–'

'Seemed the best thing to do.' Cutting off the accusation the woman glanced first at the man standing astride the fireplace then again at Henrietta before she continued in the same forthright fashion. 'I deemed you wouldn't want a wench frightened half out of her wits, a wench with cuts an' bruises to her face a runnin' off into the town; an' given the state Millie were in her were like to have done that while I were come askin' of permission to put her to her bed.'

'...*cuts and bruises ... running off into the town...*'

It was not lost on Henrietta. People would want to know how that girl had come by her injuries, her telling them Fenton Gilmore had hurled a tray laden with crockery and hot tea at her head would create yet more speculation among the town's socialites. Money afforded the privilege of keeping domestics, it did not buy the right to physically abuse them; but that had never found any place in Fenton's thinking. Looking at him now, at the disdain spewing cold fire in his eyes,

277

the sadistic smile that was total contempt, she dismissed the housekeeper, wanting her gone from the room before Fenton's anger gave rise to gossip which could go beyond the walls of Beechcroft. But the woman had barely moved a step when Fenton lashed his boot against the hearth.

'Done himself no favours has Wilkins nor Perry neither, they'll find like others afore them Fenton Gilmore don't be a man to cross...'

'Fenton, perhaps...'

'Thinks I won't find no other way does Wilkins.'

Whether oblivious of the fact of a servant's presence or else completely indifferent Fenton ignored Henrietta's attempt at caution.

'...but he reckons wrong assuming no other will take the moving of them casks, wrong in believing there be no other have dealings with ships' captains, with men who will take cargo and no question asked...'

'Fenton, my dear...'

Anxious as to where rage was leading, what in his anger he might say next, Henrietta tried again to stem the flow.

'...and Perry...'

Unhearing or unmindful Fenton raged on.

'... thinks by breaking with me, by turning collector for somebody else I'll be finished, but like Wilkins he'll find that to be a mistake, they'll see it is themselves and not Fenton Gilmore is out of pocket.'

The door closed behind the departing housekeeper and Henrietta breathed more easily, yet something Fenton had said worried at her mind.

278

'*cargo ... no question asked...*'

What cargo? Why no question? Glancing at her husband, his back turned toward her, Henrietta frowned. Was the extension of credit he had spoken of to do with the importing of tobacco?

Pouring tea into rose-patterned fine bone china cups Henrietta's mind flipped to that one word 'credit'. Asking for such had obviously not sat well with Fenton. 'A few days', he had said. Adding milk from an exquisite matching Royal Albert jug she let thought play. Surely had money been so near to hand he would never have let himself be seen asking for credit.

'He'll see...'

Another vicious swipe of his foot adding to the venom with which he spat his words Fenton was grating on.

'...Wilkins will regret refusing ... money to lay on any man's desk once that shop be sold...'

As though arriving at some conclusion he pulled in a long breath, letting it slowly free of his lungs as he turned to Henrietta's mild reminder of the danger of speaking before the domestic staff.

'Servants!' he sneered. 'Who the hell cares what servants hear.'

'It would be advisable for you to care, our standing in the town...'

'Won't count for anything shortly,' he snapped, 'Wednesbury will be in the past.'

Silver tongs still clasping small cubes of sugar Henrietta looked up. 'In the past?' She frowned. 'I don't understand.'

'No.' He smirked. 'You wouldn't; but then you see I have only just myself decided, I am putting

Lawrence Fine Tobacco, together with this house, up for sale.'

Sugar tongs clattering on to the tray Henrietta stared disbelievingly. She shook her head. 'For sale! But you can't.'

'Can't!' Cold, lethal, the glint of warning flashed. 'I ... that is...' flustered by threat darkening pale almost colourless eyes Henrietta stumbled. 'What I mean is should Emma become aware...'

'What of it!'

Snapping like crusted ice beneath a foot Fenton's retort had the teacup she held out to him rattle in Henrietta's hand. 'Emma,' she said, 'she is now twenty-one.'

'So?'

He knew what it was she was saying. Henrietta's glance fell beneath the onslaught of ice-bound eyes. He knew but would not be satisfied until it was said, until he was provided with a reason for yet another flare of bad temper. Knowing failure to answer would do no more than aggravate she replied quietly, 'Emma is of the age of inheritance, if by any chance she should learn this house has been put up for sale might she not return to claim both it and the shop?'

'Hopefully yes.' Fenton's lips stretched in a snake-like smile. Then seeing Henrietta's obvious confusion added, 'Should Emma Lawrence return to this house it will provide opportunity to deal with the last of my problems. I would have preferred it to be as it had with her sister, to have enjoyed the older one for as long as I did the younger. Such would have been pleasurable but then fate is capricious, it does not always grant every desire.'

Across from him Henrietta watched the smile fade, the glacial eyes hide beneath lowering lids, heard the hiss of indrawn breath, the guttural deep throated words, 'not *every* desire...'

Like someone caught fast in a dream Fenton's eyeballs flicked rapidly beneath thin almost transparent lids, the tip of his tongue tracing taut lips.

'...it will not deny that ultimate pleasure, the delight of watching fear grow, of seeing the body twist with pain, pain I promise will be yours, Emma, before all life is choked from you.'

'...*enjoyed the older one as I did the younger...*'

Suspicion she had not allowed herself to harbour suddenly became chains of steel holding Henrietta's every limb. 'Enjoyed' had only one meaning for Fenton Gilmore: rape. It was there on his own lips, he *had* raped Rachel Lawrence. Had he...? Henrietta gasped beneath the mountain of weight settling on her shoulders. Had he also murdered her?

'Yes,' recovered from his half-dream Fenton nodded 'I will have a sale notice posted in the newspaper, and...' he smirked his serpent smile, 'I think in the window of the shop also.'

He seemed unaware of those last whispered words, words denouncing him as a rapist, words she must not recall to him. With this warning to herself Henrietta forced the restriction from her limbs. Proffering the tea yet again she asked, 'Where will we go once Beechcroft is sold?'

'We?' The hand extended to take cup and saucer halted in mid-reach. 'We?' The brow creased as from some hard-to-credit notion. '*We* will be going nowhere.'

'But if Beechcroft is sold then we have to go somewhere.'

With a short scornful laugh Fenton looked at the figure seated a little from him, a figure the dislike of which was anathema in his throat. 'We,' he snarled, 'whatever gave you the idea you would be going anywhere with me? No,' he laughed again, 'you can go where you will, though I doubt any place other than Drew's Court will be suitable.'

'You can't...'

Flinging upward the hand reached toward the teacup Fenton sent the cup crashing against the table. 'Can't,' he roared, 'no one ... no one you hear ... no one tells Fenton Gilmore he can't, nobody, not Perry, not Wilkins and certainly no Drew's Court scum!'

'*No Drew's Court scum!*'

In the twilight-darkened bedroom Henrietta smarted under the words flung with that cup. Fenton Gilmore had conveniently forgotten the woman he labelled scum was the woman he brought to Beechcroft, it was she, her pretence of being sister to Mary Lawrence had secured for him another man's property, secured him a comfortable life.

But what had been appropriated could also be taken away, what had been gained could be destroyed.

Hands folded in her lap, Henrietta stared into encroaching night.

Misgiving she had felt over her dealings with

the man Perry had followed Fenton from the sitting room. They had died, as had all feeling for her husband; all except one.

High in the night sky clouds played tag with the moon erasing and revealing its pale silvery light, chasing shadows about the room.

Except one!

Henrietta's glance followed patterns of shadow she did not see.

Even Drew's Court scum could feel revenge.

25

She had told Timothy and Lily something of her life at Beechcroft, of how it had changed with the permanent arrival of the Gilmores.

Emma paused, her pen held still over a neatly scripted page, as she let memory carry her back to the evening they had sat together following her cries. They had come to her so quickly, Lily wrapping comforting arms about her, Timothy advising hot tea.

'You would so have loved them, Rachel.' She smiled, murmuring only to the emptiness of the house. 'Timothy and Lily would have become as dear to you as they are to me.'

Dear as Rachel had been, as memory of her still was. Emma breathed the preciousness of the thought, pulling it into her chest, into her heart.

That cherished memory had her hold back, not disclose fully the life two small girls had led under the auspices of a woman who held no love for them, of the subjection to a man who to the outside world projected the picture of a caring guardian, devoted to the welfare of the children of the sister of his wife while he raped over and again the young one, a girl he terrified into silence by threatening to remove from her life the only love she had left.

Rape! Forgotten in her hand, the pen slipped to the table.

That act was hateful, horrific for any person, how much more so when committed on a child barely at puberty, a child subjected to the added torment of blackmail, the threat to take away her sister.

'I did not tell them of that,' she whispered against tears blurring words staring up from the page she had written, 'I did not tell them, Rachel; though it can no longer hurt you I would have no more shadow cast on your memory.'

They had listened in silence, Timothy and Lily. They had put no question during her brief explanation of the life-changing consequences which had followed the death of her parents nor asked any regarding that of Rachel, only accepting what was said.

Sounds of carts rumbling past on the busy Lea Brook Road, the calls and shouts of men working on buildings being erected on the site of the old malthouse and its cottage drifted in through lace-curtained windows but did not penetrate the silence settled over Emma, the closed world that was her mind.

They had accepted but had they believed?

284

Lily's soft eyes and quiet, *'you got we now, you got Timmy and me to love you'* had been an assurance she did, but Timothy: had he been so certain?

'Beechcroft.'

Restored vividly to her mind it seemed she saw again the lad sitting beside the hearth, the glow of fire imparting a blush of crimson to the tow-coloured hair, the play of fingers twisting the laces of unfastened worn-through boots hurriedly thrust on to his feet at the sound of her cries.

'Beechcroft,' he had stared down at his hands, *'that be along of Wood Green don't it?'*

'Wood Green,' Lily had danced into the conversation, *'that be where the cemetery is; eh Emma, the house you told of, do it really be there? I mean is it one of them big fancy places with nearly a street for a path leadin' up to the door?'*

A smile touching her lips Emma saw her own smile, heard her own quiet, *'Yes Lily, Beechcroft is one of those houses.'*

'And it belonged of your father?'

Timothy's glance had not lifted with the question nor with the quiet reply saying that was correct.

'Well...'

He had paused as though trying to sort some confusion in his mind, then still not looking at her had gone on. *'I don't know the way of it, the law of such things, but seems to me what belonged of your father should rightly belong of you.'*

'Timothy be right–'

'Unless your father 'ad some lawyer paper wrote to say different, to say them Gilmores was to 'ave the keepin' of that house,' Timothy had cut through

285

Lily's support.

She could have left it at that, allowed it believed her father had indeed signed away her and Rachel's inheritance, but doing so would have been a denial of his care for his children, her silence a betrayal of the love he had always given them so she had answered truthfully.

'Mrs Coley was cook housekeeper at Beechcroft; she had been there many years and was trusted as a friend by both my mother and my father as she was by Rachel and myself. It was Mrs Coley told me it was an illness of my mother and not a holiday took them to London; she overheard the conversation between Fenton Gilmore and my father, which distinctly stated my parents would return home within a few days.'

Bella Coley's own voice intruded at that point, memory showing that woman's face as it returned her words to Emma.

'The law! And what law be Fenton Gilmore abidin' by ... that which he made for hisself!'

Was his guardianship as much a lie as his wife's claim of being sister to her mother?

'But they d'ain't,' Timothy's words overrode the thought, *'and them Gilmores never left. But that were a long time ago, you was no more than a kid, but you ain't that no longer; you be a woman growed so go see some lawyer body, have him find out if that house be yourn or whether it don't.'*

'No!' The answer had cried out as though from some physical pain. *'I can't ... I won't ... he can keep...'*

Her eyes had closed from the knowledge behind her protests, but not before she had seen the look flash across Timothy's eyes, a look which

286

spoke his belief she had not related all of what her life had become at Beechcroft, that there was something more, something so grievous she would face a life of poverty rather than go back there.

Consult a lawyer. Emma's eyes focused once more on the page as her mind returned to the present. Consultations cost money, money she did not have. But were it otherwise, did she have means by which to fight to establish any right to ownership of Beechcroft, of the tobacco business her father had owned, she would not do so.

Taking up the pen she paused once more. Claiming Beechcroft was something she must never do for even were that claim successful it would bring Lily and Timothy to the attention of Fenton Gilmore and that would invite disaster. He would find some way of venting his spite and knowing him as she did it was certain his vengeance would be wreaked upon those dearest to her.

Breath suddenly tight in her throat, a shudder banging the pen nib against the neck of the ink bottle making it shake precariously in the saucer used to prevent drips staining the tablecloth, Emma felt her whole being tremble.

Fenton Gilmore rejoiced in cruelty both physical and mental. He exulted in causing pain, the age of his victim having no account. He would delight in visiting upon Lily the horrors he had upon Rachel, each of those obscenities providing an extra pleasure, the evil of his mind delighting him with the thought that what he did would somehow be known to Emma Lawrence, that the pain and suffering of Lily would somehow transmit itself to her.

Concentration lost, she laid the pen in the saucer, the drop of her hands to her lap brushing against the small object in the pocket of her skirt.

Rachel. She withdrew the diary. Beechcroft was her inheritance also. Cradling the small volume Emma whispered aloud, 'Would your decision be as mine, would you forfeit all claim to Beechcroft?'

As the murmur faded to nothingness it seemed to Emma she felt the touch of a kiss against her cheek, heard in its ending a breath of words, a soft smiling, 'Yes Emma, I would.'

Once again she had been alone in that house. Walking with the man engaged as foreman builder Mark Halstead listened without real interest. The new iron works was going up at the rate expected, there had been no interruption to the delivery of materials, no accident suffered by any of the men. Expressing relief at the latter, giving instruction he must be informed should work be halted for any reason, he bid the foreman good day.

He returned to the carriage he invariably drove himself, resisting the urge to halt it at the house he had called at less than an hour previously.

He had seen the curtains of other houses along the street twitch as he had stepped down, guessed at the inquisitive faces carefully hiding from view, people pondering the reason for a carriage stopping there, why a man well dressed and obviously wealthy should call so often; guessing it to be for all the wrong reasons?

He had thought so, had asked was Emma Lawrence happy with her neighbours? She had smiled, her eyes lighting as she spoke of the friendliness she had met, of the help offered. It seemed the only negative thought, the only suspicion was his.

Tugging gently at the rein he guided the horse along Great Western Street, smiling as the animal made a second right turning taking the carriage into Potters Lane, following a route it was so familiar with it could have done so without human assistance.

He had given himself the excuse she might be in need of materials of paper, ink ... the same excuse he had given on that door being opened to him.

She had smiled, smiled at him as she invited him into that poky living room, as she offered tea. But the light in those beautiful eyes had been guarded, it had not gleamed directly as when she had spoken of people living close by. Was that because Mark Halstead was not received as a friend? Was her smile that of mere politeness?

But a smile of politeness was preferable to no smile at all, to driving past a house he no longer had cause to visit, to knowing the woman who had lived there was gone. It would happen. Though he had known Emma Lawrence for so short a time, had only at intervals found reason to speak with her, he knew pride would not allow her to remain in that house once work on those notes and paintings was finished.

Where had she come from? What life had she

led before arriving in that derelict cottage? Looking inwardly at the figure which came ever more readily to his mind, at the perpetual dark skirt, a blouse which spoke of its many launderings, he shook his head, It was not a life of wealth Emma Lawrence had enjoyed, but then again he felt it was not the life ascribed to her by John Adams: hers had not been the life of a gypsy woman.

Her birth family were all dead. That much he believed. So did her living in what had been a tumbledown hovel point to the fact she had no other living relative or...? The thought halted then was jolted by the next: did it mean life with them was unbearable? Had she been subjected to some form of cruelty, something which had driven her on to the streets?

She had faced him with honesty about using his property, she had been open about her immediate family, but there had been nothing of how she came to be homeless.

'...*we be children of the heart...*'

Her face had shown what these words had meant to her.

'...*where Emma goes Lily and me goes...*'

They might never know the comfort of a true home but wherever they went the lad would care for Emma Lawrence as he did for his sister and he in his turn would have her love and respect.

Guiding horse and carriage into the wide yard fronting the iron works Mark Halstead smiled wryly to himself.

He would have the love of Emma Lawrence!

Timothy Elsmore was a fortunate lad.

Wilkins had known there was no shop to be sold in Darlaston, no Lawrence Fine Tobacco remaining in any town other than Wednesbury; he had known that otherwise he would not have been asked to allow credit. How those rat-like eyes had glittered, how the tight mouth had clamped yet more on hearing that request ... firmed to prevent the smile of malice revealing itself

He had thought to have Fenton Gilmore over a barrel, he and Jud Perry both. They thought that without them Fenton Gilmore was finished, but they were mistaken. They had reckoned without Beechcroft. With that house and the Wednesbury shop sold he would have means enough to move away, start over in a new town.

A new home but the old business.

Sitting in the smart George Hotel Fenton smiled expansively to himself.

That business was profitable, very much so, and the tobacconist trade a suitable cover.

Signalling for another drink, taking it from the tray before the waiter could place it on the table, he gulped half in one swallow.

Brandy warm in his throat he twirled the fat round goblet in his hand, watching facets of light from chandeliers dance in the lead crystal.

Profit. He had let too much of that go to Noah Wilkins. But no more. He twirled the glass again. There would be no middle man to suck away the sovereigns, no go-between to arrange things with a ship's captain, he would do that himself. It would be most satisfactory.

Tossing off the remnant of brandy Fenton

nodded to the waiter then as a fresh drink was placed before him allowed the inner smile to find freedom on his lips.

He would buy his own warehouse, one where more than tobacco would be stored; his would have a space where goods other than that commodity would be housed, goods he would collect himself, where a special cask to be returned to the docks could be prepared and collected with no help but his own. But a warehouse was not the only property he would acquire.

Brandy rolled on his tongue as Fenton congratulated himself on the plan he had formulated while driving into the town. He would purchase his own 'house of comfort', a place where – for a sizeable fee – a man could relax, take a drink, satisfy all and any 'appetite', a whorehouse staffed by his own 'collection'; young pretty girls... some very young. Yes, he would include his own special preference when making those collections. He would of course need a 'madam' to oversee the running of the place, to keep a tight watch on the girls. But that woman would not be a Henrietta.

Cradling his glass Fenton smiled into the golden depths.

There would be no more Drew's Court riff-raff in his life.

'I don't want to go back to that house, I be feared of him, I be feared of the master.'

'It were Fenton Gilmore done that?' Bella Coley glanced at the woman sitting at her table.

'Throwed a tray at her head, one with a scalding hot pot of tea along of it.' Clara Thomas, cook housekeeper at Beechcroft, looked at Bella. 'You warned me of his temper afore I applied for the post so I were prepared for it but there be more than bad temper in that man, there be real evil.'

'Please, I don't want to go back, I ... I'd rather go to the workhouse.'

'You don't be goin' back to neither,' Bella answered the girl whose one cheek was purpled beneath a large bruise, the other marked with the line of a scar, 'you can bide 'ere along of Polly an' me.'

'But the mistress, her'll be ordering I work out my notice.'

'You leave 'Enrietta Gilmore to me.' Clara Thomas shook her head at the girl she had brought to Bella's house.

'Then there be my wages!'

'Wages.' Bella sniffed. 'Be as well y' forget them Millie wench, Fenton Gilmore would rob the devil of his pitchfork so I don't reckon to you holdin' any chance of seein' a penny o' what you earned along of that house an' that goes for you an' all, Clara, should you be tekin' y'self off.'

'I've got no mind for that, not for a time yet. There be things I wants to see to afore I leaves 'Enrietta Gilmore's employ.'

Waiting until Polly had ushered the tearful Millie upstairs Bella spoke warningly. 'What I said about Fenton Gilmore a'robbin' of the devil don't be the all of what he be capable of doin', and that don't just mean the throwin' of tea pots ... you look to y'self while you be in that house.'

'He won't go tryin' with me the game he played on Sally James, he won't find my bed so easy to climb into.'

'Weren't that pleasure I had in mind.' Bella gave a quick shake of her head the movement adding to the caution in her voice. 'It be what he does with his fists, using them on a woman affords him as much satisfaction as using that which swings atwixt his legs; you 'ave only to look at 'Enrietta to see the truth of that.'

''Enrietta!' Clara sniffed condemningly. 'Be no more than her deserves; but young Millie...'

'You done the right thing gettin' her away.' Bella said quickly. 'That young 'un has suffered enough in life without becomin' Fenton Gilmore's punch bag.'

'I didn't want to tek her to my brother ... he would have cared for her like her were mine, but it would have set folk talkin' what with him not bein' married. But once I be finished along of Beechcroft then Millie will live along of me.'

'That be real Christian of you, Clara, and Him whose name I've used will bless the doin'.'

'Millie be asleep.' The door opened on to the narrow twisting staircase and Polly slipped quietly into the tiny living room. 'Her were fair worn out, hardly give me time to find her a nightgown afore her were spark out.'

'It be good of you both to tek her in, I be grateful. It eases my mind knowin' her will be out of Fenton Gilmore's reach.'

She watched Polly cross to the fireplace, watched her fill the teapot once more with water from the gently steaming kettle, but Bella's thoughts remained hidden. Was the throwing of a tea tray the only cause of Millie Stokes being removed from Fenton Gilmore's reach, she wondered? Or was it something the girl had heard him say?

26

His own warehouse, his own contract with a sea captain, his own brothel. That would be Fenton Gilmore's new life. Alcohol-infused imagination painting pictures in his mind, Fenton smiled. A warehouse near to the docks would do away with the need for a railway to transport empty casks ... or one not so empty. Yes, near to the docks. He drank again. And his whorehouse, that also would be near the docks. Men home from long voyages, men who had not tasted a woman maybe for months would be more than ready to spend the money in their pockets, and his 'house of comfort' would be ready to supply much more than a taste. He would be a wealthy man, no more covert dealings with another man's property.

'Emma is of the age of inheritance...'

Like a trickle of cold water Henrietta's quiet words seeped among pleasure-giving thoughts.

'...if by any chance she should learn this house has been put up for sale might she not return to claim both it and the shop?'

The trickle a sudden icy douche washing his brain free of dreams Fenton waved aside the waiter hovering at his elbow.

Outside Wednesbury's most fashionable hotel,

waiting for his carriage to be brought from the yard at its rear, he stared toward the darkened empty market place, toward the last of what had once been a thriving chain of tobacco shops.

'...*might she not return...*'

Climbing into the carriage, taking the reins, Fenton flipped them gently to set the horse to a steady walk.

Let Emma Lawrence come. He smiled into the covering veil of darkness. She would find no home, no shops, no inheritance; but she would find a home. The smile became a low laugh. Emma Lawrence would find a home in a dockside brothel ... after Fenton Gilmore had finished taking his pleasure.

But before any of that could happen he must first empty that upstairs room of what it held, the corpse of a girl who had said she had not been stealing.

The devil so quick to leap at the base of his stomach did so now, the pleasure of it catching at his breath.

She had been afraid, the girl with the patched hand-me-down dress, the girl picking flowers to give to her mother for her birthday ... a mother she would not see again.

She had not been stealing. Nor had he. He had paid for his enjoyment, paid with a chocolate cake.

'Your mother was quite correct in her teaching.'

The murmur carried to the horse whose ears flicked nervously, expecting the following touch of a whip.

'But she failed to teach it was not only money

should be refused.'

Deaf to the sounds of the street, blind to figures coming and going from the several pubs and beer houses bordering it, aware only of the images in his mind, Fenton's smile played on in the darkness.

He should not think hard of the mother. Her failure had afforded him so much amusement, given him that very special satisfaction.

He had enjoyed it so much, the screams that had been only silence, the terror-wide eyes which had pleaded for compassion. Hadn't he shown it? Flesh already hardened throbbed against the restricting cover of trousers. Hadn't he shown that mercy, hadn't he worked that tight little cleft with his finger, moistened it with drops of scarlet blood before his entry brought blood of its own?

Recollection traced a finger along tormented flesh arousing still further the devil inside, a demon showing him yet more pictures. Breath caught in his throat, his own body reacting wildly. Fenton watched a tiny figure trying to twist free of its bonds, to escape the touch of a blood-dipped finger, the thrust of which had snatched its virgin purity; then in tormenting slowness another picture imposed itself upon the screen of memory: perspiration born of fear plastering brown hair close to the scalp of the small head caught between two hands, hands grasping so it could not move.

Darkness of night proved no obstacle to inner vision. Fenton's breath dragged in conjunction with the lurch in his loins, with the rush in his veins as it seemed he saw the hands slide about a thin neck, strong thumbs press against a tiny throat.

Mouth clamped against the demand of pulsing genitals, stifling a cry that was pure pleasure, he watched that ultimate moment, that soul-gratifying instant when a child's face twisted in fear stared up at him, when a pair of wide terror-filled eyes pleaded for life, when the thumbs choked that life away.

'What!' The loud clanging of bell signalling that a horse-drawn tram was about to resume its journey after several of its passengers had alighted startled Fenton from his reverie.

Where was he? He blinked, his glance following the candlelights illuminating the tram lumbering away, its glow swallowed almost immediately by a hungry darkness.

The carriage was not moving, the horse had halted of its own accord. But where had it halted?

The open ground! The animal had brought him to the place from where he had abducted that girl! If he should be seen here... Alarm tingling along every nerve his hand tightened on the rein fallen slack on his knees, his glance sweeping toward the church on the hill.

But there was no hill, no church.

He had heard the ring of a bell, seen the gleam of candlelight, so where was the church?

Confusion knotting his brain he stared blankly then at shouts from somewhere nearby almost laughed his relief. There was no church because he was not at that open ground, the bell and the lights had been those of a tram and the shouts which had brought him out of his reverie? They

298

were no threat to him. He had heard the like many times, they were the calls of men leaving for work or home after taking a tankard or two of ale.

They would not see the carriage. Smiling to himself Fenton jumped nimbly to the ground. Could animals possess a sixth sense? Certainly it seemed this one did. Taking keys from his pocket he opened a door let into a high fence then led the horse into the yard at the rear of Lawrence Fine Tobacco.

He had needed no lamp to lead him to that rug-covered bundle, no light to show where that body lay and he would have needed no help to lift it into a cask; except there wasn't any cask.

'Damn bloody Noah Wilkins!' Fenton swore as he had upon searching earlier for a container large enough to take that body. He had hurtled from the house after that contretemps with Henrietta, had driven here to the shop, thrown everyone out telling them it was no longer in business then had almost torn the shop apart looking for something, anything, large enough in which to place that bundle. It was not as large as some he had dealt with, and even swathed in a rug it carried little weight, yet it was still too large to fit into any cask in the storeroom. He had needed a tun, a large barrel-shaped container of the type used to import the more considerable amounts of cheaper tobaccos. But he had no tun nor any cart on which to transport it.

Mulling over first one dilemma then another, finding no answer to either, Fenton heard the soft snicker of the horse.

Sixth sense? He smiled again; the animal had solved the situation for him. He would use the carriage.

And dispose of the body where? Lifting the rug-wrapped figure once more into his arms Fenton strode out to the yard. He would deal with that problem later.

There were no more notes to be transcribed. Emma moved restlessly, trying to come to terms with the emptiness inside her. He had called in the early evening. Eyes closing momentarily she breathed hard willing away the memory but stubbornly it refused to go. She had opened the door to a knock which over the weeks had become familiar, had become waited for. It was true. Emma felt the swift rise of warmth to her cheeks. She *had* waited for that knock, had felt the sharp prick of disappointment on the days it did not come. And on those it had! Hands raised to another flood of warmth Emma faced the embarrassment of her own question. Had the pleasure of it shown on her face? Had Mark Halstead noticed? Could he possibly have guessed? No. Long-held breath released itself slowly. She had been careful to observe the niceties society demanded, had been polite and friendly but with that distance required between employer and employee.

But she was no longer his employee. As the full reality of this finally registered with her Emma sank to the chair drawn to a table set beneath the lace-curtained window of the small parlour. This was where she had worked, it was in this room she had sorted and rewritten every one of those

300

scribbled notes, had considered information contained in them with meticulous concentration, judging descriptions of the red-gold fire of sunset over deserts, of the pale pinks and pearl of dawn caressing a sleepy river; she had appraised narratives recording deep angry greys slashed with the violet of a threatening storm; the varying hues of sunlight and shadow touching the elegant façade of palaces or walls of humble mud brick dwellings. To every one she had given that same level of attention, afforded each a precise disciplined examination before matching it to its particular watercolour.

But all of that was over. He had taken the last of them.

Unaware of the clasp of her fingers resting in her lap Emma looked at the figure which had taken shape in her mind.

Hair free of the constraint of pomade allowed one dark curl to drop almost carelessly on to a smooth brow, a strong jaw defying the fashion of the day was clean shaven; but it was the eyes, deeply blue eyes with their silent words, words which it seemed even now might leave those firm lips. What was the message hidden in those cobalt depths? The words that had remained unspoken?

There had been no words! Impatient with herself she thrust away from the table. It was simply her imagination. Mark Halstead had behaved no differently from how he had on those other occasions he had called at this house. He had thanked her for the work done on his father's papers, asked as on each visit after the welfare of Lily and Timothy and then with carefully wrapped scripts and original notes in hand had turned to leave.

It had been as he stood at the open doorway that she had seen it, that sudden change of expression, a swift hard look flashing across that handsome face at the mention of leaving.

'*Why do you have to go?*'

Hard as the look accompanying it, his reply when she informed him the house would be vacated next day had snapped from a mouth suddenly drawn tight.

In the street women in dark skirts and shawls glanced inquisitively as they passed at the tall figure whose smartly cut jacket and pinstripe trousers told as eloquently as the waiting carriage he was no miner or foundry worker.

She had not wanted to answer, had not wished any discussion that could so easily be overheard by people on that busy street.

Heedless of having left the parlour for the living room Emma stared at the door which gave directly on to the street hearing in her head her own quiet reply.

'*I have told you before, Mr Halstead, I cannot stay in a house I cannot pay rent for, my mind is not changed upon that.*'

'*So you will leave!*'

It had clipped from his tongue.

'*And go where? Another tumbledown hovel ... some vermin-infested shack ... or will it be nights spent sleeping under some hedge? Then there are the Elsmores, I presume seeing you three are family those youngsters will be leaving with you, what effect will that have upon the girl? Think on that, Miss Lawrence, ask yourself can you not remain here for her sake.*'

It had been vituperative, an accusation of self-ishness, but in those moments before he had turned from her she had seen the softening of that intense blue stare, the silent unspoken request that seemed to ask: Can you not remain here for me?

'Imagination, your own foolish imagination!' Emma's self-reproof spilled sharply on the empty room but as she moved to swing the bracket with its noisily hissing kettle from above the fire she could not entirely dismiss the wish it had not been simply fantasy.

'Bit late for the shiftin' of baccy casks wouldn't y' say, Bert?'

'I would that, Alf, late and puzzlin' seeing this shop no longer be sellin' of baccy.'

Half inside the carriage Fenton stilled. Men outside the gate. Damn! Why hadn't he closed it after he drove into the yard!

'Ain't sellin' no more baccy?' Deep-voiced, the man named Bert spoke again. 'What do it be goin' to sell then?'

'Nuthin',' Alf replied. 'That be what old Tom who served back of the counter told, he said Gilmore come into the shop around teatime today his face black as thunder clouds, give Tom and the women who rolls of them cigarettes the sack, sent 'em packin' with no word other than bugger off and not to go back for he was shuttin' of the place for good.'

'That must be reason of his shiftin' stuff out.'

Beneath him Fenton felt the coldness of the dead body reach through the rug. It was no more than curiosity, a moment or two and whoever was out there would move on.

'I be understandin' of that, Bert...'

Good! Fenton breathed a fraction more freely. They understood, now they would leave.

'What I don't be understandin' of be why the shiftin' of baccy casks in a fancy carriage ... won't leave the inside of it smellin' of roses.'

The body had seemed to weigh nothing as he had carried it downstairs into the yard, he had lifted it easily into the carriage, but now still bent double over the seat he had laid it on Fenton's arms and legs ached. But to move would alert those men to his presence and that he did not want. Just a moment longer, the call of the beer house would be stronger than curiosity.

'Then mebbe it ain't baccy he be shiftin'.' Though not loud the deep voice carried clearly to Fenton. 'Whatever it be seems only neighbourly to help.'

No! Denial flared along frozen veins as Fenton jerked, setting the vehicle rocking on its springs. They must not come into the yard. But alighting rear end first proving awkward the men he had heard talking were already inside.

'Need of any help?'

Terse, empty of the respect due to a man of his standing, the question riled emotions already strained in Fenton.

'What are you doing here?' The demand was tinged with irritation as he stared at shapes solid against the violet dark of night.

Deep as shadow surrounding it a voice answered. 'We be offerin' of help.'

304

'I need none.'

'Don't seem that way to me,' it answered again. 'Y' be breathin' right heavy and though I don't see it I guess you be sweatin' like a robber's hoss.'

Was that step forward a threat? Fenton's glance flicked to the driving whip. Could he reach it?

Seeming to divine the thought the second figure moved to join the first. 'I thinks as you do Bert,' the man said quietly. 'The liftin' of casks be a strenuous job, best we lend a hand.'

'I said I do not need your help.' Tight nerves had Fenton snarl. 'Now leave my property before I summon a constable.'

'You do that, Gilmore, you call the law, tell them what it be you've done wi' my little wench.'

There were more than two! Irritation flashing into panic Fenton looked again toward the whip but even as he reached for it a black shadow streaked across the yard, a shadow shrieking as it reached for his throat.

'You took 'er,' rough work-hardened hands closed viciously on Fenton's neck, 'you took my little wench, now I be goin' to kill you.'

'No, Zach.'

Hands even stronger released those clamped about Fenton's throat. 'We 'ave to let Mr Gilmore speak, let him answer your question.'

'Answer!' Fenton choked. 'The man is a lunatic, I haven't any idea what he's talking about.'

'That be a lie, you swine, you took 'er, took 'er from the street.'

Which girl was it the man referred to? How could he possibly know? Perry? No he knew nothing of those 'special' casks and even should

305

he have known it would not have been in his interests to speak of them. Juggling with his thoughts Fenton straightened the cravat rumpled by the man's grasp.

'Who...' He swallowed against the tension built in his chest. 'Who is it I am supposed to have taken?'

'Aint no supposed.' Zach lunged again and at that same moment the curtain of cloud parted, allowing a peeping moon to glisten on a knife blade.

'I said no!' The tallest of the four caught the upraised arm, forcing it away while at the same time instructing both colleagues to hold the other fast.

Unnerved by the attack as well as the accusation Fenton tried desperately to prevent any tremor of voice or body from betraying his trepidation. Drawing a steadying breath he said. 'I don't know why you men are here but I warn you the law can be very severe and be sure unless you leave at once I will invoke it to the full.'

Obviously elected spokesman, the tallest figure answered. 'Oh, we'll be goin'. But first there be a matter needs clearin'.'

'Matter?' Despite tight nerves or because of them Fenton spat the word.

'Ar.' The other man nodded. 'The matter of Zach Turner's little wench.'

'What about her?'

'Ya knows what about 'er,' Zack exploded, 'you took 'er from Russell Street.'

Russell Street ... the girl with the beer jug! The man Turner was her father! Blood pounded in Fenton's head yet in its roar was another, a shout that said stay calm, stay calm there is no proof.

Ignoring Zach's outburst the man addressed as Bert said, 'Young Sarah disappeared while on her way 'ome from fetchin' Zach's suppertime ale, what can you tell we about that?'

Fenton took refuge in bluster. 'Sarah ... Russell Street! I tell you I know nothing of either Russell Street or a Sarah.'

'That don't be what we been told.'

Told! Beads of perspiration threaded Fenton's forehead. Who could have told? No one had seen, yet they had named the very street. But of course they would name the street, that was where the jug had been broken, this, their coming here, was conjecture, it had no foundation. Rationality a cane to lean on he said acidly, 'Then you have heard wrongly.'

'Mebbe.' Bert nodded. 'But 'til you knows what it be then you can't rightly say one way or t' other.'

He had to get these men out of the yard. Desperation lending a sharp note of anger Fenton snapped, 'I tell you one more time, I have never heard of any Sarah, nor do I recall being in Russell Street.'

'Then let we help you recall,' Bert answered flatly. *'Yes I closed Rachel Lawrence's mouth, same as I closed that of the one I took from Russell Street...'* Them do be your words, don't they, Mr Gilmore?'

'They be his words, he be the swine took my babby, my little wench, and I be goin' to cut his bloody heart out!'

Struggling free of the men holding him Zach lunged, the thrust of his body pushing Fenton hard against the carriage. Darting forward to snatch his friend away the man named Alf gasped. Almost falling backward he pointed, pointed to where lit by the same shy moon an arm lay fallen across the carriage doorway.

27

Thoughts she had tried all afternoon to push away plagued Emma's mind endlessly. He had asked why did she have to leave? Her reply had been the truth; she could not live in a house she hadn't money to pay for. But was that all of the truth? Her mind issued a challenge Emma did not want to answer yet even so answer came, bringing with it the flush of warmth to her cheeks. No, she had not told Mark Halstead all of the truth, she had not said what her heart had cried as she had looked into those deep blue eyes, that she wanted to stay, that she wished the work she had done could have gone on and on. And if he had demanded the reason for those words? Emma felt the bloom in her cheeks deepen. Could she have told him, told him that she loved him?

'*...then there are the Elsmores, I presume seeing you three are family those youngsters will be leaving with you...*'

Unbidden as the rest of her thoughts Mark Halstead's parting shot sounded loud in Emma's brain.

'*...what effect will that have upon the girl? Think*

on that, Miss Lawrence, ask yourself can you not remain here for her sake.'

His concern had been for Lily and Timothy, and she respected him for that; but only those children had caused him to ask that she consider remaining in this house.

'...can you not remain here for her sake.'

If only he had asked could she not remain for *his* sake.

Embarrassed by the thought, angry that she had let it slip so easily into her head, Emma walked quickly into the scullery. Taking the shawl from a hook set in the door she draped it round her shoulders. Mark Halstead would never say anything of the sort; the sooner she dismissed such foolishness from her mind the better. But even as she left the house she knew such a resolution could never be achieved.

'I prayed I would find you here. I have searched the town looking for you.'

Kneeling beside her sister's grave Emma had not heard the quick footsteps; looking now at the figure come to stand beside her she frowned.

'I could not imagine where else to look for you. Thank heaven I thought to come here.'

Rising to her feet Emma brushed flecks of soil from her skirts then holding the shawl close across her chest turned a glance toward a black-gowned, dark-veiled woman. She could ignore her, walk away without a word.

'I don't know what I would have done had I not found you.' In the moment of Emma's indecision the woman was speaking again. 'This was my very last hope...'

Emma breathed hard. 'I thought I had made myself quite clear when last we spoke together. I have no wish ever to see you again.'

Behind the veil Henrietta Gilmore's mouth firmed. That was not the only wish Emma Lawrence would have. Masking the acid from which the thought had been born she answered the retort with feigned sympathy. 'I understand the hurt you have suffered, my dear, but you must understand your uncle desires only your happiness, he wishes only his ward's return to Beechcroft.'

'I am not his ward!'

Contempt had trumpeted the reply. Henrietta cast a nervous look over the cemetery, her nerves quickening at the sight of a burial party entering the wide gates.

The working class of Wednesbury, the coal miners and iron workers, the nail makers and their like, folk who lived in Drew's Court and the rest of the button-small back-to-back houses lining street upon street were not often granted the privilege of burying their dead during daytime. Henrietta glanced again at the cortège winding between smoke-darkened tombstones, flower-bedecked coffin and expensively dressed followers attesting to the fact this funeral was that of a wealthy family. Would anyone among the retinue recognise her? Thankfully the veil and dark undistinguished clothing would keep her anonymous to the gentry but nevertheless Henrietta kept her voice low.

'We both know that,' she murmured as the last mourner had passed. 'But Fenton and myself have always looked upon you as our ward; caring for you has given great pleasure to our lives.'

Pleasure! Emma's stomach turned. Fenton Gilmore's pleasure was not that of a man wishing to care for and protect the daughter of a dead friend. His gratification lay in abusing her. Physical cruelty, mental torment and rape, they were the instruments of enjoyment for Fenton Gilmore, they were the medium through which he derived satisfaction. It was for that he desired her return.

Memories rising like wraiths from the dark corners of Emma's mind clamped ghostly fingers about her throat until she could only swing her head in refusal.

Veil hiding the spiteful smile curving her thin mouth, concealing the malice blazing from cold grey eyes, Henrietta watched Emma's hands clutch at the shawl, her lips tremble, and almost laughed at the emotion painting itself on that young face. It needed no special insight to understand the reason: Emma Lawrence was filled with fear, fear backed with loathing. But she would offer no help, promise no protection that would allay that dread. Henrietta's smile became a sneer. Why would she when that very fear would benefit Henrietta Gilmore?

'Obstinacy will serve no purpose, Emma,' she said, all trace of disparagement carefully concealed, 'it will simply add to the concern your uncle already feels for your safety.'

Beneath the lie Henrietta read a deeper truth. Obstinacy on this girl's part would simply increase Fenton's carnal appetite, amplify his lust for physical and sexual abuse, but despite that knowledge she went on.

'I am sure you would not want to cause either your uncle or myself further worry so please, my dear, come home with me now.'

Why would this woman not desist from calling him her uncle? Why would she not stop lying? Like a stiff breeze tossing slender branches the questions snatched at the ghosts holding Emma silent, whipping them away as leaves in a storm, leaving behind only a faint tremor as a mark of their existence.

Innate good manners prevented Emma from voicing the rush of words to her mind, words which would say the woman facing her was a liar. She stared directly at eyes she knew would be watching from behind the dark veil.

'Mrs Gilmore,' she said quietly, 'you may inform your husband I will never return to Beechcroft so long as he or yourself are living there.'

'Fenton thought that would be your answer which is why he asked should I find you I was to give you this.' Catching at Emma's hand Henrietta thrust a small package into it then before it could be returned walked quickly away.

'*...he wishes only for his ward's return to Beechcroft.*' Thoughts which had stayed with her on the walk back to Lea Brook ran like a restless stream in Emma's mind.

'*...caring for you has given great pleasure to our lives.*' Making the lives of two helpless children an absolute misery had been, Henrietta Gilmore's pleasure but that of her husband had followed a darker, infinitely more evil path.

The working of her mind allowed her no peace. Emma moved restlessly about the small living room but all the smoothing of covers and plumping of cushions did not still the thoughts churning in her head.

Fenton Gilmore wanted her return to Beechcroft for only one purpose, to use her as he had used her sister; but desire it as he would she would never go back.

'Obstinacy will serve no purpose...'

Almost on a laugh the voice echoed back, mocking, disdainful, snide as Henrietta had ever been but it was not the underlying cynicism which had Emma stare at the kettle she had lifted from the trivet.

Her refusal to accede to Gilmore's demand that she return posed a definite threat to Timothy and Lily. His continued search for her – and it would continue – could only result in his discovering those two. She had recognised this days before and had refused to do what common sense dictated, to leave Wednesbury. Now for the second time Henrietta had come upon her. It was as though Fate were warning her, but for how many more times would a warning be given? Chance was a fine thing until it was lost.

The last constituted a stark warning in itself Emma replaced the kettle, drawing the trivet away from the fire. She would take time enough to write a note to Timothy and Lily... and Mark Halstead? No, she must not even think of him.

Turning toward the parlour where pen and

paper were kept her glance fell on the package given by Henrietta. No doubt some fresh demand! Already dismissing it Emma paused at another question framing itself. Why send it in a package, why had Fenton Gilmore not had his wife deliver a demand orally?

It will take no more than a moment... A breath, a murmur, it seemed Rachel's voice whispered ... no more than a moment, open it, Emma ... open it.

Suddenly unsure, Emma stared at the neatly tied package. She could only have imagined Rachel's voice, her sister would not have her comply in any way with Fenton Gilmore's bidding. Yet the thought, imagined or otherwise, had repeated itself and each time had held that same note of urgency.

No more than a moment, that was all she would give it. Snatching the package from the corner of the dresser Emma tore away the wrapping.

A letter. She looked at the sheet of notepaper uncurling itself from around a small object. Fenton Gilmore needed to write no words, his demand could not be more explicit: it lay there in her hand.

Breath driven, from her lungs Emma stared at the dully gleaming object, a beautiful face smiling serenely from its green glass surround. She stared at Lily's treasured cameo brooch.

The crackle of paper crushed beneath tightening fingers released the trap closing on her brain. Emma scanned the words written with a confident, brazen flourish.

Emma...
The child Lily is very pretty, such lovely gold-brown eyes and pale blond hair, really quite appealing...

Appealing! Sickness rolled in Emma's throat.

...you will recognise the child I write of, a girl who, should you continue to ignore my request to return to this house bringing the diary with you, will serve in your stead.

Stunned, Emma stared at the signature.

Fenton Gilmore had Lily.

'...*will serve in your stead* ... *will serve in your stead*...'
Words beating in her brain matched the drum of running footsteps carrying her across the market square, the candlelit jars of its many stalls standing out against the grey of a storm-threatening sky. But Emma saw none of the tiny brilliant points of light, heard nothing of tradesmen's calls attracting shoppers to take advantage of 'a bargain they wouldn't see the like of again', her inner vision blocking all except a small frightened face, a child leered over, tormented by Fenton Gilmore.

The quick pain of a stitch catching beneath her ribcage forced her to come to a standstill. Emma leaned against a high wall.

How long since he had taken Lily? Where had

he taken her from? Timothy – had he also been taken? Between gulps of air dragged deep into her chest questions rapped like hailstones on the windows of her mind.

'Be you all right, wench?'

A shake of her arm alerted Emma to the attention of a woman, shawl drawn well over her head, a basket weighing on one arm.

'I asked be you all right?'

'Yes...' Emma gasped against the sharp nudge of pain.

'Don't sound like you be, nor does y' look it.'

'I...' Emma drew a long breath, 'I have run a little too quickly.'

'There be many a one o' us women done that, wench.' The woman nodded sagely. 'Run to get away from that we thought too much to 'andle, but runnin' don't tek we away from the problem, too many o' we has to go back 'ome and face it. My advice be to go in there, rest awhile, will be nobody tell you to leave.'

'No, I can't ...

Taking Emma's glance toward the grey stone Methodist Chapel, her quick 'No, I can't...' to indicate that was not her chosen method of worship the woman shook her head again, saying quietly, 'Might not be the church y' prays in normal but like John Wesley said when he stood on that there 'orse-mounting block to talk to the folk o' Wednesbury, "It don't be the walls o' buildin's houses the spirit o' the Lord, it be the walls o' the 'eart", so you go inside and sit quiet, talk to Him as I says, you'll find Him listenin'.'

She had not taken the woman's advice but

316

hurrying the rest of the way up the rise of Spring Head and on along Walsall Street Emma's prayers rose from the very roots of her soul. Drawing level with the tall wrought-iron gates of Wood Green cemetery her senses jarred. Rachel! She had not thought of Rachel in all of this! In her hurry to reach Lily she had forgotten the promise made as she knelt beside her sister's grave, a promise her diary would never be revealed to any other person... yet here she was ready to place it in the very hands of the man that book denounced a rapist.

Caught between streams of uncertainty, feeling the waters of both rising to engulf her, Emma's whole being cried disloyalty, her betrayal of Rachel.

Beyond the gates, beyond iron railings, from deep in the heart of the grounds a breeze stirred. A gathering zephyr, it brushed over memorial stones, drifted through the leaves of trees, wafting to brush gently against Emma's face, a breeze which seemed to murmur, Love them Emma, love them as you loved me.

Rachel understood, Rachel was telling her what she planned to do was right. Tears thickening her throat Emma glanced once more toward the far corner of the wide grounds, to where her parents and sister lay. Then with a whispered, 'I love you', slipping into the velvet greyness she began the final walk which would take her to Beechcroft.

'Emma.'

It came from a corridor of high hedge bordering one side of the approach to the house.

'Emma.'

317

Quiet yet distinctive it came again and as Emma halted a figure stepped clear of the masking hedge. Emma needed no second glance by which to recognise Henrietta Gilmore.

'Shhh.' Henrietta touched her lips with her finger. 'Not here, we could be seen.'

Did it matter if they were? Wanting the affair over and done Emma did not voice the question but simply followed the figure as it turned to walk rapidly away.

'It was not safe to talk there on the driveway.' Having rounded a sturdily built wall Henrietta halted before a low arched doorway. 'Fenton,' she went on, 'he could return any minute, I have to be in the house when he does.'

So why had they not entered? Why come here to the rear of the house?

As if reading Emma's thoughts Henrietta answered, 'He must not know, he must not find out it was me opened that bedroom window.' Pausing on a shudder she continued. 'I asked Fenton who it was he had brought to the house, that...' she stumbled on a sob, 'that was answered with a blow to the face and a warning to ask nothing. Later he gave me a package with the instruction that should I find you I was to give it to you. Then he strode out of the house. I ... I waited a while then went upstairs and in your room...'

What? What had she found in that room? Every nerve dancing, Emma pressed a hand to her lips holding back a scream demanding she be told the rest.

'It ... it was in your room.'

318

It, not her. Something like relief poured through Emma, relief that died with Henrietta's next words.

'I saw ... so like Rachel... Oh God not again...'

Rachel. So like Rachel! Unable to restrain the cold surge of dread Emma shook the sobbing woman. 'Tell me,' she shook again, 'tell me what did you see?'

Grey light of the dull afternoon added to the grey of eyes that seemed to stare past Emma. 'A girl,' Henrietta spoke with a frightening vacancy, 'lying on the bed, a young girl, not much more than a child.'

'Lily? Was it Lily?'

Seemingly oblivious of Emma's presence Henrietta's blank tone became that of conspiracy. Muttering quickly to herself she said, 'It was then I guessed, I guessed what that package I was to give Emma Lawrence contained, I guessed it was a demand not only for her return to Beechcroft but the return of the diary along with her. The girl, the girl you tied to the bed, Fenton, she was your guarantee Emma Lawrence would do all you desired, but desire isn't so quickly satisfied for you is it, Fenton?'

Not so easily satisfied! Blood ice in her veins, Emma stared at the woman now laughing softly. Had Fenton Gilmore already abused Lily? Was it the result of that Henrietta had seen?

'Aunt.' Concern overriding her resolve never again to use that address Emma caught at the older woman's hand. 'Aunt, the girl ... is she still in the bedroom?'

For several seconds Henrietta made no sound,

then as if waking from a dream asked questioningly, 'Girl?'

'Yes.' Emma shook the hand held in her own. 'The girl you saw in my room, the girl your husband brought to the house, is she still there?'

Recognition made a reply tumble from Henrietta. 'No, no she is not in the house. I brought her to the gardener's shed in the hope you would come, then I opened the bedroom window so it would look as if she had escaped that way; but you have to be quick, Emma, Fenton will not be fooled for long.'

The last was said over her shoulder as Henrietta led the way through the low gateway and into the potting shed.

28

'Be it 'er, be it my Sarah?'

Swallowing hard on vomit threatening to spill into his throat Alf shook his head, leaving the enquiry to be answered by anybody other than himself.

'Let me be!' Zach tried to throw off the hands holding him back. 'I 'ave to see, I 'ave to see for meself be it my little wench.'

'Alf said as it don't be Sarah.'

Rounding on the fourth of the group, a man who until now had not spoken, Zach, snapped, ''Ow would he know, go on Isaac Timmins, tell me 'ow would Alf know it weren't my wench

320

when he d'ain't look inside to see it weren't? But I be goin' to look...' Pausing, he turned a glare to Fenton. 'An' no matter it be my babby or not I be goin' to rip your bloody 'eart out!'

'Best let me look, Zach,' Luke once more intervened then at the nod of acquiescence turned to a visibly shaken Fenton and in a tone relaying the fact he was not to be played with warned against any attempt at leaving the yard. Again instructing Zach be held back he went to the carriage. Climbing on to the lower step in order to see more the interior clearly he paused before reaching inside.

'Be it 'er, Luke ... be it my Sarah?'

Zach's tormented cry pulling at him Luke stood a moment then, his vision adjusting to the extra depth of shadow, shuddered at the scene uncovered by flipping aside the rug.

'Luke, be it–'

'No!' His reply sharper than was meant Luke replaced the rug then stepping away from the carriage added more softly, 'No Zach, it don't be Sarah.'

'But I seen–'

'Ar Alf, you seen!' Luke stopped the other man's remonstrance. 'You seen what Gilmore put into that carriage, an' while it don't be Zach's little wench it does be some poor mother's babby an' Gilmore be goin' to say who that mother be.'

'You 'ad neither the knowin' nor the carin'...'

Luke stared at the man his workmates had hauled back inside the storeroom.

'It made no odds to you who the wench might be, you had to satisfy what were pushin' between

321

your legs, that which another man would pay a shilling to 'ave satisfied by any whore sellin' herself along of the railroad station or along of any public house. But that which throbbed atwixt your legs were not the all of what was desired, rape alone weren't enough to ease what burned in you. That had to be soothed in a very different way, the way I seen on the body of the child you carried from this room; you could only satisfy the evil inside by beating a child almost to death then strangling her; and that, the final act, did raping her while feeling her die in your grip give that ultimate pleasure, was that the reward of serving the devil? It could only be his evil would have a man do what you have done.'

'It was not me. I did not kill that girl.' Fenton searched in the gloom for the faces of the men who had thrown him to the floor.

'So you said.' Luke's reply came from shadow. 'What you ain't said is how, if you d'ain't carry that wench in, does it happen you be carryin' her out?'

'I explained...'

'Oh ar, you explained all right.' Alf's retort was pistol sharp. 'You come 'ere tonight and found the corpse in that upstairs room, so now explain this: who could bring a wench either alive or already dead into a storeroom secured by a padlock to which only you ever 'as the key, then tek 'er on up to another room which again is fastened with a lock the key to that only ever 'eld by you: be summat of a mystery do that.'

'Ain't no bloody mystery to me, the swine be lyin' to save his own skin, but he won't, no by

322

God he won't, I be goin' to do to him what he done to that child.'

'No Zach...'

'Be no use you sayin' no, Luke.' Zach's anger pitched him forward, only Luke's strong arms keeping him from grabbing Fenton. 'We all 'eard what were said along of that house, what he said of stoppin' the mouth of the one he took from Russell Street an' now findin' him with another young wench beaten black an' blue, the life choked from her. That be proof enough for me, proof Gilmore be lyin' an' I don't intend he get away wi' it.'

'*...said along of that house...*' Fenton's nerves jarred at the words screaming in his mind. Beechcroft! The house referred to had to be Beechcroft. Henrietta? No, no she would not dare repeat anything, so who then? Who else could have heard? There was no one else in the–

Like a speeding train jerking to a stop the thought slammed to a halt in his brain, the next moment picking itself up from the wreckage.

Yes, of course ... of course there had been someone else in the house, not only in the house but in that very room! Scarface? No, not that one, the other one, the older woman Henrietta had taken on as housekeeper. It had to be her.

'You...' He swallowed against the dryness constricting his tongue. 'You have been misinformed. The housekeeper employed at Beechcroft lied in saying she heard any mention of Russell Street, and certainly it is untrue to say I threatened to stop the mouth of any person much less that of a child.'

323

They believed him! Met by silence Fenton breathed relief. They were all at a loss, now was the time to assert himself, browbeat them into first apologising and then leaving.

'The woman is a liar,' he went on strongly, 'and she will be brought to book for it just as each of you will be brought to book for invading my property, assaulting my person and accusing me of murder, you–'

'Who said it were a woman?'

Quiet, devoid of emotion, Luke's question halted the arrogant flow. Taken aback Fenton searched desperately in his mind for what had actually been said.

'Say it, Gilmore, which one o' we mentioned a woman?'

Impatience and threat had Alf's demand throb like a drumbeat against Fenton's brain. Which one? How could he say? The darkness had hidden their faces and the rough accent made each man sound the same.

'I cannot verify which man,' he struggled to hold to righteous composure, 'but with saying the lie originated at Beechcroft–'

'Did we?' Luke intervened, that same non-emotion stilling Fenton's blood. 'Did we speak of a Beechcroft?'

'Of course you did!' Fear had Fenton flare.

'No,' Luke returned flatly. 'None of we spoke of a woman nor of a Beechcroft, that come from y'self.'

'Lawrence,' Alf put in speculatively. 'That be the name o' this shop, belonged of a Austin Lawrence killed together with his wife a number o' years gone so old Tom 'as it, he also said of a young daughter dyin' a few months since, said the whole business were kept very hush hush, that Fenton Gilmore would say nuthin' of no funeral nor would he 'ave this place closed for the day as be the usual way o' respect.'

Having listened Luke stared down at the man sprawled at his feet asking in the same flat tone, 'What've you to say to that, Gilmore?'

Unable to shake free of Alf's restricting hold Zach spat at the figure on the floor. 'He needs say naught more,' he hissed, 'think on it, Luke, think on them words. *'...yes I closed Rachel Lawrence's mouth, same as I closed that of the one I took from Russell Street...'* Put that alongside what we've found in that carriage, a young wench whipped and–'

'I have whipped no girl! There has been nothing of that here.'

'Then 'ow do you reckon to this?' At the foot of the stairs, bathed in a pool of yellow light from a candlelit lantern, Isaac Timmins held up a short-handled whip. 'Took this from a fancy bed.' He came closer to the group. Whip and lantern held out to Luke he said quietly, 'That you sees on the leather, it don't be no strawberry jam.'

Where were they taking him? Tightly gagged with his own cravat, bound hand and foot with fine leather thongs cut from several of the whips brought from the cupboard in the upper room Fenton stared into the darkness of the closed carriage. At sight of the whip, dry congealed blood dark red against the light brown leather, the man

325

Zach had seemed to go insane. Snarling again to cut his heart out he had broken free of the other man to throw himself forward, the knife he brandished a deadly gleam in the lantern's glow.

It had sliced across his cheek. Trussed on the floor of the coach Fenton winced at the constant sting. The man had been intent upon killing him; only the quick action of those not holding whip and lantern preventing the doing.

'No Zach, we mustn't kill him...'

Luke's quietly spoken advocacy rang loud in Fenton's brain.

'...we must give him time to think over what he's done, time to repent.'

'Time, the swine d'ain't need no time to think on what he were goin' to do wi' my Sarah, an' it be certain he never 'ad no repentin' of it, so I says we do for him 'ere an' now!'

Zach's kick thrust with the anger of his outburst bit again at Fenton's ribs as the motion of the coach rolled him sideward but sting as it did pain was not sufficient to still the words tumbling in his brain.

'All the more reason to give him time now.'

There had been no more discussion as far he could hear. Only whispered words as he was dragged from the storeroom.

But they were giving him time, that meant they were not going to kill him. It was probable they meant to give him a beating before releasing him. Not a pleasant prospect. Fenton grimaced at pain shooting along his ribs. But a beating could, and most decidedly would, be repaid many times over. Revenge his only solace Fenton clung to it but as the vehicle halted and he was pulled roughly from it fear knifed its way through him once more. The darkness inside the carriage had been almost a match for the night so he could see at once the place they had stopped at was devoid of buildings; no dark shapes loomed black against the sky and no sound broke the stillness.

'Take the lantern, Isaac.'

Where? Where could they be taking the lantern? He had seen there were no buildings. Wanting to question but stopped by the gag Fenton struggled wildly to free himself from the grip of his captors until a sharp blow to the head had him fall into a pit of darkness.

Seeming to float upward, rising slowly from the depths of unconsciousness, Fenton felt his head being snatched forward then something being placed about his neck. Blinking against the light of the lantern he tried to focus on the shape standing directly in front of him.

The shape bent closer and Fenton's clearing vision showed beetling eyebrows and bushy mutton-chop sideburns below which, just visible in the candlelight, was a neckerchief. Not a well-tied silk cravat! Not the groomed pomaded hair and trimmed side whiskers of a gentleman! And not the buttoned tunic of a police constable! Fenton's nerves jolted; he was still with the men who had taken him from the storeroom.

'So, y' be awake.'

The voice gruff and hard echoed and re-echoed from blackness too thick for sight to penetrate.

'That be good, we wouldn't want to leave

327

wi'out witnessin' the pleasin' of y'self at hearin' your name and title.'

Name ... title? What was the man talking about? Fenton struggled to clear the lingering haze from his brain.

'Oh we don't be wantin' of no thanks,' the whiskered face grinned at the strangled sounds emanating from Fenton's throat, 'it be only fitting a gentleman of your calibre be recognised by society.'

Placing a finger to Fenton's chest, tracing it across a torn piece of card, he read aloud.

'Fenton Gilmore. Rapist and Murderer.'

This had been their intent, to hang a placard about his neck? But why not do that in the storeroom, why bring him here to this foul-smelling hell of a place?

'All finished, Luke?'

Somewhere in the impenetrable blackness a question was asked and hearing the response Fenton sucked in a breath of relief. Whatever charade these men had engaged in it was over, soon he would be out of this vile pit and once he was free.

'Ready to go, Zach?'

'One more minute.'

The figure standing before Fenton took a leather cord from his pocket. Passing it beneath the card and round Fenton's body he secured it to a thick wooden post supporting a roof lost in darkness. 'Mustn't 'ave you fallin' over, wouldn't want you to go injurin' of y' self now would we?' Feeling again in his pocket the man withdrew a second slim leather thong and with a low laugh slipped it round Fenton's forehead then jerking his head to rest against the post knotted the ends fast together.

The voice Fenton recognised as that of Luke spoke from thick condensed blackness.

'The society Zach spoke of ... we reckon you won't be entertaining any of that seeing this drift mine hasn't been worked for nigh on thirty years, but we hadn't the heart to leave you entirely on your own so we provided you with a companion.'

The tall figure had partially blocked the light of the lantern. Now as it stepped aside Fenton saw in the full gleam another set to face him, a figure the restricting headband would not let him turn away from.

His companion! Soundless, agonised, screams ripped through his brain, screams of horror as he met wide open eyes, staring unblinking eyes: the eyes of the child he had raped and murdered.

29

Her brow creasing with distaste Henrietta looked at the plate of sandwiches left by her housekeeper before the woman took her day off. This, like her being made to keep to the less expensive establishments of Wednesbury for the making of her clothes while Fenton's tailoring was done in the city, would very soon change.

Yes, life for Henrietta Gilmore would change. Would? She smiled to herself. It already had, and the most delightful part was Fenton knew nothing about it.

To think she had resented his long absences from the house, the evenings and sometimes whole nights he had not returned. But resentment had long ago become relief, his not being here lessened the chances of her receiving a blow to the face or kick to the shins. Now relief had become gratitude. She was glad when he left, more so when bad temper had him storm off; those times she had peace of mind knowing he would be away at least until the early hours; peace which, like today, had left her to carry on her business without too much fear of interruption.

It had followed on from a visit to Powell's tailoring shop in the market place. The wife of the proprietor had a fair hand with the making of dresses but the very fact of having to use a local woman was demeaning and fear of any person of standing in the town seeing her enter or leaving that place meant she walked to and from it rather than use a carriage. That, she had promised herself, would also be a matter for change. Immersed in the thought she had not paid attention to the young girl walking like herself along Walsall Street, not until a voice had asked, *'Be you going to visit of the cemetery same as we?'* She had been annoyed at the question, annoyed at being spoken to as though she were a domestic or the wife of some factory worker.

But then it had proved a gift.

Leaving the plate with its untouched sandwiches in the sitting room Henrietta walked upstairs. Passing along the corridor leading to her bedroom she glanced toward that of Emma.

Yes. She smiled satisfaction. It had proved a gift and now she must make full use of it.

Listening for fully a minute to the silence of the house, assuring herself neither Fenton nor the housekeeper had returned, she lit the oil lamp then crossed the thickly carpeted room to where a large mahogany chest of drawers stood against one wall. Caution having her listen once more she pulled open the lower drawer taking from beneath layers of petticoats a heavily ridged blue glass bottle. Poppy juice. She clutched the bottle tightly. This had been the first of the changes she had made. The resignation of Bella Coley and Polly Lacey then the appointing of a housekeeper with whom she was not wholly comfortable had seen her wean herself off the habit of taking a drug to help her sleep. But that was a secret: kept to herself, as was the bottle held in her hand.

Much of the contents had been used. Henrietta held the container close to the lamp, its light showing a lighter expanse of blue against a lower darker level.

Just under half full. Closing the drawer she slipped the tightly corked bottle into a pocket of her gown. There would be more than enough.

It had all proved so easy.

Dressed once more in the shabby stained clothing of a man earning his living from work in one of the town's many iron works or coal mines, her own clothing together with the empty blue glass bottle left behind in the potting shed, Henrietta walked toward the town.

331

'*Be you going to visit of the cemetery same as we?*'

The voice which had piped up at her on that walk toward Wood Green sounded again in her mind. She had made no reply but her silence had not deterred the speaker.

'*It be my mum's birthday, I be going to show her the card I've made. I'll have to tell the truth, tell it were Emma helped, that it were Emma showed me how to write the word treasure.*'

At the mention of the name the snap which would have sent the girl on her way had stilled on her tongue. Henrietta smiled at the memory. That had been fortunate.

'*Emma be my friend,*' the girl had prattled on, '*her be cleverer than me and Timmy, and though Timmy don't be wi'out brain I doubt he could've wrote "treasure" exact like.*'

Emma. The name was not uncommon; perhaps the girl spoke of an older sister, Even so, a deeper sense had cautioned Henrietta to listen a while longer.

'*I be going to show my mum my new treasure, it be this.*'

The girl had proudly displayed a penny ribbon.

'*Emma said it comp … comp … set off the colour of my hair. Her wanted I wear it but I said for Mum to see it new.*'

'*Your sister is right in saying the ribbon complements the colour of your hair.*'

She had looked at the girl, at the smile of pleasure lighting eyes to gleam gold-brown diamonds, while the well-washed blond hair fell free, a pale golden frame enhancing a pretty face.

'*Emma don't be my sister … well her don't be my*'

real sister but her said her and Rachel be proud to be called such.'

The answer had bubbled back full of confidence undaunted by the additional revelation.

'Rachel couldn't tell that for herself cos of her being dead, but Emma be certain her would want to be sister along of Timmy and me.'

Emma ... Rachel ... the latter dead. Coincidence too great to be ignored. Henrietta had smiled, saying, *'Emma and Rachel are charming names as I am sure yours must be. Won't you tell me what it is?'*

'Lily.'

The eyes had danced their brilliant dance. *'My name be Lily, Lily Elsinore and my brother be Timmy. Timothy Elsmore.'*

She had to know, the child could dart away at any moment.

'Emma,' she had smiled at the girl, *'is she also called Elsmore?'*

The fair hair had caught the breeze tossing a silk cloud about the small face. *'No,'* she had laughed, *'Emma don't be Elsmore, her be Lawrence, her name be Emma Lawrence.'*

The gift had been presented! Henrietta smiled to herself. And she had grabbed it with both hands.

She had halted in mid step, her head swinging several times to simulate surprise.

'Emma! Emma Lawrence! I have not seen her for so long I thought she must have left Wednesbury, gone to live somewhere else.'

The child had looked across the street toward the cemetery and Henrietta had felt her veins tingle. She must not lose the opportunity.

'*Please,*'she had smiled at the face turned again to her. '*Emma and myself were such good friends I wonder would you take her a note from me oh – but I was forgetting,*'she had let the smile die, '*it is your mother's birthday and you are wanting to show her your card and your new treasure.*'

'*My mum told Timmy and me to help folk wherever we could so I'll wait along of you writin' your note. Besides, it will 'ave Emma happy to hear from a friend.*'

Avoiding the quieter Spring Head route to the market square Henrietta walked on toward the High Bullen. Dressed as she was in workmen's clothes, a flat cap covering her hair would be no protection were ruffians lurking in that dark thoroughfare.

But she had not been dressed in workmen's clothes when joined by that child. Henrietta's mind slipped back to early afternoon.

They had come to the gate leading into the grounds of Beechcroft, the girl making no demur when being asked to wait in the gardener's shed, '*for cook won't have the bringing of strangers into the kitchen.*'

It had been a matter of moments to gather notepaper, pencil, poppy juice and a glass of lemonade then return to the shed. The girl had smiled delight at the drink and by the time the note was written was already asleep.

The note. Deep inside the muffler Henrietta's mouth curved in a smile. It had been written to Emma as said but it had carried no word of friendship nor had the signature been that of

Henrietta Gilmore. Even so she had harboured a doubt it might bring Emma to the house, a doubt which had disappeared at sight of a cheap glass cameo glinting in the half-open hand of the child.

But Emma Lawrence had come.

Turning the corner into Upper High Street Henrietta glanced toward the Lamp public house. Perry could be in there ... he could be in any of a dozen such places but first she must try the Turk's Head.

Like the young child, Emma had made no objection to the gardener's shed. Henrietta's thoughts returned to the scene. So relieved was she to see the girl unharmed Emma had agreed that carrying a sleeping child would attract attention and should she meet with Fenton then there would be no escape for either of them. Therefore it was best they remain hidden until dark.

So Emma also had accepted lemonade laced heavily with poppy juice before she herself had left to look for Jud Perry.

Perry! A finger of anxiety touched Henrietta. What if the man should recognise the fact the person he was being asked to cooperate with, the person dressed in shabby workmen's clothes, a soiled muffler drawn across the face to almost meet the peak of a begrimed flat cap, was not a man but a woman? But then money was a perfect solvent for removing stains of doubt and Perry would wash his hands with it. No, she need have no fear of refusal. That man would collaborate with the devil supposing he paid a pound.

Drawing the collar of the jacket higher about her neck, hunched shoulders driving her chin lower, Henrietta entered the smoke-filled bar of the Turk's Head.

He was late returning home. Timothy's steps quickened as the bell of St Bartholomew's church clock rang ten. Lily would be fast asleep in bed but Emma would be sitting up. He really ought not to have stayed so long in the town but then what he had overheard while feeding and stabling the horses of carters arriving late in the yard of the Turk's Head Hotel had been interesting. The ostler employed there liked a drink, in fact he liked several drinks and so often paid sixpence to have the job of seeing to the horses done for him. That was what had happened tonight. But tonight had been later than usual and so had required payment of two sixpences.

Smiling to himself Timothy jingled the coins in his pocket. Lily could have a dress and a pair of shoes, though for sixpence they would have to be got from the pawnshop. His sister would be pleased but what would be Emma's reaction? She would no doubt chide him as any older sister might, but even had he in truth an older sister he could not love her more than he did Emma Lawrence.

Lawrence! Thoughts flicked back and forth like fireflies in his mind. It had been from the back of Lawrence's Tobacco shop he had heard voices. He had not paid much attention, he had often seen deliveries being made and empties collected from that shop and though p'raps it were on the late side that is all it would be, a delivery of tobacco.

Interest fading he had thought no more until a man's obviously angry voice had come clear across the high wall.

'I 'ave to see for meself, Luke...'

Had it been that had startled the horse causing it to snort and shuffle, the jangle of harness drowning the voice. It was nothing new hearing sharp tongues, a heated conversation between men making their way home from work after taking a quick beer. But then had come, *"Ow would he know, go on Isaac Timmins, tell me 'ow Alf would know it weren't my wench.'* Arguing over a woman. Smiling, he had returned to the job in hand. But then minutes later hearing muted voices and something sounding like a heavy object being dragged across that other yard curiosity had him listen. Being unable to distinguish with any clarity what was being said he had searched for something to stand on in order to look over the wall. It had taken several more minutes to find an empty beer barrel and manoeuvre it across the yard. The effort had proved fruitless. Timothy smiled ruefully. By the time he had clambered to where he could see into the yard of the Lawrence Tobacco shop it was too late for sight of anything other than a carriage already passing beyond the gate.

Emma was not sitting waiting as he had thought she would be and Lily was not in her room, nor was she in Emma's room. He had knocked and getting no answer had knocked louder then still getting no reply had gingerly peeped into Emma's bedroom. It had been empty. The whole house was empty. Shopping? Except for Saturdays the market closed at eight thirty and the shops at around the same time so even had they gone into the town they would have been home by now.

Think! Returned to the living room he stared at the fireplace, at the grey ash telling the fire had died hours before. Think! He pummelled his brain again. Had Emma spoken of maybe paying a visit somewhere, calling to see somebody and taken Lily along with her? Even as the thought sprang hopefully he rejected it. Emma had never once spoken of visiting and apart from neighbours no one visited here.

But one person did come, to bring work for Emma to do. Halstead. But Emma had said that work was finished, that it had been collected a day or so ago. She had also said something else. Nerves tightening like bowstrings Timothy let the memory return.

They had been clearing dishes from the evening meal, Emma handing plates to Lily, she carefully drying each one, he bringing fresh coals into the scullery.

'Mr Halstead called today.'

Hearing Emma's words in his mind Timothy only now recognised the false, almost forced brightness in the tone.

'He collected the last of his father's papers.'

'The last, do that mean there'll be no more?'

'Last usually means there ain't no more of a thing, I would've expected even Lily Elsmore to be knowin' that.'

He had teased Lily, skipping aside to avoid the

338

drying cloth she flicked at him. But when she asked the same question later when the three of them had sat round the fire, Emma had answered quietly that yes, it did mean she would no longer be working for Halstead.

This house belonged to Halstead, it went with the job. Was that the reason the place was deserted, had he come here today to demand they vacate his property? Had he put Lily and Emma on to the streets? What other reason could it be they were gone? How long since? Which way might they have gone? No matter, he would find them... but first he would find Halstead.

Reaching the street Timothy paused. He had no idea where the man lived, where to look for him. At that moment it seemed some gigantic paintbrush swept across the darkened sky turning it brilliant red-gold.

The nightly opening of the iron-smelting furnaces! Watching the spectacular scene Timothy's mouth firmed.

He might not know where Halstead lived but the men working for him would.

Perry had taken the money, his grimy fist closing over the five-pound note, beady eyes gleaming at sight of others. But the others must be earned. He knew where he could get use of a hansom, he had done business with its driver on many occasions, 'a few bob sealin' his lips tighter than any gag'.

She had stayed just long enough to arrange the hour he should bring the vehicle to the rear gate of Beechcroft, then she had returned directly. But she had not entered the house. Her housekeeper Thomas would likely have returned from wherever it was she spent her time off. Holding a match to the wick of a candle Henrietta felt the sense of unease which always came at the thought of her housekeeper. What was it about that woman? Setting the candle in a jar, placing it where its light escaped all detection from the house, she pushed the thought away. Get tonight's business over and then she would dismiss Clara Thomas and her scarfaced maid.

A soft moan recalling her attention she turned quickly. The girl was waking. Reaching for the bottle she had brought from the house, she tutted in irritation. She had used the last on Emma. But the girl Lily had to be prevented from crying out and also from trying to get away; and Emma, she also could be a problem when awake.

A glance showed rags and twine lying beside neatly stacked pots. Henrietta moved quickly. A cloth tied over the mouth, twine securing hands and feet would hold her captives until Perry could fetch both of them away. She would have been happier could the fetching have been done sooner, sitting in a musty garden shed was not to her liking, but midnight or the early hours was not an unusual time for a hansom to be coming to the house. Fenton often returned home at such an hour. Tonight's arrival of a cab would attract no undue attention.

Once she had knotted the twine securely about Emma's ankles Henrietta looked at the sleeping face. Even with the rough gag tied about the mouth it was easy to see the interest the girl held for Fenton; Emma Lawrence was beautiful.

But Fenton could not be afforded all of his predilections. The barest shadow of a curve flicked Henrietta's tight mouth. In a few hours there would be no more Emma Lawrence, no more 'niece' to tempt an 'uncle', no more threat to the comfort of Henrietta Gilmore.

And Fenton?

The smile which had been no smile faded to obscurity leaving the hardness of stone to glint in grey eyes.

Tomorrow Fenton would still be the husband of Henrietta Gilmore ... but he would no longer be her master!

30

There was no watchman at the gate of Halstead Iron Works. Maybe he was brewing a pot of tea to have with his supper but wherever the man might be, waiting for his return had no place in Timothy's plan. He would simply find someone else to supply him with Halstead's home address.

Overhead the scarlet canopy of furnace-flamed vault lost its colourful onslaught against the night, its last vestiges of blush pink defeated by the grey-black of a moon-empty sky. But Timothy needed no light of the heavens to show the way, the noise of men calling to each other, the clang of metal upon metal served as direction.

Trespass! Entering a building that stood dark

sentinel over a shadowed yard he pushed thought of consequence away. Let Halstead have his reprisal ... but first he would tell him of Lily and Emma.

'Hey!'

Already he had darted into the cavernous building, stumbling over bars of metal laid on the earth-packed floor. Timothy ignored the shout but seconds later a strong fist caught his arm and he was hauled to a stop.

'Young fool!'

Hard as the iron he worked a man's voice grated, 'Ain't you got no more sense than to come a racin' in 'ere!'

'I 'ave to speak with–'

'You be like to be speakin' wi' St Peter you go runnin' among them there crucibles, that be if he can find enough left of you to talk with. That there don't be no water, it be white-hot metal an' even after it be stood an hour an' more it still be hot enough to melt not just the flesh but bone along with it.'

'What is going on here?'

'Be a lad, I copped him messin' ...

'I don't be messin'!' Timothy flared at the accusation, 'I come 'ere to ask a question!'

'Leave 'im to me sir, I'll chuck the young bugger out.'

'No. Let him ask his question.'

Timothy stared into the face of Mark Halstead. 'Don't need to now. But there be another I'll 'ave the answerin' of.'

Something was wrong, the boy's face told as much. Rejecting a second proposal to have Tim-

342

othy forcibly removed Mark Halstead said quietly, 'If I can be of help...'

'Help!' Timothy laughed disgust. 'I reckon you've been that already, helped yourself to that house along of Lea Brook. Felt good did it, chuckin' Lily and Emma on to the streets!'

'Lily? Emma?' Beneath an unruly fall of hair Mark Halstead's brow furrowed.

'Don't come that wi' me!' Timothy's anger blazed. 'It can only be your doin', only you can 'ave them gone.'

Despite ferocious heat spewing from furnaces opened to the feeding of coke for the night-time smelt of pig iron Mark Halstead's blood chilled. Lily, Emma – what was the lad talking about?

Thanking the man for his prompt action, with a curt word Mark indicated Timothy should follow him outside. Mark turned as they reached the yard, asking in a voice suddenly raw with anxiety, 'What has happened, where are Lily and Emma?'

'That be good comin' from you, from the man who turned them out.'

Darkness hid the furrow becoming deeper but could not mask perturbation snapping in his reply. 'Turned them out, what on earth are you talking about?'

'I don't 'ave time to listen to lies an' excuses, just tell me which way they headed.'

Common sense warned that allowing consternation to sharpen his words might result in Timothy leaving before fully expounding the reason for his visit to the foundry at so late an hour. Mark forced a calmness, saying quietly,

343

'Timothy, I have not been to the house for two days, I have not seen or spoken either to your sister or to Miss Lawrence since then and I most certainly have not turned them out.'

'Well they wouldn't do no moonlight flit! They wouldn't bunk off, 'specially not without me they wouldn't; so you tell me why if it don't be you be the cause, tell me why else do they be gone?'

He needed to put no further question. Mark called for his carriage. Timothy Elsmore had the wrong end of the stick but he would have considered its full length before coming to a conclusion.

'Timothy,' he said as the carriage was brought to the yard, 'I am going first to Lea Brook to satisfy myself Lily and Emma are not there. If they are not then with or without your help I intend to search for them, though I would welcome both your company and assistance.'

It had to be an important job to have Mark Halstead at the foundry late at night. Beside him on the driving seat of the carriage Timothy kept his thoughts to himself. Yet not as important as Lily and Emma! There had been no attempt to pull the wool over his eyes but there had been the quietness of truth and the fact he had not let the workman throw him out of the foundry added further conviction: Mark Halstead had not lied when saying he had not put Lily and Emma from the house. The man had acted sensibly where he had gone off half cocked. Guilt needling at him Timothy began an apology but it was immediately brushed aside by the reply, 'I would have acted the same way myself,' almost drowned beneath the crunch of wheels and the rapid beat of horse's hooves, the animal responding to the constant flick of the rein.

They had not returned.

Bedrooms, scullery, brewhouse and even the garden privy were searched and searched again. Timothy looked at the man across the living room then as the tall figure turned to leave his glance caught a soft glint of green at the corner of the dresser. One bound taking him there he snatched up the small object.

'Lily's treasure! She wouldn't never leave this behind, it means too much to her.'

Timothy's exclamation made Mark turn about. He glanced at the glass cameo, the chill at his spine increasing as Timothy went on.

'You d'ain't send Lily an' Emma from this house but somethin' did, and whatever it were had 'em leave quick, Lily's treasure bein' left behind tells that.'

'Or perhaps its being here is meant to tell you they are not gone far, that they will be returning soon.' Mark knew his answer held little credibility but he must bolster the lad's belief his sister had come to no harm. Did he believe that himself? Or had Emma Lawrence kept to her word she would not stay in this house? Each room they had looked in had been neat and orderly, everything in its place. Despondency adding a new low to his own spirits Mark stared at a truth he did not wish to see. Emma Lawrence had left and taken the girl with her.

Emma Lawrence was fully conscious.

Henrietta looked at the figure struggling to sit up, saw the fear leap in eyes catching sight of another smaller figure bound in the same manner.

'You have no cause to worry.' Henrietta recalled the look to herself 'The girl is unharmed. But why is she here? I can see the question in your eyes. The answer is another question: would you have come had she not been? But that is not what you and I have to discuss. So far my husband does not know you are here. Oh, the letter!' She shook her head at the query in Emma's eyes. 'That bore Fenton's name but it was written by me; so as I say he does not as yet know of the presence of yourself and the child though his remaining in ignorance depends entirely upon you.'

She had written the letter, she had forged her husband's signature ... but how had she found out about Lily?

'I cannot be sure when Fenton might return.'

Henrietta's words cut across Emma's thoughts.

'And if he should...' She paused. 'I do not need to remind you of his preferred choice of bed partner. He will, I am certain, delight in the company of your young friend. But that does not have to happen. Agree to what I ask and you can both leave.'

Emma watched the figure rise and cross to where a candle glimmered among shadow, a frown of confusion settling on her brow as the faint light showed the outlandish costume. Why would Henrietta be dressed in such clothing?

Picking up the second sheet of notepaper she had brought earlier from the house Henrietta's nerves tingled. Paper had been easily hidden in the pocket of her skirt, so had a bottle tightly corked, but it could not carry an inkwell. But the pencil she had brought in place of pen and ink, would writing with that render a document invalid under the law, have it pronounced legally non-binding? She could not risk fetching pen and ink from the house; if Fenton should be there then all of this would have been for nothing, he would not hesitate to beat every last word from her ... and should Perry arrive! How many blows would she suffer when it was discovered it was she had the man leave Fenton's service!

Staring a moment longer at the wooden pencil Henrietta snatched it up. She did not have a great knowledge of the law but surely it was a signature and not the instrument it was written with which counted.

'Emma!' She held up paper and pencil. 'Set down on paper that you, Emma Lawrence, give to Henrietta Gilmore without let or hindrance the property known as Beechcroft House together with the property and business of Lawrence Fine Tobacco. Sign it and you have my promise you and the child can leave.'

Emma looked at the face, its hardness not relieved by the soft touch of shadow. She had Henrietta Gilmore's promise; a promise as reliable as that made to a friend, a promise saying she would care for that friend's daughters as though they were her own.

Candlelight, though faint, showed the look of contempt in Emma's eyes. Henrietta replaced paper and pencil on the potting bench. 'I see by your look you do not agree to my request,

347

Emma.' A few steps bringing her to where the two huddled together she snatched Lily to her feet, hauling her to the door of the shed. Pulling it open she glanced back to Emma, a smile of pure malice accompanying her next words. 'That is your choice ... as giving this child to Fenton is mine.'

'I thinks y' should wait in the carriage, you walkin' into the bar room of that place will draw too much attention. Best let me go in by meself, folk be used to seein' me in there, they won't pay no mind to holdin' a quiet tongue like they would if you does the askin'.'

Reluctantly agreeing, Mark slowed the horse.

'Not 'ere.' Timothy shook his head. 'A carriage be less noticeable outside of the George, wait for me along of there.'

The vehicle moved off as Timothy shot a glance about the market place searching empty deserted stalls, hoping to find two figures hiding among the shadows. He had hoped to see them on the drive up from Lea Brook, hoped they were making toward the town, hoped he would catch up with them there. He saw no sign of them, though, so he turned to the entrance to the Turk's Head Hotel then hesitated, a harsh, 'Quiet ... d' you want the whole town knowin'!' sending a tremor along his veins.

Knowing what? And why the snapped order for quiet? Instinct telling him he should listen he slipped quietly round the side of the building, his heart thumping at the sight of men grouped together in the yard. Sliding silently into a deep pool of shadow, hardly allowing himself to breathe for fear of being heard, he strained to catch the hushed voices.

'I tells you that one be paddlin' up to his neck an' the other'll be swimmin'; them two be hand in glove.'

'We can't be sure.'

A second voice began to answer but was halted by the first cutting in quickly.

''Ow sure does you needs be, you've seen 'em together often enough, thick as thieves they be.'

Who was hand in glove with whom? Who was it were thick as thieves? The answers would make interesting listening at any other time but right now he must continue to look for Lily and Emma. The instinct which had him slip into the yard already fading, Timothy made to slink away but another man said quietly, 'I goes along wi' Zach; I says what one knows the other knows much the same.'

'Course they does.' Zach's voice floated across the yard and into the shadows. 'We all seen that little wench's body, we all knows what were done to 'er an' I'll lay odds Jud Perry knows it an' all.'

A little wench's body! Timothy was instantly still, not even a breath moving in his chest. There had been young girls gone missing on several occasions; only a few weeks back one had disappeared from Russell Street, the jug she had been sent to fetch beer in found smashed on the ground. Now these men were talking of seeing a young wench's body. Lily? Was the girl they talked of Lily?

A cry rose in his throat but Timothy forced it

back. He could not make these men say who it was they had seen or where but if he listened he might glean the information for himself

'Zach don't be wrong when he says that pair be in one another's pocket, one man 'avin' to keep his mouth shut the other 'avin' to pay him for the doin' of it, and we've all seen Perry spendin' in the bar ... y' don't get money such as he be flashin' by humping crates along of the railway goods yard, he 'as to be up to summat else and I thinks that "summat" be the helping of Gilmore to cover his dirty work.'

'And tonight in that yard back of the baccy shop we found out what that dirty work be. Gilmore done for that babby we copped him with so it don't be wild to reason he be behind young Sarah's disappearin', and Perry – pah! Perry would skin a fart for a 'appeny then sell it back for a penny so if anybody be in it with Gilmore it will be him.'

'And if what you say proves right?'

'You knows the answer to that, Bert. We does with Perry what we done with Gilmore.'

They were talking of murder. Timothy pressed further into the concealing shadow as the men he had eavesdropped on walked from the yard. The murder of a young girl. But that girl had not been the one from Russell Street. Lily! Oh God, was it Lily! He must find out, he had to find out.

A shout bursting from his lips he ran after the men, a run that ended as strong hands caught at him, swinging him off his feet.

She had known that threat would prove successful. Emma Lawrence would not see the child given over to Fenton. Smiling to herself Henrietta watched the signature being added to the neatly written page. She had overseen the compilation of the letter, carefully making sure every word was as she dictated. Taking it she folded it once across then slipped it into a pocket of the shabby jacket beside the small book she had taken from the drugged Emma.

The diary *and* the letter.

Self-congratulation flowed like warm wine in Henrietta.

Both would be shackles binding Fenton ... and she would see they remained tightly locked.

'You promised Lily and I could leave once I had done what you asked.'

Her hand still touching the pocket, Henrietta looked at the girl she had duped into coming to this shed, then had forced to sign away both house and business; a girl who in truth she had always felt jealous of, jealous of what nature promised, beauty it had never bestowed on Henrietta Gilmore. Warm wine cooling rapidly she made no attempt at masquerade, no effort to disguise the rancour aroused by that last thought.

'I did, didn't I,' she said spite drooling with every syllable, 'I did promise that.'

'Then please untie us.'

'Untie!' Henrietta frowned. 'There was no mention of that, I spoke no such word.'

At Emma's elbow the candle flickered, its trembling flame echoing the shiver suddenly rippling along her spine, while at the edge of the shadow Lily whimpered, a cry muffled almost to silence by a gag pulled cruelly tight. Hearing the child's obvious terror Emma felt anger rise above her own fear. Henrietta was engaging in that she had so enjoyed doing to two young girls left in her care: she was taking pleasure in Lily's suffering as she had taken it in watching the anguish, the unhappiness caused those children; she was relishing Lily's fear as she had relished that of Rachel, drinking it in, savouring the taste as she had savoured it so many times before.

'You.' She swallowed the surge in her throat. 'You gave your word should I furnish you with a letter freely giving you all of my inheritance then Lily and I would be allowed to leave. You have that letter, you have the diary, you have all you asked, now untie us.'

'Emma, as I have told you I used no such word as untie. However I did promise you would be allowed to go and that promise will be kept, but first I must put *my* inheritance in a place of safety.'

A place of safety could only mean the house. Emma watched the figure move further along the bench. Henrietta had fastened her left hand to the back of the rickety chair but had needed to leave the other free in order for the letter to be written. On hand would be enough! Emma held the breath of hope. With the woman gone to the house she could unpick the twine about her hands and feet then do the same for Lily.

'It is all arranged.' Henrietta turned. 'You Emma, will be collected and removed, the girl however...' She smiled. 'The girl I shall give to Fenton. She will help offset his disappointment on finding he is no longer master of Beechcroft.'

31

'I guessed it was something you had heard said but to let you go dashing into that place like an enraged bull would have done no good, those men would most certainly have thrown you out on your neck.'

Still held at arm's length Timothy nodded. 'Wouldn't 'ave had 'em exactly welcome me with a pint.'

'Only the one thrown over your head.'

'Probably the tankard along with it.' Released from Mark Halstead's grip Timothy eased the half snatched-away jacket back more comfortably on his shoulders. Then speaking quietly but quickly repeated all he had heard said minutes before while hidden in the shadows of the hotel stable yard, adding, 'They was the same men I'd heard talkin' some hours back, I knows cos of the names they called each other. They was the same both times; Luke, Zach ... he were the one sounded real put out and d'ain't mind the others knowin' of it. Then I heard the name Isaac ... Isaac Timmins: like I says they was the same names I'd heard afore.'

'These men, the first time of hearing them talking were they in that stable yard?'

Timothy shook his head. 'No. They was the other side of the wall, they was stood back of Lawrence baccy shop.'

'Did you see them?'

Timothy shook his head again. 'I heard a noise, a scraping sound like summat being dragged across the yard. I supposed it were being made by them men earning an extra copper or two shifting of casks of baccy; I reckoned the carter who delivers the stuff had left the casks in the yard and so Gilmore had paid them men to carry 'em inside, but I couldn't say definite cos by the time I'd found a box to stand on all I seen was Gilmore's carriage drivin' out through the gate.'

'You are sure the carriage you saw driving away belonged to Gilmore?'

'Certain. I've seen it times afore around the back of that yard; but we be wastin' time standin',' Timothy turned away, 'I be going into that bar...

'Wait.' Mark caught at his sleeve. 'Has Emma talked of where it was she lived before coming to stay with you at Lea Brook?'

'What the 'ell do where Emma lived 'ave to do with this, her wouldn't never go back there!'

'Did she tell you!' Mark's impatience matched that of Timothy.

Rounding on the older man Timothy threw off the restraining hand then recognising the anxiety behind the demand answered. 'Her said it were a posh house, said it were Be ... Be ... Beechcroft, her said the house were called Beechcroft.'

Gilmore was the proprietor of Lawrence Fine Tobacco. Word had it he had carried on the business after its owner had died in an accident. Lawrence was the surname of Emma and she had lived at Beechcroft ... and so did Gilmore. Mark Halstead's nerves tripped. The house, the shop,

354

the surname: they all fitted together. Emma Lawrence was no gypsy woman, but was she owner of those properties? Had she decided to tell Gilmore so, to take back what belonged to her? And ... he drew a sharp breath. Had the 'summat being dragged across the yard' been not tobacco casks but Emma and Lily?

It seemed the thought leapt the barrier of space, slipped silently from mind to mind. 'You thinks the same as me.' Timothy breathed against bands of fear tightening across his chest. 'You thinks it weren't casks of baccy being moved from that yard but Lily and Emma, you thinks...'

'I'm thinking nothing of the kind!' Mark barked the lie. Adding to the lad's anxiety could only result in hysteria. 'What I am thinking is we will gain nothing by going into that bar room and questioning those men; were they up to no good with Gilmore they are highly unlikely to admit to it.'

'So what do we do!' Timothy snapped. 'Whatever it be we won't do it standin' 'ere!'

Glancing once more about the darkened market square Mark strode back to his carriage. He had no intention of standing there.

'You underestimated me, Emma, you and Fenton both.'

Henrietta knelt beside the figure slumped to the floor of the potting shed.

'He by thinking I would never go against him and you by thinking I would be fool enough to leave your hand untied. But Henrietta Gilmore is no fool.'

The last was said on a laugh as she knotted the gag replaced about the mouth of the girl whom a blow to the head with a clay pot had knocked unconscious.

Henrietta rose to her feet and glanced to where the younger girl lay. There was no possibility of either of them breaking free and there was time yet to take diary and letter to the house. Fumbling for skirt and blouse she could not find in darkness cast by the death of the candle flame she stood for a moment. The housekeeper would have returned and be in her bed and Fenton? He was not home yet or she would have heard the carriage on the drive. No one would see her.

Standing in the garden, she listened. The road so busy by day lay silent, the absence of sound lending an eerie sense to the night, a sense of eyes watching, of figures unseen. Those were the thoughts of children afraid of the dark! Impatient with herself she pushed the thought away. One need not be afraid of a friend and tonight darkness was the friend of Henrietta Gilmore; its cloak would cover the spectacle of two figures being bundled bound and gagged into a hansom cab, figures the selling of which to the brothels of the dockside would bring her as handsome a profit as doing the same had brought Fenton; and like him she would continue that lucrative business.

Two figures? Yes. She smiled to herself. She had told Emma the younger girl would after all be given to Fenton. But that was just another of the lies she had told her 'niece'. It was said only to increase Emma Lawrence's fear, fear her 'aunt' had derived so much satisfaction from creating. Emma had real love for that girl so giving her to think of that slight figure in Fenton's bed, to think her a plaything, a toy for his amusement, for entertainment which went beyond that of carnal pleasure, which often left his playthings bruised and battered, would cause her pain. But it would be more than physical pain Emma Lawrence would suffer, it would be the pain of the heart, the same torment she had gone through ... was still going through ... on knowing what Rachel had been subjected to. The suffering of one sister for another!

The inner smile surfaced to rest on thin lips.

Emma Lawrence would live that anguish again.

A breeze rustled leaves, disturbing the silence. Henrietta glanced across the garden, seeing trees emerge from the denseness of shadow, the house etching itself black on a background of grey. The sky which had been heavy with the threat of rain was spangled with stars, the edges of receding storm clouds rimmed with the brilliance of a golden moon. The cloak of darkness was being snatched away.

Boots crunching on the stone path sounding like the crack of pistol shots to her heightened nerves, Henrietta halted. Maybe going to the house was not such a good idea; perhaps she should hide the letter and the diary in the shed, leave them there until a more suitable time presented itself On the brink of returning there she once again hesitated. Fenton had talked again of selling the house, had said having the grounds landscaped would increase the chances of a profitable sale. Landscaping would probably include demolition of an old potting shed; that in itself was of no consequence but Fenton's volatility was; any moment could see that shed being torn down. So it must be the house, that at least would not be destroyed. Having book and letter hidden there would allow her time to find herself a lawyer, to take advice on possible ways of keeping what she had taken from Emma Lawrence out of the clutches of Fenton. Yes, it was best she did not leave her trophies in that shed.

She had not thought of this! Clara Thomas had locked up before going to bed. The kitchen door refused to open and Henrietta fumed silently. Knocking for the woman to come let her in was not an option; the noise of it would most certainly attract the attention of anyone passing. Besides, how would she explain being dressed as she was? The rear of the house was locked but the door at the front? Fenton more often than not returned home intoxicated, sometimes so drunk he could not put a key in the lock. Maybe as had been done on previous occasions the door had been 'mistakenly' left unsecured, Clara Thomas, like herself, disliking to be wakened in the early hours by a man too drunk to let himself in. Could that 'mistake' have been made tonight? Did she have time to check? Listening a few more seconds to the reassuring silence she walked quickly to the front of the house.

'He could be anywhere, there's at least forty drinkin' houses in the town not to count places such as the George or the Talbot and he could be in any one of 'em; I says we should have looked first in the bar room of the Turk's Head, we was right outside, it wouldn't have taken no more than a minute.'

'And no more than a minute for you to go haranguing those men,' Mark answered the lad climbing beside him into the carriage. 'You have no proof of what you heard them say so they would be in the right if they sent you on your way with a thick ear.'

He understood the anxiety, the pressure Timothy was under; didn't he feel the same worry for the safety of Emma? Setting the horse to a steady pace Mark answered, 'The men you heard talking, they said they would do with Perry what they had done with Gilmore.'

'So?'

'So if my guess is correct then Gilmore received a beating at their hands and the man Perry is about to be afforded the same.'

'What do that get we?'

Mark's mouth firmed. 'Answers. If we can find Perry before they do, if we tell him you overheard he is next in line for a beating but that we will see to it that does not happen provided he tells us what he knows regarding Gilmore and the child those men spoke of, then it is possible he will divulge that information.'

'And if he don't be much of a canary, if he don't "sing" then what?'

'Then we threaten him with the law. If as was said in that yard Gilmore and Perry are hand in glove then to tell him we know of the circumstances surrounding the disappearance of a girl named Sarah, that we know he and Gilmore are partners and that we will inform the police of not only our suspicions of that association but of tonight's activities in the yard of the tobacco shop, that should loosen his tongue.'

'But Perry weren't in Lawrence's yard, he couldn't 'ave been, or them men wouldn't be threatenin' to "do with Perry what we done with Gilmore", they would 'ave done one at the same time they done the other.'

'But you saw him, you saw both Perry and Gilmore climb into a carriage and drive away.'

Timothy swung to the man sitting beside him. 'No. I seen only the back of that carriage, I d'ain't see who were in it.'

Nearing the top of the High Street Mark glanced at a large ornate lantern hung above the door of the Lamp public house. 'You know that,' he said, 'but Perry does not. Neither Gilmore nor he would welcome attention being drawn to what happened tonight, the unsavoury prospect of disproving your word in full glare of a magistrate's court would most certainly not be to the liking of either man ... providing of course you were to give that word.'

'...I tells you what one be paddlin' up to his neck in the other'll be swimmin'...'

'...thick as thieves they be...'

'...what one knows the other knows...'

'...we all seen that little wench's body...'

'...we all seen what were done to 'er...'

Acrobats in Timothy's mind, sentences leaped and tumbled, a final one vaulting over the rest.

'...I'll lay odds Jud Perry knows it an' all...'

Perry! Timothy held the name, wanting to spit from his tongue. It had been Jud Perry in the cemetery along of Wood Green. Perry who had tried to snatch Lily. Perry who had snarled to Emma, *'This don't be the last of our meetin', mark that well ... it don't be the last!'*

Had the 'little wench' spoke of tonight proved a more successful effort? The one from Russell Street, had she been another? Would Perry be abducting girls for himself alone?

'...what one be paddlin' up to his neck in the other'll be swimmin' in...'

Timothy's teeth clenched. Gilmore and Perry! The waters they played in were thick with muck, they were strewn with the filth of the body trade.

Would he lie about what he had seen in that yard, would he give his word he had seen Perry when he had not?

Eyes held steady on those of the older man Timothy's reply was firm. 'Would I give my word to a magistrate? I'd give it to the Angel Gabriel hisself if it means havin' the like of Perry brought to book.'

The door had been left unlocked. A sigh of relief silent on her lips Henrietta stood listening. No sound from the downstairs rooms, only silence from upper ones but the gaslights here in the hall, though turned low, still glowed. Fenton? She glanced toward the staircase, its upper reaches almost lost among shadows. Inebriated as usual he had ignored the gaslights, probably grabbed the brandy decanter and gone up to bed. But he had not come home since her own return; she

361

would have heard the carriage. How long had he been back? Had he shouted for her? Had he gone to her room when she had not answered? Would he be in there now waiting for her to arrive? He would know seeing the clothing she was dressed in that she had not been sitting home all evening; they if nothing else would betray the fact she had been up to something, that she had something to hide and that would afford him more pleasurable minutes beating his wife until the pain of it had her hand over the diary and the letter. Quickly then, hide both and get back to the potting shed.

She glanced about the dimmed hall. No, not here, that maid had been well taught in the work-house; to leave a corner, even the darkest one, with a trace of dust would lead to the sting of a willow cane about the shoulders. No, hide what had been gained in this part of the house and Scarface would find it. But she could not risk going to her bedroom, could not risk coming face to face with Fenton. So where? Where? Insistent as a drumbeat it throbbed in her brain. Then like a reprieve the answer came. The sitting room! Put them beneath the cushion of the chair she was accustomed to sitting in, and they could wait there until the time proved favourable for putting them elsewhere.

If only it had not been necessary to wear these clumsy boots! But not wearing them, teaming work-stained labourer's jacket and trousers with women's more dainty shoes, would have brought curious stares. Should she take them off, carry them? No. Removing boots and replacing the same required time and that she could not spare.

Book and letter ready in hand, she rose ballerina-fashion to the tips of her toes only to mutter angrily as the first awkward step had her trip precariously, bringing iron-studded heels to ring on the polished parquet floor.

It was her own heart! The sound crashing in her ears was the thud of her own heart. Henrietta released the breath jammed in her throat.

She had come this far, too far to let nerves defeat her. Tuning out the rapid beat Henrietta listened a moment to the silence beneath it then, each step a masterstroke of quiet, walked into the sitting room.

32

Lying to the Angel Gabriel might receive forgiveness in heaven but lying to a magistrate in his court most certainly would not. Perjury was an offence looked on with utmost severity by the law and consequently punishment was awarded with the same intolerant measure. For himself he would take the chance of being found to lie but the lad should not be asked to do likewise.

'Timothy.' Mark Halstead spoke quietly. 'Perhaps it would be best for you to return to Lea Brook, I will find Perry and–'

'Mr Halstead.' Timothy's face as he interrupted the man beside him was tight as his voice was curt. 'Lily be my sister and it be my duty as well as my privilege to look to her wellbeing 'til the day her chooses to wed and though Emma be sister to me only through friendship and love I claims that same privilege along of her. So with respect I tells you your suggestion don't be to my likin', I be goin' to search for Perry and he'll tell me what I asks or could be he'll be afore me in talkin' with the Angel Gabriel.'

Following the curve of the narrow High Street on to the High Bullen, its wide road quiet after the day's busy traffic Mark's brief inner smile acknowledged an answer which once again showed the man in the making, a man who knew his own mind and had the tenacity to stay with it.

'You be makin' for Gilmore's place?' Timothy's question came as the carriage passed the graceful Tudor Oakswell Hall, night shadows obscuring ancient time-darkened timbers leaving chimneys seemingly floating on the grey sea of the sky.

A nod Mark's reply Timothy continued. 'Even if he be home it's likely he won't speak with you.'

'I shall at least have given him the choice.'

'Choice?'

'Of speaking with me or speaking with the police.'

The frown hidden by darkness was clear in Timothy's 'The coppers ... you don't 'ave reason to bring them in, you don't 'ave proof Gilmore be involved.'

'And Gilmore has no evidence to the contrary. Once he hears Perry has revealed everything then I think he will talk with us if only to deny his own complicity.'

'But that be lying.'

Grim in its humour Mark's answer carried on a

transitory laugh. 'It seems the blessed Archangel is due for a busy time.'

'Why not talk with Perry afore goin' to see Gilmore?'

'With so many choices of where to spend his evening it could be hours before we catch up with the man.'

'Not if you turns this carriage now.'

'Go back!' A note of recrimination laced Mark's reply. 'You mean you have known all along where Perry could be located!'

'If located means found then no, I ain't knowed it all along but I knows it now; that be him, that be Jud Perry.'

Following the direction in which Timothy pointed Mark's glance rested on a man standing in the doorway of a dimly lit tavern, a man whose narrow rat-like features showed in the flare of a match held to a cigarette.

'I don't know no Gilmore,' Jud Perry snapped at the figure confronting him, a short-handled whip tapping menacingly against a booted calf.

'That is not what we have heard.'

'Then y've 'eard wrong.'

'Seemingly!' Mark nodded. 'I hope the rest of what was heard proves equally wrong.'

'Meanin'?'

'Meaning the threat made against you.'

'Threat! Be that your way of snarin' a man into sayin' what don't be true?'

'Not at all,' Mark answered the snide retort. 'I am making no threat.'

Flicking away a half-smoked cigarette Jud

Perry's irritation at being halted flared anew. 'Then if you be mekin' no threat why stop a man in his tracks?'

'Simply to do you a service.'

'Huh!' Perry laughed. 'Be a service, does it, askin' of a man's dealin's, who it be he does or don't 'ave business with? Well this time you has your snout in the wrong trough!'

'Mmm.' Mark shrugged. 'It seems we were mistaken in our intention.'

'Ain't no mistaken about it. I've said as I don't 'ave the knowin' of this Gilmore so stand aside an' let me pass or it might be you finds y' self answerin' a few questions ... them asked by a constable.'

Having remained silent during the interchange Timothy added his own contribution. 'That be more than probable, p'raps we will answer questions put by the coppers, questions like do we 'ave any idea who it were done for Jud Perry? Who it were beat the life out of him? We could answer that while we d'ain't 'ave the seein' of it we did hear threat of the same, threat made by Isaac Timmins and Zach Fletcher as well as Alf Simkin and Bert Lloyd.'

Half recognition which had drifted with those voices playing again and again in his mind having sprung into full recognition, Timothy's naming of the men rang with a confidence that had Perry snatch a sharp breath.

Watching the other man closely, seeing the shaking hands before they plunged into the pockets of the shabby coat, Mark knew Timothy's words had gone home.

'I see you are acquainted with the men spoken of.'

'He knows 'em same as he knows what they be capable of doin'.'

'Even so.' Mark stepped aside. 'We should not delay Mr Perry any longer.'

Meeting Perry's glance full on Timothy forced a smile. 'I 'pologises for hindering of you.' Then looking to Mark added in an undertone just loud enough to he heard by Perry, 'Best let him move on while he still has legs to carry him.'

Shrill, echoing the anxiety betrayed in the trembling of his hands, Perry called as the two turned away. 'What be you sayin' regards Timmins and the others?'

Beside the carriage Timothy turned to look at the man his very soul despised. 'I were thinkin' to tell what I overheard being discussed in the yard of Lawrence baccy shop but seein' you don't know any man the name of Gilmore then the tellin' don't be important. You can explain their mistake same as you explained ours, tell Timmins and his mates they be wrong in puttin' you alongside of Gilmore.'

Gilmore had been furious when told their association was finished; furious enough to hire men to take retribution for him? Maybe it was true, what the lad said, that he had overheard some bargain being struck, a bargain that meant Jud Perry getting a hiding! A sensation like cold water plunged along Perry's spine. There could be no other reason Gilmore would take men into that yard, he wouldn't risk anyone seeing barrels far too big for the carrying of tobacco, the amounts of which would keep not four but several hundred women rolling cigarettes unless ... he stiffened as yet another thought, more icy than the rest, surged into his mind. A man with breath in his body could be a man capable of talking! Gilmore would not chance that, his money would not be spent simply on a pound of flesh. He would want the whole carcass; Gilmore was no stranger to murdering young girls but of a man ... he would pay others to do that job for him.

'Wait!' he called after the departing carriage but the carriage did not stop.

'Good evening.'

Spoken from a quiet corner of the heavily shadowed room the greeting had Henrietta choke on the sting of nerves biting at her throat.

'Fenton!'

A subdued half laugh fingered the darkness. 'No, not Fenton.'

A burglar! A thief come to rob the house! Hands instinctively tightening on the diary and letter Henrietta stood perfectly still though her mind raced. To scream would bring Fenton and that would lose her everything today had brought her and also what she stood yet to gain by selling the two lying bound and gagged in the potting shed; Fenton would take it all, but if he were too drunk to hear the housekeeper would not be, she would come downstairs. But the clothes, the jacket and trousers, she could not have the woman see her dressed as she was; and supposing she did scream the burglar would most certainly hit her over the head, knock her senseless, and if she was not in that shed when Perry arrived he would take Emma and the girl. He would pocket the money and she would be unable to do anything about it.

That was not going to happen! It had been *her* quick thinking had made that child come into the garden, *hers* the brain that produced the plausible excuse for not entering the house, *hers* the hand which had written and delivered that note to Emma Lawrence and it would be *she*, Henrietta Gilmore, and no one else, would reap the reward.

Determination stronger than the nervous hold on her throat lending her plausible confidence she said, 'Whoever you are I suggest you leave quickly. My husband is just beyond the door, he always carries a pistol and never hesitates in the using of it, and my housekeeper is in the kitchen.'

'I 'ave to contradict you again, your housekeeper don't be in the kitchen.'

Was that the way the thief had gained entrance? But the door had been locked, a window then, a window in the...

The sudden bright gleam of a gasolier turned to its full halted Henrietta's thoughts; she turned to face the intruder.

'You!' she snapped. 'What do you think you are doing, you have no business being in this room.'

'Oh, I 'ave business.' Clara Thomas's mouth held no smile. 'Seems you've had a bit an' all judgin' by what y'be wearing.'

Anger her ally, Henrietta called on its support saying icily, 'What I choose to wear is none of your concern.'

'True.' Clara nodded. 'Same as your claiming

to go visitin' of your sister were no concern of mine, 'cept I knowed it were no sister you met with.'

Had this woman followed her? Had she seen her speaking with Perry that day in the Turk's Head? Was that the reason for her sitting waiting in the dark, was that what this charade was all about? Did she hope to get money in exchange for keeping her mouth shut? Blackmail! Henrietta almost laughed. The poor fool hadn't intelligence enough to realise such an accusation made publicly could only bring herself a flogging and a prison sentence. Clara Thomas really should have sense enough to know the word of a menial would mean nothing against that of a woman of substance. The contempt behind the thought showing vividly in cold eyes she said, 'Are you calling me a liar?'

Hands clasped across dark skirts Clara chose her words. 'Liar ... yes, but that be just one of the names I puts to you, others be callous cheat, malicious deceitful impostor, a woman so mindful of her own welfare her turned not only a blind eye to the torment her husband visited on two children of a woman who believed her a friend, but also turned her back on her own family, changed her very birth name, Nellie not being posh enough.'

'How do you know–' Realising her mistake Henrietta broke off but the other woman's look said it was too late.

Clara clenched her teeth on a long pain-filled breath as she held the glance of the woman she felt only contempt for. 'How?' She released the breath in a long shuddering sigh. 'How do I know what you did, how you had brothers and sisters given over to the mercy of the parish, the kind of mercy that had the two youngest dead of fever in naught but a month, the mercy that has folk old afore their time? That be why you had no recognising of me. It were the workhouse put these lines on my face, the merciful institution that had a young girl work every God-given hour of the day in a steam-filled hell they called a laundry an' when that were done then the evenings were given to scrubbing floors and stairs then scrubbing 'em again not cos of 'em not being washed clean enough, but cos of the spite of wardresses with no other means of amusin' theirselves. Yes Nellie, they found satisfaction in causing a young wench to drop from weariness as you found yours in leavin' her to it.'

'That's a lie.'

'It be no lie.' Clara met the snarl. 'Nellie Platt had no likin' for the caring of brothers and sisters so it were the workhouse for them and the forgettin' of Drew's Court for her. But I never forgot who put us in that workhouse, I never forgot, Nellie, and I'll never forgive.'

'What do you want?'

'Huh!' Clara's smile was pure scorn. 'You give naught when we were kids and I expects naught from you now.'

'No!' Henrietta's mouth snapped on the word. 'Then why come here, why pretend to be somebody you're not?'

'That be quite a story, Nellie.'

She had to be got rid of, Perry would be here any minute! Desperate to get back to the garden shed Henrietta resorted to pompous indignation.

'I shall listen to no more of your lies, you will leave this house immediately or I will call my husband and he will put you out.'

'I don't think so, Nellie, in fact you shouldn't go countin' on seein' Fenton Gilmore, not for some time.'

'What do you mean?'

'I means he be busy explaining to a man what happened to the daughter who were snatched from Russell Street.'

So Fenton wasn't home, he wasn't upstairs in his bedroom. Wanting to keep her relief at that to herself Henrietta turned her back saying acidly, 'More lies.'

'"...yes I closed Rachel Lawrence's mouth, same as I closed the mouth of the one I took from Russell Street..." You remember them words, Nellie? Words spoke in this very room.'

Quietly said, it made Henrietta's spine tingle. But she must not allow alarm to show. Turning with slow deliberation, her tone heavy with sarcasm, she gave a brief repudiating swing of her head. 'You have no proof.'

'Ain't me as needs proof,' Clara returned. 'It be Fenton Gilmore and you be needing proof: him to convince that child's father he be no child snatcher and you, Nellie, you'll need to convince a judge you be no accomplice in murder.'

'Murder!' Henrietta gasped. 'Are you out of your mind!'

'No, Nellie, I be in my right mind. There were naught I could do for the child of Mary Lawrence, a child you knowed were being abused yet

372

did naught to stop. You helped your husband murder that girl by turning a blind eye, then you helped cover it up by claiming he were away from Wednesbury when her were killed. That be known as "accessory after the fact".'

She had to maintain a front, hold on to her composure if she were to talk her way out of this. Henrietta forced down the consternation fluttering in her throat to say with pretended coolness, 'You were not in this house, all you have is gossip, words heard from others and for which you have no sound basis, so you will simply be shouting in the wind!'

'But I were in this house when Fenton Gilmore talked of his murdering two wenches, when he said for you to find Emma Lawrence so her could be put alongside her sister, meaning her too could be put in the grave. Help him hide all trace of his lies and filth, that be all the use he has for you, Nellie, for his Drew's Court scum.'

So she had heard that also, heard it and no doubt relished repeating it; but as with Fenton she would be given cause to regret. Henrietta's mind brewed venom. Tomorrow she would lay a charge of robbery, of finding her housekeeper about to depart with items of jewellery taken from her mistress's bedroom. Clara Thomas would learn any claim made against the Gilmores would be looked on as a way of saving herself from a prison sentence and as such would be ignored.

Staring at the sister she had literally forgotten, hoping for the same blessing to be granted again very soon, Henrietta said snidely, 'So who found a use for you ... or is it no man has? That is why you came here asking to be given a post, out of jealousy for what I have while you have nothing.'

Clara shook her head again. 'Jealousy don't 'ave the feet that brought me to this house.'

Aware of time slipping rapidly away, every lost second adding to the worry of Perry making away with Emma and the girl, Henrietta began, 'I don't care what brought you...'

'Neither did you care about five kids sent to the workhouse.' Clara's hands held across her stomach clenched with convulsive anger. 'What the eye don't see then the heart don't grieve over, were your attitude. But I seen, I seen the tears of a two-year-old sister so frightened her lost the way of speech, I seen the unhappiness of an eight-year-old brother I were not allowed to meet with or speak to. Once a week at Sunday church service I would have sight of him sat along with the rest of the men and boys separated from female contact even though they be relatives, set apart as were all workhouse inmates from other members of the congregation, segregated for the paupers we were. Four years I lived with the nightmare of watching them sink lower under the oppression of life in that institution, my nightly request of heaven was to beg some miracle would see us free. It came soon after I turned fourteen, the miracle I prayed for, huh!' She laughed ironically. 'It were a miracle put me into service, put me to labour as hard and long as that I had left behind. It were years afore I were allowed an afternoon off but when I did I visited the workhouse. Always I were told inmates weren't allowed of no visitors. Then with our sister's fourteenth year I went to claim her, to bring her away from that mausoleum.'

This woman amid her lies would overturn everything; Perry would take the woman and the girl *she* had collected and no kind of threat would have him hand over the money got from a whorehouse. Henrietta's thin lips curled in on themselves, the stare of cold grey eyes signalling mounting irritation. 'So!' she snapped, 'you got your snivelling sister, what do I care...'

Calmness Clara had forced herself to observe cracked with the snap of a breaking iceberg, shards of it hurling from her lips.

'*Our* sister!' Cold, lethal as a striking sword, it sliced through Henrietta's cynical attempt to answer. '*Our* sister, Nellie ... and you are going to care, yes by God I swear you are going to care!'

33

Her head swimming from the force of the blow that had sent her crashing to the floor, eyes blind in the darkness, Emma moaned softly. Where was she? Why could she not see? Why could she not move? But questions were painful, she didn't want to think, didn't want to move. Beginning to sink back into peaceful oblivion Emma frowned rejection at the call of her mind. She wanted sleep, just to sleep. The activity of her brain was as irritating as the constant prod of a finger and she sighed displeasure. Why would this irksome thing not go away? Why... The thought died at the instant of a sound, a sound breaking through the barrier of lethargy allowing memory to return.

'...*you Emma will be collected and removed ... the girl I shall give to Fenton...*'

Senses snatched so swiftly back to reality, tingling as though touched by a hot iron, Emma's breath caught at the words pouring into her mind. Henrietta had returned, returned in order to carry out her threat. Or was part of that action, the most horrifying part, already accomplished, had Lily been given over to Fenton? Was he even now practising his depravity on the girl? No! Emma's heart screamed its silent pain. Not that, please God not that, let Henrietta do what she would with Emma Lawrence, give *her* to Fenton in place of Lily, kill her even but please ... please spare Lily.

Hidden from her in the soft blackness the shuffling step of uncertain feet brushed the stillness. The woman was searching for a candle. Hope that Henrietta would have lighted her way from the house with a lantern disappeared and with it hope that someone might have seen and become suspicious at the sight of a lantern bobbing about the garden so late at night and thus followed to the shed. Trembling with disappointment Emma released her pent-up breath only to catch it again at a fresh sound.

'...*you will be collected and removed...*'

It rang in her brain.

Collected by whom? Removed to where and for what purpose?

'Damn!'

Tension vibrated in the muttered expletive and

Emma's nerves answered with their own trepidation. It was not Henrietta had uttered that word; though her natural tone was deeper than that of most women it was not so sonorous.

Fenton!

Emma's senses rocked. He must have got from his wife the fact Emma Lawrence was a prisoner in the potting shed.

Revulsion rolling in her throat she hunched into herself, trying to merge deeper into the ink-black darkness.

Fenton Gilmore had Lily; now he had come for her.

The faint silhouette of a smile touching her lips Clara Thomas stared at the woman who for so many years had lived in her mind.

'Yes Nellie,' she said stingingly, 'you be going to care, I made myself that promise and I be going to see it through.'

Perry could be here, he could even now be in that shed. Losing money to that man was bad enough but worse still could be Fenton returning. It didn't matter if he found this woman with her stupid claims but his seeing the letter and the diary would lose her everything. Henrietta's mind whirled. She could grab the poker, strike her down, say she had done it in self-defence, that when discovering her in the act of robbery she herself had been attacked. Glancing toward the fireplace with its heavy brass fire irons she was struck by a new thought. Clara Thomas had had a lifetime of hard physical work, she was maybe strong enough to ward off an assault, possibly even reverse it. That was not the way. Henrietta returned her glance to the dark-skirted figure. Any attack she made must be the spoken kind. Heedless for the moment of her bizarre apparel Henrietta drew herself up, once more the mistress in full control, a chatelaine whose supremacy could not be held in question.

She said cynically, 'I have no interest in your fantasies and certainly none in any self-made promise but I warn you my husband will take a very different view so for your own sake I advise you to leave now.'

'Oh yes, Fenton.' Clara nodded. 'But like I said, Nellie, he be talkin' with a man whose little wench were taken off the street, a child who hasn't been seen since.'

'...*the one I took from Russell Street...*'

Fenton had screeched those words at her during a confrontation in the sitting room. Memory returned the scene to Henrietta, a scene with a maid scuffling through the door.

'She told on Fenton.' Malignant, it slid between clamped teeth. 'Scarface, she–'

With all the speed of a striking snake Clara's hand lashed a slap that had Henrietta sway on her feet. 'Don't!' Narrowed eyes, corrosive with anger, burned across the room, 'Don't you ever call her that again for if you do you 'ave my vow I'll lay the same mark to you. That scar were given for naught worse than having a heavy basket of laundry drop to the ground and the first time of my seeing it were the day I started hating Nellie Platt; yes Nellie, that scar be not only an injury to that girl's face, it be a wound to her soul, a hurt you deepened by treating her with the arrogance you thought made you a lady, and Gilmore with his vicious threats. Him and you, Nellie, together you made that wench's life a misery just as y'self done of your own brothers and sisters; but you be going to apologise.'

Pride stinging as much as her face Henrietta's composure faltered. Any of that reaching the ears of people who mattered … it must not be allowed to happen.

'Tell,' she swallowed against the indignity, 'tell Stokes she will be paid…'

Clara's scorn ripped across the quiet room. 'Another mouth shut so Fenton Gilmore and his wife can go on living in peace with their misdoings. No, Nellie, not this time; and it weren't Millie Stokes let word of Fenton's doings reach the ears it has, that act of vengeance be mine; I took it to Richard, yes, Nellie, to Richard, the brother you probably hoped never to hear of again; he let it "slip" when talking with men he works alongside.'

Richard! Henrietta frowned. So he also was in the town. 'I'd gone to the workhouse first chance I got.' Clara spoke softly as though only for herself 'It were a few weeks into her fourteenth year and I went to fetch my sister out, to bring her where I could look after her, to love her, but there were no Platt, there were no one of that name and nothing telling of any of the five of us ever having been there since a fire had destroyed most of the records. It weren't 'til I spoke with one of the wardresses who said of a Millie Stokes, a girl who'd been in that institution from being little more than a babby, p'raps if I talked with her I might learn what it were I were asking. Said Millie were in service somewhere in the town.'

Lifting out of partial reverie Clara's voice strengthened.

'I come to Wednesbury every week from then on, I come 'til I heard a stallholder say the name Millie. The wench were about to walk away when I asked would her spare a minute, p'raps her could tell me of my sister. It were when her turned to answer I seen the scar.'

'So you saw Millie Stokes' scar.' Henrietta was scathing. 'Am I supposed to burst into tears!'

'Oh there'll be a lot of them.' Clara met the sarcasm. 'Y'see Nellie, Millie Stokes be a name given when a wench wouldn't speak her own but the name of your maid don't be Millie Stokes, it be Miriam Platt ... your sister.'

Dead of fever, of an illness probably due to drinking infected water, infant twins, the carrying of whom had helped drain the life from a sick mother, had died almost at once when first being taken into the workhouse ... but the other three – why couldn't they have died as well!

Thought vitriolic as acid Henrietta glared at the woman whose very existence could prove a thorn in her own flesh. But she had not allowed her life to be blighted by them years ago and she could not ... *would not* ... have them blight it now. The poor-house had no record, no proof of having taken in a family by the name of Platt. Henrietta's mind worked like quicksilver. If Clara and Richard had, as it seemed, been planning some sort of revenge

380

then it was certain they would have told no one else of that intention. There would be nobody to connect their name to that of Henrietta Gilmore.

Folk had disappeared before as dealings with Perry ascertained; but Clara with her workworn features would be no financial asset to a brothel, and Scarface ... no customer would hand over good money to lie with that hence no whorehouse would have the buying of her.

But a house of prostitution was not the only means whereby a problem could be disposed of there were other ways. Accidents happened all the time, who was to say one befalling the Platts had not been accidental? Henrietta smiled to herself. An 'accident', a positively lethal 'accident', would be even more satisfactory; but that must come later. Right now it was essential to have the woman gone from the house.

A quick gasp concealing the truth cold in her heart, grey eyes expertly hiding the same, she injected a break in her voice as she answered, 'Miriam ... Miriam is...? Oh believe me, I didn't know.'

Clara's retort was blunt. 'Wouldn't 'ave made a difference had you knowed! You had no love for your own when you lived in Drew's Court and you be no different now; it were no heartache for you seem' them put away, it meant only freedom to go your own scheming way so don't go pretendin' a difference now. Miriam were kin you d'ain't want then and for certain her be a sister you don't be wantin' now.'

'Things were different then, I had nothing to give.'

'Y'could 'ave had love!' Clara scathed.

Repressing the retort rising rapid to her lips, a reply she knew would serve merely to prolong argument, Henrietta adopted a rueful tone. 'We all have things to regret...'

'Things!' Clara's intervention rang with scorn. 'A family be "things"! That was ever the way with you, Nellie, we were things you couldn't be rid of fast enough.'

Then as now! Henrietta held the validity of that close inside a lifetime of lies and deceit, saying next with the smoothness of silk, 'I ... I was afraid for you all, afraid I would only make life worse for you by having us stay together. But that is changed; please Clara go tell Mill ... Miriam I did not know she is my sister, tell her Felton and I will...'

'Take care of her? Oh, I be sure Gilmore would do that. But he don't be gettin' the chance and neither does you, Nellie. Should I believe what you says, which I don't, you won't be 'aving chance of caring for Miriam not for many a bright year you won't; y'see, Nellie, that husband of yourn will be hanged for murder and if heaven be right in *its* judgement 'Enrietta Gilmore'll find herself in a place worse than any workhouse.'

Pretence was sloughed away like the cast-off skin of a snake and Henrietta's look showed the full force of her disdain.

'Age has not improved a face which never was pretty nor has it been kind to a brain that was always stupid, but thinking the word of a jealous woman and a disgruntled girl with a blemished face will have either Fenton or myself suspected of any crime then you are even more stupid than I thought.'

'Miriam's face be scarred but her tongue bears no blemish, it don't be stained wi' lies nor will the words her speaks along of the law be marked by deceit. Her will witness only truth, the truth of hearing Fenton Gilmore admit to the killing of Rachel Lawrence and a young wench snatched from the street; that be what her'll testify and I'll be doing of the same.'

About to reply, Henrietta shot a glance toward the door, a sound catching her ear. Fenton! Nerves already quivering with tension vibrated like plucked strings. Fenton was back – the diary! The letter! He must not see them, he must not see them. Like a warning klaxon the words roared in her head then ... the chair, the cushion ... she had come into the house to hide book and letter beneath the cushion of the chair. Memory led her through the maze of suspense clouding her mind as she thrust them quickly into the hiding place.

Turning to face the shout, tension giving way to anger, Henrietta snapped. 'You fool ... you were not supposed to come into the house.'

'I be here for my money for what–' Frowning in confusion Jud Perry broke off, his glance running over the figure facing him. 'You,' he frowned more deeply, 'you be the one I talked with, the one sayin' you'd pay to 'ave me turn my back on Gilmore. I thought you 'aving me come 'ere tonight to collect them wenches from this place were a ruse to throw suspicion on Gilmore but I 'ad no thought...' He laughed deep in his throat.

383

'Christ, I 'ad no thought I were talkin' wi' a woman; but that meks no matter, man or woman you still be goin' to pay what were agreed.'

'Get out!'

Thin lips smeared with a rictus smile, fox-like eyes narrowing, greasy hair glinting wetly in the yellowy light, Perry replied low, the ominous threat of an animal at bay.

'Oh no,' he snarled, 'I come to do a job that already be done but that don't go to say I don't be wantin' the money.'

'Done!' Henrietta stared. 'What do you mean?'

'What I says, that shed were empty and well you knows it, Gilmore already had them wenches off to Brummajum's whorehouses afore I got 'ere.'

The rough vernacular employed in her earlier meetings with Perry forgotten, Henrietta snapped. 'Fenton knows nothing of their being in that potting shed.'

'I finds that 'ard to chew,' Perry sneered. 'Them wenches weren't like to be flies to your spider, they were 'ardly like to walk into your "parlour" so it 'ad to be Gilmore.'

'Yes, Gilmore.' Ice-bound eyes glittered. 'But not the Gilmore you think it to have been, not Fenton but Henrietta … his wife.'

'Does her expect me to believe that!' For the first time since marching into the room Perry glanced at Clara.

The jeer awakening the same resentment Fenton's sneering always aroused in her Henrietta gave way fully to anger.

'You believe what your limited mind would have

you believe but the fact remains it was I, Henrietta Gilmore, enticed that child here, I who wrote to Emma Lawrence, I who put into her hand a letter along with a cheap glass cameo, a letter saying the child would be exchanged for the diary written by Rachel Lawrence. But there was no exchange made. I drugged the child and then Emma, then while she slept bound and gagged them both.'

Perry's eyes gleamed, his brain quickly calculating what, if any, potential could be gained from that confession. 'That be interestin',' he said, self-interest thickening the reply, 'as it could be should it reach the ears of the coppers.'

Malicious, venomous in her assured superiority Henrietta answered the cynically smiling Perry in reciprocal vein. 'It would be very interesting speaking with the police, telling them how you broke into this house, how you robbed and threatened to return to kill me should I speak of it; a man with the reputation you enjoy in the town...' She laughed, a short hard sound cut off almost at once. 'Do you really think a magistrate would believe you came for any other reason?'

'Maybe not, Mrs Gilmore, but I feel sure he would believe me.'

At the edge of the doorway stood a figure, a figure that made the blood drain from Henrietta's face.

34

'*Damn.*'

The voice had her body tremble. Fenton! She had thought, Fenton had been told of her lying captive in the potting shed and had come to get her!

'*It were said as there would be two.*'

It had come from somewhere in the darkness, a voice she had realised was not that of Fenton Gilmore yet that had brought no reassurance.

'*Two you were told...*'

It had snapped agitation.

'*...then where is the second one?*'

The second one! Emma's breath tightened on hearing that question. It could only refer to herself, which meant Fenton had already taken Lily.

Sickness held back by the gag had rolled in her throat. The young girl who had trusted her, who had called her sister, was even now in the hands of the man who had abused two young women and murdered one. Lily! Her very soul had cried but in the darkness of that shed she had known it was to no avail. Lily was gone and Emma Lawrence was to blame, for if she had not gone with them to that hovel in Lea Brook, had she not stayed on with the Elsmores then Lily would be safe home with her brother.

'*There is no other here ... if you are lying, if you*'

have collected both…'

'I ain't… I swears to you I ain't; dealer said there be a pair of 'em, that I were to fetch both and do wi' 'em same as 'ad been done afore.'

'Pray, Perry … pray very hard I don't find otherwise for if I do the hangman will be far too late to execute your sentence!'

It had been fear had her mind play tricks on her, fear of being found, of where that would lead, had caused her to imagine one of those voices was known to her, then:

'…it 'as to be Gilmore 'as teken her, the one as said for me to fetch 'em must 'ave gone a changin' of the deal and sold 'em on to Gilmore, but that won't be the last of our meetin'…'

'This don't be the last of our meetin', mark that well … it don't be the last!'

As if a curtain was snatched back her mind had suddenly presented the picture of a thick-set man, eyes cold and narrow, thin mouth spilling rage as he faced a boy and a young woman who had dared defy him. The man at the cemetery! The one who had attempted to snatch Lily, whose parting words threatening herself were the same as she was hearing now. He was here in the shed.

Realisation had added to the panic already freezing her veins and she had forced her body to roll, hoping the movement would take her further into the darkness, perhaps even under the bench, but she had simply knocked against the wooden structure, the resulting topple of plant pots making the rough voice say to stand still until he struck a match.

She had heard the brittle sound of a match

head being dragged across a gritty surface, a sound that had scraped her every nerve, only the silent cries of fear drowning it in her ears.

There had come the brilliant flare of light and behind it a figure, a figure blending more into shadow as the bright gleam blinded her vision, a figure reaching for her.

Pulses skipping with the memory Emma's lips pressed together as she tried to force away the thoughts, but the past refused to relinquish its hold on her mind.

Beneath her the ground where she had fallen had smelled of must and damp yet she had pressed herself on to it in an effort to avoid those searching hands but they had gripped her shoulders, lifting her to her feet, snatching her against a hard body.

'Emma...'

Her fingers stilled, she let memory take its course, allowing herself to feel again the hand cradling her head to a chest where the beat of the heart within sounded loud as a drumbeat; yet for all its wild racing it had not silenced the words breathed against her hair.

'Emma...'

It had paused on a long breath drawn to steady the fierce tide of emotion she had felt rippling through that taut frame yet as those arms had tightened even more the break in the voice registered lack of success.

'Emma...'

It had murmured as though through teeth clenched against some physical pain.

'I... *Oh my God, I thought I had lost you... Oh*

Emma my love ... my love.'

But it had been only imagination; that tender stroking of her hair, those whispered words, had to have been produced by a mind twisted with fear, a subconscious attempt at restoring mental comfort.

How could her brain trick her that way, her own mind treat her so cruelly?

She had to stop thinking about that whole terrible evening; only that way would the pain in her heart go away. Determined to put thought into practice she crossed to the dresser with its odd assortment of cups and plates. She would put the book in a drawer, it could stay there until the rest of her work was done; but even before she reached the other side of the small cramped room the past slipped its sinuous arms about her.

Another match had been struck, its spread in the darkness revealing the face of her rescuer; a tight closed face which echoed none of that whispered softness. With the aid of the match flame Mark Halstead had removed the gag from her mouth and cut the strings binding her hands and feet then without a word had helped her from the shed.

'Lily?' she had choked the name.

'Lily is safe, she is with her brother.'

'Thank heaven.'

It had been a whisper but the words coming to her in that shadowed garden, the *'Thank heaven you are both safe! You should have...'* had throbbed with an undercurrent of tension, which might have gone further had not a small figure hurled itself forward and Lily sobbed her own relief against Emma's skirts,

'*Lord, Emma, you two 'ave had the life scared outta Mark and me...*' Timothy's arms had joined those of Lily, his hug fierce.

Mark and me. Emma's wry smile reflected an inner hurt. Mark Halstead had not echoed that sentiment; instead he had glanced beyond her to the man who had followed from the potting shed.

'*Remember our agreement, Perry,*' he had snapped, '*keep to it or take the consequences.*'

He had turned to her then with a curt order for her to stay with Lily in the carriage drawn against the rear gate. Had it been the brusqueness of those words or disappointment at realising the trick fear had played on her which brought her own sharp refusal?

The momentary silence following had the hallmark of an explosion but then with a word to Timothy to keep firm hold of Lily he had turned on his heel.

She didn't want to remember. Emma stared unseeingly at crockery set neatly on the dresser. She did not want to see the pictures in her mind, the dreams which plagued her sleep, she wanted only what could be seen and touched; the rest, the memories, must be blotted out. How otherwise could she live, how to go on day to day while her heart cried out for something she could never have? Tears crowding her throat, she clasped the book to her chest. 'Help me, Rachel,' she murmured, 'help me to forget.' But before the whisper dropped into silence the pictures returned with perfect clarity.

Timothy walked to one side of her with Lily at the other, both holding tightly to her hands. The door to the front of the house stood open.

Caught fast in the net cast by her yesterdays Emma relived the events of a week ago.

They had followed after Perry and Mark Halstead, he again softly reminding the other man of some prearranged agreement before they entered the house. But only Perry had stepped into the living room while they had listened from the hall, listened to Henrietta confessing to abduction and enforced theft. Then Mark Halstead had entered the room, saying, *'Maybe not Mrs Gilmore, but I feel sure he would believe me'* had Henrietta snarl, *'Get out ... get out of my house'*.

Emma 'watched' herself release the hands holding hers, 'saw' herself walk into the living room hearing again in her mind her own words, *'No, this house is not yours it is mine.'*

A face drained of colour had swivelled toward her, the breath in Henrietta's throat a strangled slush of sound, but almost immediately she had recovered from shock.

Standing in the quiet emptiness of the house Emma saw again the exultant smile, the flush of triumph return a bloom of colour to sallow cheeks.

'No,' Henrietta had virtually crowed. *'Beechcroft ceased to be yours the day your parents died. From the very moment of hearing that news this house, the business, everything you might otherwise have inherited became ours, mine and Fenton's. We always intended it to be that way and now,'* she had laughed, *'I have your signed deed of gift.'*

The letter and Rachel's diary: she had handed them to Henrietta in exchange for Lily's release. But Henrietta had not kept to that agreement. Saying so, repeating to her the words written in the note given with the cameo brooch had brought another laugh from the woman she had once believed to be her aunt.

'Lily!' Henrietta had scoffed, 'I know of no Lily nor of any note.'

'That don't be what you said two minutes gone.'

Switching a glance of pure malice toward the retort Henrietta had snarled, 'If you be thinking to save your own skin Perry you'll do it best by keeping your mouth closed.'

'Like Fenton Gilmore closed the mouth of a little wench he snatched from Russell Street.'

She had paid little attention to the figure opposite but at the cold flat remark she had looked with questioning intensity at the lined face of the woman stepping back from the reach of Henrietta's clawing fingers. Clara Thomas. Emma felt a warmth of gratitude. She had taken the letter and the diary from beneath the cushion of a chair, returned them to Emma, then as Perry and Mark Halstead had taken the screeching Henrietta from the room had said, 'Nellie would 'ave taken everythin' from you, there can be no denying of that and while my apologisin' be naught set against her spite still I offers it.'

There had been pain on that face, pain that spoke of much more than had been witnessed in that room, and its parallel resounded in the next quiet words.

'God knows I promised meself her would pay for ...

392

for what her had done, for the selfishness which left...'

Caught in her private world Emma seemed to see the woman pause and in the instant before the glance fell away saw the grey eyes dulled with ancient hurt.

'...I 'eld that promise...'

The voice murmured on.

'...I lived on the sweetness of it for years but...'

The glance had lifted, bringing with it a brief smile yet the shadow of pain did not lift from Clara Thomas's eyes as she went on.

'...but tonight I realises that also were a selfishness, one which won't 'ave the wipin' away of another and though I knows Nellie has to be brought to book for the wickedness done to you and to that child I feels summat of a sorrow for her cos no matter the sentence of a court Nellie's true punishment would lie in her biding the rest of her life in the like of Drew's Court.'

Remembering now, Emma felt the compassion she had felt at that moment, the urge strong in her to say she would make no complaint though some inner voice had reminded her Lily too had been subjected to fear and abuse and though Emma Lawrence could forgive she could do so only on her own behalf. She had begun to say so when the youngsters had come into the room Lily clutching tightly to a brother whose face was pale and drawn from hours of anxiety.

'We 'eard what were said...'

Timothy had looked first at her and then at Clara Thomas, saying to the woman, 'Lily and me was taught the holdin' of a grudge serves no purpose, that heaven would right the wrongs of folk in its own fashion, that be the way it has to be with Gilmore and *his wife. As for meself the having of Lily and Emma, my sisters, the two people I love most in the world, having them safe be all the satisfaction I asks.'*

Looking to where they stood, a brother's arms wrapped protectively round the slight figure of his sister, a young lad ready to fight the world in her defence yet one whose heart possessed the magnanimity of forgiveness, she had felt a fierce sweep in her chest, a great tidal rush along her veins. She had run to them, scooping both close, love for them flooding through her, emotion welling up from the very depths of her being, brimming over, filling the well of her soul.

'*...my sisters...*'

'I love them Rachel.' Tears wetting her lashes Emma touched the small book with her lips.

'I love them as you–'

The murmur interrupted by a sound from behind Emma turned, her pulses leaping as her eyes met those of the figure watching her.

Seeing fear drain the colour from Emma's face Mark Halstead crossed quickly to her side, his hand reaching to steady her, but feeling the shudder ripple beneath his touch stepped away.

'Forgive me,' he said. 'I remembered being told people hereabout leave rear doors on the latch so when my knock at the front wasn't answered I took the liberty of letting myself in. I shouldn't have, I frightened you.'

'I...' Emma's reply trembled. 'I thought...'

'That it was Fenton Gilmore.'

'Has ... has he been arrested?'

Controlled but far from extinct anger was

reflected in Mark's reply. 'No; apart from finding his carriage where it had been left outside the railway station the police have nothing to go on. They presume he must have come to the house, heard us talking and guessed his little game was over so run while he had the chance.'

'Leaving Henrietta to bear the consequence.'

'Unfortunately, yes.'

'Couldn't she...? I mean...'

'Be spared a prison sentence? That is the way you and the Elsmores would have it but by allowing their crime to go unpunished could allow them to repeat it on some other young women. No Emma, they have to be stopped.'

'But Perry,' Emma countered, 'he was involved yet he is not in custody.'

'That I confess is my doing. I made a bargain should he take me to the place arranged between himself and the person who had hired him then I would say nothing of his dealings; thank God you were still there.'

'I thought I had lost you ... Emma my love ... my love.'

Soft, whispering in her mind as they had whispered against her hair, the words brought a swift blush of colour to Emma's cheeks. Seeking a way other than the truth to account for the emotion that was its cause she glanced at the brown-paper-wrapped package held in his hand.

'Your father's papers, has there been some mistake?'

'Ribbons for Lily, she said she lost her new treasure when...' He paused, placing the package on the table and for a moment it seemed he would leave then in a voice throbbing with vehemence, a rawness that seemed to tell of emotions too long hidden said thickly.

'Yes, there has been a mistake, but it is mine, not yours. I made the mistake of not telling you I love you, a love which began the first moment you came into my office and if I let you leave without having told you then I'll be an even bigger fool. What I am saying is I love you, Emma, I am asking you to be my wife.'

His wife! For a long moment Emma existed in a world of pure happiness then with a crash it fell around her feet, fragments of it spearing her senses. How could she become his wife ... how could she go to him after what Fenton Gilmore had done!

'I can't ... Fenton...' The murmur meant only for herself slipped into silence that seemed to vibrate.

Gilmore. Mark Halstead watched the crestfallen look, saw the abhorrence. Was that man the reason behind her refusal of marriage? If so it was not from love, the look in her eyes bore witness to that and to something more. Emma Lawrence was afraid.

'Emma.' He spoke gently, hiding the sting of rejection. 'You need not fear Gilmore, he won't dare approach you ever again.'

'You...' She swallowed against the choking force in her throat. 'You don't understand.'

No, he didn't understand, but then he would not ask. Taking a moment to quieten the surge of desire to take her in his arms, to close the protection of his love about her he said,

'I understand what can happen when we let the past govern the future, when we let what has gone before affect all that life might yet offer. The past is the past; let it lie there, Emma; when you find the man you *can* love don't let the past come between you.'

I have found the man I love. Silent on her tongue it cried in her heart. Mark Halstead was the man she loved.

Tell him ... tell him, Emma.

Somewhere amid the clamour of unhappiness, tender as a soothing kiss, the murmur sounded in her mind, the whisper she had seemed hear tell her to love Lily and Timothy, a voice she loved and trusted; but this time she must not be led by it.

'Rachel...' it was a sob, 'you don't know.'

At the scullery door Mark turned at the soft cry, his glance taking in the trembling figure staring down at the book clutched in visibly shaking hands and in two strides was beside her. Driving away the urge to draw her to him, to hold her firm against him, he eased the book free of her fingers, placing it beside the package on the table.

'Emma,' he said quietly, 'if that is the book Henrietta Gilmore took from you, if as I think it is your sister's diary then let it go, let it rest with her. You have no need of words set down on paper to remind you of the love you shared. That is engraved in your heart; cherish it, Emma, as I treasure what I feel for you.'

'I can't – you don't know!'

A cry of sheer despair, it snatched at him

releasing words meant always to be kept inside, his own heart aching in secret; but in the emotion of the moment it came tumbling out.

'I know only that I love you, that you are the beat of my heart, the breath of my soul and that without you I have nothing. John Adams was correct in calling you a gypsy woman, in saying you take what you want without account of the effect.' He smiled ruefully. 'You availed yourself not only of my property but my very heart; give it back to me Emma, give it back with yours.'

Yes, yes she would tell him. The answer soft in the silent reaches of her heart Emma lifted her face to the man she loved, her eyes smiling through a sheen of tears.

'You and Rachel, love of both of you is engraved in my heart.'

A low cry erupting in his throat he caught her to him. 'Emma,' he breathed, 'Emma my love, my love.'

Long moments later, her mouth released from his kiss, Emma said teasingly, 'You know it is said a gypsy wedding requires you to jump a broomstick.'

Looking down into soft dewy eyes Mark Halstead smiled to himself.

For his gypsy woman he would jump the moon.

The publishers hope that this book has given you enjoyable reading. Large Print Books are especially designed to be as easy to see and hold as possible. If you wish a complete list of our books please ask at your local library or write directly to:

Magna Large Print Books
Magna House, Long Preston,
Skipton, North Yorkshire.
BD23 4ND

This Large Print Book for the partially sighted, who cannot read normal print, is published under the auspices of

THE ULVERSCROFT FOUNDATION

THE ULVERSCROFT FOUNDATION

... we hope that you have enjoyed this Large Print Book. Please think for a moment about those people who have worse eyesight problems than you ... and are unable to even read or enjoy Large Print, without great difficulty.

You can help them by sending a donation, large or small to:

**The Ulverscroft Foundation,
1, The Green, Bradgate Road,
Anstey, Leicestershire, LE7 7FU,
England.**
or request a copy of our brochure for more details.

The Foundation will use all your help to assist those people who are handicapped by various sight problems and need special attention.

Thank you very much for your help.